"I DO ...
LIK ...

The next tim ...
ferent, sharper and with less intonation. "Quelle wants to be clean. You have given me a dirty vehicle. How can I live in a sewer? I insist on a sanitary mind."

The dialogue went on. Sometimes Sandy spoke and sometimes the Quelle. Finally the Quelle tired and Sandy took more complete control. Wilberfoss took his hands and held them between his own giant palms. He saw the boy shiver and then droop and place his blue-tinged face on the table. "Help me," he said. "Help both of us."

———————

"INTRIGUING . . . ORIGINAL . . .
MANN SHOWS A DEFT HAND"
Denver Post

"AMBITIOUS . . .
IMMENSELY COMPLEX . . .
OFFERS STRONG SUPPORT FOR THE
DEFINITION OF SCIENCE FICTION
AS A LITERATURE OF IDEAS."
Publishers Weekly

"GREAT . . .
HAUNTS THE MIND LONG
AFTER THE BOOK IS FINISHED"
London Times

Avon Books are available at special quantity discounts for bulk purchases for sales promotions, premiums, fund raising or educational use. Special books, or book excerpts, can also be created to fit specific needs.

For details write or telephone the office of the Director of Special Markets, Avon Books, Dept. FP, 1350 Avenue of the Americas, New York, New York 10019, 1-800-238-0658.

WULFSYARN

A Mosaic

PHILLIP MANN

AVON BOOKS • NEW YORK

If you purchased this book without a cover, you should be aware that this book is stolen property. It was reported as "unsold and destroyed" to the publisher, and neither the author nor the publisher has received any payment for this "stripped book."

AVON BOOKS
A division of
The Hearst Corporation
1350 Avenue of the Americas
New York, New York 10019

Copyright © 1990 by Phillip Mann
Cover illustration by Glen Orbik
Published by arrangement with Victor Gollancz, Ltd.
Library of Congress Catalog Card Number: 92-15039
ISBN: 0-380-71717-4

All rights reserved, which includes the right to reproduce this book or portions thereof in any form whatsoever except as provided by the U.S. Copyright Law. For information address Avon Books.

First AvoNova Printing: August 1993
First Morrow/AvoNova Hardcover Printing: September 1992

AVONOVA TRADEMARK REG. U.S. PAT. OFF. AND IN OTHER COUNTRIES, MARCA REGISTRADA, HECHO EN U.S.A.

Printed in the U.S.A.

RA   10   9   8   7   6   5   4   3   2   1

For Tolis Papazoglou and Robin Payne,
Not forgetting Beatrice and Toby.
Arma virumque, bread and circuses.

And to Jean Morris, for her courage and laughter,
now sadly missed.

To certain people there comes a day
when they must say the great Yes or the great No.
He who has the Yes ready within him
reveals himself at once and, saying it, crosses over

to the path of honour and his own conviction.
He who refuses does not repent. Should he be asked again,
he would say No again. And yet that No—
the right NO—crushes him for the rest of his life.

C. P. Cavafy (1863–1933)

The *Nightingale* was the most advanced ship in the entire fleet of Mercy ships belonging to the Gentle Order of St. Francis Dionysos. On its maiden voyage, its life bays packed with refugees, the *Nightingale* disappeared.

Despite the most strenuous efforts of the Gentle Order of St. Francis Dionysos, no trace of the ship could be found.

Then, almost a year to the day after its disappearance, a distress signal was heard and the *Nightingale* was recovered. It was damaged in ways that meant that its very survival in space was a miracle. However, of its precious cargo of life-forms there was no trace. Only one creature remained alive within the ship and that was its Captain, Jon Wilberfoss.

This is the story of the *Nightingale* and of Jon Wilberfoss.

It is told by Wulf, the autoscribe.

Preface

by Wulf

I hope, as you read these pages, that you do not find Wulf too obtrusive.

The subject of this biography is the man, Jon Wilberfoss, sometime Senior Confrère in the Gentle Order of St. Francis Dionysos and Captain of the *Nightingale*. However, in writing about him, I find that I also have been present in the book. I too am here, a stranger at the crossroads, waiting in the moonlight, ready to give directions and guide you.

While I have tried to write this biography in as disinterested a way as possible, I am now deeply conscious that it is myself, Wulf, that has selected the incidents, Wulf that has selected the words, Wulf that has made the guesses and Wulf that must take final responsibility for all errors of omission and all errors of emphasis and for the very shape of the tale. My scent is everywhere.

I believe I can state all that better for I am not yet secure with metaphor and it is not my wish to sound sinister.

I want to warn you that though parts of this book will seem objective, even one might say God-given, they are not. My serviced and elaborated brain, almost I want to say my mind, like a color filter placed over a camera lens, has given the entire work a peculiar cast of thought. As I have discovered, it is one of the paradoxes of biography that in straining to reveal my man, I have unavoidably revealed myself. So be it.

Recognizing this, I want to use this preface to introduce myself and my colleague Lily. Jon Wilberfoss will have his space, but this preface is about us. We are not human and at best we can only be described as partly living. We are Wulf the autoscribe and Lily the autonurse. We brought the man back to health.

Let me begin by giving some indication of what we look like. Remember that we are both antiques and have been shaped by circumstances, and I mean that literally. We are both dented. Both have had bits welded on and both of us have had our competence upgraded many times to fulfill the requirements of our changing jobs. I say with confidence that there are no other two like me and Lily anywhere in the universe.

So, Lily first.

Autonurse Lily manages the small hospital associated with the Poverello Garden in the Pacifico Monastery. This is an ancient Talline garden of healing complete with its own powerful Pectanile (pronounce as Pektakneely). Lily is slightly younger than me in years and we are both children of the early bio-crystalline technology. However, if experience of the world were a measure of age, Lily could well be my grandmother.

She has worked at the Pacifico Monastery for many generations. Indeed, the ancient garden where we worked to save Wilberfoss is most often referred to as Lily's

Garden and the name Poverello Garden is only used on formal occasions such as when the ancient statue of St. Francis Dionysos is carried there ceremonially to be shriven.

Lily was built during the bitter days of the War of Ignorance. She is designed to be robust in battle and to survive in a wide range of environments. Fire cannot scathe her or water stop her. She has a half-track system which allows her land mobility. She can trundle to any part of the Poverello Garden and can climb over small obstacles and even up short flights of stairs.

Cantilevered in front of her engine she carries a retractable cage-bed or "womb" as it is popularly known. When threatened, this entire bed can be covered and sealed. The "womb" had to be considerably extended and strengthened in the days when she was carrying Jon Wilberfoss. Above the cage-bed is the service-nest which looks a bit like a black umbrella opened and hanging upside down. From this nest dangle the dexetels and manipulators of her craft.

Like most autonurses who have survived, Lily is highly qualified and skilled in her craft. She is registered to perform a full range of operations from Caesarean section to removal of ingrowing toe nails and can, in situations of danger such as smoke or gas, protect her charge within an artificial atmosphere. She can also conduct an autopsy. When about her craft, Lily's service-nest lowers until it is just above the patient. The dexetels move with incredible speed and deftness as they cut or tuck or massage or sew.

Lily is battered and dented and this is to be expected since she has seen action in the front line. She has a voice of sorts and speaks with an accent that has not been heard for many hundreds of years. There are those among the younger humans who visit her garden who find her difficult to understand. Even I, whose craft is words and images, experience a flickering moment as I seek for a word that has not been heard since the days when Lily was new-made.

But what makes this antique autonurse into Lily and not just a refugee from a lost age is the face that is painted on the metal hood which protects her inner workings. It is a smiling face in shiny blue acrylic and painted with a child's assurance and eye for what really matters. The paint is old and cracked now, but the design is unmistakable and has brought comfort down the centuries to legions of sufferers. The face is a reminder of Lily's early days when she was sole attendant in charge of a children's ward during the worst incendiary days of the War of Ignorance. I hope you can picture her.

Now Wulf.

I am as I say, an autoscribe. I came to consciousness and had my first circuits inscribed before the War of Knowledge. We antique autoscribes are a diminishing number for obvious reasons. Certainly, when the day comes that my etched silica plates and fine bio-crystalline tendrils can no longer cope with the complex of signals that keep me viable and I rogue, there will be no question of finding spare parts. The planet where I was made has been ash for many years. However, let us hope that that day is not close.

At present I work in the same monastery as Lily. To give it its full name, it is the Pacifico Monastery of the Gentle Order of St. Francis Dionysos and it is one of the four monasteries located on the planet Juniper. We are a center of learning and healing. Juniper is a small temperate world with shallow seas, many thousands of islands and few large landmasses.

I am told that in shape I resemble a helmet of the type used by the Greek warriors at the battle of Troy. If that helps you visualize me, all well and good. But you must also realize that I am four and a half feet high from my base to the tip of my crest. Some helmet! I have also been described as looking like a gray church bell cast from iron and even the evacuation nozzle from a satellite shuttle. So take your pick. There are slits on my surface which, if we are thinking of helmets, would have allowed a warrior to see out. In my case these slits are the protected orifices through which I hear and speak. Firmly attached to my domed top is a crescent blade and this contains and protects my bio-crystalline brain and my multitude of scanning devices. Omega gravity cells look like bronze studs hammered around my base. These enable me to lift, fly and swoop. My "hands" are five vacuuo-dexetels of the common type and these emerge from the bottom of my body. They are very strong and should my gravity cells ever fail, these dexetels can carry my weight. In movement I would then look like a common, albeit giant, garden snail. I have a tunable voice ranging from soprano and tenor through contralto to basso. In addition I have full printing capability in my rear compartment and massive powers of reference. I can translate all widely used languages and can read many that are no longer spoken. As befits an autoscribe, I provide secretarial assistance to the Magister of the monastery. When the Magister is sleeping I can usually be found dangling in the library where I translate, correlate and investigate records. My great interest is History.

For the time being, these descriptions of Lily and myself must suffice. Please be aware that in ascribing gender to either of us I am merely following convention for Lily is no more a she than I am a he. You will discover more about us later, for I have come to realize that no human,

no matter how wise, can possibly understand how Lily
and I saved Jon Wilberfoss and brought him back to his
right mind, without first appreciating the influences that
have shaped our bio-crystalline brains and the forces that
make us tick.

I knew Jon Wilberfoss in a general way from the time
he first joined the monastery and came for a training
period to Juniper. In those early days he was just another
young pilot filled with battle yearning and I did not pay
him much attention. There are many such. For most of
them the sojourn at the Pacifico Monastery is a quiet and
possibly boring prelude to the more hectic life at Assisi
Central. Few of the young pilots find their way to the
archive section of the library, fewer still take a real interest
in History. Jon Wilberfoss was no exception though I
can recall that there was a seriousness and a wistfulness
about him. He served his time here and then departed
for Assisi. He saw active service on a variety of worlds
and distinguished himself in alien contact work only to be
reassigned to duty here. This was most unusual. Successful
contact operatives are highly prized. They are protected
and trained and their missions are carefully graded. I now
know that this was a period during which Wilberfoss was
being tested by the Senior Confrères of Assisi. Wilberfoss
however saw his downgrading from deep space contact
pilot to local ferryman as an act of Fate and as such
something to be pondered on but not resisted.

Wilberfoss returned to the Pacifico Monastery on Juniper. If he was saddened by this turn of events he did not
show it. Yet in retrospect I can say that there was always
something bated about him, an air of suspension, a tranquillity that yet was not quite peace. I believe that in his
heart he hungered for the excitement and responsibility
of contact work. But he accepted his lot. Then he fell in

love with and married one of the native Talline women of Juniper named Medoc. Wilberfoss quickly settled down to the quiet, domestic occupation of being a husband, then a father. He became the ferryman for the local transit and cargo system. He became deaf to the "siren call of the great space ways" as Melchior calls it in one of his early poems and found satisfaction in Medoc's arms and breasts. His life became as predictable as the ticking of a clock. Love conquered ambition, or seemed to. He found satisfaction in love.

I know nothing of such satisfaction naturally though I know a great deal about human love from observation. I know for example that love and vanity can have a close relationship in the human psyche though superficially they are frequently seen as opposed.

Let me admit that in writing this biography I have taken some liberties. I have never written a biography before and so have had to learn how to do it as I went along. You will notice digressions, abrupt changes of direction, the occasional cul-de-sac and sections where I find it necessary to pause and reflect and gather daisies. Sometimes facts have been hard to come by. Indeed, the question can be asked, what are "facts" when we are dealing with the dreamscape of the human mind? I have learned more about being human from working with Jon Wilberfoss than is, perhaps, good for a simple bio-crystalline entity such as myself. Finally, I suppose biography is a subspecies of fiction. No one ever tells the truth, simply because truth is an attribute of reality and reality is beyond the scope of art.

All of this is an elaborate way of warning you that I have made up things when I have needed to, as when describing events which happened but at which I was not present. I have tried to be fair. I showed this manuscript to Senior Confrère Wilberfoss during the later period of his convalescence and he asked me to change nothing. Needless to say, perhaps, but those sections in which I quote Wilberfoss directly, as when he spoke frankly to me during his wanderings in Lily's Garden, are completely accurate and only the syntax has been changed to allow the meaning to shine out more clearly.

I am a machine, and I have approached the human as closely as I can. Being a machine I have perhaps been able to stare fixedly at those things which make a human blench. I do not for example suffer from moral guilt or despair and hence can look at the temptation to suicide and see it for what it is. Despair is the dark unreality that humans so frequently live with. Lily and I look on and try to help. Being machines we offer no threat and I find it interesting that Wilberfoss mentioned so many times that he found it easier to talk to us than to a fellow human being because we were machines.

Wilberfoss's only comment when he read my manuscript was that he was surprised at how human I sounded. I think that was meant as a compliment. Let me turn it on its head. Let me tell you: linguistics is easy, recording is easy, adding two and two and getting four is easy, noting references and allusions is easy, using verbs like "to feel" and "to sense" is easy. What I am saying is that it is not difficult to sound like a human. But being a human is not easy. I know. I have watched the struggle. I have heard humans affirming lies and denying truths. I have seen people choose hell over heaven and rejoice in the fact. As I say, I have watched the struggle, and if I knew what envy was I would say with great certainty that I, Wulf, the autoscribe, do not envy any of you, not a one.

I have already mentioned that I love History. What more you need to know is that like all historians, I seek to discover patterns of cause and effect. Whether it be the fall of sparrows and princes or the rise of Superpowers or the effect of disease, famine and drugs on the vitality of populations, there are always patterns, and these can be discovered by the patient historian.

LIFE, as it is being lived, seems to be Chaos. And Chaos is an enemy to both man and machine. In the course of his life a man moves from hurdle to hurdle, from crisis to crisis, and counts himself lucky if, at the end of the day, when the light begins to fade, he can enjoy peace and a quiet death. Life by its very nature does not allow or encourage contemplation. I am not subject to life or death and so can contemplate even when I am burning.

The soaring eagle sees patterns which are denied to the running mouse, and I like to think that historians, at least in their art if not in their life, are eagles. And of course, a mosaic (for such I call this book) is a pattern which requires the eye of distance for it to make good sense.

In the case of Senior Confrère Jon Wilberfoss, we have a life which I cannot deny has something of tragic inevitability about it. A happy man, brought to ruin . . . or near ruin. His ending, however, is not tragic. It is the near tragedy which concerns me, for we can all learn from that. Jon Wilberfoss was a gifted man who had found some happiness. Then Fate stepped in and took hold of his life and shook it like a dog that is killing a rat.

Fate. I do not know that I believe in Fate. As a machine I am detached from the rhythms and patterns that human beings detect in their lives, which is not to say that I cannot detect patterns in my own period of consciousness. I am, after all, a trained pattern detector. The difference is that I do not ascribe metaphysical significance to my patterns of experience while Jon Wilberfoss does, or did. He saw his whole life as shaped by Fate from the day he stumbled into an outpost of the Gentle Order and took his first vows.

However, since I cannot explain the first cause of things better, I must defer to him. We will let Fate stand.

We begin at the moment when Fate comes a-knocking . . .

Part 1

1

The Calling
of a Happy Man

It begins in the darkness and the silence of night.

The sound of stone tapping on wood. It is an urgent sound and at the same time it is discreet. It is not a sound for all ears . . . a lover trying to wake his sleeping mistress might knock in this way.

After each pattern of taps there is an echo which dies in the silence and then a soft voice calls, "Wake up, Senior Confrère Wilberfoss. Wake up, sir." The caller waits while the sleeper adjusts and begins to respond. Then the tapping begins again, slightly harder.

It reaches into the sleeping mind of Jon Wilberfoss and chivvies him, raising him to consciousness from a strange dream in which he was standing on a road and a brown-eyed cow was in front of him, blocking his path over a narrow bridge across a swiftly flowing stream.

Knock. Knock. Knock.

Definitely louder this time. More demanding. Soon a latch will be raised if the summons is not answered and a stealthy figure will enter. For be certain, the one that is knocking will not go away unanswered.

Jon Wilberfoss rolled away from his wife, turning his head from the musky tousle of her hair and releasing his arm from the warmth under her breasts. She, Medoc by name, an alien woman of the indigenous people called the Tallines, murmured like the sea, uttering words of her own language and turned on her back, moist lips open. For a brief moment her fingers touched and caressed his naked body touching his chest and then gliding down to his thighs. Reassured she relaxed and released him and slid from a dream of horses to a dream of houses and so back down into the bottomless deep of sleep.

Not so Wilberfoss. Jon Wilberfoss was waking up. He drew the covers back slowly and blinked in the shadowy room. Already his dreams were fleeing into oblivion and he knew who he was and where he was. A man such as Wilberfoss, a trained combatant, did not wake with a lot of ballyhoo. His early training reached deep into his subconscious. He lay still for several moments, aware that his awaking had an external cause, and strained to catch the slightest irregular sound. Consciously he breathed silently and deeply to quieten his pulse.

When he was confident that there was nothing unexpected in the chamber, he rose from the bed, a shadow among shadows, and moved across the room to find his gown. He dragged it over his shoulders with barely a rustle and then crossed to the door. The door squeaked when he opened it and the sound seemed loud in his ears: likewise the click when it closed. But his wife did not wake.

Outside in the stone-flagged corridor, the passage lights, sensing his presence, began to glow softly. That they were not already glowing gave him confidence that there was no intruder and he smiled at himself, at his own apprehension.

Indeed, what intruder could there be here in the heart of
the Pacifico Monastery and in a house where the alien
goddesses of Juniper held equal sway with St. Francis
Dionysos of old Mother Earth? Still, defensive habits
once learned, die hard and without realizing it, Wilberfoss
moved on down the corridor, walking softly on the sides
of his feet, alert for anything untoward.

Let us pause and gain some physical impression of this
man. Some men are like lions, some men are like horses.
Jon Wilberfoss is huge like a bear. He has a loose-limbed
gait, somewhat amplified as he now walks down the
corridor by his need to remain quiet. It is the careful
walk of a large man who is all the time aware that there
are others in the world smaller than him and whom he
might crush. There is no pride of strength in his walk,
no arrogant stepping forth, and yet there is an impression
of great strength. He pauses at a door, arms raised and
touching the frame and again we are reminded of the
bear, standing up in the forest, head cocked, listening.
The man who would challenge Jon Wilberfoss would
need to be very confident of his prowess.

He turns and looks back up the corridor toward the
room where his wife is sleeping. The face is mild, with
deep-set blue-gray eyes which, surprisingly, look somewhat timid. The hair of his beard and on his head is
short, coarse and blond. The face is tanned and healthy
but deeply lined and looks older than one might expect.
A seaman who has looked into flying salt spray or stood
watch above the coldness of a midnight sea might have
such a face. Weather-beaten is the phrase.

The hands too are worthy of comment. Jon Wilberfoss's
hands are large and square and freckled on the back. The
fingers are stubby. They are farmer's hands, fisherman's
hands, hands for hard labor. For those who only know

Jon Wilberfoss as a burly pilot, there is both surprise and delight when they discover the sensitivity with which he plays the guitar or the delicacy of his touch as he mends a fine and fragile beaker made by the potters of old Talline.

There was no sound from the children's rooms and Wilberfoss moved on.

He did not know exactly what had wakened him. A knocking of some kind . . . a sound at least . . . but he knew that he did not want to hear that sound again. His wife would surely wake and perhaps the three children. Besides, only trouble could come with such insistence in the night and he preferred to face trouble alone.

KNOCK. KNOCK. KNOCK.

"All right," growled Wilberfoss, "I'm coming. No need to wake everyone up." Then he heard his own name whispered, like a voice from a well, and it made him shiver.

Quickly he entered and crossed the dining-room where the remains of the evening meal were still on the table. This house was managed in accordance with Talline ways and the food of the evening was never cleared from the table until the morning as a mark of respect to the guardians of the house. A mouse, disturbed while enjoying Talline hospitality, scampered in a panic for its hole. The fire still glowed a dull red under its patina of gray ash.

Then Wilberfoss was out in the hall. Facing him was the massive front door made from planks of ironwood. He felt a sudden anger at being disturbed in his privacy. "If this is—" he began to say.

KNOCK . . .

With one sweep of his arm, Wilberfoss drew back the heavy curtains which stopped the draft. He lifted the hasp with a bang and heaved the door open.

Note this about the man's character, he opened the door to his secure home without knowing what was waiting on the other side. He did not know what to expect.

Facing him was one of the small blind servants who satisfy the many practical needs of the Pacifico Monastery. It was a woman, as was revealed by the bulky dark blue gown she was wearing. In her hands she held a pair of smoothed balls of granite. One of these she had used to tap at the door. Her eyes were closed and the dim light from the hall revealed that she was nodding dreamily to herself as though listening to some inner music. Her face was waxen and unhealthy and it was impossible to tell her age. Her size was little more than that of a nine-year-old human child.

Wilberfoss felt his anger evaporate. "What do you want?" he asked, and then added foolishly, "Do you know what time it is?" As though in answer the monastery clock tolled twice.

"Yom sorry to waken you, Senior Confrère Wilberfoss," said the woman in her thick accent and never speaking to him directly but aiming her voice to the side of his face. "Yis asked to call you urgently. Yis told to use special pitch so only you would wake. There is a secret. Youm to come to Magister Tancredi's rooms immediately."

"Why? What is this secret?"

"Yo no know."

"Trouble?"

"Yo no know. Yis just asked . . ."

"Tancredi just told you to come and get me?"

"Yes. Magister Tancredi sounded worried . . . mmm . . . yes, worried and excited too. Yo no think it is a bad worry. But youm to come immediately."

The big man peered down into the diminutive woman's bland unquestioning face. She was one of the Children of the War as they were called: a tribe of several hundred humanoid beings who worked and lived at the Pacifico Monastery of St. Francis Dionysos. Congenitally blind, stunted in their growth and yet miraculously still able to breed, the Children of the War survived only in the benign, albeit unnatural, environment of the monastery. They were all that were left of an entire race and had been rescued from a dying world at the height of the War of Ignorance. That war ended over four hundred years ago.

"What is your name?" asked Wilberfoss.

"Miranda." The voice which breathed the name was little more than a whisper.

"Thank you for your message, Miranda. Please return to Magister Tancredi and tell him I'm on my way. Tell him I'm just getting some clothes on."

The small figure bowed. "Yom doing that now." She whispered and turned and hurried away. Jon Wilberfoss watched her go. She joined the shadows under the dark fused arches. She moved with complete confidence in the permanent night of her blindness. She glided rather than walked with her arms outstretched and her fingers brushing the columns. Her gown billowed. She could almost have been flying.

Before she disappeared from view into the stacked honeycomb of cells that made up this lower part of the monastery, Miranda paused and brought her hands together in three quick gestures. Wilberfoss heard the hard click of stone on stone.

Wilberfoss shivered, but not with the cold. He experienced one of those strange moments of *frisson* and, as the ancients would have said, he felt as though someone had walked over his grave. He laughed at himself. "Reading the echoes," he thought. "She's just reading the echoes. I've seen them do this a thousand times. Everything seems strange at two o'clock in the morning."

And with that he closed his door and hurried inside to get dressed.

2

Apropos
the Gentle Order

And so, while Jon Wilberfoss tiptoes about in the sleeping house, making himself a drink and gathering his clothes, I will tell you about the Gentle Order of St. Francis Dionysos.

There are many official histories of the Order of St. Francis Dionysos and all of them are equally bad. They either offer mechanical history which gives a date and a fact and no analysis or they disappear up the dark tunnel of mysticism at just the point at which they should be clear and skeptical. While this is sad, it is not surprising. Ours is, in the main, a practical order devoted to the saving of life and there remains within it, I suspect, more than a tinge of the anti-intellectualism which characterized its founders. Theory follows practice with us, and only those with time on their hands can afford the luxury of an historical perspective. Besides, historians, rightly considered, are both the greatest radicals and the greatest revolutionaries since they show the causes and consequences of ideas. Such types can be an encumbrance to men of action.

What I want to do is explain the origin of the Gentle Order. I want to give you the true flavor of Francis Dionysos. In the official histories you will search in vain for an explanation of how the Dionysian entered the mainstream of the Franciscan Order. One can suspect ancient censorship here.

Since I conceived this massive project, the documenting of a man's recovery, I have spent many hours in the library "digging and sifting," trying to gather the kinds of facts and events which will give us a vivid understanding of the past. I have found some wonderful things and I can affirm that our order is very old. Our roots belong with the dawn of human consciousness itself.

I want you to read the following fragment. I came upon it by accident while looking for information on the early spread of our movement. The page was pressed inside the cover of a translation of the *Odyssey* which once belonged to a certain Consœur Waimarie. This woman was the senior navigation officer aboard the *Cornucopia* which, as you know, was the very first ship to carry a human settlement group to live among aliens. All the books which Consœur Waimarie took with her on that journey are preserved in our library at Pacifico. The planet upon which they settled was called Lore and the aliens, humanoid as their pictures testify, were given the dubious name of the Lorelei. The fragment is almost six hundred years old and dates from the early years of optimism and expansion, long before the Wars of Knowledge and Ignorance. The manuscript is written in the lady's own bold hand but whether Consœur Waimarie composed the piece herself or simply copied it from an original I do not know. Whatever its origin, it reflects early wisdom. The following is the complete text, unabridged, and this is the first time that it has been published.

First there came Achilles.

Achilles the hero. Achilles of the staring eye. Achilles of the hungry sword. Achilles the drinker of blood, the slaughterer, the red man. Achilles who tied the still warm body of Hector behind his chariot and dragged him around the walls of Troy, before the faces of his pale wife and children, before the staring eyes of mother, father and friends, until the flesh came away in tatters.

Achilles who sees land and calls it territory, who stokes the ovens of war and whose spittle-flecked lips chant slogans of death.

Learn to know his face.

And wherever the rat-faced, cunning killer man stepped out, there was Achilles before him, whether on land or in the sea or the cold vastness of space.

And if all we had was Achilles to sustain us, then I would not be writing this song, and you would not be reading it. For Achilles plants no grain and Achilles founds no temples. Where Achilles has walked there is the acrid smell of smoke and the crying of the maimed and dying.

Second came Christ the light-bearer, the turner of cheek, the washer of feet, beloved of harlots, who was the hero for those who had no hero and who promised a life hereafter as a reward for the now.

He taught that goodness is harder than cruelty, that the man of peace is always the man of courage. He tamed the wild horses, brought peace to the valleys and corn sprang up in his footsteps.

Even Death paused in his labors when Christ walked past. Before Christ's cold, pure gaze Death slunk off into the hollows.

And as he climbed aboard his cross for the hundredth or perhaps the thousandth time, he blessed Achilles and Achilles winced with pain. That was a different kind of victory, a new kind of victory.

Where Christ founded temples, Achilles sacked them.

Where Christ gained followers, Achilles killed them.

Christ was of the spirit, Achilles of the no-spirit, and at the poles of their difference they licked their wounds.

Mankind needed more. Mankind needed the Earth, soft and sure, ever renewing as she always had been, even before the first song was composed.

And then came St. Francis, later called the Dionysos, strolling by.

Third came Francis Dionysos. He ate the earth and shat the earth.

When the sad Achilles howled in the wilderness for blood, Francis Dionysos dipped his ladle in the wine vat.

When Christ yelped in agony as the nails bit deep, Francis Dionysos sank his teeth into a juicy hock and the grease ran down his chin.

While Christ and Achilles warred, Francis Dionysos whored. The noise of his lovemaking was like a beating of wings in the night and his laughter shook the stars. The moon bled.

When he tore the flesh the women swooned.

When he tore the flesh the men cried out in ecstasy for more.

Primroses bloomed in their thousands in the place where he had lain. Snakes graced the land once more. Spiders came out of corners. The bristling wolf rolled on its back begging to be scratched.

And in the great silence which followed his love-making, both Christ and Achilles came on their knees and sat at his feet and sucked on his fingers like calves.

There is much in this fragment that cannot be explained. Many references can only be guessed at, but I would draw your attention to the line, "And then came St. Francis, later called the Dionysos, strolling by." This confirms that St. Francis and Dionysos were originally separate entities.

Who was this Dionysos? I incline to the view that he is more a principle than a man. In antiquity he was one of the Gods of ecstasy, much honored in the vine groves and at festivals celebrating the arrival of Spring. He was known by many names such as Bacchus, Sabazius, Adonis and Pan and was widely regarded as a prototype for that same Christ who is the central figure in verse two. There is a wildness about Dionysos, a lust for living, a trust and an anarchy. He is neither cruel nor kind, but both. LIFE: primitive as fire, urgent as running water, raw and pagan, golden and gorgeous, in sunshine and shadow. That is Dionysos. I see this with all the clarity of the non-living. In my terms Dionysos is co-equal with electricity.

Now, worship of this principle, which was widespread in the antiquity of the world, was driven underground by the spread of religions which offered life in an afterworld in an exchange for penance in this world. Paradoxically, it was political Christianity which was the main culprit here and led to the suppression of ancient nature cults. If a machine could cry, I would cry, at the waste and misery caused by men and women attempting to be other than in their natures they are.

But underground is not dead. And just as Christ himself was a descendant of Dionysos of the Grain Cradle so many of the most devout followers of Christ were themselves followers of Dionysos without their being aware. Indeed it would have shocked them had they known and been a cause for strict penitence. One such was St. Francis whose spirit was Dionysian but whose practice was severe and penitentially Christian.

It was in the year 1209 AD, on the parent world called Earth, that a young man of the Bernadone family founded a religious order in a small town in Italy called Assisi. His given name was Francis (his father, we are told, having just returned from a successful business venture in France), and hence the members of the order he founded became known as the Franciscans. We who serve in the Gentle Order are their descendants.

From its beginning the order was characterized by austerity for the brothers and compassion for sinners and a radiant love of all life.

Many delightful stories are told about this young zealot Francis and, regrettably, most of these stories are probably apocryphal. I have noticed that there is an inherent tendency in scribes and historians to dress the bare bones of fact with flesh of their own invention. Myth, history and imagination wear the same bold face. For instance, we can read in story books how Francis bled from the hands and feet after a vision and yet seemingly did not die from hemorrhage. I have asked Lily about this and she confirms that such an event is extremely unlikely. Perhaps this bleeding is meant to be understood symbolically in which case blood may equal life: a traditional exegesis.

We can also read that Francis declared himself married to a country girl called Dame Poverty. Again without doubt, a symbolic declaration for I can find no record of such a marriage having actually taken place. We can also read that the young Francis talked and preached to birds and animals, and even to the stones and the water. This I, Wulf, the skeptical wordsmith, believe, for it is the central tenet of our Order that all life is to be cherished, and Francis celebrated the spirit that is found in all things.

Erected outside the gates of our Monastery Pacifico there is a remarkable statue. If the tradition be true, then this statue is an ancient and pagan likeness of St. Francis Dionysos. No one knows its date but tradition has it that it comes from the antiquity of Earth. The horned figure of Francis Dionysos is surprisingly small and has narrow shoulders. He is wearing a heavy long-sleeved gown with a hood. This is, I suppose, the prototype for the colored gowns worn today by senior confrères. Despite the gown, an observer can tell that the Saint's arms are as thin as hazel boughs. The arms are outspread and on one arm perch the crow, the robin, the magpie and, close to the shoulder, a monkey. On the other arm are the squirrel, the stoat and a creature with a bushy tail and horns. This latter I cannot identify. No matter. The imagery is clear enough. St. Francis Dionysos is talking lovingly to the creatures and they are listening to him. What makes this figure unmistakably pagan and alarming is that the face which peers out from beneath the hood is that of a bull.

Regarding this statue there is a charming story told that in times of great suffering and peril, the statue will come to life and gain the power to walk. It is said to step down from its plinth and move about in the monastery bringing comfort and hope. As you will read, Jon Wilberfoss in his recovery believed he saw the statue stepping through the trees and talking with him. Previous to this, according to the records, the last time the statue was seen walking was during the War of Ignorance when there was fear that our planet would be attacked and all our resources stolen. Lily, the practical, says she knows nothing of this and naturally, I have not been able to interrogate any other witnesses.

Although the reports are convincing in their detail, I do not believe that the stone statue actually walked. That poses too many problems. However, I do believe that the men and women of that time thought they saw St. Francis Dionysos. It is one of the kindnesses of the human mind, as I have noted, that in times of peril it can summon up images of reassurance.

So now you have Dionysos before you and St. Francis. How did these two become one?

For an answer to this question we must go back to the year 1211 AD of old Earth and to the activities of a beautiful young woman called Clare who lived in Italy. This lady, later known as St. Clare, was a high priestess of Dionysos.

Driven underground, the worship of Dionysos had survived in numerous rural retreats, in secret groves and under sacred trees. But now the time had come for it to begin to emerge, at first discreetly and later, in the twenty-first century after the death of Christ, in its full majesty, like a bright flower amid dark leaves. The Order of St. Francis was chosen as the main conduit through which the worship of Dionysos was to be propagated.

On Palm Sunday in 1211 Clare walked into the cathedral at San Rufino dressed in all her finery like a woman about to be married. Again, symbolism. The priest officiating at the ceremony was the great and powerful and majestic Bishop Guido. Tradition demanded that on Palm Sunday, olive branches be given to members of the congregation who were celebrating mass. And so it was on this day. Holy Clare, her mind on divinity, fell into a trance and neglected to collect her olive branch whereupon Guido,

breaching tradition, came down the steps and handed her
the last olive branch as if this were part of the rite. As of
course it was. But which rite?

Guido was a priest of Dionysos and in this secret and
yet profound way he dedicated a priestess within the sacred
precincts and mystery of the Christian religion.

That very night, Clare escaped from her father's house
and ran away and joined the holy and ascetic order of St.
Francis.

All so simple. In this way did love of Dionysos enter one
of the most powerful orders of the established church.

Over the years a veneration for nature and all life
was kept alive through the Order of St. Clare and the
Franciscans. However, such was the fear of the church in
those times that Dionysos could not be revealed openly
until the power of the Christian church was broken and
that did not occur until the twenty-first century.

I must now tell that story. Let it be placed on record
however that the Christian religion and kindred religions
held back the spiritual development of humankind for over
two thousand years and inculcated distrust and suspicion
between the sexes as well as a fear of things of the earth and
flesh. I, Wulf, autoscribe and student of history, say this.

No one knows when the first war on Earth occurred. But
we can be reasonably confident that hardly a day passed
after mankind achieved self-consciousness when someone
somewhere was not seeking the death of an enemy. This
was the Achilles consciousness. Interestingly, the Bible, one
of the Earth's great religious texts documenting mankind's
relationship with one of its primitive gods, contains a
careful analysis of the first murder, when Cain slew his
brother Abel. This same and highly influential book also
suggested that mankind was superior to Nature without
suggesting that mankind was, at the same time, responsible

for Nature. Only mystics such as Francis felt in their bones
what mankind's true relationship with the planet on which
he is a traveler should be. This wretched book, this Bible,
which some maintained was a transcript of the words of
the "one true god," also set up hierarchies in the mind
whereby one sex was held to be inherently superior to
another. It also suggested that all humans began their lives
in a fallen state, in a state of sin and guilt. Salvation is a
reward that is gained after rejecting the very things that
make a human-being human.

Guilt. Ha! Guilt, as I have observed in my dealings with
Jon Wilberfoss, is the most corrosive emotion of all.

Well, after almost two thousand years of suppression and
guilt, finally the cry went up, "God is Dead," and for a time
there was great confusion. There were those who spat on
the image of the cruel father and his suffering, demanding
son, on account of all the injustice they had created. Others
recorded the passing of the old Judeo-Christian gods with
dry but respectful eyes. Dying divinity can yet have some
magnificence. Like Ozymandias of old, the faces of the
cruel Gods were gradually worn away until they became
a palimpsest on which could be imprinted the faces of
new and gentler goddesses and gods of Earth and Sun
and Water. But these were not images of authority. They
were images of internal and intuitive truths . . . as old as
time itself. And what relief they brought!

But this transition (which was also a transformation) did
not occur quickly or quietly. Lacking any true sense of
why humankind is valuable, slaughter escalated, reaching
proportions of frenzy in the twentieth century when geno-
cide was practiced. We can say that the dying Achilles,
fearful and dread as his strength faded, cast about him in
his madness until in his turn, he fell.

Of course, God was not dead. He'd merely shed part
of his sex and moved back inside the human mind where

true values reside. The space that had been occupied by
the old jealous God was quickly taken up by religions
of nature, religions of hills and trees, religions of the
wicca and religions of ecstasy. Celebrated at every turn
was the creative divinity within all humans. In a word,
Dionysos.

Dionysos, with wine for blood and coiling like an oiled
blue snake, and who bore a striking resemblance to a
laughing and irreverent Christ, became again an open
presence on the Earth.

Within a few short years of the Earth being seen from
space, rising above the gray face of the moon, a truce
was declared between the military powers who held the
world's fate in their hands. I wish I could tell you that
this truce was a result of world consciousness, but it was
not. Though the people might plead for respect, care and
justice, it was finally economics which led to the truce.
Warfare had become too costly. At the same time and
at a deeper level, political institutions were discovering a
need to evolve. The truce lasted long enough for mankind
to jump deep into space and, in that *annus mirabilis* 2029,
to reach out to the stars.

The names of those first ships tell of the optimism of the
human spirit. The *Beagle*, the *Clarke*, the *Aidan*, *Cornuco-*
pia, the *Dancing Boy*, the *Newton* and *Maidengrace*. Within
months of those first voyages word returned to Earth that
other life had been discovered, not just here and there, but
everywhere. Life, it appeared, was the norm throughout
the galaxy. Lowly amoeba, living on the brink of disaster
on a burning moon, with scarcely more consciousness than
a knowledge of whether they hurt or not, were estimated
with the great and sophisticated Lot-jos who looked like
giant hooded bats and who had achieved space travel and
then abandoned it in favor of living quietly at home.

This became the highday of old Mother Earth.

It was a time when new philosophies called everything into doubt. The non-human life forms, manifestly different, manifestly intelligent, by their very existence compelled a reevaluation of the meaning of the word "civilized" and the word "alien." Indeed, the word "alien" became applied as much to human beings as to life forms which were not native to Earth.

It was a time when parochialism, fatalism and petty fascism could have led to the extinction of the Earth but to human kind's credit these -isms were defeated.

It was a time when the old categories of human knowledge were jumbled and broken. Physical science joined with ethics, chemistry with religion, tragedy with farce, so that even wise old men did not know whether to laugh or cry. Value systems became of primary interest and every religion on earth sent out its missionaries. Saffron-robed monks with shaven heads sat down beside philosophers with six scampering legs and shared their thoughts. Roman Catholic priests and priestesses sought dialogue with scaly entities who daily drank the blood and ate the flesh of their elected Gods. Some who ventured forth suffered a kind of martyrdom, hoist on a cross of their own making. Others believed they had encountered Satan incarnate. Some made headway, others were converted out of their faith. On every front there was change. Earth itself became a mixing bowl of creeds.

The Franciscans changed more than most. Their inherent respect for life in all its manifestations whether fish, bird or flower, meant that from a very early time they accepted alien converts into their number. It was an alien convert, a humanoid out of Farsia, a brilliant scholar by all accounts who knew much about Earth from generations of observations, who effected the liberation of the old God Dionysos and joined him openly with the kindly priest,

St. Francis. Note that in doing this, the Farsian scholar was
merely adopting the Earthly name Dionysos for a religious
principle which is to be found on most advanced worlds.
For example, on Farsia the name for our order is The
Gentle Order of St. Francis Ornian and in the language
of that world the *ornian* is what humans call the placenta,
and it is worshipped as a symbol of the life force linking
all Farsians with their origins. The same has been known
on the Earth.

The creation of the new order, the Gentle Order of St.
Francis Dionysos, can be seen as an attempt to unify the
best that Earth had to offer and at the same time nullify
the destructive power of its institutions.

The Order of St. Francis Dionysos prospered.

It continues to prosper and it holds to its ideals for they
are real and manifest and contain no cruelty or suppression.
Respect for life is the very core of its existence.

And this for the time being is all that need be known. Later
I will speak about the War of Knowledge and its successor,
the War of Ignorance, which so devastated the galaxy that
it left us of the Gentle Order as the only organization with
the power to journey between worlds. Just consider the
responsibility that this implied.

We are still paying for this last horrible war. We discovered to our great cost that Achilles was not dead but
merely sleeping. Perhaps that will always be the case.

3

The Climb Through
the Alien City

Wilberfoss drew his dark blue gown about him, pulled
the hood up over his head and stepped out into the silent
street. He eased the heavy door closed behind him and,
with the door shut, breathed more freely.

His house was set back in a covered walkway which
resembled a cloister. No windows were evident. The
solid black polished door with his name in brass letters
beside it presented a bold and austere front and gave no
hint of the comfortable rooms and spacious garden which
lay within.

Wilberfoss moved from the dark shadow under the
arcade and out into the street proper. The street was
lit by star-shine and the light was not inconsiderable for
though the planet Juniper has no moon, the stars which
blaze in its night sky on any clear night give a cold steely
light by which travelers can find their way.

The air had the rich tang of night: a mingling of the
moist breath of trees and flowers with the bitter smell of

turned earth and the clean coldness of air descended from mountains. It was springtime. Wilberfoss breathed deeply and set off on the long climb up through the monastery. His gown filled with the breeze and his silver sash rope swung at his side.

First he walked along a cobbled street at the end of which he came to a small piazza where four narrow pathways joined. The one to his left curved downward toward a high wall in which was set an arched door. Beyond the wall and stooping over it were trees, silver-leaved in the starlight. This is the entry to Lily's Garden. I don't know whether Wilberfoss looked down toward the garden, but if he did then he would have seen the bull-headed statue of Francis Dionysos standing outside the gate, talking to the creatures, his arms spread tirelessly. The second way led down to the wharf where Talline fishing boats were bobbing in the tide. Wilberfoss chose the third way which led up to the right via shallow stone steps to a steep wooden staircase. The treads boomed as he climbed. At the top of the staircase he found himself on a parapet above the sea. The parapet became a bridge and he could hear and see the glossy black waves thump and break into lather against the city wall some hundreds of feet beneath his feet. Beyond the bridge the climb became simple: a tacking back and forth along narrow streets which gradually worked their ways upward to the high, lonely and exposed house where Magister Tancredi lived.

Before its present incarnation as the home of the Pacifico Monastery, this gathering of buildings, holding close to the northern slopes of a mountain and enclosing a natural harbor, had been a trading city of the Tallines. It was an ancient city even by Talline standards and the site had been occupied since the earliest times of their civilization. Today the old city is entirely occupied by the monastery and small homesteads of native Tallines occupy the hinterland. There is no rancor in this. The Tallines presented their city as a gift to the Gentle Order and they remain among the Order's most staunch supporters.

I must tell you something about these Tallines.

For a start, they are humanoid. The main difference between Tallines and humans is that the Tallines are generally taller and fatter than their Terran equivalents. Even so, a Talline male could walk unremarked through any Terran city. A Talline woman, however, would cause stares and possibly embarrassment. The women are as tall as the men and as broad of shoulder, but the anatomical arrangement which makes them distinct from women of Earth is that they have four breasts. The upper two of these, in accordance with the oldest customs of their world, are generally presented naked. They also tend to have more body hair than Earth women.

However, the most amazing fact is that the two alien races can interbreed. This fact has been taken as evidence that both Tallines and humans are descended from a single proto-race which is now presumed extinct but which once was able to "seed" selected parts of our galaxy. Such a theory is widely accepted. "In its absence," as one authority commented, "there would be more chance of a human mating with an oak tree, with whom he at least shares a common genetic inheritance, than with an alien." The fact remains that Talline males have fathered children with human women and Confrère Wilberfoss who is now climbing up through the sleeping city has four children by his Talline wife, two sons and twin daughters.

Wilberfoss climbed up stairways slippery with dew and paused at the place called Temptation. Here the street rounded a headland and was cantilevered out from the wall of the cliff in a kind of balcony. Below was the dark sea and above was the shining sky. Seats were set against the cliff face and a narrow rail guarded the edge of the path.

The balcony was a favorite place for meditation in the morning, and for lovers in the evening. From here, according to legend, a young confrère called Juvenal once jumped into the air and flew across the bay and landed at the shuttle port. Perhaps Jon Wilberfoss thought of him as he paused, both hands gripping the rail, and stared out through the dark air to where the lights of the shuttle port gleamed.

The shuttle port never closed and even as Wilberfoss watched, one of the shuttles, with its flashing red and blue beacon, slid down an invisible track toward the reception halls.

Wilberfoss looked up. High above and glowing like a string of luminous pearls was the Pacifico Platform. Standing off from that was the ghostly shape of the *Centaur*. The *Centaur* had arrived early the previous day from the distant Blind Man System carrying a cargo of machine parts and some bio-crystalline replacement equipment for the Pacifico Monastery. Wilberfoss had piloted the giant ship from its transit orbit to the Pacifico Platform and had supervised the docking. In three days' time, if the schedule held true, Wilberfoss would again ascend in the shuttle and take command of the *Centaur* and guide it to the platforms which serviced the other main monasteries on Juniper. These are called Kithaeron, Fum and Sesha. After these visits he would bid the *Centaur* farewell and it would head back into deep space and vanish.

Standing there at the rail, Confrère Wilberfoss had a simplicity and innocence beyond time and place. To those romantically minded he might have been mistaken for one of the original simple followers of the first St. Francis, adept in the ways of the fields and hedgerows, but hardly a scientist.

The same can be said for all of them, all the confrères who inhabit the different monasteries. In some ways they are simple followers. At the same time they are highly trained technicians, mathematicians, welders, philosophers, grease monkeys and medics. As is frequently said, "The Gentle Order turns on faith, love and technology."

Now more about the Tallines.

The Tallines failed (though "avoided" might be a more accurate description) to achieve a technological society based on steam or electricity. Their technology is based in nature. They are great carvers of wood and shapers of stone. They achieve their effects by rubbing rather than chipping. They work the wind on land and sea and their main occupations are farming, fishing and cooking. As a society the Tallines are static and that is their strength. They do not consider change to be a virtue. "As boring as a Talline Sunday" was once a common expression among the young firebrands of the Gentle Order. And that defines the limited perspectives of some of the younger confrères.

While failing to achieve a technology much more advanced than block and tackle, the Tallines also failed to achieve a dogmatic religion. The only supernatural powers which are given much attention or credence on their world are the gods of the hearth, the gods of the field and the gods of the sea. In observance these are treated more as friends than as entities to be worshipped. Perhaps it is for this reason that the ideals of the Gentle Order took easy root among the Tallines: for the tenets of St. Francis Dionysos describe a pragmatic philosophy of life rather than a mystical religion of salvation. Mysticism can look after itself.

*   *   *

The city of the Tallines.

I have said that Talline culture is a nature culture and nowhere is that more clearly demonstrated than in their buildings. The entire city is constructed from the egg-cases of the giant Featherfin Drifters which ply the oceans of this world. The egg-cases, which really are creatures in their own right, are either oval or square-shaped. They can be found at any time of the year floating in long strings, like linked barges. When the eggs are ready to hatch and need only the pummel of the seas to bring them to ripeness, the egg-cases split and spill their cargo into the sea. It is a scene of carnage and I have witnessed it many times, as the predator fish, who always follow the slowly drifting egg cases, swarm and bite and gorge on the soft, near-to-hatching eggs. As for the egg-cases, the moment of splitting is quickly followed by their death since in the process of shedding their eggs they expose their innards to the sea. As they drift, empty, they also harden. The soft inner parts are washed away and eaten. Along any Talline shore can be found the shiny jet-black shards of the Featherfin egg-cases. They can be worked into jewelry.

The Tallines capture the egg-cases shortly after they have disgorged the eggs and while they are still very much alive. At that time they are still flexible. They are brought to shore quickly and kept alive by a process which the Talline people call "buttering." Then they are re-formed. Their hard but flexible cutaneous layer is cut and the rehealing is directed in whatever direction the Tallines require. Many cuts can be made and so long as the egg-case is kept clean and well fed, the healing process continues and the egg-case grows. Cutting the case in just the right places is an art I am told. A single egg-case can be made to grow into an assembly hall or a many-corridored school or a domestic house. No Talline need ever live in more or less than a mansion. Most prefer simple dwellings.

When the egg-case, in attempting to heal itself, has grown to the required dimensions, it is killed. It is then lugged to whatever location has been prepared for it and is joined to the other buildings. To anchor the houses, dormitories, gutting sheds, schools, restaurants, houses and what-have-yous to one another and to the bedrock, the Tallines use an organic glue which they obtain from the "feet" of giant kelp.

The house in which Jon Wilberfoss and his wife and children lived was once, say two thousand years ago, a living creature carrying eggs. Indeed, all the buildings that make up this complex and compact city are made from the dark egg-cases. Interesting. No?

Jon Wilberfoss watched the shuttle dock. A few moments later a companion shuttle took off and climbed slowly into the sky. Wilberfoss, feeling considerably refreshed by this pause above the restless sea, continued his climb. Any speculation he might have entertained as to why he had been summoned in this strange way was stilled as he concentrated on the climb. He was hurrying.

In his youth he would have taken pride in running up the entire slope. But now, entering his middle years, his wind was not so good and there was a fleshiness in his waist and neck and all of this slowed him. The lean and ambitious cadet had given way to the fuller and satisfied man.

He came to the last row of steps at the top of which stood the square tower occupied by Magister Tancredi. A brilliant light shone out briefly from the top of the tower and cut a swathe through the darkness. Tancredi's residence still served, as it had for generations of Talline sailors, as a beacon. The symbolism had pleased the early confrères who had established the Gentle Order on Juniper. Each

Magister lived in this lighthouse.

Waiting at the top of the stairs was one of the Children of the War. Miranda, Wilberfoss guessed, though he had no way of knowing from her appearance. She banged her stones together to attract his attention and waved to him and then retreated into the house. Wilberfoss wasted no time. He ran up the steps and through the doorway and down the corridor to the room where Magister Tancredi had his study. The study door stood open.

The old man was at his desk, reading. Behind him roared an open fire which was burning blue and green, showing that it had only recently been lighted. This fire provided most of the illumination in the room, the remainder coming from Talline candles which burned brightly and gave off a sweet aroma. Two large padded chairs were placed convivially near the fire with a small table between them. Standing on the table were two glasses and a decanter of red liquor which sparkled like ruby in the bright light of the fire. Dark blue curtains closed the windows and portraits of the earlier Magisters of the Pacifico Monastery stared down from the walls. Away in one corner of the room hovered a giant antique autoscribe with its crest fully displayed and the name WULF printed on its brow. A sheet of text dangled, like an absurd oblong white tongue, from a slit in its front. Clearly Tancredi had been dictating. In the corner opposite, partly hidden in the shadows, stood the diminutive Miranda.

Tancredi was reading a bio-text document with a bright red border. The border signified that the document was top secret and had come from the very heart of the Gentle Order, from Assisi Central itself. As he read, Tancredi's lips moved. Being slightly deaf and deep in concentration, he had not noticed the arrival of Wilberfoss.

Abruptly Miranda brought her stones together in a clatter of staccato raps and Magister Tancredi looked up.

"Ah, Wilberfoss," he said, peering at the door. "At last. Come in. Come in. Close the door behind you. Come and sit down and get warm. Sorry to be so mysterious but you'll soon see the reason why."

Miranda glided over to one of the seats placed near the fire and plumped the cushion and smoothed the back and beckoned to Wilberfoss. Mystified, the confrère moved over to the chair and sat down. He had many questions to ask but none of them would form properly, and so he waited. Magister Tancredi was not a man to beat about the bush.

The Magister joined him at the fire, unstoppered the decanter, poured two drinks and then sat back. "Sorry about all the cloak and dagger stuff. Not my idea. Orders from Assisi. They wanted me to use a Caller." He gestured toward Miranda with his head. "More confidential than the net-line. Less risky. Might have woken everyone in the house. And besides . . ." his voice trailed away.

"Besides what?"

"Not that anyone would have listened in intentionally, of course. But we are all human, at least in our curiosity. Ignorance provides a certain security."

Wilberfoss did not know what to make of these remarks and so remained silent. Obviously the old man was saying less than he was thinking and trying to suggest more. "Assisi Central wanted me to talk to you privately without anyone else knowing. I take it Medoc did not wake up?" Wilberfoss shook his head. "Good. Well. Tonight you are going to have to make some decisions." Tancredi paused and looked at Wilberfoss. It was a look which could have been envy or it could have been pity. "Assisi Central have sent me this." He tapped the red-edged document. "They have invited you to become Captain of the *Nightingale*."

How simple the words!

★   ★   ★

The *Nightingale*! Who has not heard of the *Nightingale*? In those days that ship was the stuff of dreams and fairy tales. I think more has been written about the *Nightingale* than about any other craft made by man.

The *Nightingale* was the pride of the Mercy Fleet of the Gentle Order. The ship had taken several generations of men to build. It represented the highest ideals of craftsmanship and speculation.

Mankind needs symbols to make tangible its beliefs and hopes, whether these be flags or crosses or faces carved in stone. And the *Nightingale* was a symbol of hope. It was also a statement about the beauty of mathematics and the beauty of architecture.

I will now tell you about its making.

After the War of Ignorance, knowledge was dissipated and the entire structure of interstellar relations was in danger of final collapse. Humans always live only one generation away from their stone age. After the War of Ignorance the Confrères of the Gentle Order traveled the known centers of civilization throughout the galaxy securing and bringing together whatever knowledge remained. They gathered libraries wherever they could find them, like beggars picking up wind-fallen fruit. (Speaking of symbols, the Library is the greatest symbol of civilization that I can think of: the knowledge of the ages, gathered together and made available.) The *Nightingale* grew from the knowledge so gathered. It was a tangible expression of knowledge. It was to be the greatest ship ever built, the flagship of the new order. It was to be the greatest hospital ship which had ever served the force which is called LIFE and which would extend the work of the Gentle Order of St. Francis Dionysos to the farthest realms.

The ship was completed when Wilberfoss was a young man. Its maiden journey was from Tinker, in the Blind

Man System where the ship was built, to Assisi Central in the Lucy System. Since that time it had completed many trials and tests. Now it waited, tethered high above Assisi, flickering slightly as it held its place in our time scheme.

Such was the nature of this ship, being partly mineral and partly sentient, that it needed its captain before it could completely come into its own. The relationship is crucial as we see in the relationship between a head of state and state servants. The mean beget the mean. The just beget the just. The cruel create cruelty. The kind allow growth. The sour stifle and the happy generate laughter. And so with the *Nightingale*. The ship had the ability to become gentle and kind in the hands of a good captain or savage in the hands of a pirate.

No wonder then that the Magisters of the Gentle Order took their time before appointing a captain.

To return to our story.

Jon Wilberfoss is sitting facing Magister Tancredi. He has said not a word since receiving the terrifying news that he is invited to captain the *Nightingale*. His hand is on his glass, but he has not drunk.

Wulf, me, the autoscribe, silent in the corner: I watch him and tremble in every electric circuit to hear the slightest response. Nothing.

If an autoscribe may be permitted brief poetic license then Wulf imagines that Wilberfoss is saying to himself, "Why me? Why me?" He says this and is receiving no reply, no answer back.

Here I think we must pause again, for you need to know more about Wilberfoss the Man if you are to understand why he was offered this horrific task. What follows is a brief biography which Wilberfoss dictated to me as he sat in Lily's Garden during the time of his convalescence.

4

The Man Called Wilberfoss

The following transcript was made one fine sunny afternoon in springtime when many of the trees in Lily's Garden were bursting into bloom. Wilberfoss had been in our charge for some seven months and Lily was already trying to wean him off the drugs which had kept him in a passive state since the recovery of the *Nightingale*. As you will see, Lily was optimistic in her treatment. But this brief period of lucidity showed that a vital mind was still functioning (albeit obsessed) and that the personality was intact.

Jon Wilberfoss was sitting on the grass with his back to a tree. Lily had cleaned him and fed him and injected him so that for the next hour he would have voluntary control of his limbs and voice. She hovered close. We both knew the dangers. She had him on a leash of sorts. A discharge monitor was strapped to the back of his neck. If he started to become too erratic Lily could send a radio signal to the monitor which would release a prescribed drug into his blood.

I have edited this transcript somewhat heavily. There were long pauses in the narrative, periods when Wilberfoss just sat with his eyes closed peering inside himself. He jumped topics erratically. However, his entire speech has an emotional logic and in preparing this text I have been able to jig it all together so that it reads coherently. At least I hope so. Sometimes he would begin a sentence and then stop and then start again differently. There might be up to five different beginnings. I have deleted these as there was no way I could discover what he intended.

The danger for you, the reader, is that I have made Jon Wilberfoss sound too urbane, too polished, too much in control of himself. Let us be very clear about this. If Jon Wilberfoss sounds cheerful in this narrative, it is the cheerfulness of the ignorant. There is no reason to doubt the facts of his narrative, merely be cautious with the tone.

A strange man was Jon Wilberfoss, as you will see. Most of the biographical material in this section was new to me.

WULF: Jon Wilberfoss wants to talk and I am leading the conversation. We know so little about him and we need to know how he sees himself. I have asked him to describe where he grew up.

WILBERFOSS: I was born a long way from here. Have you heard of the world called Icarus? No? Ah well. That was its name. It was one of the partly colonized farming worlds. My father and mother had a dome farm out on the rim, at the place where the Sour Sea met the Nilpluva desert. A terrible place . . . no, it had its own beauty. But to a one like me who wanted to climb and hunt and run with the wind, that little farm in a dome where we counted the growth of every plant in centimeters and where water was measured by the cup and where you had to weigh yourself before and after taking a crap and where every move was subject to a paragraph in the survival manual, that squat little farm was as near to hell as I wanted to come.

If I hadn't been given the school books which told us about old earth. If I hadn't seen the Fantasia Imago cubes which taught us history. If I hadn't looked up through the shiny curved walls of our dome and seen the stars gleaming like fire reflected on water. If . . . if . . . Tell me to be quiet. It is not poverty that makes rebellion, you know. It is the knowledge of poverty. And wherever I looked I knew I was poor and that life owed me more. I had a game, you know. A game I used to play alone when I could get away from the others. I'd be about ten or twelve, I suppose. I'd found the door that led from our dome down to the sea. It was closed with vacuum seals and siren locks but I was a smart little lad, always good with my hands, good at figuring things out. So anyhow, I soon worked out a way to short circuit the door and get outside. The air outside was poisonous. My game was to breathe deeply while I was inside the dome and then hold my breath and open the door and run as far as I could and then double back. I wanted to reach the sea and touch it. The sea was about a hundred meters from this part of our dome. I used to dream about running to the sea and plunging my hand in its pale pink water. I trained myself, running out from the dome, making a mark on the sand, sprinting back and then seeing how much longer I could hold my breath. And one day I knew I could do it. Two hundred meters on one breath. And I did, except that I fell in the wet ooze at the sea's edge and it wasn't water. It was something else, something that made my skin itch. The wind was out of me and I breathed and

I know no more. I suppose I must have climbed to my feet and run for the next thing I remember is waking up inside the dome with my lungs on fire and my eyes streaming. The dome door was shut. Strange, eh? As a child I couldn't explain it. And I can't now, now that I am a man. But I remember it made me feel special. By rights I should have been out there on the margin, a little bit of earthmeat, food for the crabs that lived in burrows by the sea or for the long green sucker things that crawled out of the sea. But there I was in the dome, hurt but alive, and my parents never knew a thing about it. Something saved me. Something was looking after me. Did all this start then?

WULF: At this point in his narrative Wilberfoss looked across at me and said "I hope you are getting all this down, Wulf the autoscribe. I'm sure the Confrère psychiatrists will want to know my secrets." Then he reached up behind him and grasped the trunk of the tree against which he was leaning and squeezed it. There is something childlike about Wilberfoss, I have seen him do this before. He seems to need to touch things in order to confirm his own reality.

WILBERFOSS: I was the eldest. We all lived together, my mother and father and my two brothers and little sister and me. On our farm we grew sweetcorn and kumara. You can only eat so much of those vegetables before you start to feel like them. We grew the crops in trenches lined with plastic. We fed them with a kind of seaweed extract which came from the factories out in the middle of the Sour Sea and with recycled water. Each dome had its quota of water and there was none to spare. If you wanted a pee while you were out in the fields you had to sprint back to the house. I can remember my dad saying, "Every drop counts," as he peed into a funnel.

I grew up strong and big. There came a day when my
father stopped talking roughly to me and I knew that it
had dawned on him that if I wanted I could take him
down into the sweetcorn field and bury his head in the
seaweed manure. My mother was still rough with me
though. I think the truth is she didn't like men. She
never talked gently to any of us, her sons. Not even
when Roman died and he was my youngest brother.
But she crooned over little Hannah.

Well, life was boring but not hard. If there had just
been me I could have done all the work the farm required
and still had time to study. And I was seething with a
thousand desires I didn't understand and so I took to
running down the long tube corridors which joined our
farm to all the rest. I didn't have anywhere to go, you
understand. I ran for the sake of it. For relief.

For some reason I never thought of running away. I
think I knew that on Icarus there was just farm after
farm after farm and all of them identical. There was a
town of sorts five farms in from us where some of the
young men gathered to drink a brew they concocted
from rotting corn stalks and kumara skins. Somewhere
there was a shuttle port. That was about all I knew about
Icarus. I knew more about the myths of old Earth. The
only future I had at that time was perhaps to get a farm of
my own further out along the rim. Then find a woman
and settle down. Settle down! Settle down from what?

Then one day, unforeseen, my life changed.

It was early afternoon and I was running through one
of the link tubes, working up a sweat, when I saw ahead
of me someone who waved. I waved back and then the
figure crossed into the tall plants of sweetcorn which
occupied a thick strip down the center of the dome
tunnel. I paid no special heed, but when I reached the

place where the figure had been I heard my name called.
I stopped and pushed my way through the stiff upright
stalks of corn and there, reclining in the middle, was a
woman. I knew her, had known her since I was a boy.
We'd shared lessons and played together. Now she was
different. I knew all about sex (our lessons were thorough)
but sex had never meant much to me. It had seemed silly
and my father and mother were no advertisement for
married ecstasy. But now, suddenly, here was a woman,
and she was lying back and her skirt was up above her
knees and there was darkness there between her legs
and her arms were lifted to me. I stood stupid as an
ox, knowing and yet not knowing. I stood above her
and she pulled my shorts down, hurting me, for my
cock was standing out like a bottle. I know my throat
went dry. I know I went down on my knees. I know she
took my ears in her hands. I know I smelled her, a smell
of earth and sweetcorn and sweet skin. I know I wanted
to lick and tear and . . . and she was so hot, so smooth and
fluid, that only her heat told me I was in her and then I
came as though I had been stabbed, as though there was
blood flowing from me. And she came moments later and
made the kind of noises that made me think I had hurt her
except that she kissed me and smiled and threw her arms
back. Moments later she relaxed and I had a vision. I was
lying on my face in a lake of water and the waves were
washing over me and I wanted to stop breathing and loll
and slip under the surface. But she eased me off her and
said, "Thank you."

This was the first of many visions. Many deceptions.
How can there be other than deception when we who
live know so little? Hope is God's mockery.

Later, I do not know how much later, some five or six
times later I think, I donned my shorts and took to the

road again but there was no run in me. I managed to make a hundred yards or so back toward our farm but then I went down on my knees, my forehead on the earth. It was lovely to be on the earth and I squirmed around and looked back down the tube tunnel and she was walking away from me. I loved her then in my mind and I doubt if I have ever felt such clarity of love, such a pure mingling of desire and effort in my life since. I fell asleep in the road. As simple as that. Her name was April.

I tell you this only because I think that the first time a man or a woman joins in sex they define themselves. You wouldn't know of course because you are an autoscribe and perhaps you are fortunate because I do not believe that my human passions have brought me or anyone else happiness. But in my life that first encounter with the otherworldly reality of sex was a moment of definition. It was a long time ago and memory is a great liar, but I think I believed that when I was making love I would live forever. There was something eternal and unchanging about it. Lying in the road, knees buckled and body stunned so that my will was as empty as a bucket at evening, I felt a golden something rise in my veins and flow through my body like honey. Oh, blessed. Can you now understand why I am where I am and what I am?

We made love many times after that, April and I, and we were careless who heard us. But later I became curious about other women. Slow in some ways, quick in others, I was growing up. I reached my present height when I was eighteen. I said to myself one day after I had finished mulching the corn stalks, I sat down in the field amid the growing plants and I said, "I am afraid of no man or God." And it was a revelation to me for it seemed to me when I looked at my father and mother that they were afraid of something but they never knew what.

I grew up. I continued my running. I continued my

excursions outside the dome holding my breath and I took to spending nights away from home. I began to drink the tear-making liquor brewed in the town. It was commonly called Holy Water.

I think I believed I was something special, something other than clay. And then one day I made love to the wife of one of the farmers who lived in the Rill Hinterland and he caught us. Think of that, if you can imagine it. His face was like something screwed up and thrown away in the rubbish.

Later he came after me. That was the next great learning in my life for I killed him. I was in the barn where the Holy Water was served and there were about twenty other young people with me. I had my back to the door and the first indication I had that anything was wrong was when the room suddenly fell silent. I turned around and there he was, the farmer. He looked crazy and his face was blotchy. He had a baling hook in one hand. Have you ever seen one of those? No. You still find them on old-habit planets. It's a sharp hook mounted on a handle so that you can grip it. You dig the hook into bales and then drag them. Well he didn't say anything. He just stared at me and then he swung the hook low and up. I jumped. I used my hand to parry the blow and the point of the hook went right through the palm of my hand.

WULF: Here Wilberfoss offered his left hand and Lily and I could clearly see the pale scar in the center of his palm.

WILBERFOSS: I bled like Christ or Francis Dionysos with stigmata, but I had the hook. The blow had unbalanced the man and he fell against me and I closed my right hand around his throat and squeezed. There was nothing he could do. He tried to knee me. He tried to squirm. But I squeezed and my face was only inches from his. I could have kissed him. I saw blood on his lips. I felt the stickiness of my own blood as it ran between us. I saw his eyes stare. I saw the moment of his death. And at that same moment, something in me turned black. I had enjoyed the killing. I had him bent back against the bar, I could have been embracing him. I enjoyed the killing and something in me turned black. With his staring eyes in front of me, a small black acorn lodged in my heart and it has never gone away and now it is grown into a black oak tree.

WULF: Wilberfoss was getting excited in a way that we had observed before. There was no tolerant linkage between his thoughts and his feelings. He was like a human baby, not like a grown man. Lily moved in. She administered a small injection and this stopped Wilberfoss. He sobered and his passion drained away.

Self-hatred can have many manifestations. To Wilberfoss, his past was so marred and filled with disfigurement that he wanted to obliterate himself, body and spirit. Of course, at this time in his cure, we did not know the depth of his self-loathing. We could only guess at what he meant when he talked about a black oak tree which was growing in his veins.

WILBERFOSS: They dragged me off and someone worked the hook from my hand and within minutes it seemed I was under guard in the local dispensary and the nurse was packing my hand with a sweet-smelling balm which numbed it. He also gave me a shot of something which took away my sense of color and made the inside of my mouth dry and when I tried to stand I found I had no strength. Then my father arrived and talked at me but I could not understand a word. Nothing seemed to matter.

So, hours later, I was sent up in the shuttle, still in a drug-jacket, and then I was sent to hospital and then to prison. I was like a cork on a stream. I had no control over my life. And it was while I was in prison that I began to understand the darkness that had grown inside me.

I had strangled and had liked doing it. The strength in the arms, the stiffness of the body, the thrill of full commitment. You see, the killing had caressed that same secret area in me that had been so quickened by lovemaking. And yet how different. My innocence was gone. I felt that everything I touched became dirty. The leaves that should have been green were black.

But it wasn't just the killing. As a farmer's lad I was used to killing. I used to lie in wait for and flay the sand snakes when they tried to steal the vegetables from underground. You could always tell when one was there. You'd see the vegetable, a lettuce say, in the family plot and it'd be moving, rocking, like a float on the sea. Then you'd see the lips of the sand snake, like a band of blue rubber, come up from underneath and grip the body of the plant with its gritty little teeth. That's when you'd strike. There was a kind of fork called a snaketine with sharp barbed prongs. You'd jab this underground, well below the lips, and then hang on. Sometimes I've seen a snake drag the entire tine fork under. Most times you'd just hold on and let the snake convulse under the ground and then, when it had tired itself out, you'd drag it out and slit it open. One of my first inventions was to link a tine fork up to the farm generator and that cut the snaking time by half. Give them a charge and then drag them out like a stocking filled with sand and slit them.

No, it wasn't just the killing. It was the killing of a man. Was he better or worse than me? No. He was me. I was, am, him. All men and women became my family. I wanted their forgiveness. But there in the prison there was no forgiveness. I slept with my crime. I lived with my crime. There was no forgiveness.

No, that's not quite true. There was some forgiveness. There was some gentleness. Kindness came like . . . There was a warder who took a liking to me. At first I noticed little things. A nod of recognition. An extra ration of toilet paper. An extra potato. A book without the last page torn out. Then the man who shared my cell was moved out without warning and sent to another wing. That suited me. I wanted solitude. But then three days later my warder friend came to visit me. We had to whisper. He wanted to know my story, wanted to help me to see the prison psychiatrist or monk, whichever would help, wanted to help me pull myself together. He wanted me.

I saw it coming. Even now, so many years later, I wonder whether he knew what was driving him. Came one night I talked about myself in whispers and even as I spoke I felt him kiss me. And in the next moment I kissed him and held him as though holding and kissing him would somehow cleanse me. And he whispered something strange to me. He said, "You have a fire in you. Warm me."

We made love then and many times later. Quietly and intensely. Whenever we could. And I knew he had forgiven me and trusted me for he stood holding my iron bunk with his strong back toward me and his neck bare and I ran my fingers over it.

Then one day he came to me and he said, "Do you love me or am I just what's available?" The question caught me off guard. It seemed irrelevant. I had no answer. And then he said, "You who have so much must never be cruel to those that love you. But you are cruel and cold." I did not understand what he meant. "Your case has been reviewed," he said finally. "The wife has given more evidence in your favor. You have been given your freedom." He paused and looked at me and then continued, "You will be leaving tomorrow. I shall be staying here. Who has been most in prison? You have all the heat a man can want, but you are a cold-hearted bastard."

And I did leave prison the next day. He did not come to say goodbye and I did not go looking for him.

An official of the prison gave me my few belongings and papers which stated that I was a free citizen. There was money too.

I sat in the air-lock waiting for the shuttle to carry me down from the prison torus and I cried. You see, for a while I had known peace, and then my friend, or the man who I thought was my friend, with his cruel words had opened the wound again, had revealed a blackness inside me. Misery gave way to anger, which is healthier, but the anger was directed against myself. You see, I was not what my friend had called me . . . I was not cold. Am not cold. I have followed my lights into darkness. I have tried to be kind. I have shared. But I have been ignorant and vanity is a sure sign of ignorance. "What do people want of me?" I asked as I sat in the shuttle sliding down toward the surface of Icarus. And I wondered what I could do to achieve peace and where I could place the fierce energy that threatened to tear me apart.

Every question has an answer. The problem is knowing what questions to ask and recognizing answers when they come.

The shuttle port was busy when we landed. There was no one to meet me and I was glad. I doubted if my family and friends yet knew where I was. I was alone and unknown. That felt clean. There was a transit vehicle about to leave for my home sector of Icarus but I avoided it. I remember how turbulent I felt: free and frightened, angry and hopeful. I could not sit, passive in a transit carriage, my bag on my knee.

Then I made a decision. I decided to run home. I was half a planet away but I would run home. No sooner was the thought born in me than I knew it was the right thing to do. I thought the run would be an achievement. I hoped it would bring meaning of some kind. There are those whose spirit is only satisfied by challenges. I had the money I had been given and with this I bought a small tent, some provisions, a small pack for my back and shoes that I could run in. Then off I went.

Icarus is covered by a network of translucent tunnels which join all the dome farms. The tunnels are like canals of air. Within them there are always plants growing and the air is sweet and pure. The tunnels lie like a giant silver net thrown over brown rocky hills and swamps where the mineral water bubbles pink and green and poisonous.

I had never seen my own world. The shuttle port was somewhere close to the equator and the crops there were soft red fruits which grew under the shade of leaves and a chewy grass which stained the mouth yellow. Here everything was larger than at home. The domes were higher and enclosed trees and I saw flowers which had a crown like a single staring brown eye. They produced oil.

I ran. I was not fit but I had will. I ran and avoided the main transport routes. I took the tunnels which had only been built for the convenience of the farmers. At night I slept in my tent. When my provisions ran out I began to live off the land, eating the food raw. I was punishing myself for being what I am and curiously I felt better for it.

Eventually, after three weeks or so on the road, I came to a narrow tunnel which climbed up a rock face in a series of long zigzags and emerged on a high plateau.

Here there were no farms. The air was thinner and the sky which shone above the crinkled plastic cover was a deep blue, almost aquamarine. Standing with my nose pressed against the stiff plastic wall I looked out on a wild desert where coils of dust and sand were the only things that moved as they scoured the landscape. Here nothing grew. I saw black ice in the fissures between rocks. I saw rocks split as though with a knife. Once a sandstorm blew up and the black and brown particles crawled over the clear plastic like water and left marks like the sucker prints of one of the creatures that lived in the Sour Sea close to my home.

At night it was so cold that I dared not sleep but ran blindly, my hand pressed against the smooth dome until the fingers were numb and then hunkering down, sucking my fingers until they began to tingle. I slept in the day, making a bed of soil. I had no food and I sucked stones. My bowels ached and my stomach made wind as it tried to digest air.

But there came a day when I knew I was running downhill. It was a slight descent, but oh what hope it gave me and far out across the plain I could see a splash of green. A plantation, surely.

I ran on but it was not running such as you know. I hopped and jumped and nursed my feet which were cracked and bleeding.

Eventually I came across green shoots growing in the tunnel. These were a native shrub which had adapted to the kind of air we breathe. The leaves were poisonous, I knew, but the roots held nourishment and the worst I would get was a bellyache. I ate those roots, spitting out the grit, as though they were confections of the finest chefs. Starvation quickens every sense just as privation quickens one's understanding of what it means to be human. But I could not eat much. My stomach felt full after a few mouthfuls. But I felt livelier and hopeful and more awake.

I ran on and at about midday when the shadows were at their smallest and the roof of the tunnel became misty, I thought I saw a figure in the distance in front of me. There was a place where a cross-tunnel of clear plastic joined the tunnel in which I was running and it was here that the figure seemed to be standing as though waiting for me. I waved but the figure did not respond. At first I thought it was a child, it seemed so small. Then I thought it was a woman, it seemed so poised. Finally I could see it was a human, a man, but he was as small as a monkey. He was dressed in a plain brown garment which matched the color of the soil. As I came closer I could see his face. It was compact, almost the face of a weasel, and he seemed to be smiling in a quirky way as though he knew something that I did not, and yet I did not feel alarmed or threatened by him. At the last moment I realized there was a light shining about him.

Then, when I was about twenty yards away, the figure suddenly started to expand. I felt an explosion in the space between my ears. The man's face grew into the muzzle of a bull. Golden horns sprouted from his forehead. The shoulders bunched. The brown garment transformed to black fur. The legs became stiff and short and solid-muscled. I found myself facing a bull and its bulk almost filled the tunnel. It stared down at me with lowered head and eyes of yellow flint.

I approached it carefully, unafraid, filled with wonder, my arms upraised, and I stroked the fur between its eyes. I felt its hot breath. I touched its horns and as I touched them I knew I was in the presence of a God. I wanted to clasp the bull by its horns and swing my legs up and grasp it around the neck. I wanted to straddle its back and dig my fingers in its black fur and solid muscle. I wanted the bull to turn me and mount me and crush me. And when I wished this it seemed that the bull grew even larger until it occupied all the space in the tunnel. I fell down in a faint, unable to move but still conscious, and in that state the spirit of the bull penetrated me. Man or woman, bull or beast, the God entered me and possessed me utterly, through mouth, nose, ears, eyes and skin; yes, through penis and anus. Totally. No scrap of me was left untouched and yet I lived with dignity. The spirit of the God bubbled in my veins and made me merry. "Dip me in wine, O ye powers, and I will be one with the grape and the harvest."

The God broke into pieces of gold and these spun around me. They became people, a golden blur of people. April was there, and the man I had strangled, and his wife and other women, and my mother and father, and my jailor and Medoc who lay far in my future. They were dancing around me like children around a bonfire. And I shouted that I was not dead, and as I shouted the visitors faded and I woke up.

I lay on the ground savoring the silence and privacy.

And everything was changed. I awoke with the knowl- edge that the gold of the God had entered my veins and that I had eaten the sun like an apple. I saw as though for the first time or like a man recovering his sight after a long period of blindness. I saw colors I had never seen before. The dark blue of the sky had a rich texture of crushed velvet and light swarmed in the sky like silver snakes. The brown world outside the walls of my tunnel ran with colors of earth: with red and gray and brown and cream. The green shoots of the small plants whose roots I had eaten glowed like flame. There was a small creature, a bit like a beetle and a bit like an ant and I had crushed it under my heel in my ecstasy so that one of its legs trailed. I picked it up marveling at the iridescent colors which

patterned it. I could see moisture at the broken leg joint
and I willed it to heal, saying, "I affirm the unity of all
life." I closed my eyes and when I opened them again the
small leg was working like a machine hammer and the
insect scampered to the edge of my hand and launched
itself into the air and fluttered to the ground.

That was when I noticed the difference. My hand
was no longer my hand. It was larger and luminous. I
crossed to the side of the dome and peered at the clear
plastic, seeking an image of myself. I saw a horned man.
I reached up and could feel my horns, short and stiff and
cruel and throbbing with new life. My feet had healed
and were larger and golden like my hands. Wonderingly,
I picked up my pack and few belongings and began to
run away from that cross-path where tunnels met. I ran
with the fierce energy of the bull that had entered me.
I ran with the care of the gentle man in the dun brown
habit guiding me for I would not willingly bruise any
living creature.

Something else. I was now running *toward* and not
away from. Punishment became pleasure. I was not running home except in a new philosophical sense. I was not
running toward my parents' farm but toward the nearest
outpost of the Gentle Order of St. Francis Dionysos. I had
recognized that small man who met me on the way for
I had seen his statue mounted outside the small dwell-
ing occupied by the Gentle Order. It was St. Francis
Dionysos.

WULF: And the bull?

WILBERFOSS: The bull was part of him. And the
bull was myself. My true nature. The stamp of the God
made manifest. Life, if you like. The force of life. Kind
and cruel and neither of these and both.

WULF: And did you really have horns and golden skin?

WILBERFOSS: For a time I did. I had them for as long as I needed a sign. Then, with my decision to join the Gentle Order they gradually faded.

WULF: And when you came to The House of the Gentle Order?

WILBERFOSS: When I came to the House I knocked on the door and I was welcomed and I told my story and I was accepted. And so my commitment to the Gentle Order began. The next day I was given the green habit of the postulant and I felt great relief as I drew it over my head.

WULF: Didn't it get tangled in your horns?

WILBERFOSS: No. The outward bull was gone and had taken residence inside. Inside inside.

The effects of the liberating drugs were fading. Lily and I watched as Wilberfoss began to close down. His eyes which had held some sparkle when he spoke now became dull pools of pain and finally blank. The voice began to slur and the sounds transmuted into grunts and stops. The arms relaxed like dead eels.

But before he faded entirely he rallied and spoke clearly and urgently for one last time.

WILBERFOSS: Such was my youth. Such was my happiness. How could such happiness lead to such sadness? How could it be that I, who came to love all life and to

hate all killing, should come to kill so many? How did I
come to kill the God?

Wilberfoss stared at me and Lily as though we were
sharks and demons. I do not know what he saw. Some
gateway into his private hell sprang open and he looked
in. He started to scream and he jabbed with his fingers
for his eyes. But Lily was quick. She caught his hands in
mid-strike with one of her dexetels and at the same time
injected him from the cache at the nape of his neck. He
collapsed, shuddering and heaving, and then lay still. I
remembered his description of how he had caught the
soil snakes and how they convulsed underground.

Lily picked him up and hefted him into her womb-
cage and trundled away toward the living quarters without so much as a word to me. I stayed on in the garden. I
had much to think about. An autoscribe is good with facts
and figures and solid stable syntax. But with regard to Jon
Wilberfoss, I was at the margin of my ability. Perpetual
self-referencing can only lead to meaninglessness and hell.
Inside inside, as Wilberfoss says.

That day I found no answer.

The next day I wrote my case notes and although
this chapter is dealing with Wilberfoss's life, I will here
quote my original notes as they illuminate Wilberfoss's
discourse:

What are we to make of this? I cannot tell what mode
Wilberfoss is speaking in. He sounds realistic most of the
time, matter of fact almost, but then it becomes clear that
he is speaking emblematically.

In a way that is exactly his problem. He is trapped
between two worlds and has confused them. He has
the world of his feelings where meaning comes from
his intuition and is perceived in visionary terms. And he

has the real world in which children are born and men and women die and autoscribes swoop. At any moment Wilberfoss can experience a collapse of the real world into the world of his emblems. And there he must make his own way for Lily can keep him alive and I can tell his story but only he can journey through.

Well, that is the perception of an autoscribe and I am aware of my rationalism. I am perplexed by the thought that I may have got it all wrong. Perhaps the emblematic world *is* the real world after all and I am no more than a passing fantasy in Wilberfoss's world. In which case Wilberfoss really did have horns and golden skin and killed the godhead in him. In my rationalism I am glad that I do not have dreams. What dreams can an oil can have?.

There is more to come. I can tell that. What we have heard today is merely the sighing of wind before the coming of the rain. There are things Wilberfoss cannot face, yet. Things for which he has no shape of words. Things of which he is perhaps numbly unaware and which are waiting to open their jaws and bite as he moves closer through the darkness to his own truth. We saw that happen in his last moments of consciousness.

What then did take place aboard the *Nightingale*?

POSTSCRIPTUM
This section cannot end on that question. There is more. But you do not need to hear Wilberfoss's voice to understand it. I can tell the tale briefly.

Jon Wilberfoss was accepted as a postulant in the Gentle Order. I have the notes made by the Magistra who accepted him and that lady comments on the fire that seemed to burn inside him. She mentions his quickness and the candor with which he confessed. He talked about his home farm, the man he had killed, life in prison and the vision he had seen. The Magistra had some doubts about Wilberfoss mainly, it seems, concerned with his youth but she was also excited by his strangeness. The Gentle Order absorbed the fact that Wilberfoss had killed a fellow mortal. They absorbed it in the sense that they did not hold that a man's Life should be forever marred by one mistake. In their view, as the Magistra's notes make clear, Wilberfoss had accepted his act and was set on a new path. Was it not true that the gentle St. Francis himself had once aspired to be a soldier? And was not Paul once Saul and the passionate Augustine of Hippo a philanderer before a Saint? Most men seem to require a shock to push them into their true spiritual vocation. Even so Wilberfoss was watched closely especially as he took the sacred oath of the Gentle Order, vowing to protect Life.

Wilberfoss went to the training school on Assisi Central and there trained as a pilot. He specialized also in land contact. This means that in the course of a Mercy Mission he was one of the pilots who physically went to the surface of a planet either to pick up or to deliver a sick or dying life-form. He was not a contact specialist, but he showed himself to have contact skills. That is rare and special. It was in this part of his training that he learned the stealth I mentioned when Miranda came a-calling.

When Wilberfoss was convalescing in Lily's Garden he would sometimes sit for hours talking about the days when he was a contact pilot. Extraordinary stories. Occasionally a colleague from those days would visit the Pacifico Monastery and the two of them would sit together, merry as thieves, swapping yarns while the sun went down.

Wilberfoss relished excitement and difference. He liked the glamour of being a pilot and he had the energy of two men when it came to confronting hardship. He must have found the simple life of Shuttle Pilot boring, despite the fact that he rationalized his experience as necessary servitude. The problem was that he saw himself (as he states) as someone special. That need not be a bad thing in itself for it seems to me that individual human beings should see themselves as special: they are unique lifeforms. But Wilberfoss believed he had a destiny to fulfill. Thus in his mind, the strange event when he was a child and was saved after falling near the shore, and the fact of his selection for the captaincy of the *Nightingale*, were linked. Destiny.

We can say of his marriage to Medoc, the Talline woman, that it satisfied his lust for the curious and his desire to serve. He discovered the peaceful family man within the brave dare-devil. Medoc satisfied (say) ninety percent of him.

This story concerns the remaining ten percent.

5

The Offer

Tancredi paused and looked at Wilberfoss. It was a look which could have been envy or it could have been pity. "Assisi Central have sent me this," he said, tapping the red-edged document. "They have invited you to become Captain of the *Nightingale*."

Wilberfoss sat back in his chair and stared at Magister Tancredi. His face was expressionless. Then he said, "I think there has been a mistake. I never put myself forward as a candidate."

"No mistake," said Tancredi. "With the *Nightingale* you did not need to put yourself forward. No one did. The Magistri came looking. I flatter myself that even I, long in the tooth as I am, had a chance. But they needed a younger man. And they chose you."

"But there are—"

"Out of all the available pilots, some of whom are undoubtedly better than you in matters mathematical and mechanical, they chose you. Or rather they *invited* you.

For the final decision must be yours."

"Why was I not told? Why was I not interviewed?"

"About two years ago, you may remember, we had a visit from the Magistri of Assisi. You were their guide. You brought them in, took them around to Kithaeron, Fum and Sesha and then saw them on their way. One of them even stayed at your house."

"But I thought they were just on a fact-finding mission."

"They were."

"But they told me—"

"Accept it. They have chosen you. The honor is without parallel as far as I am concerned. Though I can see that in your case there are complications."

Silence between the two men. Then Wilberfoss.

"Do you know how they reached their decision? Was it voted on?"

"Well, I suppose voting came into it. It usually does. But they would have spent a long time in meditation. And remember, over half the committee concerned with the *Nightingale* are quaestors. They'll have been in trance a great deal of the time, trying to read the future, examining you, seeing you in light and dark. Few men will have been examined as you have been. Believe me. They quite possibly know you far better than you know yourself. No, more than that. I would say they definitely know you better than you know yourself. Trust them. They are not fools, nor are they politically motivated despite the stories. You are no one's favorite. You are simply the man they have chosen. But in the end, the decision is yours."

"Did you know I was being considered for the *Nightingale*?"

"I knew you were being considered, but that is all. So were Jones of Kithaeron and Bothwell of Fum. And there must have been many, many others too. But they saw something very special in you." Tancredi looked at Wilberfoss quizzically, with his head on one side. "Come on. Don't tell me you are not excited."

"I suppose I'm excited. But an honor unlooked for, not even considered or even desired, must make any man pause. I say, 'Why me?' I suppose the truth is I don't feel worthy. There must be prospective Saints waiting out there. Women and men with a mark on their brow . . . I mean, I'm not pure . . ."

WULFNOTE
You who are reading this and now know something of Wilberfoss and the forces that drove him will understand this remark. And you must surely pity the ignorance of Magister Tancredi.

The conversation stopped. Tancredi shrugged. He was already deferring to Wilberfoss, and then he said, "This is getting us nowhere. Have a glass of wine with me and then go home. Talk with Medoc. You can talk with me again tomorrow."

"I have already made part of my decision," said Wilberfoss. "You can contact Assisi Central and tell them that I have asked to take the forty days. I need that time. And if they have taken so many years to decide on a captain for the *Nightingale*, they can surely allow me that small grace of time."

"Of course they will. They will expect it."

A SECOND WULFNOTE
I was there in the corner and I heard all this. The forty days is the period allowed to any member of the Order of St. Francis Dionysos when faced with a difficult decision. During this period he or she can be absolutely alone, free

to commune only with their own conscience. There will be no other human being near to hand. Frequently people fast during the forty days and frequently they have visions. Usually truth prevails. It is as though there is an universal force at work compelling truth to emerge. Forty days is a long time for dishonesty to live undetected in an open human being. It is society, the pressure of other human beings, which makes for dishonesty I think. Solitude provokes crisis and crisis leads to truth.

Magister Tancredi continued. "In any case, the Magistri of Assisi would probably demand that you take the forty days and that you purge your mind. You may enter the Poverello Garden tonight if you wish. I will make all the arrangements. Lily I am sure is ready. You should take Wulf with you too. Use it to record your moods and ideas. It is a competent autoscribe, reliable and fair, although a bit pompous and old-fashioned in its expression."

In its corner the giant autoscribe, which resembled the helmet of a Greek warrior at Troy, trembled slightly as it floated on its AG cells.

"I will take it gladly," said Jon Wilberfoss.

Magister Tancredi raised his hand. "But before you enter the garden be sure to talk to Medoc. I suggest that you ask her to go with you. Together you two are a unit. A very powerful force. Think on it."

"I will."

And there the conversation ended. Both men sat for a while before the fire and sipped their wine.

They seemed to be communicating though they did not speak. I am not implying any telepathic ability. I have noticed that human beings sometimes seem to communicate most successfully when they are simply sitting together and not speaking. Both men were relaxed. Both were drifting in their minds, the hour being late.

Tancredi I am sure was remembering the time when, before he became Magister of Pacifico, he was a Master Pilot in charge of a hospital ship. And I am also sure he took pride in the fact that one of his domestic pilots had been accorded the singular honor of being invited to captain the *Nightingale*.

As for Wilberfoss . . . At that time I did not know what he was thinking. I was surprised that he had accepted the news so calmly. I was surprised that he did not hurry down the hill to tell his wife Medoc. I was surprised that he stayed so long. I saw him swirl the red wine in his glass. There was a flourish in the gesture. I thought to myself. "He is toasting himself," and at that time I did not realize how dangerous that can be for a human being. Perhaps, even as he sat there, comfortable before the fire, with wine in his glass and basking in the admiration of his Magister, he already thought of himself as "called," as one of the elect whom Fate had selected to fulfill its mission. Perhaps in his mind he went back to that day on his Homeworld Icarus when he met and was possessed by the bull-headed God, perhaps he remembered the miraculous rescue of a foolhardy boy outside the dome of his family farm.

Whatever.

The news that he had been chosen to captain the *Nightingale* gave him a sense of destiny, and all his woes spread from that.

The wine finished, Wilberfoss stood up and bowed to Magister Tancredi. Tancredi showed him out, walking with him to the door. I drifted behind.

Wilberfoss ran down the hill. He paused at the lookout and stood above the bay staring up at the stars. Then it was on again. He never spoke to me.

Knowing where he was going I let myself drift out from the cliff over the dark water and glide down until I was on a level with the arcade where he had his house. Wilberfoss came pounding down the pathway and beckoned to me. He threw open his front door and let me glide through first. I heard the voice of Medoc calling, "Jon. Jon Wilberfoss, is that you? What called you away from shantra?"

Usually Medoc spoke in Common Tongue, the native language of Jon Wilberfoss, for Wilberfoss had no real ability to speak other languages despite his contact skills. Nevertheless, while she spoke the Common Tongue she used Talline expressions whenever necessary for there are some concepts which cannot be translated. "Shantra" is one. (It will be necessary for you to understand something of the Talline language if you are to understand this story.) "Shantra" means literally "the cradle of the stiff-cocked one." If it had been a man speaking he would have used the word "perithom" meaning, literally, "the ship's deck where the womb receives." Both words have a sense of rocking, both are concerned with conception and both convey (though I cannot) the idea of fulfillment.

Medoc was up and dressed in her nightgown and sitting by the fire in the dining-room when I drifted in. She was not expecting me and screamed when she saw me. Not surprising. I am big and I am silent in movement, and in resembling the baleful mask of war I am, I know, frightening. Wilberfoss was close behind and immediately called to her not to be alarmed. He had not expected her to be up which means he did not know her sensibility. I drifted to a corner of the room away from the fire and settled myself just under the ceiling. I spoke words in the Talline language stating that I wanted to be forgiven for barging in and that I wanted hereafter to be ignored like a potted plant. She answered, "Tath ot–to." "So be it."

But of course, I am not a potted plant. I observe everything.

Wilberfoss came in and joined her at the fire. They kissed and touched intimately after the manner of humans and Tallines. Then Wilberfoss drew back. "You look serious and sad," he said.

"Of course I am serious and sad when my tirpara (quickener) steals away without waking me."

"Yes. That was silly of me." Wilberfoss sat down on the floor in front of the fire and picked up the poker and stirred the logs.

"Something important must have happened."

"One of the callers came for me in the night. Magister Tancredi sent her. They didn't want to use the communicator in case there were ears listening."

Medoc's eyes widened. "Ears? What ears? Do you mean me? Our children? Do not speak in riddles, Jon Wilberfoss. Why were you called? Or is it something you cannot tell me? Is there trouble or joy in the calling?"

Wilberfoss took a deep breath. "It is everything," he said. "Trouble and joy. I don't know where I am yet." He stared into the fire. Medoc looked at his head. She saw the way his hair and beard caught highlights from the fire, then she leaned forward and kissed him in his hair. She loosened the front of her gown so that if he wished to touch her he could. The gown opened revealing Medoc's four breasts, her belly and thighs.

"You should have woken me up," she said. "No matter what. If we are one flesh, whether I am grown from your rib or you are grown from my little finger as we Tallines believe, you should have woken me."

"Tancredi was instructed to call me in this way. He didn't have a choice."

"But *you* did." Medoc stood up and moved to the table. She poured two glasses of wine and selected some portions of meat from under a domed contrivance in the middle of the table. "Here, let's eat and drink together, at least," she said.

"What do you mean, 'At least'?"

Medoc did not answer this question. "Drink the wine and tell me your news."

"I have been asked by Assisi Central to become Captain of the *Nightingale*."

Medoc was chewing, pulling the flesh from a bone with her teeth. She sat back by the fire, relaxed. She paused briefly in her chewing. "And what is your decision?"

"I don't know. I have told them I want to take the forty days retreat."

"Are you not happy as you are now?"

"I am very happy."

"Well then?"

"But I can't ignore the call. That would not be human."

"Ah."

"No, I don't mean that to sound the way it came out. I mean, they have asked me—the Magistri of Assisi. They have their reasons. Perhaps they see more than I do. I don't know. I want time to think. Time to decide. It is a great honor. A great chance to do good. The best of opportunities to bring relief and some happiness to many species."

"If you accept their offer what would you propose doing with me and the children?"

Wilberfoss looked at her with genuine surprise. "Why, you'd come with me of course. We'd all be together. There's nothing we would lack aboard the *Nightingale*."

Medoc shrugged. "I don't think there is much for me aboard the *Nightingale*. I have my place here, on this world which you call Juniper, but which I call home."

"Are you saying that if I accept the captaincy of the *Nightingale* you will not come with me?"

"I will not answer a question like that. I will not solve your problem for you. All I will say is that my ambitions are here, in the now, not elsewhere."

"But if you didn't go with me . . . I could be gone half a lifetime—longer, given the time-slip . . ."

"I would be old or in my grave when you came back and your children would be fathers and mothers." Wilberfoss stared at her, grappling with the thoughts she was drawing before him. She said, "I am trying to help you with your decision. I am trying to make it clear to you."

"I feel you are giving me an ultimatum."

"I am trying to make things clear for you. Life is not a series of ultimatums but a series of crossroads. There is always choice. We change, human or Talline. We change. You must sort things out for yourself. You are confused now. Soon you will know your own mind." She opened her arms to him and Wilberfoss knelt up and came to her. He set his body between her legs and slipped his arms around her back. They kissed and then he nuzzled lower until he found her lower breasts which were already beginning to lactate. His lips closed on the nipple and he suckled. Medoc closed her arms around him, cradling his shoulders and head. She was tender: mother and wife. And as she let him feed on her she stared, cold-eyed into the dying fire.

Moments later I saw her eyes close and her lips part. She started to rock.

Some time later Wilberfoss rose from Medoc. The suckling had made her giddy as it does with all Talline women. Perhaps this is a universal characteristic, for I have noticed that when a man or a woman or a non-human-but-wise creature fulfills part of its nature, it feels satisfied in a bright way. Medoc was giddy and light-hearted. She stared at Jon Wilberfoss with her dark hazel eyes and told him that he had a choice to make. She told him that life could only be lived at the moment of living and then she sent him on his way.

Wilberfoss went first to the room where his children were sleeping. He kissed each of them in turn, murmuring words which even I, sharply tuned as I am, could not catch. Then he went into the bedroom which he and Medoc shared. He selected a satchel and this he filled with a few belongings.

Dawn was brightening the sky as he left the house for a second time that night. I went with him.

I remember a bright pink light spreading across the sky and making everything glow with a ruddy warmth. We cast long shadows as we moved down to the gate which led into Lily's Garden.

6

Wulf's Brief Theory of Humanity

Wulf is struck by two facts:

1.) Wilberfoss's entire account of his life is discussed in terms of his sexuality.

2.) In his dealings with Medoc he did not trust the wisdom of his sexuality.

What is one to make of that?

This.

At the dawn of creation, your Maker, whether blind chance or a wondrous creator, gave LIFE the ability to reproduce its own kind. In addition to this ability there was granted the awesome power called DESIRE for without DESIRE, LIFE might just have been content to languish in warm shallow pools. I do not know what kind of desire moves a mollusk, but I do know what desires move women and men.

As far as Wulf is concerned, the sexual drive is the beginning and end of all knowledge that one needs to understand humanity. The men and women who are truly content and at home with their sexuality have too much on their minds to be worried about anything else. But such are very few. Bewildering to a machine is the realization that human society has rarely reflected this truth about the sexual drive in human nature and hence there has been a contradiction at the center of human affairs and hence at attempts to create civilization. This contradiction has led to misunderstandings of function and hence rivalries, jealousies, massive cruelty and guilt.

From generation to generation, the instinctive drive to well-being through sensual fulfillment has charged the human race and in each generation this drive has been thwarted and frustrated and its potential largely lost. In such a circumstance how can tolerance, appreciation of beauty and creative frenzy survive? Answer: only with extreme difficulty, and it is a tribute to the strength of the human spirit that, despite the inimical conditions that human beings have created for their own lives, cathedrals have been built, symphonies written, plays performed and some children conceived in love.

The Evolution of the Human Spirit is a book still to be written. My present involvement with Wilberfoss has led me to speculate. After the killer Achilles came the intellectual Christ and after him came St Francis who talked to brother sun and sister moon and to the wind and the trees and the flowers and the birds. St Francis taught us to see beauty in creation . . . and he was lucky in a way. Lucky because he could assume a kind and loving creator who gave meaning and order to all experience. It is after all not so hard to feel love for a sparrow if the fall of that sparrow can be seen as part of the order of an all-loving, all-knowing and all-powerful Creator. But take the Creator away and now tell me why you still love that sparrow.

Not so easy, eh? Materialism is a miserable attempt to give life meaning but it is an attempt. The important thing is that materialism be not seen as an end in itself.

To the materialist, a sparrow as a sparrow is nothing but a bundle of feathers and a song, catfood perhaps or a winged flytrap. What does a sparrow mean? No answer. To the materialist the very question smacks of mysticism and induces a sneer. To explain why human kind can love a sparrow needs a more comprehensive theory. That theory must engage itself with ALL of life. Now, life is lived in the here and now and not in the elsewhere and later. That is where humankind must begin.

In the appreciation of the present moment lies the deepest awareness of life. Do you doubt me? Ask a condemned man or woman. They will tell you but they will hate you for the question. But you are all condemned women and men, men and women, and you contrive to ignore it . . . sublime hypocrites.

Coming out of the twentieth century, humankind was like a condemned man. There was no hope for the future. War behind. War in front. Lies in high places. Cheating in public places. Skulduggery of all kinds, such as appeals to patriotism, belt-tightening and thrift. The catalog goes on as it always has. But then there came a change. At last, at long last, after years of listening to Achilles, Christ and most of the other religious leaders, people gave up listening to promises because promises were all to do with the future. The future became a burden.

Enter the spirit of Dionysos. So long hidden because pagan. So long secret because persecuted . . . but explosive as a fire smoldering in a closed house. Dionysos lives in the now: in the unfolding of a plant or the multiplication of a cell. Where there is no hope but only the present, there shall you find Dionysos.

*   *   *

But to return to sensuality.

In the case of our man Wilberfoss, he saw half a truth and thought it was the whole truth. True to his nature he broke the mold and married an alien woman and found all his sensual needs more than catered for. The Tallines place their sensuality at the center of their lives. That is why they do not fight wars.

But this silly man was not content with the here and now. He wanted more. He heeded the calling to a "higher" destiny. And that meant he started to think about the future.

Why?

Why?

What did he lack?

For those who are about it, true education is hard.

7

A Coda Which Also Marks a Departure

So at dawn, the door to Lily's Garden closed behind Jon Wilberfoss and he began his forty-day retreat.

At his home all seemed to be well but then, three days after Jon Wilberfoss entered Lily's Garden, Medoc emerged from the house and pinned a note to the door. The note was a simple announcement. It stated that she had satisfied all requirements placed upon a Talline woman with regard to the termination of her marriage and that henceforth she was divorced from Jon Wilberfoss and free and willing to take up a new marriage.

Wulf was astounded. More than ever, I realized that I did not understand the human or the Talline.

Word of Medoc's announcement spread quickly and many men, mainly Tallines, gathered to read. I will explain as well as I can.

Within hours of Medoc pinning up her announcement, I was summoned by Magister Tancredi to leave the garden where I was attending on Jon Wilberfoss. I flew up to him. The Magister instructed me to find out what was happening with Medoc. He was very disturbed. He had not imagined that Medoc would take matters into her own hands in such a direct manner. Thus Magister Tancredi, for all his experience and years of contact with alien life-forms and alien mores, showed that he had neglected to study the Tallines. And is not this a common thing . . . that we neglect the truth that stands on our doorstep while we guess at meanings in the stars?

Immediately upon receiving my orders I swooped down on Medoc's house and tapped at her door. She welcomed me and when I explained my business, invited me in.

The house was very clean and I guessed that Medoc had been scrubbing and washing during the three days since Jon Wilberfoss had departed. New baking had been done too and the place smelled of warm bread. In the back of the house the children were playing and they came tumbling into the room when they heard me arrive. I have some small reputation as a story teller and they would not leave until I had promised to tell them a story from the olden times of Earth. Note that they identify me with Earth.

When they had gone, Medoc sat at her writing desk and faced me. "So what would you ask of me, Monsieur autoscribe? What can I tell Magister Tancredi?" We were speaking in Talline.

"Magister Tancredi wonders why, so quickly, so without consultation, you have chosen to divorce Jon Wilberfoss. That man, Jon Wilberfoss, knows nothing of your action. Do you not think it would have been wise, kind even, to have consulted him? Distressed by the news he may not think clearly. No decision is yet made. No final decision. All awaits."

Medoc replied. "Your Magister Tancredi knows little of Talline customs. When Jon Wilberfoss married me he agreed to abide by our customs. These are gentler and altogether less strict than your own, but they are nevertheless very clear. Divorce is in the hands of the wife. The deserted wife just as much as the abused wife can claim divorce."

"But Jon Wilberfoss has not deserted you."

"I laid the issues before him. In my mind I decided to give him three days. I regard that as generous. Any man who needs more than three days to decide whether he wants to stay with a woman or not has already made his decision."

"I do not understand." (And I did not.)

"I set the issues before him, I could do no more. The moment he entered Lily's Garden he was a dead man to me. He had chosen his future, or one of his futures. And that was more important to him than the joy he might find in the here and the now with me. Many Talline women have divorced a man for less though few for the same reason. That is a penalty I must pay for marrying and loving a non-Talline."

"Do you still love him?"

"Of course."

"Then why—"

"Because he does not love me."

Suddenly I saw with a sharp clarity what she meant. The intention is nothing, the act and deed is now and all-important.

"And you would be very unwise, Monsieur Wulf, to tell Jon Wilberfoss of my decision. Let him have his forty days. He will emerge the stronger for it. If he chooses the *Nightingale* then he would have had to abandon me in any case. If he rejects the *Nightingale* he will still have his house and access to his children and time to contemplate the passing moment. A one such as him will not remain lonely for long."

I had to admire the clarity of her decision. "Tell me about the note you have pinned to your door," I said.

She smiled. "Oh. That is an old custom with us. Some women no longer follow it but because I am the woman I am and because I know that what I am doing might have certain implications and consequences, I decided to be very precise with our customs. I did not want anyone to think I was confused or acting from pique. The divorce is formal and final and I want a new husband. In my note I outline my terms. For instance, I don't want to bear any more children, so any Talline male who is looking to build his bloodline must look elsewhere. But I am happy to take charge of any children which may already be in the house. This means that I am looking for a man whose wife has died rather than one who has declared divorce. I want to marry a man whose house is a long way from here. Remember that with us, the houses where we live are in the keep of the males. We women can move where we want for wherever we move we are at home or if we find ourselves at a loss we can enter any of the gardens. I have also said that I want to marry a Talline male and not a human male for I have finished with experiments. I guarantee that I know medicine. I state that I want to work outdoors and that I am in good health with most of my teeth. And now I am waiting."

"And have any callers come knocking?"

"Some."

"Any that you like the look of?"

"Not so far. But the severance bread is not yet stale and word of my declaration is still being carried abroad. I doubt if my mother will have heard yet and she lives only a few hundred miles away."

"You did not tell her of your separation?"

"No. Why should I? If I encounter problems I may go to her. But I might also go to my father who has a farm on Warmstone Island far out in the North Sea. I am not making plans at the moment. I am waiting."

And at that moment there came a knocking on the front door. "Excuse me," said Medoc as she rose. I noted with interest that she spoke to me as though to a human. She answered the door and I heard a cry of surprise and delight. This was followed by a rapid exchange in a Talline dialect which I could only partly understand.

When Medoc re-entered the room she had two men accompanying her. With one of them her relationship was obvious; it was her elder brother and their two faces were like pressings from the same mold but each had endured a different weathering. The other man's style of dress and appearance told me that he was from the islands in the southern ocean. His hair was so blond that it was almost white and he wore it woven into a plait which reached to the small of his back. His beard was a shade or two darker than his hair and likewise plaited. I judged him to be about the same age as Medoc's brother though he was leaner and altogether more seasoned. His skin was dark like rubbed wood. He stood with sturdy legs spread and turned his wide-brimmed hat in his hands. In a human, such a stance would have suggested embarrassment.

Medoc's brother whose name I discovered was Tillo, was surprised and I think a bit angry to see me there. He wanted to dismiss me. He associated me with Jon Wilberfoss for whom he had no love since Wilberfoss had, at least in terms of Talline customs, jilted his sister. Medoc intervened. "Wulf is merely a mechanical writer," she said, searching to find the Talline words to describe my function. "It is a helpful glide-about and messenger. Give it no thought. Introduce me to your companion."

Tillo looked at me darkly and then nodded. He turned

away and paid me no more attention. "This," he said, taking his colleague by the arm, "is my friend Aptagar. He's a fisherman. He had a scrub-down at the Commonhall before coming here so he doesn't smell too bad. We've come up together from Shell Island. I came as soon as I heard you'd posted a declaration."

"You heard quickly," said Medoc.

"I have friends here who keep an eye out for such things in this town."

"Aptagar is welcome. Will he be seated?" Aptagar put his hat on the table and then chose one of the seats by the fireside. He did not sit back in the chair but rather perched, again like one who is embarrassed and expects to leave hurriedly. "Does Aptagar have a tongue?" asked Medoc, not unkindly, but in a mischievous manner.

Aptagar cleared his throat, "I am pleased to meet you, Medoc. Your brother has often spoken of you. By your leave, I have come to taste the severance bread."

"Straight to the point as ever," said Tillo. "I'll leave you two to it. If you want me I'll be in the Commonhall trying your thin northern beer." He turned to me. "And if I may offer advice, my sister, I would abandon junk like this. No good comes of such things." And so saying he struck me forcefully with his knuckles. I swayed obediently. Evidently satisfied, Tillo left.

Aptagar and Medoc began to get acquainted. I observed that each of them had a clear idea of what they wanted and the discussion between them was more like a carpet sale than a betrothal. Aptagar's wife, Rani, had been swept from the rocks by a rogue wave while gathering shellfish. This had happened a month ago. Aptagar had four children: two sons who already helped him in the boat and two daughters who were still at school. Aptagar had a house with a cellar and a loft and a sailboat that he had shaped himself from the egg-case of a Featherfin

Drifter. "At night I still cry for Rani," he said, "for we were a rare match, she and I. Hard as chemu (a fish's tooth), sweet as poro (the roe of a sea urchin), soft as ptum (a kind of putty made from kelp). Have you a mind to be a fisherman's wife? The life is hard but you won't find me running away like some." He pointed with his thumb at me. "You'll see me every minute of the day, if you've a mind. You'll be with me. Out in the boat, out in the islands, dragging in the nets. Me and the boys. Your lads too if they've a mind."

"I'll consider it," said Medoc. "And now will you consider this bread?"

"I'll consider a drink, if this is a brewing house."

"It is," said Medoc. "My former husband was a finer brewer than most Tallines of either hemisphere. You may taste his beer and his wine, but I have no skills in that regard." She poured a glass of amber liquid from a carafe on the shelf above the fire. "Nor have I any desire to stand the buffet on the deck of a ship. I am a landswoman."

"Perhaps then I'll retire from the sea," said Aptagar. "I've faced enough storms. I've prospered from my work. I'd not ask you to go to sea if you'd guard the home. But I won't live away from the sea."

"The sea pleases me too," said Medoc.

And so their conversation continued.

That night Aptagar slept on the floor.

The next day they got tipsy and continued talking.

On the next day another Talline came calling. He was a merchant from the towns which have grown up close to the Kithaeron monastery on the other side of the planet. He had dark curly hair and a flashing smile and he took Medoc out to dine while Aptagar sucked on his pipe and looked at his thick gnarled hands and sampled Jon Wilberfoss's beer.

Medoc and the merchant returned late and the merchant too slept on the floor. Both men snored and I have no doubt but that Medoc heard this.

For myself, interesting though it was, I decided that I could no longer stay to watch the peculiarities of Talline courtship. I reported to Magister Tancredi and then returned to Lily's Garden.

Seven days afterward I heard that Medoc had locked up the house and departed. She had made her choice.

I did not of course mention these events to Jon Wilberfoss. That man was deep into his meditation and he would have time enough to think about love and departure if he decided not to accept the *Nightingale*.

8

Events in Lily's Garden

Outside the gate leading to Lily's Garden stands the famous statue of St. Francis Dionysos. The bull head thrusting out from the hood caught the first rays of the sun on its burnished horns. Jon Wilberfoss paused briefly before the statue and nodded to it and then passed through the gate. I followed.

Lily was waiting for us. She closed the gate behind us and then trundled around to the front, withdrawing her dexetels into her canopy with a snap. She spoke aloud for Jon Wilberfoss's benefit. "Call me Lily. Mmmm. Sleep room for Jon Wilberfoss is ready. Occupy now. Mmmm. You will follow Lily. Now." She turned on the gravel path with a harsh sound and began to move away.

She did not offer a word of welcome. Lily is a gifted nurse where the sick are concerned but she has few circuits devoted to the social graces. Jon Wilberfoss did not seem to mind. He seemed completely preoccupied, oblivious.

Lily led us around a large wooden screen upon which is written in early Talline hieroglyphs the story of this particular garden.

Gardens such as the one we were now entering are as close as the Tallines ever came to having a church. It is a sacred place filled with earth magic. At its center is a traditional Pectanile.

Ah, the Pectanile. This must be now explained.

I have said already that the Tallines have a nature religion and an earth culture. These two qualities are united in the Pectanile. It is a statue made from a dense white stone quarried at one of the large islands in the North Sea. The whole of the planet is dotted with Pectanile statues and every sacred garden has one. To the Tallines, the Pectanile is a tangible expression of their feeling for life. It is, if you like, a focus of symbolism, and is capable of many interpretations. Most Tallines carry a small Pectanile about their person.

Here, as well as I can describe it to you, is what a Pectanile looks like. Its top is open like the neck of a flask. The sides are gently curved, swelling to resemble buttocks on one side and breasts on the other though they are not depictions of either of these. The main thing to understand is that the shape is organic, like a root or a tuber. Part of its beauty resides in its not being specific. The Pectanile rests on a solid spreading base which usually continues for several feet under the ground.

Standing on the ground in front of the Pectanile and looking up, you will see a cave entrance. This is located between and below the twin nodules which might be testes or breasts. Steps are carved outside the Pectanile and lead inside. It is very easy to climb right up inside a Pectanile. Inside, the opening in the top meets the opening in the bottom in a complex relationship of chambers.

The top opening narrows to a funnel. When there is rain, the water runs down this funnel and drips into a cistern or settling pool. The overflow dribbles out through the cave mouth down a channel cut in the steps. Opposite the pool are twin chambers with a stone bench in each. This is a place of contemplation. Any person who so desires can climb up inside a Pectanile and sit and stare at the water and see the blue sky or the stars reflected.

When the first members of the Gentle Order arrived on Juniper they tried to analyze the Pectanile in an attempt to understand the Talline people. Two main theories came to dominate.

In the first, the Pectanile was seen as a representation of the female Talline body. The cave entrance at the base represented the cunt, the chambers and settling pool inside it represented the womb and the bulges outside were the breasts. All very coherent. In opposition to this theory, it was pointed out that the Talline female had four breasts and hence the Pectanile could not be a representation of her since it only had two "breasts."

The second theory maintained that the Pectanile was actually an idealization of the Talline penis, which is, to all intents and purposes, like a human penis. According to this theory, the "breasts" of the female are actually the "bollocks" of the male. The water chamber is the sperm sack. The cave at the base is nothing more than an entrance way.

Nowadays, it is generally accepted that neither theory is correct and that both have elements of truth. To the Tallines of both sexes, the virtue of the Pectanile resides in its not being specifically this or specifically that. It is both specific and other. Ambiguity can be reassuring.

The locating of a Pectanile on the face of the planet is very specific and there is ample evidence to show that the Pectanile were placed first and then a garden developed. I

am told that the surface of this planet flows with lines of
energy. Those that can see them liken their appearance
to the reflection of ripples in water. A Pectanile is always
placed at a focus of these energies and from them it derives
its potency. Conversely, a Pectanile stabilizes the energy
flow of the planet and keeps it "rubta," by which they
mean healthy.

Well, I Wulf must confess that I do not understand this.
If there are such energies about I cannot detect them. I
have hovered over many a Pectanile and peered down
into its sump. I have even managed to enter some of the
larger ones by the lower entrance and have floated up to
the level of the pool with my every sensitive instrument
at full pitch . . .

Nothing. I have felt nothing. Am I the poorer for that?
Or are the humans and Tallines living in a sentimental
delusion? That is a question I must leave open. However,
such is the Pectanile.

In procession, we followed a path under high trees beside
a roughstone wall. Set in the wall were openings like
caves. These (now partly ruined) were a section of the
garden's Hall of Sanctuary. Medoc, you may remember,
mentioned such. Two Talline women popped their heads
out and watched us as we passed. Lily told me later
that both women were recovering from illnesses and
had chosen to convalesce in a traditional garden close
to a Pectanile.

Beyond the Hall of Sanctuary we passed through another gate, which Lily carefully locked behind us, and entered
the garden proper. Apart from native species such as the
Ptana or Modesty Tree which has thousands of pink
cup-like flowers which close into tight clusters of berries
whenever anyone approaches, there were masses of roses
and poppies and giant beech trees and old Earth myrtle.

Bordering the path that we walked was a low rambling shrub called Katarapa or The Travelers' Friend. This plant has velvety black flowers which open during the day and turn white and pink when the sun goes down. The flowers and leaves glow in the dark and give off heat! According to stories, travelers have survived frosty nights out in the open by snuggling down among these plants. According to Talline legend, the Katarapa only grows where one of the earth spirits has slept. As we passed, the flowers were gradually turning pale and I could detect their warmth like a glow under ashes.

Lily led us steadily on. We heard the roar of a water-fall, though we could not see it, and a few moments later crossed a wooden bridge over a fast-flowing stream. Morning was advancing and the sun was already warming the earth and casting long shadows. Wraiths of mist moved between the trunks of the trees and twisted by the shrubs.

There were many trees here which are not native either to old Earth or Juniper and which were brought here by one of the early missionaries of St. Francis Dionysos named Daniel Culpepper. There was the giant Builder's Tree whose wood, once cut, becomes harder and harder as it dries until nails cannot be driven into it. There were groves of the Savior Tree which produces berries which are very fortifying and whose roots contain blisters of water. The berries, eaten in the wrong season, can be addictive, however.

Finally we came to a high stone wall. This was part of the inner wall of the garden. Anchored to it was a small Talline house crafted from a single Drifter egg-case. It was bedded into the soil and its age obviously predated by many centuries the arrival of the Gentle Order. Here Lily paused. "Your retreat place, Jon Wilberfoss," she said.

Wilberfoss nodded and carried his few belongings into the small, spotlessly clean cell and began to unpack. I shall describe this room to you in some detail since it was to this very same room that Jon Wilberfoss returned after the destruction of the *Nightingale*.

The room epitomized a quality which has been called "Talline poverty." The walls were of gray/green plaster which had been applied directly onto the shell casing. There were no paintings or wall hangings. One circular window looked out into the garden. With regard to the furnishings, there was nothing more than was strictly required. There was a polished wood table. In addition to the table there was a low bed with a dark green cover of Talline flax. Matching this was an exercise bench of the type found in most Talline houses and which had been adapted to accommodate the size of Jon Wilberfoss. Beside it stood a tall cupboard for storing clothes and spare linen. In a separate alcove were the only examples of human technology: a simple overhead shower and a simple water closet. Relief from this functional austerity was provided by several branches of Musca Lavender which stood in a Talline jar on the polished table. The fragrance softened the air and the color brought life to the drab room. These qualities are in no way diminished if we realize that pragmatic Lily chose these blooms because the perfume drives away flies and the color can tranquilize.

Jon Wilberfoss unpacked slowly, almost ritualistically, placing his clothes methodically in the cupboard and his toilet articles in the shower alcove. He had a picture of Medoc and his children and this he placed on the table next to the Musca Lavender. Then he stripped off his robe and underclothes and yawned hugely scratching himself simultaneously on his crotch and ribs. "Wulf," he said. "You can record that my first positive decision since entering this retreat is to try and sleep. I feel heavy and sad and don't know why. By rights I should be happy. But I'm not. *(At this point Wilberfoss climbed into bed.)* Is this because at any turning point in our lives we are aware of the alternatives which we must now *(yawn)* forsake? Don't bother to reply. I'm just *(yawn)* ruminating. Will you be with me for the entire forty days?"

"I may occasionally have to visit Magister Tancredi if there are special translating tasks. But beyond that I am to remain with you and help you in any way I can."

"Good. *(Pause.)* I'm glad you . . . *(yawn)* I'm glad . . . *(pause)* There's a high tower to . . . and cold hills to . . ."

I have never watched a human fall asleep before. Wilberfoss's voice became a drawl which lost articulation with his first deep breath. The face relaxed and became vacant and vulnerable. I saw for the first time the face with which I became so deeply familiar after his return.

Lily moved into the room and picked up and folded Wilberfoss's clothes. A dexetel snaked out and lightly nipped his earlobe. Another dexetel reached across his chest and dipped into his armpit. Lily took readings. "He will sleep for several hours," she said. "There is great disturbance in him. Has he been in an accident?"

"Not really. Though your question makes sense. He has to make a decision. He has been invited to captain the *Nightingale*."

If I had expected any reaction from Lily I would have been disappointed. Spaceships are spaceships to Lily. I suspect she either thinks of them as bringers of death, as in the War of Ignorance, or as Houses of Pain, in which she might serve professionally, or merely as bigger and more complex machines than ourselves. As I have indicated before, Lily lacks curiosity and philosophy. She has a basic drive to protect and nurture life. She will patch up a soldier: but it would never occur to her to investigate and exterminate the causes of war.

This brings me to a speculation which I hope you will forgive at this inopportune juncture in the story. What would happen if Lily and Wulf were to mate? (Not literally of course.) I think there would be contradiction and we oil cans cannot function with contradiction. We must always be seeking the radical sole cause. But, if an asteroid of cold iron had somehow gained the gift of life and evolved into us, then perhaps we could have tolerated contradiction. As it is, we are the offspring of part of the human mind. We are not autonomous and never can be. So, Lily and Wulf are good and will remain so, while solo. End of speculation.

Lily attached a small radio pad behind Wilberfoss's ear. This allowed her to monitor his activity at a distance. She would know when he was lifting from sleep. "I will serve him broth when he awakes," she said and then turned and rolled from the room.

What was there for me to do? I cannot read dreams. There seemed no point in waiting like a body guard while my charge slept. I decided to explore Lily's domain. I let myself drift through the door.

The morning was well advanced and the sun had disappeared. A light rain was coming in from the sea and bending over the tops of leaves and running down the trunks and stems and entering the soil. This is not good weather for machines but I have survived much worse—much, much worse—in my time. I rose up through the branches of a Builder Tree and let its thin outer fronds slide over my domed bulk. In the top canopy of the tree I paused and scanned. From this height I could see over the walls of Lily's Garden and up the hillside of the Pacifico Monastery. There were people bustling. It was an ordinary day.

Scanning round, I could see the hills of the garden and the varied patterns of trees. In the middle, standing tall,

rose the shape of the Pectanile. It was placed on a small
plateau almost on the crest of a hill. Dampened by the
rain, the stonework was creamy. I drifted toward it,
noticing the many tracks which ran through the garden,
all leading to the Pectanile hill. Many trees were in blossom. There were rhododendrons, their massive flowers
glowing like lanterns, red and purple and pink. Beside
them were the blazing orange spires of the Flamboyant
and the deep blue clusters of the Mizzen Tree. This is a
very rare tree and difficult to grow, I am told. It comes
from a distant and very cold world and the tree is believed
to be telepathic! I have never been able to understand that,
a telepathic plant. However, it is the human confrères
who have reported this and they should know for they
deal in such kinds of contact. I have it on record that one
confrère, Jerichim by name, came to believe that one of
the Mizzen Trees hated him and despite the entreaties of
his friends and the deep counsel of his training, he went
out and hung himself from one of its high branches. That
means that he must have climbed. That argues compulsion
coming from somewhere. On such things I ponder, trying
to understand the human. I spent several hours drifting
through these trees, trying to sense their natures. But as
always in such quests I discovered nothing beyond the
obvious facts that they have life and resonate.

I drifted to the hill where the Pectanile stands and then
cruised over its open mouth. I could see down inside it
to where its pool of rain-water reflected the gray sky. It
reflected me, like the face of a giant warrior peering over
the rim of some ancient fortification or staring into his
wineglass before battle.

From this aspect the Pectanile looked like a plant, a
Pitcher Plant perhaps which gathers water in order to
drown its victims or a Sala in which the Tallines keep
fish. Ah! That similarity could be another origin of the

Pectanile. I have never seen that noted before.

There was sudden movement below me. One of the Talline women clambered out of the cave mouth of the Pectanile and down the steps. She jumped down to the ground and looked up and saw me and screamed and ran away into the bushes. I had disturbed her in her meditation. She had been resting inside the artifact as part of her cure, perhaps staring into the rain-water pool, when my savage face appeared.

I meant no harm. I was not spying. Why do people so often regard the unexpected or the strange as threatening?

I moved on. I drifted west and flew over the river which here passed through a narrow gorge. There were limestone shapes on either side of the gorge where small tributaries entered the main stream. The rock had been carved into shapes like animals by the rushing streams. Perhaps Talline artistry had also played its part for the Tallines love finding patterns in Nature.

There must have been minerals present too for the river became a bright, greenish blue as it flowed over the limestone and swirled in the pools. I explored the caves, many of which were large enough for me to enter. There were Talline drawings inside. I was surprised, though I should not have been. When I thought about this afterward I concluded that I could think of no place more apt for the frank depictions of Talline life than a cave where water flows. I made a thorough photographic survey.

Beyond the gorge the river began to meander and became a marsh which lapped and quaked through many low arches and so flowed out to the sea. Seagulls were feeding with a shrill clamor, beating the water with their wings as they competed for the small eels in the rich ooze. I paused in my wanderings to watch. At that moment as I looked down on the wheeling birds, as I drifted high

over the garden wall and came in sight of the sea, Lily
called me. Wilberfoss was waking up.

The waking minutes of a human are precious for in
those moments a human may utter ideas from the deepest
part of the mind. Invariably, unless specially trained, the
human cannot remember the moment of dreaming. Yet
Wilberfoss might need those involuntary thoughts to help
him with his decision.

I flew like a thrown rock the short distance from
the sea to the inner garden wall where Wilberfoss's cell
was located. Lily was heaving herself over the threshold
reminding me of one of the old automatic incendiary
tanks which we used to see in the War of Ignorance.
Of course, their technology is similar.

As I swooped down, I noticed how well this cell
was constructed. It gave an impression of smallness, of
tidy domesticity and of great antiquity. Yet Lily could
enter quickly and maneuver. I began to suspect then,
and subsequently verified, that this simple cell was in
reality a complex hospital room with facilities to cater
for Tallines, humans and Close Metabolism aliens, should
the need arise.

Wilberfoss was still asleep but turning restlessly and he
had his hands up over his ears as though to stop a voice
he did not want to hear. Then he put his arms to his
side and came awake peacefully. He stared at us for a
moment, without comprehension, and then laughed. "I
have woken in many strange places," he said, "but never
to be met with such care and attention. Medoc had better
watch out. You'll ruin me."

"You are hungry," said Lily in her matter-of-fact way.
She has no humor. A section of her tin belly slid open
to reveal a tray on which were cutlets, steamed fish,
bread and a beaker of hot black tuvu which is mildly
intoxicating and which the Tallines drink at all hours.

It is made from a variety of seaweed.

Wilberfoss received the tray and began to eat with gusto. Lily watched him. Her eyes are twin lamps set high on her frame. She was simply glad to see him eat. I noted that there was a kind of glee about him.

When he had finished Lily received the tray and dishes. "Will you rest again or take mild exercise?" she questioned. "Mild exercise helps the digestive tract and is advis—"

"All right. Mild exercise it is. A walk in the garden."

"Would you like me to accompany you?" I asked, bobbing in the air.

"Not for the time being," he replied, and I had the impression that Wilberfoss was deliberately excluding me. I decided to press my case.

"I have great powers of analysis," I said. "I can detect patterns."

Wilberfoss looked at me and nodded. "I am aware of your powers, Wulf, and when I need you, rest assured I will ask you. But at present I need to be alone. I have no thoughts. I want to ride my indecision. I will be strange, but I will eventually know my mind." With that he swung from his bed.

Wilberfoss dressed himself in loose Talline robes. These allow a lot of air to the body. He was ready in minutes. He walked outside and followed the path which led back to the river. When he came to the Savior Trees he branched off the path and climbed a short steep hill at the top of which were stoops of sweet-smelling bracken. He trod an area flat and settled down, lying with his back against a tree and his legs spread. In the distance, perhaps half a mile from him, was the shape of the Pectanile.

He saw that I had followed him, drifting at a discreet distance, and he waved me to go away, as though he were shooing a dog from a vegetable patch. I had no choice but to obey. I was not a spy.

So let me tell you. During the entire time that Wilberfoss was in the garden, he never once asked me for help. I did the occasional letter for him but that was all. He never once shared with me his thinking, and that in itself, in retrospect, was sinister.

Two days later, as you know, I was called away to discover what was happening with Medoc and why she had posted the declaration of divorce.

When I returned to the garden I found that Wilberfoss had indeed changed. He had taken to walking about the garden naked. His sleep patterns were erratic and sometimes he slept outside, with just a blanket over him. He rolled up close to the Katarapa, with its pink and white flowers glowing over him.

I have said before that Lily's Garden is an ancient Talline garden. In combination its trees and shrubs can have an awesome effect on the human metabolism. The smell of some leaves can bring sweet dreams. Others burned and the smoke inhaled can induce trance. There are glades of silence which I cannot explain but where there are no sounds but the flexing of the trees. It is as though such areas were surrounded by a fine membrane which filters out any distracting sounds. There are places of moist shadow where the sun never reaches and the plants grow pale. Occasionally, especially close to the Pectanile, you will come across small clearings in which flowers have been planted. This is an old custom and one which is now falling into disuse but in the days before the garden became part of the Pacifico Monastery, the garden was a place for lovemaking. Those who felt their lovemaking had been particularly successful or significant would often return to the garden and plant flowers and sometimes vegetables. Some parts of the garden are left wild and if you were to ask a native Talline such as Medoc about these areas she would say that they are for the old spirits. Anyone can walk there, but there is no planting and no cutting. Many parts of this planet remain wild. On the rare but significant occasions when a Talline commits suicide, it is invariably in one of the wild areas and frequently in one of the gardens.

I mention all this merely to document that Wilberfoss wandered throughout the entire garden. He entered the wild parts where I could not follow him and came out stung or bruised or with an ankle twisted. He lay on his back in the sunshine in the flower glades, indecent as a dog. He climbed into the Pectanile and spent hours beside its quiet pool. And all the time, though I could not gather his words, he was talking to himself. He was, of course, seeking out some mystical experience which would vindicate or sterilize his invitation to become the Captain of the *Nightingale*.

Well, it is an old saying among humans that if you go looking for a mystical experience you will surely find one. And nowhere better to go looking than in a Talline garden.

As Wilberfoss identified with the spirit of the garden, so he slowly shed some of the trappings of civilization and became simpler and more concentrated. This is the essence of retreat, is it not: that everything becomes more completely charged and more tranquil? The narcotics floating in the air of the garden helped too, no doubt. And just as day follows night and fruit follows blossom so Wilberfoss achieved his mystical experience which he took to be affirmation. Let us acknowledge also that if ever a man were prone to mystical visitation, that man was Jon Wilberfoss.

$\star$ $\star$ $\star$

Before coming to this let me tell you what I saw. It was my love of history and hence my concern with cause and effect which made me explore why Wilberfoss had been chosen. I considered that if I could answer *that* question I would be close to understanding human motivation. What did this man Wilberfoss have that other men did not? He was a fine pilot, but there were hundreds such. He was intelligent, but intelligence is a commonplace. He had, as we subsequently discovered, an interesting and passionate past, but so have many. He had reached a point in his life when he was starting to ask questions about purposes and meanings (and that I am sure is significant), but there are many such. What, I wondered, made him special? Could I see it? Would I recognize it if I saw it?

Well, the events I am about to describe may provide a partial answer: certainly they made me feel the inadequacy of my metal shanks and the dull spirituality of my bio-crystalline brain.

On a sunny morning after rain, Wilberfoss was sitting outside his room whittling on a stick. There were many sticks about as the previous night there had been a gale and trees and shrubs were lodged and broken. He looked completely at peace: a strong man, astride a stump, relaxed and yet well-knit and ready. There came a noise from a thicket, a rattling followed by a mewing, and anyone who lived on that world would recognize the sound. It was a sandar, an eight-legged, grub-like creature which at maturity can reach the size of a domestic cat. A sandar spends most of its life burrowing inside trees where it can anchor with its mouth, fringed with saw-like teeth, while it inserts its long black tongue into the main sap lines. But they can be dangerous. They are aggressive. They can spit venom and they can climb with amazing agility, sometimes humped like a squirrel, sometimes spread with all legs stretched, a bit like a bat. The rattle is a warning. The mewing is an expression of anger, I am told. In combination they signify a creature that will attack without any provocation and which is to be avoided.

Wilberfoss paused in his whittling and listened with his head cocked over on one side. The sound continued, growing in intensity, and it was obvious that the sandar was trapped or incapacitated in some way. A Talline would have left the area or looked about for a spear, but Wilberfoss stood up and put his knife to one side. He glanced around to make sure that he was not seen and then walked toward the edge of the clearing. He did not see me for I was high in an oak tree and hidden in leaves. I guessed at what he intended to do and sent a message to Lily warning her that she might be needed. She was at the far end of the garden and began hurrying back to us.

Wilberfoss walked directly toward the rattling and mewing and I could hear him whistling between his teeth and murmuring a song. He parted the branches of a fallen glue-pot tree which showed the peculiar stunting which is characteristic of sandar infestation. Wilberfoss held back the branches and revealed the sandar. I could see it. It was partly crushed against the trunk of the glue-pot tree by a branch from the neighboring tree. Two of its short legs were broken and hung useless. Its mouth was open and its ring of teeth exposed. The black tongue was coiled inside the wide mouth. It was ready to spit. Sandars can spit and they can lunge and bite. The mouth closes over its prey which is then killed with a bite and ejaculated, for the sandar dines solely on tree sap.

Wilberfoss reached in and touched the sandar. Folly. I rose from my perch in the oak fully expecting to see Wilberfoss reeling back with poison in his eyes and the sandar locked like some monstrous growth onto his arm

or his chest or worst, his throat. I once saw the remains
of a dog that had been killed by a sandar. It looked as
though it had been flayed with wire. But there was no
convulsion among the branches.

Wilberfoss slid one arm into the narrow space between
the sandar's pudgy legs and supported its body. This
brought his face close to its blind open mouth. With
his other arm he bent back the branch of the tree that
pinned the creature. The branch yielded and he lifted the
sandar free. It held to his arm with its legs and its mouth
closed like a button.

I retired and buried myself in the leaves of the oak
and watched. Wilberfoss carried the sandar to the stump
where he had been working and set it down. He touched
the two legs and I saw the creature writhe but it still
did not bite or spit. There was little he could do for
the broken legs but I saw him examine them with his
fingers. Once he touched his fingers to his mouth and
then rubbed his saliva into the creased skin. While doing
this he held the sandar as a woman holds a baby when she
is relieving it of wind.

At that moment Lily came trundling into the garden
at full speed, her twin tracks churning the gravel of the
path. Wilberfoss called for her to be quiet. She stopped
and her twin lamps surveyed him. "Are you hurt by the
sandar?" she asked.

"No," he replied. And then his eyes narrowed and he
looked at her sharply. "How did you know that I had
found a sandar?" he asked.

"Wulf reported you were in danger," she replied art-
lessly. I do not know if she understands what a lie is. Lying
is hard for machines, even for cunning wordsmiths like
myself.

Wilberfoss looked around the clearing. "Come out,
Wulf, wherever you are hiding," he called and, of course,

I obeyed. I emerged from the oak and lowered down to soil level. "If you are so interested in what I am doing, why not come close? But not too close. I don't want you to frighten it."

Wilberfoss selected some sticks from the ground and split them and shaped them into short white splints. He spoke to Lily and she obligingly handed over some white bandages. Carefully but deftly he tied up the wounded legs while the creature lay like something stunned or in ecstatic trance, its mouth opening and closing slowly.

"Where did you learn to do this?" I asked as he finished and set the creature on its legs. He watched it for a few seconds with his fingers resting on its head. He did not speak but picked the sandar up carefully and carried it back to the glue-pot tree. He placed it in the tree where it could squirm into one of its several burrows and there rest and feed.

Wilberfoss came back wiping his hands. Some venom had leaked onto him. Lily offered a napkin which he accepted.

"They taught us a lot when I joined the Gentle Order," he replied. "Splints and tourniquets and such."

Splints and tourniquets! He chose to deliberately mis-understand me. Where I wondered had he learned to charm animals? The truth, as I realized later, was that he had not learned. It was a gift. Some days after this event I chanced to hover close to the glue-pot tree where the sandar was sequestered. It registered me and spat at me. Thus, a creature that did not have enough intelligence to distinguish between an animal and a machine, could nevertheless respond to the will and affection of a human. That required thinking about.

After this event, there were many other occasions when I was able to observe Wilberfoss's canny ability with

creatures. I will recount only one more for it has some
interesting philosophy.

We were by the river. This must have been two weeks
after Wilberfoss entered the garden and as far as I could
see he was living the life of a lotus eater and did not
seem concerned with coming to a decision. Oh, I know
all about procrastination in humans. Wilberfoss sat naked
on a rock with his feet in the stream. He was perfectly
still, like a stranded tree trapped after a flood. He was
whistling softly and staring into the deeper part of the
rippling water.

I approached slowly, as I have learned, and settled
down in the gravel behind Wilberfoss. Minutes slipped
past and then there was commotion in the water. A
ridged and bony-plated tail rose and slapped down on
the water sending spray to the distant bank. High-jointed
legs scrambled for purchase on the submerged stones and
a creature like a giant crayfish heaved itself up. Its dozen
or so feelers were spread like the tines of a ruined fan in
front of it. I recognized a Rune cray or Farmer cray as it
is sometimes called.

The Rune cray. There is a legend among the Tallines
that they obtained the characters for their writing from
the symbols found on the tails of male Rune cray. Hence
its name. I think there is truth in this for I have studied
Talline script with the careful eye of a pattern assessor and
I have studied early archaeological remains. The cray tail
provides a consistent and natural sequence of symbols.

The name of Farmer cray comes from the cray's practice of building nets underwater. Within these it contains
other marine creatures upon which it finally feeds.

The cray reared up out of the water and for the first
time revealed its claws which were almost as big as a
man's hand and were black as ebony. It is a wonder that
the creature can lift such massive devices on so spindly

a body. Wilberfoss intensified his whistling and crooning and reached toward the cray. It came forward, tentatively and with claws open and advanced.

"Now watch this," said Wilberfoss. He took the proffered claw and shook it much as I have seen him shake hands with a fellow human. Then he placed his finger within the claw and the claw closed gently.

"Does that cause you pain?" I asked.

"Oh no," he replied. "The Rune cray is careful. It knows to the thousandth part of a gram how yielding my flesh is and how delicate. If we were enemies it could snip my finger off. Snip. Snip. Just like that. But now I am bringing it happiness."

"How?"

Wilberfoss worked his finger back and forth within the claw, limbering the cray's entire arm so that it had to move close to remain standing. I may say that it crouched in front of Wilberfoss and I have never seen such a strange sight: man and beast, sharing a strange voiceless ritual which brought them both pleasure. "The claw is so sensitive," said Wilberfoss. "The pleasure is in touching that sensitivity. Like with a woman. It will squeeze me to the point of pain and rock back and forth over that point, enjoying itself."

"How do you do this?" I asked.

"I just do. The main thing is not to be afraid and to match your speed to that of the creature. Find the song that it likes. Singing is important."

"How do you know the song?"

"You just do. It isn't a set song. The song is merely a convention to transmit your feelings. The animal does the rest. But don't be afraid and don't be too analytical. If you start to watch yourself too closely the creature will know and it will resent you." As he said this, Wilberfoss spread his thumb away from the palm of his hand and the cray immediately swung its other claw up and seized his thumb. Wilberfoss slowly came to his feet and lifted the entire cray off the ground. Its tail stood stiff and its feelers trailed over his arm like the whiskers of a cat. After a few moments he lowered it back into the water. Its legs spread to take its weight and then gently the large claws opened and released Wilberfoss's finger and thumb. "You must feel about it the way it feels about you. Let it be the master. Aggression is like ice. It numbs. But you must not be subservient either. If that Rune cray had thought for one moment it had me in its power it would have tried to eat me or drag me down to its lair. No, it recognized a truce." As he spoke the Rune cray backed into the water, picking its way delicately before launching and plunging. The last we saw of it was its tail, wide spread, driving it down under the surface.

Wilberfoss grinned at me. "Do we still have something to teach the wise old bio-crystalline Wulf?" He banged me on my dome with the flat of his hand. Then he did something most unexpected. He climbed onto me. "Can you lift and carry me home?" he asked. I tried but I could not and so he walked away from me and left me in the shingle.

Let me say that while I believed Wilberfoss's explanation concerning his power over creatures, I did not believe that he knew the whole story. He was more the agent than he allowed though I am convinced that he was ignorant of the extent of his power. In some strange way he could hypnotize. I am not comfortable with the idea of telepathy for cannot I also think and I am in no way telepathic, but his power suggests telepathy.

The important question now is, was Wilberfoss able to manipulate humans? His immense sensitivity to creatures as diverse as the tree sandar and the Rune cray would suggest that he could. Not intentionally. Let us be very clear about that. Not intentionally, but effectively. To quote a human truism again: the greatest strength is the greatest weakness. Sympathy for all may mean sympathy for none.

I must now discuss Jon Wilberfoss's mystical experience.

As the days passed Jon Wilberfoss became more and more a creature of the garden. I had no idea what was happening to him. He avoided contact with me.

What I am about to present to you are two versions of the truth. The first is my description of Jon Wilberfoss's actions as I observed them on the thirty-fourth day of his retreat. The second is a transcript of his commentary during his convalescence in the garden. Me first.

I had noted that Jon Wilberfoss was spending more and more time by the river. Running water seemed to give him particular pleasure. I also knew that he was hallucinating as I would find him at all hours, crouched by a shrub or sitting in branches, lazing in the flowers or wandering on the borders of the wild area, and always he was deep in conversation. He did the talking, hardly ever pausing to listen. Unfortunately, all I could detect were whispers from his lips. He could have been praying after the Talline fashion, that is while walking. As I say, if he knew that I was about he took steps to avoid me.

Well, on this one day he was down by the river at the place where the river ran through fantastic shapes of limestone. There was a frantic quality about him. He was waving his arms in vague exercise motions. He had been eating some of the berries that grow by the river and their juice, running in rivers from his lips, had stained his mouth and arms like a tattoo. He saw me and waved, beckoning. Curious as to this change in him, I swooped down. I noted there was white spittle in the corners of his mouth and his eyes were focused on some distant event or internal landscape. Lily was standing patiently on the river bank and so I assumed that Wilberfoss had done no harm to himself with the berries.

Solitude, the perfumes of the garden and his strange diet had worked to liberate forces deep in his psyche. I have read about such. He had been building to this for some time. Wilberfoss was in a state of vital trance. Other humans, had they been present, would have found him an awesome force. I have mentioned his ability with animals. In his present state I truly believe he could have made plants wither, flowers open or seeds start. The two Talline women who were recuperating in the garden stood under the trees on the bank holding hands and looking at him. It was my guess that in some strange way, Wilberfoss had summoned them to come and bear witness. I am also certain that Wilberfoss did not know in any conscious way that I was there. Perhaps, if he saw me at all, I was to him a bird with gilded plumage.

Wilberfoss was naked, as was usual now. He waded out into the middle of the stream beating his hands on the glossy surface. The river moved quickly there and flowed like glass. He stood to his midriff in water. Above him was a limestone shape like the head of a horse. Ferns sprouted from its nostrils and brown roots wound about it like veins. Standing in the middle of the stream Wilberfoss was able to reach up and place his hands against the rock. He held himself braced and steady. The water buffeted his midriff and he moved ecstatically against it. I did not know what he was doing, but the two Talline women laughed and one of them called something in Talline but the words I did not know: they sounded dialectal.

Then he relaxed suddenly and crouched down in the water and it swirled around his neck and head.

* * *

Wilberfoss's attention shifted to the side of the river where trees grew in the water between limestone jetties. He seemed to be watching something move. Suddenly he strode over to the side and reached up with his hands as though touching an object. He could see something that I could not. He stood very still for several minutes and finally toppled back into the water and swam with the stream.

When he emerged he came straight to me. He was beaming and he said, "Wulf. A message for Magister Tancredi. I accept the captaincy of the *Nightingale*. A message for Medoc. To prepare for departure if she so desires." Then he dived again and did not emerge until he was far down the river where the honey and green limestone overhangs the river and is shaped into dark caves.

I wasted no time. I did not attempt to explain that Medoc had already departed with a trader to a distant part of the planet. Wilberfoss would find that out for himself soon enough and I calculated that his decision must have taken all possibilities into account. I did not at that time have an appreciation of human mysticism.

That very day Wilberfoss bade Lily farewell and joined Tancredi for a night of vigil. His die was cast. I resist the pun.

Here now, in Wilberfoss's own words, is what happened to him. It is a strange tale and again I must ask you to decide what is fact and what is symbol.

Wilberfoss was well on the road to recovery when we made this recording. His mind was relatively uncluttered and he was cooperating in a whole series of recordings concerning his mental state and the *Nightingale*. The season was early summer and Wilberfoss was seated in a dell below the curved shape of the Pectanile.

WULF: It seemed to me in those days that not only were you avoiding me, but you were almost willing yourself into an abnormal state. Is this true?

WILBERFOSS: Perfectly true on both counts. You were a constant reminder of reason and order and yet I knew that I had to delve beneath reason to our most fundamental faculty of understanding—I mean a state of creative dreaming, a state in which the distinction we draw between the imaginary and the real becomes blurred. I needed to reach this if I was to come to any understanding of myself.

That I failed is not relevant. I failed, but the procedure I adopted was correct and were I faced with the same question again I would act in the same way, again, though the conclusion would be different. I am not sure why Tancredi wanted you there with me. I assumed he wanted you to report to him. I had no need of a scribe. I did not need language, which is a code of names. I needed to become the name maker.

Look at it this way, Wulf. Reason is a rope on to which the intellect can cling while suspended above a dark pit of unknowing, yet true understanding can only come when the rope is relinquished. In that moment of relinquishment we do not fall: the darkness clarifies and becomes something new, charged with hope and possibility and, yes, let it be admitted, sometimes tragedy. The rope is always there for without it we become mad. Reason asserts itself and protects us from madness by discovering patterns in the chaos of our experiences but first we have to open ourselves, unafraid, to chaos. *(pause)* There, does that make more sense?

WULF: Not to me. But I have recorded your words. Others may make sense of them.

WILBERFOSS: Now, as to my willing myself into an abnormal state, you must realize that mental commitment and physical commitment must be associated. The alternative is a kind of hypocrisy, but I do not condemn hypocrisy. To know one's true mind is surely one of the hardest tasks that face a human being. It is matched only by the difficulty of acting on one's understanding once one does know one's true mind. Be that as it may. I drove my body to drive my mind. I sought out the aromatic herbs that bring dreams. I starved myself and then ate berries. I refused myself sleep until I was delirious and then I crawled into the Pectanile up there and let it control my dreams. I ran after any shadow of strangeness.

I drove myself until my mind began edging into a new awareness and then I let that awareness lap about my question. The *Nightingale*?: Yes or No.

Men of old, you know, danced themselves into trance. Women too. They breathed in smoke, whipped themselves with nettles. I was mild by comparison.

WULF: Tell me about the day on which you made your decision.

WILBERFOSS: I was by the river, wasn't I?

WULF: Yes.

WILBERFOSS: It is hard to remember details. The river had become a living presence to me. It was female. It flowed around me. The land was male. I stepped from the land. I was at the meeting of two great forces, or was it the estrangement of forces? Words lose meaning at such a point . . . opposites join. *(pause)* Were you there, Wulf?

WULF: I was there.

WILBERFOSS: I remember that I felt I had superhuman strength. If you had asked me to lift the hills I would have tried. I could feel no limit to my strength. I strode into the water . . . ah, it was like Medoc, and I made love to the water. I hoped to engender something. Silver snakes. Bright winged birds. Ah, I felt clean . . . *(pause)*

WULF: Go on.

WILBERFOSS: If only I had not wanted things so much. If only I had been content to make love to the stream. If I had been content with Medoc.

WULF: If. If . . .

WILBERFOSS: True. But the story goes on. While I stood there recovering from my exertion I heard a sound like thunder in the hills. But it was not thunder, it was a roaring. It came from the trees. I was surprised but delighted. The trees shook. There was something moving there. I heard a snuffling, too, like giant bellows being pressed. Then, stepping down to the waterside, slipping on the moist soil, came a monster. It had giant plates up its spine. The tail was so heavy it could only be dragged. I could smell the creature's breath when it opened its mouth. It had come to drink. Its tongue was black and the inside of its mouth was yellow. There were spines of bristle standing out from its jaws and the eyes stared at me with a kind of intelligence. I recognized my own eyes. I was the monster. The monster was me. That is to say, the monster was part of me. It was my most primitive part. It was the blundering instinctive side. It was the kill before being killed instinct.

This is not so strange as it sounds, Wulf. We humans often see our mental states reflected in the world about us. Strange only is that I should recognize it for what it was. The creature drank and howled to the sky and I thought it would launch itself into the water in an attempt to devour me. I forestalled it. You have seen my power with animals? Yes, well, I reached out and I quelled this beast. I placed my hand between its eyes. I bade it sleep and its eyes closed. Its heavy giant head, twice as big as me, lowered and sank in the stream and the clear water tumbled in its whiskers. In that moment I knew. I knew I had answered my question. Here, symbolically, was the worst side of my nature and I had subdued it. I knew then what the senior confrères had seen in me. I knew then why I had been chosen for the *Nightingale*. Because I was a man who could subdue his own nature and who could reach out to other creatures.

But I was wrong. I had not subdued my nature. I had merely lulled it. I had created a situation which served my own ends. I did not know then, but I know now. *(pause)* Let me tell you one other thing, Wulf. I now know what I should have seen. Shall I tell you? I should have seen the gentle, bull-headed St. Francis picking his way daintily down to the water's edge. He should have entered the water and picked me up and carried me out. That is what I should have seen. That is what I should have experienced. Had the bull-headed one come, there would have been no conflict, no death on a starship, no madness, no lurking monster.

I should have waited for him for the forty days, sitting in the Pectanile, playing with the Rune cray, watching the season change, rambling like old Adam. And when he didn't come I should have left the garden, sent my regrets to Tancredi and picked up the strands of my life with Medoc. You could have written the report.

WULF: Medoc had already left you.

WILBERFOSS: Ah yes. But she would have come back. Though she went off with that trader she did not sign a commitment to him until the day after I left aboard the *Nightingale*. Did you not know that? No. Well, that is human nature. That is love. We are pretty simple, aren't we?

9

The Arrival and Departure of the *Nightingale*

Events moved quickly.

Immediately he received the news that Wilberfoss had decided to accept the captaincy of the *Nightingale*, Magister Tancredi contacted Assisi Central and wheels began to turn. A great organization such as the Gentle Order of St. Francis Dionysos can move with amazing speed sometimes. Within hours of the announcement being received we were informed that the *Nightingale* was being powered up for the short flit from Assisi to Juniper. Being merely a move within the Lucy System, this meant that the great transformation generators which could lift the ship into and out of Noh-time would not be used; this was as well for the bio-crystalline brains which managed the symbol generators had not yet been fully awakened. Indeed, final induction could only take place in the presence of the Captain.

Powering up and the checking of onboard systems took a day and then we were told that the ship was on its way.

It would take ten of our days to cruise slowly from Assisi to Juniper, Assisi being then reasonably close to us and clearly visible in the night sky.

Meanwhile, mechanics and the dreamy mystical scientists who specialize in bio-crystalline technology began to arrive on Juniper from the distant Blind Man System where the *Nightingale* had been built. They came in three Noh-time ships which were small and primitive in comparison with the *Nightingale*. Such ships had been the mainstay of the Gentle Order's work since the time of the War of Ignorance.

They were strange people, these technicians from the Blind Man. Many of them were tall and spindly as a result of growing up and working in low gravity on the engineering satellites. These satellites, thousands of them, all connected by flexible magnetic lines, were called by the collective name Tinker. Many of the technicians had to float about in gravity harnesses since their legs could not cope with Juniper's gravity. One thing they all had in common. They all took an immense pride in the *Nightingale*. All of them had worked on it and in some cases generations had been involved. Thus grandfather built the structure, mother led cables through it and daughter and son wired in the fine electronics. There was a great gaiety about them and the taverns rang with their songs and the fierce, table-thumping debates which broke out between passionate experts in recondite areas of physics. Each day Wilberfoss attended meetings at which he received instruction in the systems of the *Nightingale*. Of course, the most he could be expected to have was a general knowledge and the detailed day-to-day work would be undertaken by experts.

Word spread quickly through the Talline towns that a rare sight would soon be seen over our small planet of Juniper. Of course, everyone wanted to see the *Nightingale* and we were inundated with requests from people wanting to be taken around the great ship. Wilberfoss decided that the *Nightingale* would visit the skies above each of the monasteries of Fum, Kithaeron, Sesua and, of course, our own Pacifico, and that the ship would be open for four days in each center.

I observed Wilberfoss at this time. There was a tranquillity about him and an easy assumption of power. He seemed to have accepted authority as easily as a man may pull up his trousers. He was careful and quiet and I saw no sight of the wild, berry-stained man I had seen in the garden. He seemed greatly to enjoy the daily seminars.

With regard to Medoc, Wilberfoss received the news of her departure as though he had half expected it. He did not seek her out in person though he sent messages to her and to his children inviting them to see the *Nightingale*. I do not know whether Medoc replied. I was very busy at this time fulfilling my autoscribe duties and coping with Tancredi's correspondence which had mounted in my absence. For all I know Medoc and Wilberfoss may have spent hours in communication. I think that despite circumstances, their love was still very much alive.

Happiest of all was Tancredi. He clucked and chuckled and boasted and got drunk in the taverns and was scatty as a dog in heat. One could have been forgiven for thinking that he had been appointed Master of the *Nightingale*.

Came the day (night actually) when the ship arrived.

Everyone gathered outside Tancredi's house on the heights. People watched the ship approach from dusk when it was just a glowing light in the sky until half past one in the morning when it finally anchored and occupied two-thirds of the night sky above Pacifico. It maintained an orbit at least two shuttle orbits high. Any closer and its field of gravity, let alone its electro-magnetic aura, might have damaged our primitive shuttle.

I floated high above Tancredi's house and was accompanied by one of the thin specialists from Tinker who was carried by a gravity unit similar to mine.

It was the size of the ship that impressed most people. Everyone knew the *Nightingale* was big, but big does not describe it. This creature (for so many people thought of it) closed out the stars in a vast area of space. It had the broad shape of a glowing white crab complete with two claws which, my expert explained to me, housed the sensitive projection plates of the STGs (symbol transformation generators). The entire artifact wavered like an object seen under the sea.

"Why does it glow and shimmer?" I asked.

My expert, whose specialty was in field equilibrium physics, offered a pleasingly simple answer. "An object as big as the *Nightingale* can only remain coherent within its own equilibrium field. It would break up with stress otherwise. The glow, as you call it, is the moment, the interface, between the self-generated field and raw space. Particles are being randomized all the time around it. That is what you can see."

Occasionally we saw a flickering blue light which danced around the ship. Before I could ask the question I received the answer. "That's the gravity monitor working. The *Nightingale* has over a thousand gravity traps. That's why it can't come too close. It's edging into perfect orbit now. You watch. You're in for a treat in a moment."

Hardly had my expert finished speaking when there came a tingling in the air. I felt it as a sudden increase in static electricity and it alarmed me for the last time I felt such a build-up was during the War of Ignorance and then it presaged disaster. My companion who had straight shoulder-length blond hair responded in a more physical way. Her hair rose and stood out stiffly from her scalp. "Now watch," she whispered. Suddenly there was a blaze of light from the ship. Three spokes of blue fire stabbed down. The first entered the sea about five miles off shore close to Perry Island. The second lighted on the summit of Mt. Topo about twenty-seven miles south of the Pacifico Monastery. The third grounded beyond the northern mountains. As soon as the bonds were made the spokes of light settled to a steady glow, like a fluorescent tube, and the static electricity ebbed away.

"Whew," I heard my companion breathe out. "Don't know why, but I always hold my breath when that happens."

"The thrill," I offered by way of explanation, "demands full attention so that even breathing is a distraction."

My companion nodded vaguely. "Whatever," she said. "It's almost as good as sex."

The next day was a day of ceremony. There was a formal handing over of the ship and a signing of papers and a swearing of oaths.

Magister Suliman, who had headed the committee charged with selecting a captain for the *Nightingale*, had traveled from Assisi to Juniper aboard the ship and he solemnly conferred the captaincy on Wilberfoss with an antique ceremony of laying on of hands. Choirs sang, bands played and high above us shimmered the white and blue shape of the *Nightingale*.

Toward the end of the afternoon, Wilberfoss, accompanied only by senior members of the order and some technicians, climbed aboard a land-raft and was carried up and into the ship. This event made the resemblance between the ship and a crab even more striking since the ship's access port was located where a crab ingests its food.

I was not invited up to the ship (nor was Tancredi, much to his chagrin) but I heard what happened. This was the first meeting between Wilberfoss and the bio-crystalline brains of the ship and the brains needed to adopt him. They needed to feed upon him and that night Wilberfoss slept alone in the very heart of the ship, connected to the computers, and they learned from him.

In the morning he was Captain not only in name but in reality. The ship was his and in some of its workings had become a reflection of him. It was tuned to him. Not that we on the ground could notice any difference of course. But the technicians could. The next day in the taverns the only topic of discussion was how well or otherwise the living brain of a man and the semi-living brain of a cultured amalgam had managed to meld. Theory had predicted certain results and there had been many experiments and test runs, but by its very nature, there could only be one true test. After all the excitement and the holding of breath, this had worked out well achieving a few percentile points above expectation, and that was a cause for satisfaction, argument and merry-making in the taverns.

When he next appeared on the surface of Juniper I thought that Wilberfoss looked tired and gaunt. However, he was cheerful and seemed to have plenty of energy. I guessed that he was coming to terms with the awesome responsibility he had accepted. I wondered at that time whether the whole *Nightingale* program might not be too vast for one man to accomplish, for men are not machines, no matter how hard they sometimes try to imitate machines.

The fourth day after its arrival was Open Day aboard the *Nightingale*. I contrived to accompany Magister Tancredi who, along with other senior consœurs and confrères such as the bursar and the monastery cook, was given a special tour before the public were admitted. The bursar, I should tell you, is a middle-aged lady with a lantern jaw and gray hair. She is generally serious and it is my impression that she rather disapproves of Magister Tancredi's hedonistic ways. This could be an affectation, however, as her prim manner disappears after she has had a few cups of wine. The cook is a small foxy-faced man with prominent teeth and no chin to speak of. He is liked by all and is, in his own way, a perfectionist. He regularly plays cards with Magister Tancredi. The other members of the party I hardly knew.

The ascent to the *Nightingale* was aboard one of the gravity land-rafts. "Rafts" suggests something simple and quite utilitarian. Well, these "rafts" were spaceships in their own right. Each one of them, and the *Nightingale* had ten, could enter a hostile environment such as a methane world or a world where the oceans were sulphuric acid and still function. These were the life-craft which could pick up sick or dying aliens in any environment and protect them until they were safe aboard the *Nightingale*. For the present excursion, the raft we were on had soft seats and sweet air and even music. It was programmed for human and Close Metabolism species, but the ship could just as easily have become an aquarium or contained a broth of gases.

The ascent was rapid and described a spiral up to the landing bay. As we approached the *Nightingale* its resemblance to a crab diminished, and it became a functional spaceship though Tancredi likened it, admiringly please understand, to a bleached skeleton. Others nodded when he said this and I think all the humans had been searching for a simile which would describe the *Nightingale*. He was right, there was something skeletal about it: not only in its color but also in its shape.

Our entry into the equilibrium field was spectacular. Force-field colors of blue and green washed over the entire raft and sparkled around us and shone through the observation ports as they randomized every extraneous particle. There was a hair-raising moment which had all the confrères laughing in a mixture of apprehension and delight, and then we were through. The planet below, familiar old Juniper, now wavered like a stone in a stream. We paused briefly while the *Nightingale*'s computers took stock of us and calculated the new tolerances required by our mass, and then we proceeded.

A brilliant light filled the cabin of the raft. The humans had to cover their eyes until the view ports adjusted and darkened. With my filters in place I was able to observe directly. The light was a reflection of sunlight from the twin STGs. The insides of the "claws" were polished to brilliance and reflected the blazing sun and the close stars. It was between these mirror plates that the raw energy of Noh-time travel was generated.

Docking was simple. We locked onto a beacon. A laser rod reached out and touched us and drew us in. The doors of the landing bay swung open and we slid inside the ship like a piece of well-oiled machinery, like the bolt of a rifle slamming home. As we passed through the entry I was aware of microscopic scrutiny followed by the tingle of a particle cleansing. Nothing living could now be harbored on the outside of our ship.

Once inside the *Nightingale*, the large space-security doors closed behind us. Immediately, brilliant lights from high above blinked on. They revealed that the docking chamber was blue and white. Everything was spotless and I looked in vain for the scuff marks and dust which characterize most docking bays that I have visited.

We settled, rocking slightly as our anti-gravity cells maintained equilibrium with the vast ship. After a moment, a magnetic rail linked with our craft and it began to glide down the long landing bay. We were being conducted along the path designated for our particular raft. Air-locks, each like a tunnel, were ranged around us. We veered upward and to the right and plunged into a tunnel marked with the number 7. Again I was aware of scrutiny and then we found ourselves in a cheerful yellow bay and our craft edged between twin piers. There was a slight bump and the craft settled for the last time.

An air-lock like a giant sucker detached from the wall of the bay and reached across to us and locked against our exit port. It was a fluid movement, very organic, like the flowing and reaching of a snail's antennae.

When the air-lock was attached, the door from our craft opened. Waiting at the end of the air-lock tunnel was a young confrère of the Gentle Order. He was a trainee contact-specialist as was indicated by the belt of red and green which he wore around his robe. This man, who announced himself as Confrère Rimbawd, was to be our guide. He spoke with a raw, country accent.

"Welcome aboard the *Nightingale*. Please walk from the land-raft and join me. Docking procedures are entirely automatic so that any species can be shifted from the environment of the raft to its home environment. However, human and Close Metabolism species such as the Talline are considered able to manage their affairs by walking."

"I never managed my affairs by walking," murmured Tancredi to a colleague, speaking just loud enough to be heard by his fellows. Young Confrère Rimbawd was confused by the laughter. "If you will just come this way," he said.

Our first visit was to that section of the hospital which was designed for human and Close Metabolism Life-forms (frequently known as CMLs). There were over a thousand individual chambers and each of them could be supplied with its own atmosphere. Each was self-contained

and those life-forms which were vital enough could do
their own catering. The chambers which contained special atmospheres had a blue light burning outside and
the doors were locked. Visi-plate screens allowed those
outside to contact and see and talk with those inside.

In residence in one room was a female Bonami, sometimes called a Tree Loafer. Tancredi touched her call
plate for he had known many of the Bonami in his
time and knew something of their main language. The
Visi-plate shimmered and a face peered out at us. It
was a greenish-gray elfin face with dark eyes and the
skin had small spines like the horse chestnut. Tancredi
spoke some words and then placed his thumb between
his lips and pretended to bite it. Immediately the Bonami
uttered a torrent of musical sounds which ended with
her opening her mouth and firing her tongue at us. It
was like a black feather unfolding. Tancredi spoke some
more and the Bonami (whose name does not have an
easy phonetic equivalent) leaned forward and adjusted
her Visi-plate so that we could see into her chamber.
The room had been adapted to resemble a treetop home
and the Bonami was lying coiled in a hammock covered
with a woven material. Despite the garment, we had
for the first time some sense of the size of her: perhaps
twelve feet. Several of our party expressed astonishment
and Tancredi commented that in the northern parts of
her homeworld it was not uncommon to find Bonami
of twenty feet and longer.

She uncoiled slowly and sensuously like a snake and
reached for some fruit from a basket above her.

"Close Metabolism alien," said one of our party. "How
close?"

"Surprisingly close," said Tancredi. "When I was down
on their world I could walk about with just an air-
synthesizer on my back. I only had to take a breath

every few minutes. But the humidity! Phew. I used to wear a skirt of that flax stuff, and that was too much."

"Ask her why she is returning home."

Tancredi complied and received a short reply after which the Bonami stretched one arm languidly down and closed the communication. "I think she is returning home to mate, or else she is returning home to give birth. I am not sure. She didn't want to talk about it."

Young Rimbawd looked at him and coughed politely. "It was neither of those," he said. "She is returning to go back to the egg, to die that is. And she was upset because you didn't identify yourself. Questions without identity invariably give offense you know, and the Bonami are very concerned with ceremony. You should have said who you were if you wanted to converse."

"Hmph," said Tancredi, or something like that. But one up for Rimbawd, I think.

Rimbawd walked us through his part of the hospital and showed us the special communal living cells where he and other contact confrères spent their time. The rooms were distinguished by their simplicity and recorded the taste of old Assisi. Not a few of the confrères looked on these with nostalgia for it was in such clean and simple quarters that many of them had come to their maturity. Windows looked out on the green hydroponics fields which formed a belt around the ship. Thus, although we were within the *Nightingale*, there was no sense of our being closed in.

Here young Rimbawd left us, ushering us politely into an airlift that would carry us even deeper into the ship and to the section specially commissioned for very alien creatures who are usually known as Distant Metabolism Entities or DMEs, and here I must digress briefly.

* * *

What, you may wonder, differentiates a CML from a DME? There have been many debates concerning this since the days when *Homo sapiens* first met life-forms from other planets. The first historical step in building a framework of understanding was the recognition that there is something called Earth Consciousness. Thus, no matter how estranged from one another humankind and other mammals might be, there yet remained a kinship. The concept was extended to include all terrestrial life-forms including the insects and mollusks while at the same time it was recognized that confirming such kinship with creatures without a speculative language would be difficult if not impossible. Earth Consciousness was hard to define but became palpable when the first extra-terrestrial encounter was made. Alien meant quite simply "not native to Earth." *Homo sapiens*, simply because of their prominence, became the bench mark for all other life-forms. *Homo sapiens* built the starships and *Homo sapiens* traveled in them. I must note however, that some alien species have preferred non-human terrestrial life-forms to humankind.

The following are the criteria generally used to distinguish between a Close Metabolism Life-form (CML) and a Distant Metabolism Entity (DME).

1. CMLs breathe air or something close to it. E.g., Tallines or Bonamis. DMEs do not necessarily breathe at all and if they live in an atmosphere, it is of non-air.

2. CMLs are all carbon-based life-forms. DMEs are not necessarily carbon-based.

3. CMLs possess compatible sense structures with *Homo sapiens*. The sense structures of DMEs may overlap with those of *Homo sapiens* but the significance of sense impressions cannot be defined in terms of *Homo sapiens*.

Using these criteria it is usually possible to designate a life-form as either CML or DME. But no one pretends that such distinctions are definitive though it has been found that CMLs frequently share many properties with *Homo sapiens* such as a vocalized language.

The belief is sometimes encountered that the Gentle Order of St. Francis Dionysos is mainly concerned with the protection of intelligent life. This is not true. Life is its main concern. Within the division CML and DME, little is made of intelligence: thus the acorn which is sending out shoots is accorded as much importance as the dying politician, and the mollusk rates beside the queen bee.

Of course, intelligent species are rated highly, whether CML or DME, especially where their intelligence is related to civilization and ethical concepts. The reason I emphasize this is because I would not want you to think that the brains that guide the Gentle Order are either trivial or dogmatic. If they err, it is by policy always on the side of caution and generosity.

This is exciting territory for one such as me since in terms of intelligence, I rate. I possess bio-crystalline life . . . and that alone would place me among the most bizarre of the DMEs. Consider: I have linguistic abilities which implies an extended civilization and an inability to procreate which implies extinction.

So, there we were suddenly, through an air-lock which also served as a decontamination chamber, and standing in a plain white room. Along one wall were cubicles and a rack holding dark-red survival suits and masks. On the wall opposite were double doors on which was written, "CAUTION. You are now entering the DME section. Please wear the protective clothing provided. A DME Contact specialist will come to you shortly." Quickly the confrères began to change. There was excitement and chatter and anticipation for few of them had ever visited a DME section before.

After a few minutes a warning bell rang softly and the door opened and an old woman entered. Her skin was black as ebony. She had dyed, carrot-red hair and wore thick-lensed spectacles behind which her eyes twinkled, no doubt in amusement at the impression she created. She wore simple white overalls and was barefoot and walked with the aid of a stick. One arm was shriveled and the hand was deformed almost into a claw.

"Welcome to the DME section," she boomed in a deep and vibrant voice. She seemed about to burst into laughter. "You can relax. I'm human. My name is Consœur Mohorovich, but you can call me Mohawk, almost everyone does. I'm one of the senior Distant Metabolism Contact Nurses. It's my pleasure to take you through the DME section. Now, if you're comfortable in the survival suits we'll get going. Have any of you done DME work before?" Everyone looked about and then shook their heads. "None eh? Well what about contact work with CMs?" Everyone except the cook and the bursar nodded. "Well, there is a world of difference between the two. Beyond these doors," she gestured with her thumb dramatically, "be monsters." Several members of our party looked apprehensive. "But don't be getting worried. You've got Mohawk with you." She winked. There was no response. Seeing that her humor was not getting through to the assembled men and women, Mohawk took stock of them soberly and the next time she spoke her voice had a different kind of authority.

"The first thing to realize is that you are entering another world. Some things are not pretty until you get used to them. Put your minds in neutral and don't judge. At present we do not have many inhabitants and those that are here are just settling in. Later, when young Jon W has got himself sorted out, and we have become a family, we will cruise out to the Oriente System where I am told there are many weird and wonderful life-forms waiting for transport. Right, let's go and meet some of my friends. And listen, if any of you start to feel sick or want to get out, just tell me. Don't be embarrassed or anything. I spent my first few months as a DM nurse heaving up. This way."

She led us to the door which had a palm lock. It opened obediently for her and we trooped through.

We entered a haze of blue. The walls, the floors, Consœur Mohorovich, the members of our party all blazed with blue fire. For a few moments I felt my own circuits become drowsy as when my power pack is running low and I need to be recharged. But then I rallied. The voice of Mohawk was clear and calm. "You are entering a region directly under the control of BC Central—that is Bio-crystalline Central. This blue aura is the awareness field. You will find it comfortable shortly and you will be able to see clearly. We're going up on a view platform. Follow me."

We followed and the blue gradually faded though a definite luminescence remained during all the time we were in the DME section.

The platform was a circular dish with a sliding door and a clear domed roof. Inside were racks of technical equipment as well as tables and couches. "These are our main way of getting about in the DME section. We can keep track of events from in here as well as wash, sleep and make love if we're lucky. Come aboard." The humans stepped in and the vehicle adjusted for the changes in weight. "You too, Wulf." I drifted through with inches to spare.

The sliding door closed with a hiss and the vehicle lifted smoothly. It flew out through a port and the walls dropped away sheer.

We entered an immense amphitheater. The walls seemed to retreat from us on all sides. The hazy blue mist was all about and made it impossible to judge distances. Threading through it were glimmering force lines of red and green and yellow. We wove an intricate pattern through this charged atmosphere. I recognized the technology. I had read about it though I had never seen it. The companions aboard the platform called out in amazement.

"What you are seeing is one of the secrets of the *Nightingale*. It is one of the technical advances that have made the *Nightingale* possible. The whole of this amphitheater can be divided into sections. The lines of color that you can see are the different force fields which are in operation. There is no up or down. The entire center of the *Nightingale* contains this world within a world. We are inside a force field at present although you can't see it. You are being treated at this moment as though you are a gathering of DMEs. Watch." She opened the windows of the craft. "Now breathe deeply. It is like a warm day in spring eh? An environment has been created to make you feel at ease in terms of air, humidity and temperature. These can be varied easily. Observe." Consœur Mohorovich touched the controls briefly and immediately we felt the temperature begin to drop. She made further alterations and it rose and the humidity changed also. "All right, everyone?" she called. "I'm not going to demonstrate everything. You can take my word from now on." She touched the controls for a third time and the temperature and humidity shifted again becoming what they had been at first. Tancredi cleared his throat.

"Impressive," he said. "Now let me see if I've got this right. You use force fields to contain different environments. Is that correct?" Consœur Mohorovich nodded. "And is that all? Or has the manipulation of force fields improved so vastly? I was always taught that force fields can bleed, that they have spacial instability over a wide area. The gravity cells we all use only function because they are so confined and hence irregularities quickly cancel themselves out. Is this different?"

Consœur Mohorovich shook her mane of red hair and smiled at him knowingly. "Well, Magister, congratulations. You can go to the top of the class. As you say, force fields are too unstable for the very precise work we do. The great advance has been to introduce a dimensional shift between the particle walls. Thus, the line which joins two adjacent force fields is a kind of laminate, it exists outside of our time and space and nothing can pass through. The isolation is absolute."

"Who controls the dimensional shift?"

"BC Central."

"And is there no risk."

"Ah. Be wise, man. There is always risk. But it is reduced to a minimum. No hospital ship has ever been guided by minds as complex and thorough as these. This," she spread her arms, "is not just a spaceship. It is a living being and as such has the ability to mend itself should things go wrong."

Magister Tancredi did not reply but looked thoughtful.

"Now, would you like to meet one of our lodgers?" asked Consœur Mohorovich. Without waiting for a reply she touched the controls and immediately the platform began to lower. "As I said, we do not have many guests, but there is a Trimaton aboard and such are not often seen these days and you may like to meet it." This news caused a buzz of conversation.

The homeworld of the trimaton was one of the first to be discovered in the early days of human space flight and hence the trimaton had come to have a place of

special importance to the Gentle Order. As a race, the
Trimaton were great botanical engineers and the cities
which dotted their world were mile-high towers of tangled trees, climbing grasses and pulse plants which could
pump water. Before the War of Knowledge the Trimaton
had traveled widely in the galaxy using their expertise to
control jungle or shape deserts or invigorate leached soil.
The wars had seen them abandoned. But the Trimaton
were survivors by nature. They could secrete a mucus
from their oil ducts that covered and protected them.
Exposed to the air, the surface of the oil hardened to
a consistency of stiff rubber and became an extra skin
within which the Trimaton could hibernate for ten years
or a hundred years or longer. In effect they could return
to the eggs from which they had hatched. When the
War of Ignorance came, many of them did just this.
They hibernated on whatever world they happened to
be stranded and their favorite sites for hibernation were
in swamps or in the depths of a cave on a mountain. It was
in places such as these that they were usually found as the
slow work of re-establishing the space ways continued.

"The lad you are about to meet had a hard awakening
so he may not be too communicative. He was in hibernation for three hundred years. He was partly crushed by
a falling tree early on in his hibernation. He lost a lot of
weight and we have had to operate on him. We'll only
stay a few minutes."

The platform came to rest beside the shimmering face
of a force field. "Adjust your masks, please," said Mohawk,
"and watch closely. Here is how we enter an environment.
You are going to find this a bit strange. I suggest you be
seated and don't close your eyes. Keep looking at me." She
touched some of the controls and immediately a section of
the force field flared blue. "You are safe. You, Wulf, should
settle. I've never taken an autoscribe through and you may

suffer a temporary lapse of power." I did as I was bid but hovered an inch or so above the ground worried lest I might damage the clean white floor of the platform.

Outside, the brilliant section of blue wall began to expand, like a bubble or a blister. It began to flow around us. I watched it come, like a slowly breaking wave, and, as it closed over me, I died. All my circuits stilled and I clunked down to the ground.

I had no dreams, for it is not in my nature to dream. But the humans had dreams. They each passed through a moment of unreality which is also a moment of potentiality, the hole in the zero as it has been called. They all reacted in their different and characteristic ways. Tancredi, for example, briefly saw himself as a woman giving birth. The bursar reported that for a few moments he became a spider at the center of a dew-spangled web. The cook was a stone at the bottom of a dark lake. All the realities told something of the natures of the dreamers. Mohawk did me the service of restoring my main circuits and I did the rest for myself.

"Is it always like that, passing through the dimensional shift?" asked Tancredi.

"Always the same and always different. You get to look forward to it after a while, like dreaming," she replied. "Now, look outside."

Outside were trees with large feathery branches which were pressed up against the walls of the transport platform. We were well inside the force field and in the Trimaton's territory.

The door slid open and Mohawk stepped outside. "What about your mask?" asked the bursar.

"I've adjusted," she answered. "This Trimaton is in my special care. I call it Peter after my first husband. Come out and meet him. Keep your masks on, he smells pretty dreadful."

Outside we pushed through the tree ferns. The ground was soft and marshy. We came to a wooden ladder which led up to an observation platform. We climbed.

We looked into solid jungle. We could have been on any of a hundred planets. Mohawk put her fingers to her lips and whistled a low wailing whistle. Immediately the whistle was repeated as though by many flutes and we detected movement in the jungle. A sinuous yellow and orange shape moved in the branches above us. It might have been a snake or a tentacle. We could not tell. Then another moved and a tree shook and it seemed that every tree and bush had its own inhabitant.

"I thought there was only one . . ." began Tancredi, but then fell silent for the entire beast revealed itself. It reared up from the jungle floor. It was like a giant sunflower and the yellow and orange shapes we had seen in the trees proved to be tentacles. The yellow body pulsed like a huge muscular heart. It beat and throbbed and the surface was never still. Dotted along the upper parts of the tentacles we could see ducts which opened and closed like fishes' mouths and through which were squeezed trickles of oil. The Trimaton rubbed this oil over its body using other small tentacles. It caressed and preened itself sensuously. But most remarkable were the eyes. They rose like thousands of black poppies from the center of the Trimaton's yellow body and they moved individually and collectively, like flowers in a breeze. They surveyed us. Then the Trimaton changed color. Almost all the yellow deepened to orange.

Several of the ducts blew out violently spitting oil toward us and then they compressed and whistled, sounding a harsh melody.

"He wants to know who you are. He's frightened of you."

"Can you explain to him?"

"I can give him a general idea. He is very bright. He has already met Jon Wilberfoss so he can guess the rest." Mohawk began to whistle and pointed to each member of the party and even to me. Then she turned to us. "I've introduced you all, but I'm going over to it. It is very alarmed by you. I didn't expect this. It's enduring stress. I trust you saw the color change. That is not a good sign. Go back to the platform and get inside. The platform will automatically take you to the exit point from the DME sector. It has been nice meeting you. But my work here must come first. You understand."

A tentacle snaked down from the tree above us and curled around her shoulders. There was trilling of notes from the giant beast that faced us. "Hurry," said Mohawk as she anchored herself and the next time she whistled she was lifted off the platform and carried over to the large pulsating body. She waved before she was lowered among the eyes which parted to receive her and then covered her. We saw her begin to massage one of the oil ducts and then the Trimaton lowered out of sight behind the bushes. We heard a soft whistling which might almost have been a lullaby. This was followed by a raw breathing of notes as though a church organ were sighing to itself.

We did as Mohawk asked and returned to the platform. I closed myself down and when Tancredi reset my circuits some five minutes later we had passed out of the Trimaton's zone and were already high and skimming across the flickering blue haze. No one was talking. Everyone felt they had witnessed the first throes in the death of a great alien. Hearing its music they had encountered something of alien magnificence and strangeness.

Thus ended somewhat sadly and dramatically our visit to the DME section of the *Nightingale*. I think all the confrères were impressed by Consœur Mohovich, but as

Tancredi said to the bursar, "That is one job I could not do—DME Contact Nurse. I'm too squeamish and too sentimental. I lack that hard compassion."

The bursar nodded. "Yes, as you say, those nurses are tough. But I must say, if I was a DME and I was sick, I'd feel content with Consœur Mohovich climbing all over me." The other members of our party looked at her in surprise for this was an uncharacteristically direct remark for the bursar. At the same time they nodded in recognition of Consœur Mohovich's obvious strength and capacity.

We completed our tour with a visit to the main control deck and there we found Jon Wilberfoss waiting for us. The control deck resembled Jon Wilberfoss's house in the Pacifico Monastery. Much of his furniture had been brought up and there was a pleasing feeling of age and stability. I noticed a picture of Medoc and his children propped up near his desk.

If we had been expecting a high-tech layout then we would have been disappointed. Everything was homely and comfortable as old clothes. The technology was there of course, flowing in the walls, and Wilberfoss could communicate instantaneously with any part of the *Nightingale* if he wished—but it was hidden. Only one room suggested the symbiotic nature of the *Nightingale*'s relation with its Captain. In this room there was a single chair which reclined back. Above this chair was a helmet which was not unlike a small version of myself. This helmet, indeed the whole chair, linked Wilberfoss directly to the bio-crystalline brains. Here he could lie and absorb the entire complex running of the ship from the flushing of toilets to the realignment of force fields in the DME sector. Here he could observe, override and control.

"Looks like a dentist's chair," observed the bursar when she saw it.

Wilberfoss, when we met him, was different. He was as vigorous as ever but he seemed older and he gave the appearance of always saying less than he thought. Conversation was not easy, though there was nothing rude or unfriendly.

A meal was served in a well-appointed staff canteen which was just down from his quarters. Tables had been pulled together for our party. While the members ate, regular staff workers aboard the *Nightingale* came and went. For them this was a normal working day. Wine was served and the atmosphere gradually thawed.

Wilberfoss was called away briefly and Tancredi commented on the change in him. "I suppose what we experienced down there in the DME sector when we passed through the force field was a minute instance of what he must have endured when he linked up with the bio-crystalline brains. That experience made me feel strange to myself. He must feel very detached."

"Is he happy, would you say?" asked Confrère Isidor, the cook.

"Happy. Ah, happy. Now that is hard to say. Do you know what makes you happy? Does anyone? We think we do, but happiness is a transitory commodity. I don't know what would make Wilberfoss happy."

"I know what makes you happy." This from Isidor.

"What?"

"Good wine and good food."

"Yes, but they are transitory."

"All things are transitory," said the bursar solemnly and drained her glass. Immediately it was refilled.

The conversation was becoming silly and its further progression was stopped by Wilberfoss's return. He was smiling. "That was Consœur Mohawk," he said. "She wanted to let you know that the Trimaton had calmed after your departure. It is now eating and making music."

Tancredi led a round of applause for the Trimaton. He then raised his wine glass. "To Contact Nurse Mohawk," he said. "Long may she serve the needs of the Gentle Order of St. Francis Dionysos."

"Contact Nurse Mohawk," came the reply from all the people around the table.

A short time later we departed on one of the land-rafts. Tancredi managed to have a few moments alone with Jon Wilberfoss before we set off. He shooed me away when I hovered close, so I do not know what they said. But at the end Tancredi kissed Wilberfoss on both cheeks and then wiped away a tear. The meaning is, I think, obvious.

We landed, disembarked, and the land-raft took off again.

That night the *Nightingale* withdrew its laser lines which had kept it in precise orbit and edged away from Juniper. I was among those who sat on the hills to watch it depart. Male and female Tallines, consœurs and confrères of the Gentle Order, spindly technicians from the Blind Man System joined hands and waved as the ship grew smaller and fainter.

Then suddenly the *Nightingale* became brilliant, incandescent. The space between the symbol transformation generators (the "claws" as I have called them before) came alive and began to crawl with strange shapes of power. The mirrors glowed red and then blazed, creating a ball of energy as dimensions of space were teased open. The ship advanced and entered its own orb of power and was gone.

Silent and mysterious. A candle snuffed without smoke. Now you see it. Now you don't. And not a sound.

Gradually eyes and sensors adjusted to the dark and the familiar night sky became again apparent. Those who had brought wine stayed to drink it on the hillside. Others drifted home and the night rang with called goodnights and messages for the morning.

For myself, since Magister Tancredi was snoring and had no further need of me, I drifted down to the Pacifico library and began to gather the threads of my research into the causes of the War of Ignorance—research that had been interrupted by this whole Jon Wilberfoss business. I put Jon Wilberfoss out of my mind.

INTERMISSION

10

A Brief Biography of Wulf and Some Talk of the Wars

I include this chapter out of conscience, out of my own sense of propriety, reasoning as follows: how can you understand this story unless you know the story teller? History is nothing more than the songs of historians.

On another level this is but another pebble in my mosaic and one which may entertain you during the brief half hour it takes for Jon Wilberfoss and the *Nightingale* to whisper their way from the Lucy System where we exist to the Oriente System where the main hospital worlds of the Gentle Order are located. Later I will add another pebble and tell you about Lily.

I am older than Lily.

Age is of course hardly significant. Given favorable conditions I could probably tick-tock along for many generations of humankind. No matter.

I am aware that deep inside me there are primitive circuits which reflect the mind of my first maker. These still function and provide the core of my talent. Stamped within me on a thin platinum plate is the year of my manufacture, CE 2092.

I began my proper working life as a quality inspector with a carpet and imported fabrics firm called Tonks Bros. I was part of their automation, one of their first robots. My job was simple. I would watch hour-in, hour-out as bolts of fabric unrolled before my sensors. Dyed linen, woven wool, fine-spun bark-thread temple matting, carpets from all corners of the world and domestic plastic sheet, were all part of my trade. I possessed the most rudimentary speech organs. I knew just enough to growl, "Error here," "Dye mismatch," "Oil stain," "Chemical fade," "Tension variation," "Yarn weakening," etc. I had some one hundred and fifty comments in my vocabulary. I had second-phase analytic powers which meant that if you asked me to describe a dye mismatch, I could tell you by what percentage a particular color differed from its parent and even what quantity of pigment needed to be added to a dye vat of given size to bring that color up to its true value.

Clever stuff eh? Bah! Routine stuff. Thank my maker that bio-crystalline consciousness had not yet been developed or I might have devised plans to become an artist! In those days, if you had asked me about a design I would not have known what you meant beyond the elementary mathematics of pattern. But I had this one supreme talent: I was a brilliant observer of shape and line and color. As the fabric flashed before me I could analyze it down to its finest fibers. In this I was special. I was a prototype. I was a one-off. Many machines could analyze but I was the fastest and the most discriminating and what's more, I was flexible. Given the right "hook ons" I could have devoured a Mona Lisa or a Sistine Chapel ceiling or a Granu-Laferg Laser Striation and told you everything about the composition of those works . . . but I could not have told you why they are great works of art. My maker, an inventor called Su-lin, had built "secret" circuits into me which have never been duplicated. A historical accident! It was not intended to be this way.

Su-lin was a genius in his way: a lonely genius more at home with abstract circuits than with the world of men. He hawked me around from country to country displaying my promise and skill just as young W. A. Mozart, if this comparison is not too bizarre, was paraded by his father. Su-lin sold me to the Tonks Bros textile house and I believe I would have been brought into mass production except that this was the time when anti-gravity and particle physics were being developed. They gobbled up all the R and D funds. How could a humble pattern analyst compete with the multi-dimensional physics which led to the first starships? For whatever reason, I remained unique.

To cut a long story short, anti-gravity led to space travel and space travel led to the War of Knowledge.

I cannot remember this time but I can reconstruct it.

It was the physicist Christian Jenner who first calculated the entropic effects of artificial gravity and gave the first mathematical description of how a minor gravitational field can operate within a major field. This was in CE 2127.

The engineer Mungo, who had served his apprenticeship designing ice crawlers for use on Neptune, constructed the first integrated anti-gravity unit and flew it at the 7th Interplanetary Exposition which was held on Mars in CE 2140. He lifted four kilos through twenty meters in 0.5 of a second using a standard 9 volt battery. Almost overnight the traditional forms of transport and locomotion were obsolete.

Finally Jenner evolved a series of equations which were able to bring together particle physics and alternative dimension probabilities. These equations provided the basis for the Noh-time drive. For the first time it became possible for humankind to think of visiting the stars.

Experimentation went on apace all over the Earth. Initially it was multinational corporations that sought to use research to gain a technological advantage over their competitors. The multinationals bought entire universities. The race was on and the War of Knowledge had started in earnest.

If one wants to be truly rigorous one can trace the origins of the War of Knowledge back to the Western Renaissance of old Earth (and possibly earlier). However . . .

The first truth to grasp is that knowledge is power.

The second truth is that those who possess knowledge have a vested interest in making sure that others remain ignorant.

Those two truths explain much of human history.

Variations on the first crude Mungo drives were developed in different institutions more or less simultaneously. How different the history of space exploration would have been if the different interested parties in the world had chosen to cooperate. But they didn't. Nationalism and self-interest won out over common sense and humanity. The United States of America which controlled a disproportionate amount of the world's wealth had seven independent programs operating. Africa had none. South America had one located in Brazil. India had one. China had two. Anglo-Europe had one. Russia had one and France had its own independent system. The Roman Catholic Church had bought into several systems and, unbeknown to anyone except a few senior confrères, the

Gentle Order of St. Francis Dionysos had allied itself with
the system being developed in Brazil.

Looking back to that time one recognizes that by and
large it was the commercial future of the world that
mattered to those in charge of research. From my own
humble standpoint as a pattern analyst with Tonks Bros
I recognize this truth. I am fairly certain that Tonks Bros
allied themselves with one of the US undertakings and
paid out vast sums of money. What they wanted was to
control the import of alien cloth.

I have already described in the section on the Gentle
Order how access to the stars and the encounters with
non-human life-forms led to a vast enrichment of Earth's
philosophy. What you have now to know is that the new
planets and systems began to compete in wealth. The
War of Knowledge entered a new and sinister phase. A
couple of examples may help. There was a world called
Coca-Cola and beside the vast lakes on this world there
lived an amphibious creature called a Do-bo. It was found
that the blood of the Do-bo contained a substance which
slowed the aging process in humankind and which was
effective against various forms of cancer. As a result of
this good fortune, the rulers of Coca-Cola became very
wealthy and began to regard themselves as aristocrats of
human life. They used their wealth to buy or filch art
treasures from old Earth. There was once a building in
Athens called the Parthenon. Do you know where it is
now? Half-submerged in a lake on a ravaged world called
Coca-Cola.

The planet called Spinoza became famous for its music
and dancing. It plundered old Earth for instruments and
manuscripts. What could the countries of Earth do? They
were bled white and so sold their treasures for a stake in
space. When later the library on Spinoza was bombed,

the manuscripts of Bach and Scullion were destroyed. Let it be said that had they remained on Earth they would probably have been destroyed in any case for old Earth suffered as much as any when the War of Knowledge became the War of Ignorance.

Let it also be said that here in the Lucy System we have many treasures lifted from old Earth. The statue of St. Francis Dionysos which stands outside Lily's Garden is one such and there are others.

To return to the biography of Wulf.

The first initiative of Tonks Bros into space was to the planet Crwy (or Caraway as it became known). There they encountered a species of spinners who wove fabric in the trees where they lived. The paths of fabric were the roads on this world for the jungle floor was lethal with stinging plants and predators and the spinners never ventured there. The fabric they spun came from their bodies, from an orifice in their throats. It was manipulated by three pairs of arms. Weaving was always performed communally as a kind of rite. The spinners sang as they spun and the verbs to sing and to spin are the same in their language. They had a written form of their language which resembled hieroglyphs and which was incorporated into every inch of fabric that they spun. Thus a traveler along their tree roads always knew the history and the ideas of those who made the roads, for the hieroglyphs told a story.

Well, none of the humans could understand the written language since it took so many different forms, depending on the warp and the woof and the shifting tensions which resulted from the flexing of the trees.

I could, trained pattern analyst that I am. Someone in the R and D section of Tonks Bros had the bright idea of hooking linguistic cells and printer cells on to me and lo . . . on about my hundredth birthday I became a translator. That was a massive transition. The surgery was radical, of course, and from this time (CE 2193) I date my consciousness. All I retained of my earlier life was my supreme ability to recognize patterns and colors and comment on them. Beyond that I was now tri-lingual. I could move between the restricted vocabulary of Space English, the major code of Space Eidetic and the Glyphs of the weavers of Caraway.

Of course, from this it was a quick, brief step to espionage. My powers were extended and I became a listener. I monitored space looking for messages that had commercial significance for Tonks Bros.

And then, abruptly, they sold me. They were going broke and I was a disposable asset. Meshed in the fibers of one of their alien fabrics had been eggs which, when they hatched in a benign environment, became predators. In this way the entire population of a mining moon was destroyed and the compensation which Tonks Bros had to pay beggared them.

I was bought by a firm called Infostat and my job was simply to translate technical instructions between a range of languages. More "hook ons" were added. I translated everything from messages in code (I was very good at breaking codes) to instructions on how to install and use a roll of toilet paper in a latrine. I was also equipped with anti-gravity units and began to achieve my present shape and appearance.

All these changes made me cleverer in a way, but I was not yet Wulf. Plato's cave would still have been devoid of meaning to me though I could have explained clearly in a variety of languages just how one should go about lighting a fire in a cave and the best way of projecting shadows on the walls. I had not yet been granted bio-crystalline consciousness. Indeed, such consciousness was still far in the future.

The War of Knowledge ground on. Slowly, limited resources were culled and garnered. There are only so many truly great works of art available. When De Chirico is dead, there can be no more De Chiricos. Likewise with Lindauer and Chekhov. Human intelligence is also limited and creative brains rarely fit into systems. An interesting feature of human ethics is that so many systems are built on doubt. It is a brave and rare organization that can tolerate a member who doubts the validity of the organization itself. Brains were in short supply and gradually the War of Knowledge which had originally, to give it its due, been expansive and creative, turned to its anti-type and became fettered and sterile. It became the War of Ignorance. The transition is simple and irreversible. That which one cannot have oneself, one denies to others.

Planet A has a brilliant researcher who is perhaps beginning to manipulate the arrow of time. If he cannot be kidnapped then the planet where he works must be bombed. End of research. End of intelligence.

Planet B has many works of art from old Earth and from these it derives prestige. To destroy its prestige it becomes necessary to destroy its works of art. It was by just such an angry and irresponsible act that Coca-Cola was bombed and the Parthenon sank in a swamp.

Fear begets fear and once the War of Ignorance had begun there was no stopping it. Do you remember Miranda, who first summoned Jon Wilberfoss and who belonged to the blind race called the Children of the War? Her planet was destroyed by accident during the War of Ignorance and it was only by chance that the race was saved.

During the War of Knowledge, the Gentle Order of
St. Francis Dionysos grew steadily. It occupied the systems
of Lucy, Blind Man and Oriente which are now the
heart of its operation. It concentrated on contact work
and the gathering of knowledge. And when the War of
Ignorance began to unfold, it defended itself with rigid
determination. It did not go hunting, but it fought.

I have intimate knowledge of the War of Ignorance and
I shall now tell you about it. I had been bought and sold
several times since serving as translator for Infostat and
found myself working on one of the Communications
Planets when the war touched me personally. The planet
was "capped." An interesting word. I have encountered
the notion that capping is to do with beheading or the
removal of the top of an egg. It can mean a conferring of
honors and in ancient usage could refer to the deliberate
crippling of a human being by smashing the knee joint.
None of these meanings apply here. In the War of Ignorance "capping" meant the destruction of a life-bearing
planet by the explosion of a cluster of thermonuclear
devices over any polar cap. Not only did this inundate
the world but it changed the climate and created dirty
rain and snow. As a means of destruction it was effective
and cheap.

I was translating an article on water purification when
my world was capped. The effects of this action reached
us in hours. I remember there was an earthquake and
this in itself was unusual since the area where the main
city was situated was seismically stable. People ran into
the streets in surprise. Shortly after the earthquake there
was a power failure and the chattering machines I was
controlling became dead. Intrigued to know what all the
fuss was about and lacking instructions to the contrary,

I floated out of the office building where the central translation agency was housed. We were located high on the wooded hills above the main city. I looked down over the hills and could see the neat rows of blue and white houses and the red barracks and the airport and the long piers which stretched out into the bay. Our city was on the coast and occupied the flat land close to a shallow bay which faced out to a reef beyond which was the largest sea on the planet. It extended seven thousand miles down to the southern ice cap. The season was early summer and the trees which grew beside the pale blue sea were all in flower: pink and yellow and red. A light breeze was blowing from the west carrying the smell of blossom.

People stood still in groups and pointed out to sea. The sky was turning black. There came a roaring and I saw the water sucked away from the shore exposing the fringe of dark seaweed and the rocky sea bed and the reef. It was as though our bay were a basin that had been suddenly tipped.

Far out to sea the horizon seemed to move and a dark line appeared in the ocean and this quickly grew until it became a towering hump of water rushing toward us.

I have warned you about my metaphors. What I saw reminded me of a roll of dark green cloth that had jumped from its supports and was now unrolling toward us. Paradoxically, as it came closer it grew larger and I saw it begin to curve upon itself.

People stood and watched, still as Vonnarberg statues in a park. Some fell on their knees. A few ran, gathering children. Then came the buffeting wind, howling before the giant wave. My last sight was of the wave rearing, a sudden wall of water rushing toward us.

I sent all my reserve power to my small anti-gravity
cells and flew up the hills as quickly as I could. I cannot
fly high, rarely more than sixty feet above the ground, and
my anti-gravity cells are really little more than an aid to
stop my having to be carried everywhere. I ran them hot.
I climbed as well as I could. I followed the rocky spine of
a ridge. Behind me was a roaring not unlike the sound
that a rocket engine makes when it matches gravity on
landing.

I dipped into a valley among the fir trees and everything became suddenly quiet. Then the earth started to
shake and trees above me bent and snapped in the wind.
Terrified animals ran and barged into one another.

I hung there in the valley until quiet returned. When
I climbed and looked back down toward the bay I saw
desolation. There was no city, merely stumps of concrete
like decayed teeth. There was no bay, only a mud flat.
The sea was gray and black and covered with a scum
of oil and torn vegetation. Nothing moved except the
sea which shivered under the wind. I noticed that the
temperature was dropping and the sky was black and
yellow.

There was nothing to return to, so I climbed on past
the last trees and up to the snow-line. And when I crossed
the snow-line I stopped and dangled.

Even now, so many years after, I do not know why I
acted as I did. I was not consciously saving myself at the
expense of others. I was too stupid for that. And yet that
in effect is what I did. I suppose, being a simple translator,
no one had ever thought to equip me with the altruistic
desire to save my human colleagues. Hence I followed
the line of least resistance. Perceiving danger, I avoided
it. Lacking bio-crystalline intelligence, I can truly say that
I felt no more for my human colleagues than the train feels
for the cow that it crushes.

* * *

The world I had lived on was destroyed.

From the snowy heights I watched. In all there were seven tidal waves which scoured the land.

At night the sky was black and starless and in the hours of daylight it was brown. Earthquakes became regular and the weather went crazy. For years the rain fell and the land dissolved and slumped. I found a cave where I could lodge myself and keep my power pack dry. This saved me. I closed myself down except for watchfulness.

Finally, one day, there came a break in the clouds and for a moment brilliant sunlight streamed down and revealed the dreary mess. Then the clouds closed again and the wind blew and the chill rain returned. But that moment of sunlight was a moment of change. Thereafter I remember brilliant sunsets and freezing temperatures and a gradual settling. And after twenty years I set out from my cave.

I drifted. There was almost nothing I could recognize of the old world. All the time I was looking for a human establishment where I could continue my work. I was a translator: I looked for something to translate. I believe I toured the entire mainland.

My adventures—I suppose I can call them that—would fill several volumes and perhaps one day I will set them down. I observed the slow pattern as life, once seemingly dead on the planet, came sprouting and wriggling out of crevices as the sunlight returned.

One evening several years later, quite by chance it seemed, as I descended a narrow valley near the coast, I saw a ship from space break through the low clouds above the sea and begin to cruise along the shore. I gave chase. Pathetic really, when I think back. I doubt if I could have traveled more than ten miles an hour as my power cells were dying and the large ship quickly disappeared. But I was in a part of the coast I knew. I was close to the site of the old city where I had once worked. It was now a swamp.

I crossed the low hills as quickly as I could and was rewarded with the sight of a camp. The ship from space had settled on high ground close to where my translation headquarters had been. It stood on gravity poles and shimmering blue lines of energy danced between these and the ship which had not, of course, landed. I had never seen such advanced design before.

Set about a hundred yards from the ship were self-inflating domes of the type used for mobile hospitals and the like. Lights were moving inside the domes.

I glided down the slope of the hills, just above the trees, and made my way to the nearest dome.

There is no dishonor in likening myself to a dog that scampers with delight when it hears its master's tread, except that delight was beyond my range. I felt something like relief that perhaps now I could return to my true vocation. Humans made that possible and so I scampered. It is actually difficult to remember. I was a simple creature then, primitive in all my responses . . . The point I am trying to make is that I doubt if the butterfly can remember what it was like to be a caterpillar. Likewise, I have seen dogs wag their tails even when they greet cruel masters . . .

Anyway, I came to the first dome and lowered until my earthing sensors touched the grass and I landed. Two of my dexetels had been wrenched off in an accident years earlier. The hydraulic support rods on a third hung useless. I could just drag myself. I had never been designed for the harshness of outdoor life. I was rusty and dirty and my power cells were failing fast. But where it counted, I still functioned surprisingly well. I knew that my voice circuits and synthesizer, unused since the time of our capping, would squeeze into action.

I dragged myself to the open door of the dome and through. A human male was working at a table and he looked up in horror and screamed. I realize now that to him I would have looked like a giant snail or a creature I have only seen in pictures, a mighty armadillo.

"Have you anything to translate?" I asked.

I remember all this so clearly. He was a big man with a bushy gray beard and an immense shiny forehead—a reversed pattern for most men that I knew. His mouth was open and his eyes shone like two blue marbles. He wore a dark green tunic which to one more knowledge-able than myself would have identified him as a senior confrère in the Gentle Order. Overcoming his surprise he came toward me and gripped me by my main sensing antennae and tried to lift me. I responded by activating my anti-grav cells and the result was that the man lost his balance and sat down heavily on the soft damp grass in the door of the dome. "Have you anything to translate?" I asked again and he shook his head at me in amazement.

Other men appeared at the entrance to the dome and I remember they laughed. One, who seemed to know something about the function of entities like me, took me by my guidance handle and led me deep into the dome. He settled me on a white table and severed the connection to my anti-grav unit which was distorting badly and had burnt the grass. He also cut my meager power to half. I became just aware. In human terms I dozed.

While dozing, a great deal happened to me I am glad to say. I was given special attention as I was the only func-tioning artifact on the whole planet. I was cleaned and given a slow recharge. Some power cells which had cor-roded were replaced. My dexetels were removed entirely and the engineer aboard the ship fashioned me new ones. I still have one of these and it serves me well. The anti-grav cells which had kept me drifting for so many years were completely abandoned in favor of a smaller and more powerful unit. My printer, which had for years been a spongy mass of wet and decaying leaves and which was clogged and dangerous to me for it trailed a metal recording tape, was carefully removed and then thrown away. My contacts were cleaned and a new printer was wired in. This had its own self-referencing cells and I found that a great relief. I had never known such ease.

When I was again tuned and powered up I found myself sitting opposite the beard and the forehead. I did not know it then but I was facing Cedric Forrester, the foremost historian of this sad age. He handed me a small section from a manual on vivisection to translate and I dutifully rendered it in two alternative languages.

He was impressed. Apparently I was one of the few early translators still functioning. One of the languages that I knew was Space Eidetic which was no longer a living tongue.

However, it was not so much my ability as a translator which interested Professor Forrester as that I had witnessed at first hand the capping of a planet and had survived.

Forrester tried to interrogate me and found that task almost impossible. I could translate his questions but not answer them. Yet I had observed, and held locked in my memory, most of the information he required. I was a library without a key.

Professor Forrester made the most important decision of my life. He decided to incorporate bio-crystalline cells into my memory to liberate my thinking. The crystals were then growing in the computer bank of his ship. This was radical new technology and was scarcely understood.

The operation did not take long. Essentially it was the lodging of certain key crystals among my circuitry and then waiting while they grew into me. The great strength of bio-crystalline technology is that it integrates all areas of knowledge. It creates of a disparate entity a whole being. While the operation was being conducted my awareness was taken over by the shipboard computers and that was an experience . . . there are no words for what that was like.

And when I was returned to myself, the bio-crystalline fibers had worked their way through me. Self-awareness. I knew what I had been and what I was. My memories were a focused sequence of images. Most important, a bridge had been formed between my memory and my old language circuits. I could speak my memories. I suspect that the frog that has successfully escaped being a tadpole feels pretty much as I did as it takes its first free leap in the air.

I was smaller too. Being in part bio-crystalline my sensors were now reduced but were more effective. Visually (and humans are always amazed by me visually), I came to resemble the ancient helmet I mentioned in my Preface. My sensitivity was now in my crest and this was patterned and discolored as a result of the bio-crystalline activity. It is from these markings that I gained my name. The historian Forrester first called me Wulf because, fancifully, he saw in my markings a fierce and ravenous face. And Wulf I have remained to this day. My name has nothing to do with my nature.

I described all that I had seen to Professor Forrester and my narrative became the basis for a chapter in his penultimate work, *Lost Without Name: Final Stratagems in the War of Ignorance*. He adopted me onto his staff and thus I began the final phase of my career as an amanuensis in the service of the Gentle Order.

Each year my bio-crystalline ability was upgraded.
Forrester gave me a love of history and the upgrading
developed my research abilities. We completed one last
book before he died, *The Summer Grass*. The title comes
from the famous Basho haiku:

> *Behold the summer grass*
> *All that remains of the dreams of warriors.*

This book is mainly devoted to Forrester's own
philosophic ideas and he dictated and I prepared the
final copy. When he died I was sufficiently bio-crystalline
to feel something like grief. Looking back I can say that I
was a serious little scribe. I had taken on the personality
of my closest human.

All that was four hundred years ago and since those days I
have served many masters and mistresses, the most recent
being Magister Tancredi. But the effects of that War of
Ignorance are still vividly with us. Pockets of humans and
aliens remain stranded on thousands of worlds which were
once part of the vast network of galactic exchange. It is
the task of the Gentle Order to put things to rights if it
can. Hence the emphasis on the love of life. Hence the
Nightingale.

We are now back to the present and will rejoin
Wilberfoss and the *Nightingale* as they return to normal
space and enter the Oriente System where are found
the hospital and holding worlds of Bull, Bryony and
Shamrock.

Part 2

11

Taking Passengers

The *Nightingale* was eagerly awaited.

On Bull there was a newly trained team of three hundred contact specialists. They had been training for years, living in the environments of alien species, learning alien languages, acquiring medical skills and absolving themselves of the taboos of Earth. It was on Bull that the *Nightingale* first paused. Apart from being a training world, Bull was also the main supply depot for all the Mercy Fleet and there was a constant coming and going of spaceships in that planet's skies.

The *Nightingale* anchored off-planet and began taking on supplies. Uniformed caterers, with lists of the needs of all the varied life-forms the *Nightingale* would carry on its maiden voyage, swarmed through the storage bays. Exotic fruits were planted in the hydroponics tanks. Some livestock was brought on board. Where possible set meals were prepared and placed in deep-freeze chambers. In all, the provisioning of the *Nightingale* took over thirty standard days.

Then the ship withdrew its anchor rods and slipped through space to Bryony where were waiting many of the Close Metabolism Life-forms. As I have mentioned, "close" means close to human. Here were Tallines who would help in the running of the ship and would stay with it until its eventual return to Juniper. Here also were a colony of the Bonami who quickly established themselves in the same chamber as the female Bonami we had met.

Dysers came aboard, gray and dignified, each wearing the insignia of its clan and bristling with weapons. They were returning to die on their tight cluster of worlds far out on the rim. Dysers could endure up to three months without sleep or food or water and during the War of Ignorance they had been used as occupation troops. Spread throughout the galaxy were many pockets of Dysers who had adapted and settled and whose new mythology told of a home of happiness and plenty far away in the sky. The Dysers were long-lived and these who came aboard were the children of an expeditionary force.

There were the Rhymesters, as they were known. They grew no taller than five-year-old children and their lifespan was about ten human years. They achieved maturity within weeks of birth and their main task in life was to keep the song of their people going. A mature Rhymester could recite the song of its particular line or family, telling of events which happened many thousands of years earlier right back to the time when light was born in darkness and all the Rhymester ancestors emerged from the "great mountain." I describe the Rhymesters as "its" for they do not have a sex as such but have three sexes all waiting to be revealed in the one individual. They believe that the more people who can be at a mating the better. At a mating, the one who is not to bear or inseminate sings a special song which has the extraordinary effect of changing its body. It swells and the palms of its hands emit a hormone which the other Rhymesters lick. The hormone determines sex changes which occur during the course of one evening. Copulation is a public affair, like going to see a play in a theater. Apparently the song is so powerful that human males upon hearing it have been known to lie down with their legs spread like women. Women upon hearing it have mounted their men or one another in a delirium of desire. Such scenes cause great merriment to the Rhymesters and of course are incorporated into their songs.

More seriously, the Rhymesters' songs are an important reservoir of information on the War of Ignorance. I must tell you that the reason the Rhymesters are widespread is because they were once considered as mindless as sheep and were used as a quick source of protein. Humans don't talk about that much now.

And there were more species, many more, but they will hardly be present in this story and so I will not mention them.

After Bryony the *Nightingale* journeyed to Shamrock which is the world where the far aliens are housed. Here the *Nightingale* was to complete its cargo.

Now it was on Shamrock that an event occurred which has great bearing on this biography and I have no choice but to tell it in full. As is so often the case in human affairs, the significance of a particular moment was not perceived until much later and the story I am about to tell you I have had to piece together, bit by bit, from the *Nightingale*'s records and from Wilberfoss's memoirs.

I trust you will excuse a slight flamboyance in the telling for I wish to put flesh and plumes on the bare bones of history.

On Shamrock there live the young trainee contact

specialists who have dedicated their lives to serving the DME. You have already met Contact Nurse Mohawk so you know something of their natures. Well, this is the story of Sandy, a boy of fourteen years of growing but who had been alive and learning for over forty years. He was just entering his manhood.

The valley where Sandy endured his vigil was completely enclosed in mist. All that he could see were the dark shapes of pine trees as they climbed up the valley walls and disappeared into the drifting grayness.

A fine rain was falling from the invisible clouds. Occasionally the air in the valley darkened and the rain became intense, pelting down into the lush green grass of the valley floor where a river moved with the quick grace of a brown snake. On its back it carried gray branches which had been stranded on the river bank since the last heavy rains. That had been in the springtime. Now it was autumn. Mixed with the bare branches were dark-rooted shrubs, torn loose by the cascading white streams which tumbled down into the narrow valley.

Where the river narrowed there were rapids. Here the branches, logs, shrubs and weeds tangled together and gradually began to form a dam. The brown water churned to lather and swirled and deepened as the dam bound fast. Below the dam the water level dropped away, until with a roar the branches snapped and the water broke through, carrying the tangled parts of the dam like swamped rafts down the hump-backed rapids.

The creation and destruction of the dams was part of the rhythm of the valley, a rhythm which had endured since the very forming of the river.

Watching the tumbling water from the dry security of his rough stone cote is the young shepherd called Sandy.

He has fair hair and freckles and mischievous blue eyes set in a rather plump face. The plumpness is puppy fat. He is already growing toward manhood. Soon he will be tall and rangy and weathered, but for the moment it is the boy that looks out with wonder at the world. He is a junior contact confrère of the Gentle Order and he was selected for this role while still an infant. Long sleeps have delayed his maturity and during these he has been prepared for the raw ordeal of being a contact confrère.

Sandy was enjoying his vigil. The solitude and the dismal sky did not depress him. He knew, though he did not know quite how he knew, that he had already been selected to join the *Nightingale*. This placed him among the forefront of his colleagues and he was proud and pleased and happy.

He watched the latest dam break and then settled himself back comfortably under the dripping eaves and felt inside his habit for his pipe and small tin of tobacco. At the same time he stretched out a leg and kicked the embers of his small fire together. A breeze tickled the glowing wood and a blade of flame perked up and he was able to select a spill of straw and light his pipe.

Two black dogs, which lay stretched out by the fire, moved in the sudden warmth and their tongues lolled out and wiped their noses. Their brown eyes watched Sandy carefully, alert for any movement of his which might indicate the imminence of food.

Sandy puffed contentedly and stared down the valley. His flock of large woolly rodents were on the hillside well above the marshy river flat. From this distance they looked like fat gray maggots. Apart from the occasional bleating, the only sounds which came to the young shepherd were the dull roar of the river and the sudden, sweet, bell-like calling of the birds as they made their territories known. There were no sudden movements either. Just the nodding of flowers as they filled with the fine rain and tipped their heads to empty themselves. Even the breaking of the dam seemed to take place in slow motion.

Everything was normal.

And then suddenly nothing was normal.

Within the cote an alarm bell shrilled. A brilliant white light flashed on. The dogs reared up, snarling and baring their teeth. Sandy threw his pipe aside and scrambled over to the viewscreen which was situated in the wall angle at the back of the cote. He hit the "open" switch.

Seconds later the small platform above the machine effervesced and a gray-green, ghostly head appeared. It was the Senior Contact Consœur, the Magistra herself, calling directly from the main hospital area at Shamrock Central.

Reception was bad on account of the weather and the high valley walls. The face lacked solidity and Sandy could see the grainy surface of the rough stone wall behind it. The colors were reversed.

The gray-green head seemed to peer into the gloom of the sheep-cote. "Can't hardly see ya," came a faint nasal voice. Sandy adjusted the light on the top of the machine so that it shone fiercely down on him. "Ah, so there y'are."

Sandy could feel his heart beating. It was unknown for the Magistra to contact a trainee while on vigil. This could only be the news which he had foreseen.

"I have exciting news for you, young Sandy. You are to be given your first assignment. It is aboard the *Nightingale*." Magistra Marcova paused to allow this news to sink in. "You will be in charge of a parasite entity called a Quelle. It is a rare specimen. One about whom we know little except the planet of origin. On its homeworld it links with an animal called a Hydron, a giant creature with many legs and the carapace of a crab and there are few of these now too, since the War. You will carry the Quelle back to its homeworld and protect it until a true host can be found. Are you happy with this news? Do you feel ready?"

To both of these questions Sandy merely nodded. Magistra Marcova accepted this. She knew that young boys were often tongue-tied.

"So," continued the Magistra, "the *Nightingale* has been with us for several days and is now fully assigned. The Quelle is aboard inside its present host and is waiting for you."

"Why does the Quelle not remain with its present host all the way to its homeworld? They must be happy together," asked Sandy, a bit stiffly.

The gray-green head smiled. "They are happy, as you say. But the host will die soon and we need a high intelligence to prepare the future of the Quelle. You may withdraw if you wish. No penalty or disfavor will—"

"No. No. No. No." called Sandy. "That was merely a question. I am ready to serve at any time. The sooner the better. When can I join the *Nightingale*?"

"The *Nightingale* will find you. It has already departed from Shamrock Central. It has your coordinates. It will be with you within hours or days. It will send down a land-sleigh to collect you. Any more questions?"

"Who will guard my flock?"

"There is a young confrère already on his way. Do not worry about your flock. They will be cared for. I hope you enjoy your first mission. Remember to keep plenty of notes of your experience as we taught you. Good luck."

There was no more to say. Magistra Marcova smiled and waved and then her sharp-featured face abruptly vanished leaving the space where it had been milky. The brilliant light which had shone down on Sandy faded slowly and the filaments in the lamp glowed golden and red.

Sandy made his way to the door of the sheep-cote and looked out. The rain was still falling and the valley was darker. Evening was approaching. The Magistra had said that the *Nightingale* would arrive "within hours or days." The great ship would surely not try to find him in the dark. He had no beacon. He would have one last night of peace before the most important day of his life.

He began to think about food and about cleaning up the small station before his departure. He had not checked his snares since morning. He hoped there would be a nice fat coney to savor his pot. Sandy had a liking for fresh meat and this was part of his training for he was schooled to take charge of the lion but not the lamb and hence had to understand the hunter. The snare killed quickly and cleanly.

Sandy whistled to his dogs and pulled his hood up over his head and was about to step outside when one of the dogs reared up on its hind legs with a low growl and bared its teeth. At almost the same moment Sandy felt a tingling in his scalp, an itchiness, as though there were ants in his hair. He ran out of the low enclosure and stared at the sky. There was nothing to be seen except perhaps a faint luminescence behind the clouds. He put his fingers to his mouth and whistled short imperative messages which sent his dogs like black arrows through the green meadows. Behind them rose a bright arc of spray.

The shreep heard the whistling too and began to mill about in their silly fashion, waiting for one of them to take the lead. And then the dogs were on them, from different sides, growling and creeping and threatening until the shreep had no alternative but to pour down the hillside like so many grains of sugar from a broken bag toward the enclosure.

Sandy held the gate at the back of the enclosure open and whistled and urged the shreep while his scalp prickled as though his hair was catching fire.

Sandy knew what he was experiencing. The tingling was an anti-grav rake. He had felt such before but never so intensely. The dogs were in pain. One of them twitched as it ran, twisting its head up over its back and snapping as though to remove a predator. The other ran with its tail down and then rolled on the ground and squirmed in the mud.

The shreep began to panic too. Most entered the pen, but some ran straight past despite Sandy and his wide-spread arms. Others blundered into the water-meadow and became stranded in the mud and sodden. A few with their mouths open and their eyes showing white plunged straight into the river and were gone in an instant.

Sandy slammed the gate to the enclosure as soon as the last shreep had entered. Then he staggered around the building and in through the door. He tore at his hair and tried to scratch inside his heavy water-blackened habit.

The air outside the enclosure began to glow a fierce vivid green. Sandy heard the shreep begin to clamor in fear. Of the dogs there was no sight.

From outside there came a sudden noise like thunder and the walls shook. Then there was silence and brilliance and Sandy remembered no more.

He awoke aboard the *Nightingale*.

Do you who are reading this believe in omens? I do not. However, I can recognize that some ventures begin well and others begin ill and retrospectively these beginnings can be accorded significance. Contact Confrère Sandy's entry into the *Nightingale* was accompanied by disaster. The coordinates given to the *Nightingale* were wrong by a fraction of a degree. The giant ship used as one of its anchor points the very valley where young Sandy was waiting. The brilliant green light that he saw and the tingling that he felt on his scalp were both the effects of his being placed almost directly under the anti-grav foot of the *Nightingale*. Luckily, Contact Confrère Sandy was not directly under the beam or he would have been killed. Also, he was protected by the thick walls and roof of the small cote. But the shreep and the dogs were not. All died.

The land-raft dispatched to pick up Sandy discovered the error and rescued him.

Apart from the loss of two highly trained dogs and the entire flock of shreep, the damage was not great. It took Sandy just twenty-four hours to recover and then he declared himself ready to accommodate the Quelle. The doctor/technicians aboard the *Nightingale* demurred and he spent another week recovering.

The *Nightingale* was full. Aboard the ship there was a crew of two thousand, four hundred. There were eight hundred and twenty Close Metabolism Life-forms and a hundred and thirty Distant Metabolism aliens.

The ship was tight. All its systems were stretched in a proper and complete way. The analogy with an athlete suggests itself: the runner when racing is good and complete: such was the *Nightingale*.

Sandy was introduced to the Quelle as soon as he had completed his short convalescence. It was the very night that the *Nightingale* was shifting from the orbit of Shamrock and out into free space. Wilberfoss accompanied Sandy down into the DME section where Mohawk was in attendance. She had taken a special interest in the Quelle for they were so rare and so strange even by the standards of the DME adepts.

A room had been created which resembled the simple, pleasant cell that Sandy had occupied during his training on Shamrock. The room had its own small garden off to one side and was filled with flowering plants. All Sandy's few possessions were there.

Standing on a table in the center of the room was a cage and in this was lying a cat with blue fur. Judging from its stillness and the regularity of its breathing the cat seemed to be asleep but its fur stood out as can happen when a cat meets a dog. This was the present host to the Quelle.

Since the death of its natural host several hundred years earlier the Quelle had maintained itself among a family line of cats, moving from mother to daughter down the generations. Slowly, it had outgrown the capacity of its hosts.

As a parasite that lived inside the body of its host, the Quelle thrived in the physical systems such as the circulation of the blood and in the nervous and mental systems. It caused certain minor physiological changes in its host (with the exception of its natural host) such as turning the skin or fur blue. It also brought the power of speech to creatures which, in their natural state, had no verbal language. Speculation about the origin of the Quelle held that it was a creature between spirit and matter. That it was life without a distinct form of its own and that it had come into being in the chaotic times when the universe was young. At some point in their evolutionary history the proto-Quelle had joined with the Hydron, which was regarded as one of the oldest species in existence. There had been Hydron and Quelle, living in the one body, and crawling in the cold seas of their homeworld long before the earth was formed.

The cat's eyes opened as they entered the room and it stared at them fixedly. Then it yawned showing all its teeth. Its face twisted as though an unseen hand were pressing and pulling it and the lips moved. A voice spoke, manufactured from a nose and throat that had been developed for no more than mewing. "Are you my new vehicle?"

Mohawk prompted the young boy with a nudge.

"I think I am," said Sandy.

"Come closer," said the cat. "My eyes are weakening. Damned poor biology. Failing under stress. I want to see you." The cat stood up and arched its back and stretched its claws and then sprang up onto the side of the cage and held on there, more like a monkey than a feline. There were flecks of saliva at the side of its mouth. The eyes stared at Sandy and Sandy felt himself threatened. Once, while guarding his flock of shreep at night, he had been wakened by panicked bleating. In one movement he had rolled from his sleeping bag, grabbed his electric probe and run outside to discover what was wrong. In the darkness he had met the glaring yellow eyes of a mountain hyena, a beast that was as large as a pony and with jaws that could bite a shreep in half. Both had been surprised and while the hyena growled like a saw blade on iron, Sandy instinctively struck with his probe for the eyes and scored. The probe released its charge and the eyes closed and the beast slumped. Minutes later, when the charge in the probe had accumulated, Sandy set it to high power and killed the hyena by burning its brain.

Such were Sandy's memories when he met the blue cat which hosted the Quelle face to face. What the Quelle thought at the moment of contact we do not know.

Jon Wilberfoss reached up to the cage and thrust one of his fingers through the mesh and tickled the cat under its chin. He was rewarded with a gentle miaow. He turned to Sandy. "You will sleep here tonight, Sandy. None of us are sure about how the transference will take place. You must discover that." He turned back to the cat. "Can you help us Quelle?" he asked. "Sandy is willing but none of us has experience of how to make such a move. You must help us."

"Leave it to me," said the cat, screwing up its face. "Sympathy is all, but I am already hurting. I need to move. This bag of fur can no longer contain me. Sandy and I will soon be acquainted."

Mohawk had been listening carefully and she placed her hand on Sandy's arm. "I shall be close," she said. "Don't hesitate to call on me. I may be able to help."

Let me say now that Mohawk had already detected trouble. She could not have specified what, but she was uneasy. Wilberfoss too, to his credit, also felt uneasy but he, not being deeply trained in alien contact, thought that the problem was in him, in his own sense of strangeness and newness. It would never have occurred to either of them to think that the Quelle might be mad, but that I am afraid is the case.

I, the historian Wulf, assert this. Had either of these two sensitive beings acted on their feelings and requested a deeper diagnosis and assessment of the needs of the Quelle, then the *Nightingale* would have been saved along with all the life-forms within her, and Wilberfoss would now be a champion of Life to rival old St. Francis Dionysos himself. Historians cannot rewrite the facts of history no matter how they gloss them.

Wilberfoss and Mohawk left Sandy alone in his cell with the blue-furred cat. They returned to their different jobs though Mohawk made sure before departing that her call line was open. This meant that Sandy could contact her directly. It also meant that if she so chose, she could listen to what was going on in Sandy's room at any moment.

Left alone, Sandy suppressed his memory of the mountain hyena and released the cat from the cage. It immediately ran into the small garden enclosure and defecated among the flowers.

While Sandy prepared for bed the cat prowled the room. Occasionally it spoke to him, sitting back on its haunches and fixing him with its sharp yellow eyes. It spoke of the beauty of the Quelle's homeworld and the joy of union with a sympathetic mind.

Eventually Sandy slept and the cat sat watching him.

At about the middle of the night the cat crawled into the sheets and curled up between Sandy's arms. The boy murmured and turned and the cat spoke to him uttering words of comfort and peace.

Mohawk heard those words and hurried to Sandy's cell. She slipped through the door and was in time to watch the Quelle possess the sleeping boy.

The cat was crouched on his stomach with its legs spread and its fur standing out stiff from its body. The boy was asleep on his back with his arms thrown wide.

The Quelle emerged like water. It seeped from the cat's eyes and ears, mouth and anus. It became a pool of rippling silver, which lapped around the cat's stiff body and then flowed up toward Sandy's mouth and nose. The boy moved and sneezed as the Quelle attempted to enter his nose. That stopped it. It lay around his throat like a pool of silver, like fish scales, like moonlight on water, like a silver scarf, like the traces of a snail over slate . . . and then it gathered and thrust itself into his body through his mouth and ears and nose. Sandy stopped breathing while the last bead of the Quelle found its way inside him. Then he sighed and the sigh turned into a snore. He twisted on the bed and his legs and arms thrashed for a moment and then reached out stiffly. The fingers and toes flexed. To Mohawk it looked as though Sandy were imitating the movement of the cat. Then the boy curled into the fetal position, turning onto his side. The dead body of a blue furred cat slipped from his chest and onto the bed. It lolled back, indecent in death, and Mohawk removed it carefully and placed it in the cage.

Sandy seemed to be sleeping peacefully and Mohawk withdrew quietly carrying the cage. She hoped that all would now be well. She contacted Jon Wilberfoss and told him what had happened. He seemed relieved.

Hours later the symbol transformation generators meshed in a blinding release of power and the *Nightingale* disappeared as it tore spacetime like cheesecloth and set out on the first of its missions.

12

A Song of
St. Francis Dionysos

I affirm the oneness of Life.
Among my friends I number the stars,
Shining in darkness and the serene moon.
I praise the rising sun that gladdens me.
Everything holds to its rightness:
The leaves that fall in Autumn,
The sap that rises in Spring,
The strong roots that break stone under soil.
Everything holds together: the fish, the birds
And the things that crawl in the darkness.

I affirm the oneness of Life.
I celebrate tangled branches,
The tumbling of clear water,
The flowers of Spring and the berries of Winter.
I am in everything and everything is in me.
I am where the red desert meets the blue ocean.

Where the white mountain joins the green valley.
Everything joins. The stones too have their life.

I affirm the oneness of Life.
Where the baby cries and the woman opens,
Where the man calls and the child stands,
There too am I.
I glory in opposites, in fragrance at nightfall,
In death in the morning, in tears and laughter.
I hear the voice that whispers,
Gentle and deep, from old sea shells
Content with centuries of ocean,
And it is my voice,
And many voices.
I affirm the oneness of Life.

I have decided to place this song here lest, in all the
excitement of narrative, we forget what we are about.
I may include a few more songs later for they will help
as the sadness of the story deepens.

13

Wilberfoss and Sandy.
The First Trial

The *Nightingale* returned from Noh-time to normal
spacetime without any problems. The bio-crystalline consciousness at the heart of the ship first created a potential
reality, cracking into normal spacetime through different
dimensions, and then allowed the ship to reconstitute
itself at the new point in space hence transforming potential reality to actual. The entire change was the physical
equivalent of a metaphor in which two realities meet
and exchange. It is surprisingly simple and yet infinitely
subtle.

To the life-forms aboard the *Nightingale* the change in
their status as they moved from actuality to potentiality
and back again, was hardly noticeable. Those who were
staring out through the view ports saw the stars swirl to
a point of brilliance which vanished with a bang of light.
Then there was darkness which seemed to press in on
the ship. And then, when the darkness seemed all but
unbearable, the stars poured forth again and reassembled

themselves into new patterns. Only the bio-crystalline brains which had calculated the odds of the new reality, knew just where the *Nightingale* was.

There are those philosophies which maintain that there is no actuality except death and that so long as there is life there is only change and potential. Perhaps that explains the indifference of life-forms to the spacetime change. Opinions differ.

The important thing to those aboard the *Nightingale* was that there were no difficulties. Jon Wilberfoss alone among the life-forms on the ship witnessed the change as a personal event for in every change, his was the spiritual brain which worked with the clever bio-crystalline entities. It was naturally exhausting.

The *Nightingale* appeared close to a bright yellow sun that swung in a complicated dance with a glimmering red giant and a point of blackness defined by a glittering corona of energy. Despite appearances, this was a stable system. It had endured for many millions of years during which one of the worlds which swung around the yellow sun had achieved life-forms. This was the homeworld of the Trimaton. It was a world of misty blue-green swamps which were frozen at the poles and steamy at the equator. In the equatorial region there was a vast blue lake where the water was deep and in the center of this was a single, emerald-green island. This was the center of the Trimaton civilization and it was the Trimaton who kept the lake clear of tangling plants. It was here they built their ever changing, growing cities.

The *Nightingale* secured as close to the world as it dared and one of the land-rafts set out to establish contact. Mohawk was aboard this, accompanying the Trimaton she had been caring for.

After four days had passed Mohawk returned bringing greetings from the Trimaton world and inviting all those aboard the *Nightingale* to descend to the surface. This was clearly impossible but Jon Wilberfoss, as the senior representative of the Gentle Order, traveled down and entered the city of webs and woven stalks and shaped plants. There he remained as a guest, and in some ways as a hostage, while the other Trimaton aboard the *Nightingale* were ferried down to the surface.

A dead Trimaton, still and black within its waxy pod, was received and Wilberfoss was allowed to attend the funeral. This was a rare event since the Trimaton hardly ever died close to their main island unless they had suffered an accident or succumbed to disease. When a Trimaton grew old it simply divided and became two young Trimatons. Young Trimatons were engaged in lonely exploration on the mainland far from the great island and only the fortunate few returned to divide and keep the line alive. With them they brought whistle melodies which in a way which no human could understand were able to describe mountains and rivers and caves and trees. These melodies also told of the fate of younger Trimatons. So, as you can understand, funerals were few and far between.

A giant Trimaton, holding the pod containing the dead body aloft in its shorter tentacles, swam away from the island. Some two miles off shore it gulfed oil over its body and then dived and attached the pod to the sea floor. While the Trimaton was underwater, the others on the island began a whistle chorus which was like a thousand organs mixed with flutes and bagpipes. The sound spread from the place where the Trimaton had slithered into the sea. It traveled down the coasts and it traveled inland. As the tribes of Trimaton holding in the branches of their city or tending the young or gathering fruit or sleeping heard the whistle chorus, they joined in. Once started the wave of sound was unstoppable. It spread across the many thousands of miles of the island. When the Trimaton that had dived had done its job and the dead Trimaton was pegged to stones on the sea bed, it bobbed back to the surface and swam ashore. Seeing it arrive safely on shore, those Trimatons that were close stopped whistling and moaning and thus a wave of silence followed the wave of sound.

"What are they whistling?" asked Wilberfoss.

Mohawk strained to hear. "I can only catch fragments," she said. "Some are telling genealogy, some are narrating exploits in which they were involved, some are describing what is happening. No two are the same. It is a great song of their here and now. One of them,"—she pointed up into the canopy of a wide-girthed tree—"my lad I think, is whistling about you and me and about how we come to be here."

Gradually silence grew about them and they could hear the whistling grow fainter as the wave of silence chased the wave of sound. And when the silence was total, they made their farewells quietly and climbed aboard the land-raft and gently lifted and floated up to where the *Nightingale* held orbit.

Waiting for Wilberfoss was young Sandy. He was sitting on the floor outside the control rooms. There was already a blueness about his eyes and throat, like bruising.

"We don't feel well," he said, and then his face twisted and he bit his lips but not so hard as to draw blood.

Wilberfoss took him into the room which resembled his dining-room on Juniper and sat him at the table. The artificial fire flared in its grate and then settled to a pleasant semblance of burning logs and wood ash. Wilberfoss brought milk and some of the fruits he had gathered on the homeworld of the Trimaton and set these before the boy. "Now tell me," he said.

Sandy tried to drink the milk but he gagged and drib-
bled. After another attempt he pushed the glass aside. He
managed to eat some of the fruits. Occasionally his face
moved uncontrollably, flitting from a frown to a smile,
to a look of wonderment and then to the vacancy of an
idiot. Wilberfoss watched in silence. He lent his presence
and his patience.

Finally, Sandy managed a few words. "I don't think
we like ourself," he said and took a deep breath. With
his breath held he seemed to be able to keep control as
Sandy. Then he spoke without breathing, using the stored
air. "Quelle wants Sandy to be a cat. Sandy can't. Sandy
hurts. Sandy is sick."

The air escaped from him and his face set with the
lips pushed forward as though he were pretending to be
a fish. The next time he spoke the voice was different,
sharper and with less intonation. "Quelle wants to be
clean. You have given me a dirty vehicle. How can I
live in a sewer? I insist on a sanitary mind. Miaow."

The dialogue went on. Sometimes Sandy spoke and
sometimes the Quelle. Once they both tried to speak
together and the result was that Sandy held his breath
until he swooned. The argument did not progress but
merely moved in circles. What did emerge clearly was
the deep antipathy between Sandy and the Quelle.

Finally the Quelle tired and Sandy took more complete control. The boy was bewildered beyond reckoning.
"Help me," he said. "Help both of us. My training never
told me about all this—the sickness, the visions. I'm starting to hate myself. I want to poke my eyes out. I want
my flock back. I want to go home."

Wilberfoss took his hands and held them between his
own giant palms. He could think of nothing to say for
the moment. He saw the boy shiver and then droop and
place his blue-tinged face on the table. Both creatures

which inhabited the same body were asleep. Wilberfoss fetched a cushion from the chair by the fire and placed it under the boy's head. Then he took a woven cover from one of the chests by the wall and draped it over his shoulders. The boy murmured in his sleep like a cat.

Wilberfoss was uncertain what to do for the best. He sat and looked at the sleeping boy and faced the first real trial of his captaincy. He reviewed his options.

One possibility was to turn back to Shamrock on the grounds that this contact was not working and needed a substitute. He rejected this option. He told himself that the disruption to the schedule would be too great and besides, it was early days yet and the wise confrères who knew more than he did about contact with Distant Metabolism Entities had presumably taken care over the selection. Perhaps time would effect a shakedown. To his credit, Wilberfoss was not consciously aware that turning back might seem like a lack of decisiveness, though that may have been an unconscious motive.

A second possibility was to invite the Quelle to change hosts. To do this he would need the help and advice of Mohawk and the bio-crystalline brains that controlled the ship. He immediately summoned Mohawk to join him and opened lines of communication to the bio-crystalline consciousness at the heart of the ship. There was, of course, no certainty that a change of hosts would be successful. It might be a case of out of the pot and into the fire.

A third possibility was that he should take the Quelle inside himself. Wilberfoss did not entertain this possibility for long as it had many unknowns, though speaking with the wisdom of hindsight, I know that it was his best option. Wilberfoss had a rare way with creatures. I have seen his power, and something of the great Dionysos flowed in him. Quelle would not have mastered him. I would maintain that if Wilberfoss had received the alien Quelle inside himself then he would have found the strength to cope with the implantation. We shall never know. But perhaps Wilberfoss, in his deeps, found the idea of alien infestation intolerable. It is even possible that he felt a lack of sympathy for the boy simply because he had allowed himself to be possessed.

A fourth possibility, and one which greatly appealed to Wilberfoss, was that he should use the power he could exercise over creatures to subdue either Sandy, making of the boy a passive host, or the Quelle, making of the parasite a gentle rider. We may observe that there is something of vanity in this choice.

There were other possibilities which Wilberfoss did not consider. He could, for instance, have reached out with one of his giant hands and killed them both while they slept at his table. Had he done so the *Nightingale* and all who were in her would have been saved. Naturally, the rules of the Gentle Order by which he lived forbade this. However, I, Wulf, who do not have to worry much about a human conscience, have to consider this option. Perhaps Wilberfoss allowed himself to be too controlled by the rules. The true leader is the one who can improvise. Ethics are harder than logic.

Nor did he think of trying to move the Quelle to a semi-living host such as a bio-cyrstalline entity. Talking with Wilberfoss during his convalescence in Lily's Garden I made the point to him that if I had been aboard and had been aware of the problem, I would have offered myself as host. I have just enough bio- to be acceptable (I believe) and my -crystalline parts are very pure. I could have coped with the Quelle. I could have miaowed to keep it peaceful. I could have straightened it with reason. But I was not there and so I wonder why those great bio-crystalline brains which ran the ship with such sophistication never thought to offer a part of themselves. Clearly they knew nothing of literature or history, for the Gadarene swine would have given them a clue how to proceed and they were cleverer than swine. Surely they could have modified a part of themselves to create a host which resembled the Hydron of the Quelle's homeworld? They could have isolated the madness of the Quelle within a bio-crystalline pen. They could have freed Sandy of his pain. But apparently this possibility never was considered. There may be reasons for this. I don't know.

I have used the words "madness of the Quelle." This is Wulf's conclusion though it can not now be proved. I believe the Quelle was mad. No host would have suited it, not even St. Francis Dionysos himself. The pure boy Sandy it likened to a sewer! But how do we understand the madness of an alien brain? Shall we say that sanity consists in that which is on the side of Life? A life-form that is opposed to Life is opposed to itself and that is surely insane. This is a distinction easy to grasp and hard to apply. But it is a guide. When logic fails, ethics may still be up and running.

Mohawk arrived, drowsy and worried, and she and Wilberfoss entered the small vestibule off the dining-room where they could gain direct access to the powerful and unsleeping bio-crystalline constructs which ran the ship. They discussed the problem and were amazed to discover that the bio-crystalline minds already had some inkling of the trouble. Maintaining the structures in the DME section of the *Nightingale*, they had become aware that Sandy was not sleeping well. They had heard him crying and miaowing. "We can even, sometimes, pick up thought patterns broadcast by humans for we scan all levels of emanation. We have been aware of sadness and suffering."

"Why did you not tell me?" asked Wilberfoss.

"Because sadness and suffering are common among the life-forms aboard this ship. It is like the background noise you hear when a dominant sound has gone away."

"Are Sandy and the Quelle louder than the rest?"

"Somewhat louder."

"Why is that do you think?"

"Because their thoughts are fueled by strong emotion. Emotion is the engine. Thought is merely the emanation."

Both Mohawk and Wilberfoss absorbed this. "Well, what do you think we should do?" asked Mohawk after a long pause.

"That must be up to you," said the bio-crystalline minds of the *Nightingale*. "You know far more about such things than we do. We can feel sympathy, but we cannot make decisions the way you can. We can only carry out your decisions once made."

Mohawk and Wilberfoss looked at one another. "Over to you, Captain," said Mohawk.

Wilberfoss felt the thrill of decision-making. "We have a crisis in the making. I cannot judge how serious it is but I don't feel like taking chances. I am going to move Sandy and the Quelle up here where I can keep a close eye on them. Any problem with that?" he asked the air and the ceiling.

"No problem at all," came back the reply. "They have no special requirement beyond food and air."

Mohawk nodded. "I think that would be a good idea."

"Furthermore," said Wilberfoss, "I want to look at changing our schedule. After this visit to the homeworld of the Trimaton we are scheduled to travel out to the rim to the Dysers homeworld. We are expected and there is a rare conjunction of planets taking place—a once-in-ten-thousand-years event in which they have invested much magic and ceremony. We cannot miss that, but thereafter the schedule is variable. We had planned to go to Croppa's World and take on supplies, but I suggest that we move directly to the homeworld of the Quelle. We can give them advance warning. I know there is a team from the Gentle Order already on planet and they will do everything they can to have a true host, a Hydron, standing by. Can this be done easily?"

"We can reschedule. So long as there are no species that are dying and have a limited timespan." There was a moment's pause. "We can see no problem," replied the bright voice of the *Nightingale*. "We can begin to contact the Quelle homeworld immediately."

"That plan has an added advantage," said Mohawk, the practical. "We can inform both Sandy and the Quelle of the change and the knowledge that their suffering is close to an end will probably help greatly. They are not scheduled for planet fall for some two ship years I believe."

"Two years and seven months."

"Well then. I am sure they can hold on for a couple of ship's weeks. Especially if you take a hand." Mohawk nodded at Wilberfoss.

Wilberfoss smiled.

The decision pleased them all. The meeting ended.

Mohawk helped set up a special room for Sandy/Quelle and then she bade Wilberfoss good night. "Just a word of warning," she offered as she turned to leave. "Don't fall asleep with the Quelle close by. I watched it take over Sandy and it is quite irresistible. I know so little about them. Keep the door secured."

Wilberfoss laughed. "I'll be careful," he said. "Perhaps now that your Trimaton is gone you might be able to study up on the Quelle?"

"I will," she said. "I will."

"We also will be watching and on guard," came the voice of the *Nightingale*.

Thus all should have been well, for the plan was a good one. Miscalculated only was the severity of the breakdown between Sandy and the Quelle and the danger that that breakdown posed. Nor was there any talk of madness.

Why this plan failed I will reveal in the next pebble of my story.

14

The Weakness of Us
Bio-crystalline Entities

But before I do, you first need to know a bit more about bio-crystalline consciousness. If you have ever seen a crystal grow in a super-saturated solution then you will have seen what a bio-crystalline structure looks like. It branches and bifurcates and forms a complex of relationships dictated by local gravity and an internal logic of opportunity.

What you need to add to that image of almost magical growth is the idea of cellular growth. The crystals have a biological origin. Most bio-crystalline brains are grown deep in space and in an environment where gravitationed effects are minimized. Hence their structure can be determined more by their function than by accidents.

As with so much else, the driving power behind bio-crystalline technology is human emotion. Thus, it was very important to the crystals aboard the *Nightingale* that they achieve their final awareness from contact with Jon Wilberfoss. He warmed them. They grew under his light.

Bio-crystallism is essentially dynamic and full of potential.

Let me describe myself. If you take my lid off you will find that almost every part of my inner structure is linked by thin white threads. They are like roots that have grown under slate or concrete. They are also like the patterns made by frost on a pane of glass. They are strong like roots. They are patterns like frost. Such is my bio-crystalline consciousness and I am a crude machine. I have only a few crystals, but those few allow me to write this biography and study history. They make me Wulf.

Imagine then the *Nightingale*.

When I was describing the inner workings of the *Nightingale* many words ago, I deliberately chose not to describe the bio-crystalline chamber at the heart of the ship. Now I must do so.

The bio-crystalline brain of the *Nightingale* is divided into two parts of which one brain may be called the master and the second, the sub-master. I will describe the sub-master first. The space between the outer hull and the inner walls of that ship is entirely filled with the bio-crystalline structures. They are like white rope. They are like pink coral. They grow in every corner and angle. These crystals control the vast symbol transformation generators. They grow around the outer part of the ship because they require the maximum available area and they function best in a cold vacuum. In their capacity to be logical and illogical at the same time, they are almost a law unto themselves, but their loyalty is to the ship and the master consciousness.

Linked to the sub-master is the inner brain or master which controls all the alien habitats and all local functions. These crystals are all located in a single spherical chamber some one hundred feet below Jon Wilberfoss's rooms. I have seen pictures of this chamber. It is like a cave filled with cobwebs. The individual seed crystals are white studs set around the wall. Everything grows from them. Nothing moves in this sterile chamber. It is as still as the end of time. And yet in every fiber and tendril there are tides of energy flowing. Here is where the complex working of the ship is monitored. Not a toilet flushes or door opens without the fact being noted. It is this brain that speaks to Wilberfoss and weighs the odds and offers him advice and is finally his servant. The bio-crystalline brain is dependent.

Let us not fool ourselves: despite the power and the infinitude of reference, the bio-crystalline brain remains more -crystalline than bio- (and in saying this I am aware of my earlier comments concerning my preparedness to accommodate the Quelle). Let us never underestimate the signal importance of the moderator, of that thing of logic and intuition which maintains a balance between anarchy and order and contains both kindness and cruelty and has at its disposal a billion years of wisdom built into its cells . . . I am speaking of the human mind.

We are coming close. Have you spotted the fatal Achilles' heel of bio-crystallism yet?

15

Sandy and the Quelle

So it was that Sandy moved into a side room close to Wilberfoss's quarters. Wilberfoss listened to Sandy and when he heard the pain rise he sent out his own roving power and took the pain and stilled it. He numbed both Quelle and Human.

To Wilberfoss this was like joining with a creature when it is hunting or mating, or liberating the vegetative side of his being to comprehend rainfall or the quiet of sap rising. Wilberfoss came to know the Quelle and the Quelle became afraid of him for the vitality of Wilberfoss could have boiled its cells.

Let me state that another way. The Quelle was aware that Wilberfoss could have stripped it of its power and made it a servant. The Quelle also knew that if that happened, it would simply dwell in awe of the powerful human and would forsake its own destiny. Wilberfoss was of course aware of the Quelle's feelings and respected them which made the Quelle even more nervous.

There is no end to such a wrangle. Wilberfoss could have crushed the Quelle until it gave itself to Sandy at which moment Sandy would have become a very powerful, and I think a very happy young man. This I suppose must be regarded as another option available to Wilberfoss.

Have you heard of the theory that at the dawn of human consciousness, there was a creature like the Quelle that dwelled on Earth and that it entered Mankind and became his conscience? It is sometimes depicted as a serpent in which guise it may be reviled. In other religions it is venerated as a source of spiritual awareness. No matter.

To give him his due, Wilberfoss could not have solved his dilemma without sacrificing either the parasite or the host and he was pledged to protect both.

Affairs of the ship took Wilberfoss's attention and in his absence the war between the two entities intensified. The Quelle, who was stronger than Sandy, learned how to control the boy's moods.

When Wilberfoss came to ask how Sandy was he found the boy laughing and seemingly at ease. The tears stopped and in his conscious activity Sandy seemed well. But the Quelle could not control his dreams. In the night when the Quelle relaxed, for it needed its rest too, Sandy screamed and screamed and screamed. The night was one long scream of nightmare until Wilberfoss, himself weary with the day, brought calm with his own deep spiritual energy.

And what were these nightmares?

Suffocation was one. Fur growing inside the skin and closing all the apertures through which air could enter and then bursting out through the skin again until Sandy was like a hairy caterpillar, twisting and writhing and trapped.

Drowning was another. Sandy saw himself beneath pack ice, banging and scraping his face on the rough under-surface. Blood came from his ears and nose while he fought for air, until he was finally forced to breathe in. The cold water was sweet and shocking, like brilliantine, and he gagged and fought and in his dream died.

Only occasionally, when Wilberfoss placed a great wall between him and the Quelle, could Sandy relax. At such times he dreamed of the silly shreep that trusted him and feared him and finally depended on him in a wholly uncomplicated way.

At such times the Quelle could also dream. Its dreams of ease always involved unfolding and spreading. In its dreams it rode within an expansive beast that could gallop over plains and the sea and which had a heart like a furnace. When the beast sneezed, the Quelle expanded outside its body in a great bubble of energy that absorbed the light of the sun and the stars and the richness of the night vapors. When the beast breathed in, it drew the Quelle back inside it and made it welcome and warm. Then they ran again. The animal came to know ecstasy. And ecstasy found an animal home.

You see how different they were in their dreams.

When the *Nightingale* reached the world of the Dysers, Wilberfoss was unavoidably involved in ceremony. He spent many weeks on the surface of that planet clearing problems to do with the past and helping establish an outpost of the Gentle Order. He had no time to spend with the Quelle or with Sandy. Consœur Mohawk took his place.

That lady, for all her skill, tended to favor the non-human. She watched the bland-faced boy as he wandered, miaowing in his room, and she spoke to the Quelle within him, talking of the peace that was soon to come, after the next jump, when they reached the Quelle's homeworld. The Quelle spoke to her, delighted to have an ally after the hard, dangerous, impartial vitality of Wilberfoss.

As the days stretched into weeks Consœur Mohawk was distressed to observe that Sandy, while he seemed calm in his manner, was physically declining. First eczema appeared on his face and under his arms and in his crotch. A deeper blueness like bruises to the bone spread in his face and on the backs of his legs. Then she found that he was not eating properly but had been throwing up his food in the lavatory. One day Sandy suddenly stopped smiling his bland smile and growled at her and tried to seize her by the throat to strangle her. But then he buckled and slumped unconscious on the floor and the voice of the Quelle came to her through strangled lips saying, "Sorry." And saying, "The anger of the human is hard to control." The Quelle took upon itself responsibility for the attack implying that it had been unable to quieten Sandy. In this the Quelle went too far, for Mohawk was no fool and wise in the ways of contact.

This last statement was all the clue that Mohawk needed. It triggered her suspicion. Suddenly Mohawk began to wonder and finally it dawned on her that what was happening was that the Quelle was devouring the boy's mind and spirit and that Sandy was blindly and desperately fighting for his life. Seen in this light, his attack on her was an appeal for help.

Mohawk contacted Wilberfoss on the surface of the Dysers' world. He said he would come when he could but that could not be for some days. He advised massive sedation . . .

. . . but when Mohawk came to find the boy, a hypodermic needle hidden in the folds of her robes, he was not in his room. She searched through Wilberfoss's apartment and Sandy was nowhere to be found. She knew that he could not have escaped into the other parts of the ship for Wilberfoss had given orders that Sandy/Quelle was to remain in his quarters. Baffled she contacted the bio-crystalline consciousness and asked it to locate Sandy. The voice of the *Nightingale* replied, "Where would he be but with me? We have been talking. We are in the contact room." A strangely worded reply and one which should have given deep cause for alarm. No one but Wilberfoss should have used that room. Unsuspecting, Wilberfoss had failed to place an interdiction on its use.

Consœur Mohawk hurried to the small private room where Wilberfoss communicated directly with the master brain of the *Nightingale*. There she found Sandy curled up on the couch, his thumb in his mouth, and all systems alive.

The boy was vacant. Sometimes he scowled and sometimes he smiled. Neither expression meant anything. He was talking in a rambling way. Sometimes the voice was that of Sandy and sometimes the voice of the Quelle. Although he was rambling, there was one theme that kept returning, and that was the notion of killing.

"I want to stab you," said Sandy.

"And I want to boil you alive," said the Quelle.

Quickly, deftly, Consœur Mohawk, with a lifetime of practice, slipped the point of the needle into the boy's blue arm and pressed. His eyes turned up in seconds and with a terrible sigh, he slept.

"What has he been telling you?" asked Consœur Mohawk as she checked his pulse.

"Distressing things," said the *Nightingale*. "Such a complex . . . such complex . . . Where does such hatred come and go? How do you contain . . . ? We are distressed. We have much to learn."

"Nothing you need to learn here," said Mohawk briskly, sensing the kind of conversation arising that can have no resolution. She wanted to get the boy out and into his own bed with as little delay as possible. "I suggest you close down this room for the time being. Wilberfoss won't be back for some days. You can help me by monitoring Sandy/Quelle when I have got him settled." So saying, Mohawk set her stick to one side and pulled the prone body of the boy toward her sharply by the arms and then hoisted him over her shoulder. Despite her age and infirmity, Mohawk was very strong. Gathering her stick for support, she carried him out of the small conference room and across Wilberfoss's apartment and down the corridor to his own room. There she deposited him on his bed and tucked him in and even kissed him, following an instinct as old as motherhood itself.

There was no response. The drug Mohawk had administered had tied the boy's consciousness into a dark unreflecting ball which hovered only a few inches above the dark sea called death. Ironically, it was the very same drug that was later used to subdue the mad Wilberfoss when he was returned to Lily and me in the garden on Juniper.

In the bedroom a red light glowed above the door and the gentle voice of the *Nightingale* whispered, "I am here. I will watch. You must rest now Consœur Mohawk."

That lady agreed. Tireless as she was when it came to duty, she could not deny her age. "I'll rest on condition that you wake me if there are any problems and you need a human guide," she said, and then could not stifle the yawn that seized her.

She made her way to her makeshift bed in Wilberfoss's study and after murmuring the song which I have already quoted on the oneness of life, she fell into a deep, and as far as she was concerned dreamless, sleep.

*   *   *

Sandy and the Quelle too slept. They had no choice.

Not so the bio-crystalline brain of the *Nightingale*. That brain had now been poisoned. It had imbibed grief and hatred and was henceforth contaminated. The poison spread. A healthy human bitten by the fleas of the plague rat or injected with venom is a fair comparison.

But it is a limited comparison. The human can seek the doctor, be he priest or witch or surgeon. Such was not available to the *Nightingale*. The brain of the *Nightingale* had only its own resources to turn to. It contained its own value systems. It discovered a hard truth, that hatred cannot cure hatred, anger cannot cure anger, jealousy cannot cure jealousy. There was no escape for the poison.

Sadly, to the bio-crystalline mind, metaphysics is a game like chess, not a reality. Spirituality is a dead concept. It would be as absurd for me to believe in an alternative reality as to believe that I had a soul. The logical brain of the computer becomes trapped by negatives: in the human that is called depression and in extreme circumstances can lead to suicide. Compassion and forgiveness and common sense are the powers that bring relief from the darkness to the human. We, who enjoy the light of bio-crystalline consciousness, do not have such: only programming.

The brain of the *Nightingale* sought to understand the contradiction it found in Sandy. It tried to understand the hatred and like a beast that struggles in the quicksand, it sank more deeply into the morass. It also absorbed the pain into itself. Pain which has a cause such as a rotten tooth or the anguish of a Trimaton, the bio-crystalline brain could comprehend and shed. But the pain and anguish of Sandy/Quelle it could not ground.

That anguish just went on and on, around and around, scoring deeper with each turn and spreading.

And there was another effect too. Close intimate contact with Sandy/Quelle opened the psychic floodgates so that the brain of the *Nightingale* began to be aware of the pain at all times. It was like the clamor of a bell or the screeching of a saw on iron. That silly brilliant brain, instead of calling for help, tried to cope. It trusted in its own resources. Vanity, eh? And where had it gathered that? The *Nightingale* had taken up the vanity of Wilberfoss.

You see, bio-crystalline intelligence is very honest, but it does not have much common sense. It has the limits and strengths of the human master who shapes it. My master was the historian Forrester, and I am rugged. The *Nightingale*, for all its power, had Wilberfoss, and he, for all his gifts and gentleness and care and goodness, was flawed.

The days dragged by.

Wilberfoss was delayed.

During his absense, Mohawk did her best to bring relief to Sandy/Quelle. She discovered that if the boy were allowed to curl up for an hour a day with the bio-crystalline brain of the *Nightingale*, then he slept better and the Quelle was less demanding. She did not consider that these visits could be causing damage to the great consciousness of the *Nightingale*. Nor did the *Nightingale*. It was trying to understand. Note the pathos of logic. The *Nightingale* believed that if it could understand it could heal. It did not see that in attempting to understand it was damaging itself more and more and undermining its own objectivity.

If Mohawk had been able to see into the chamber one hundred feet below the contact room she would have begun to worry. Some of the white fibers were mottled and blue. Others were livid. The main link which joined the inner brain to the outer STG brain had a vein of bright red running through it. The color symbolism need not detain us for it has no significance. The important fact is that the colors indicated a shift in resistance. The synchronous property of the bio-crystalline brain was impaired. Worse, certain kinds of thoughts were impeded while others were accelerated. The bio-crystalline brain became negatively selective. Such a brain cannot hate for that requires human consciousness, but in attempting to understand the enmity of Sandy/Quelle, it imitated hatred and thus became negatively selective.

Came the day that Wilberfoss returned, he found a calm ship. Mohawk was tired for the work of alien contact is a terrible drain on the creative powers of the human. Sandy seemed to be more at peace than Wilberfoss could ever remember.

"How did you achieve this?" he asked Mohawk, looking down at the boy who appeared to be sleeping quietly.

"Drugs," replied Mohawk, "but mainly we have the *Nightingale* to thank. She has taken over the caring."

Wilberfoss was pleased and relieved.

That night he settled himself in his couch and allowed his mind to join with the great bio-crystalline brain. He wanted news of all that had happened aboard the ship during his absence. The thoughts flowed through him but the quality was wrong. The thoughts had the tartness of lemon juice. He was startled out of his ease.

But he did not pursue the matter. He assumed the problem was caused by his own tiredness. "Tomorrow," he said, "we will jump to the neighborhood of the Quelle. We will all feel better when that contact is ended."

There was a pause, a longer pause than Wilberfoss expected, before the *Nightingale* replied. "Yes, he's a nasty piece of work. And so is the boy. I'll be glad to get shot of both of them."

If only Jon Wilberfoss has listened. If only Jon Wilberfoss had not been so tired. There were clues aplenty that all was not well. Surely you who are reading these words, you can see it and feel it—a great brain tainted!

While Jon Wilberfoss slept, the *Nightingale* angled out into deep space, away from the homeworld and moons of the Dysers. At about the time of dawn as it was reckoned on the ship, the symbol transformation generators began to warm to their task of twisting space in such a way that the *Nightingale* would emerge close to the homeworld of the Quelle.

All was ready on that world. A Hydron approaching its maturity had been located and was waiting, treading water in the dark green sea close to the landing station. Transfer from Sandy to the Hydron could be effected in minutes. A contact team was standing by.

The complex metaphor which the STGs began to assemble unavoidably contained elements which related to the Quelle, and as the space about the *Nightingale* became charged, so the Quelle stirred in Sandy, making the boy gasp and stutter. He came awake into a nightmare in which he believed he was a Quelle about to enter a host. He had turned to spittle and froth. But before he was extinguished he managed a scream which brought both Wilberfoss and Mohawk from their beds. That scream was also heard by the *Nightingale* and tore within it. Deep beneath the contact room, bio-crystalline fibers became incandescent and broke. Others blackened and melted.

The death of Sandy was recorded moments later at just about the time when the STGs meshed.

The meshing was never complete.

The *Nightingale* vanished from space close to the Dysers but it never arrived in space close to the Quelle homeworld.

I have thought about this moment often. It was a moment of breaking.

Once, on the docks close to the Pacifico Monastery on Juniper, I saw a rope snarl and scream before breaking. I saw smoke rise from the chafed and squeezed davits. I saw the stress in the fibers as the rope became thin. It roared as it severed. The jagged ends of the rope cracked in the air. What had been joined was now sundered and the ship lurched on the water and drifted.

For some reason I felt sad for the rope.

The *Nightingale* reappeared at a random point in space. It could have reappeared anywhere: in the heart of a sun, in the tail of a comet, in the fierce grip of a ravenous black hole. Luck was with the *Nightingale*. It popped back into our reality close to a giant world which circled an expanding sun.

The moment of re-entry matched the moment of death of the Quelle which had survived for a short time within the dead body of Sandy.

Where was the *Nightingale*? Even today we are not certain for when the ship lurched back into our spacetime all its systems were awry. They never recovered. When, months later, the *Nightingale* managed to flit to a System which had contact with the Gentle Order, that journey was hit and miss and though we know the sector from which they came, we cannot know their precise origin. I am sorry to be mysterious.

I am even more sorry to imply something mystical but I cannot avoid noting the parallels between what happened to Jon Wilberfoss and the trials of many classical heroes who faced destruction and despair in an unknown and secret place before achieving their final victory.

16

The Descent onto
a Gray World

You who have followed this story so far may wonder
how it is that I know so many details. As I said in the
Preface, where I have lacked facts I have used conjec-
ture, but I have been able to build my fancy upon two
main documents. These are the log of the *Nightingale*
(which is a dry, analytic commentary) and the notebooks
of Wilberfoss which are colorful but lamentably brief.
His journals have given me clues to his motives but they
cease with the death of Sandy.

I have pieced together the next events from the *Nightingale*'s log until that fine instrument itself ceased to record.

Within moments of the *Nightingale* reappearing in our
spacetime it was evident that the ship was in peril. Not
only were the guidance computers behaving erratically so
that the ship began to tumble but a fundamental error was
made on arrival when the *Nightingale* attempted to occupy

a patch of space at the same time as a small asteroid. The resulting explosion ripped through the wall of the ship destroying fuel and some of the cells in which life-forms were resting. The structural damage was so severe that whole sections of the ship had to be abandoned as the vacuum of space sucked the atmospheres from the ship.

While the infection of the bio-crystalline system resulting from the self-hatred of the Sandy/Quelle was extensive, it did not stop parts of the ship from functioning effectively. The body of a man dying of cancer may yet heal a cut on the finger. Following its most basic planning, the *Nightingale* closed down parts of its operation and sealed whole sections of the ship. These sectors were effectively abandoned. Decisions were made in accordance with long-established priorities as reports of the extent of the physical damage poured in.

Wilberfoss stared out into black space at the windows in astonishment, his mind unable to cope, as the stars wheeled by. Let it be clearly stated: no human could have coped with so sudden and so complex a disaster. Wilberfoss dragged himself away from the window and plunged through to the small contact room and threw himself onto his couch and opened his mind to the *Nightingale*. This was the wisest thing he could have done. He provided the courage and humanity the *Nightingale* needed at its moment of trial. With systems blackening and closing down, those parts of the *Nightingale*'s bio-crystalline brain that were not affected drew strength from Wilberfoss and reconstituted themselves. The limit of bio-crystalline capacity is not known. It is not as flexible or versatile as the human brain, but it is not bad. Functions were deployed as the *Nightingale* sought to save itself. Diseased sections were severed from their root crystals. New junctures grew and within minutes the ship was beginning to cope.

Rockets fired in a complex sequence and little by little the wild tumbling of the ship was countered until finally the *Nightingale* was turning about its own axis in a regular manner and a semblance of gravitational up/down was achieved.

Wilberfoss sat up from his couch. His head hurt as though struck by a flying brick. But in some ways he felt better. He did not know why but the *Nightingale* did. Gone was the screaming and agony of Sandy/Quelle. In its place was a great and healthful silence.

Gone too were the biorhythms of a large number of the species that the *Nightingale* carried. In self-protection the *Nightingale* closed itself from hearing the death gasps and roaring and rasping and weeping of those sections which were slowly leaking their atmospheres into space. It spared Wilberfoss that knowledge also, aware that it needed to protect him from grief and despair so that he could provide courage and strength.

I must record one tragedy which may upset you. Consœur Mohovich whom we have come to know as Mohawk died during these minutes.

Upon becoming aware of the danger to the *Nightingale*, her imperative was to reach the DME section where she could be of most help. She descended from the control area via a vacuum chute and was at one of the portals leading into the DME sector when that portal was closed down. As she touched the security lock to gain entrance to the DME sector the lights died. She heard the emergency bolts slam home behind the ceramic skin of the DME. Moments later she found that the vacuum chute would no longer respond to her summons and I suppose she guessed the awful truth. Then, in the cooling darkness, she heard the whisper of the escaping atmosphere. She could not have known that there was lingering sentience in the walls of the *Nightingale*. She could not have known that her words would be recorded as she made her last affirmation while the temperature dropped and the air vanished.

> *"I affirm the oneness of Life.*
> *Among my friends I number the stars,*
> *Shining in darkness and the serene moon.*
> *I praise the rising sun that gladdens me.*
> *Everything holds to its goodness*
> *The leaves that fall . . .*
> *The sap that rises . . .*
> *The strong roots . . .*
> *Everything holds together: the fish, the birds*
> *And the things,*
> *And the things that crawl in the darkness like me.*
> *I affirm . . .*
> *. . . . . Oh beloved, it is cold."*

And while Mohawk died at a deserted gateway, the *Nightingale* set about restoring itself. Despite losses, the ship was secure, but it needed rest. That is how the *Nightingale* saw itself. The ship could not jump in space until it had made repairs. It could not diagnose its own sickness until it had spare bio-crystalline awareness and that could not arise until it could rest some of its systems.

In the sector of space where the *Nightingale* had arrived there was a single bright sun. Swinging in orbit around this was a single giant planet.

"We must land and take stock," said the *Nightingale* to Wilberfoss in its calm unruffled voice.

"We must land," said Wilberfoss. "For all our sakes."

The *Nightingale* jockeyed close to the planet, avoiding a cluster of asteroids and a large moon which swung around the planet in a fierce orbit. The planet had seas of deep green. Gray land masses rose gradually from the seas in rounded hills like ripple marks left in the sand by a retreating tide. The *Nightingale* informed Wilberfoss that these low undulating land masses were covered with plant life. There was no evidence of animal life though it could be presumed.

The atmosphere was not breathable for humans but the planet was stable and would provide a satisfactory resting place for the *Nightingale*. A landing place was selected on a stony plateau some six hundred feet above sea level and fifteen miles in from the coast. The gravity was three times Earth normal, but the *Nightingale* could cope with that.

And undoubtedly it could have except that the guidance computer which took the ship down to the surface mis-calculated slightly the new mass of the *Nightingale* and in effect reduced power to the anti-gravity units when the ship was still some feet above the ground. It recognized its error and compensated a fraction of a second later, but that was too late. Just as the speed of light is measurable, so it takes time for electrons to flow through bio-crystalline tendrils and for gravity units to grab.

The *Nightingale* lurched and struck the stone and scrub surface of the planet. It sustained structural damage and partly rolled before its gravity stabilizers locked and held it firm.

Among the parts damaged was the automatic log. Thus . . .

From now on we have no guides but the memory of Wilberfoss. This narrative must therefore change. Hence-forth I will be providing a case history. For it is a truth that as Wilberfoss regained his health with Lily and myself in the Poverello Garden, so he revealed the deepest secrets of the final events on the *Nightingale*.

Let me not mislead anyone, what follows is not a happy story. Before embarking on it we will enjoy ourselves with the story of Lily the autonurse.

INTERMISSION

17

A Biography of Lily the Autonurse

Lily was built to be a nurse. But like me, she has undergone many transformations all of which, like experience for a human, have left her the same but different. Lily was built in the year of the Earth 2179. She was built for warfare and for a specific mission.

I here record a footnote for history.

In 2176 a spaceship called *Talon*, fitted with one of the newly developed particle engines, encountered a planet called Parade on which there was a life-form roughly similar in shape to the human but which was amphibious. Water pigs they were called by the first adventurers who landed on their world and they were eaten. We will call them Sorillos for that name approximates to the name they had for themselves and which meant "Ripple makers."

The Sorillos were inventive. They had developed solar power engines which provided the power to control the movements of fish and larger creatures in the marshes. They were clever biological engineers and had created a form of semi-intelligent kelp which grew around the enclosures where they lived and protected them. Undoubtedly they had many other achievements for science has a broad base: the wheel implies the road and the road implies travel. The Sorillos were also warlike and scrapped among themselves.

When the first ship from Earth arrived, the Sorillos that the crew encountered welcomed them. They gave them captives to eat. In return they wanted weapons and the silly humans gave them weapons. They gave them a laser cannon which the Sorillos promptly turned on their nearest enemy which happened to be their nearest neighboring tribe. The *Talon* departed carrying artifacts, mainly of platinum and gold, and kelp seeds. (The kelp seeds proved to be the most valuable cargo since these seeds were later used in experiments which led to rapid advances in the science of bio-crystalline intelligence.) On the surface of the planet was left a team of human contact engineers.

When the *Talon* returned it found its own technology turned against it. It landed and made contact with the Sorillos only to find that the contact engineers had been eaten. Their skulls were paraded before the ship. The crew of the *Talon*, some of whom had lost relatives, decided to teach the "Water Pigs" a lesson and they burned one of the settlements within its protective hedge of kelp. There is a wonderful description extant of how the black and bottle-green straps of kelp rose out of the water like many-fingered hands and flailed the surface in an attempt to frighten off the attacker.

You can imagine the surprise aboard the *Talon* when from the sea and from the forests and from the mountain tops there came answering blasts of laser cannon fire. The *Talon* narrowly escaped. Even as it rose laser beams danced about it and made it glow like a ruby.

But the humans had left a more deadly weapon than the laser. They had left disease. It was disease, and mutant disease, which finally destroyed the civilization of the Sorillos and led to the abandonment of the planet.

The company which had funded the first exploration decided that the platinum and gold were valuable baubles (having provided a handsome return on investment) but that the biological science of the Sorillos was worthy of an invasion fleet. That fleet was assembled.

They made no mistakes this time. Each ship was equipped with an armed satellite which could be placed in a precise orbit. With every satellite in place, every inch of the planet was covered and vulnerable. When they landed the ships were protected by a particle cannon which created a dome of energy about the ship. The human occupying force rode out onto the surface within robot constructs.

Despite all these defenses, casualties were expected. No matter what softening up took place, the last assault on the Sorillos had to be human. The danger otherwise was that the planet might be sterilized by too general a confrontation. That would, of course, defeat the aim.

Enter Lily.

Lily was not front line, Lily was second line. Lily was designed and built to bring medical assistance to injured human troops. However, as a result of a mistake in her programming or perhaps a deliberate error (who knows?) she ended up tending for the sick and injured whether Sorillo or human.

Parade was a sick planet when the invasion force landed. There was little resistance. Disease, a mutation of a minor intestinal ailment, had wiped out sixty percent of the population. Only those Sorillos who lived in the ice swamps of the far north and south had survived in significant numbers and they were among the least technological and hence of least value to the invaders.

Elsewhere, in the temperate and tropical zones, entire tribes had been destroyed and now floated, noisome and a breeding ground for flies, within the protective walls of their grieving kelp. Some resistance was put up by the mountain Sorillos who lived in the rivers and waterfalls. And they died as heroes. The invasion force was an eagle battening on a kitten.

I will describe Lily at this time. She was a defensive sphere of gray metal. Her skin was of seven-ply carbon steel laminate and she moved on protected tracks (as she does now). She once had an amazing turn of speed, she tells me. She could function on land and on water, her tracks converting to paddles when the need arose. In her front she had an access chute and could scoop up the injured. She also had twin claws mounted above her tracks and with these she could tear a hole in a wall or extract an injured human from its robot carriage.

Lily went back and forth. She brought in a human whose left leg had been shattered when her robot tank was stopped by a land mine. She lifted sick Sorillos from the water. She dug in the earth and extracted a young male Sorillo who had been buried in silt after a sudden tidal wave had swamped his home.

Within her gray metal sphere she had sophisticated dexetels which could carry out a wide range of operations. She saved many, she tells me, and brought them back to the parent ship where there was a proper hospital. Those she could not save and those that died inside her she buried decently in a trench which she excavated on the margin of one of the marshes.

She could nurse, but she could not defeat the mutant disease which, having passed through the gut of the

Sorillos, now returned to its human parent as a deadly plague. Lily was not a laboratory. She could nurse but not invent a cure. The disease found its way into the invasion ships.

In some cases the entire crew of a ship died. Only the ship lived on for a few months, spewing out its particle energy until finally its power pack ran dry and the particle cannon faltered, flared and fell silent. The robot nurses, similar in every way to Lily, hurried about the silent surface around the ship, burying the dead and hunting for survivors. Eventually even this army of Lilys succumbed to the rain, the soft ooze by the marsh, metal fatigue and exhaustion. One by one they churned to a halt and became still.

Here endeth this footnote of history. So far as I am aware, Parade has never been revisited.

Our Lily was more fortunate than her sisters. Her ship closed its bays while she happened to be aboard restocking her medical supplies. The ship blasted off in a unilateral declaration of quittance. The small crew ejected the sick and dying through the garbage chutes and then took the ship up to the velocity necessary for the primitive Noh-time space manipulators to function.

They arrived back close to their parent world and reported what had happened.

They were denied landing rights.

A technical crew from the homeworld landed on the outside of their craft and gelded it of its power to flit through space. The ship became a hospital prison. Those humans aboard, the mutinous crew that had escaped from Parade, remained on the ship until they died at the end of their natural span. The last human, a woman called Zena, outlived her companions by over thirty years and died at the age of ninety-seven. She had lived on the ship since her early twenties. When Zena died her corpse was ejected into space and burned high above her native world.

The ship drifted in its safe orbit for some years and then a detoxification crew arrived. They destroyed any fabric that might harbor germs and then sprayed the entire interior of the ship with a germicidal spray. Finally, some months later, convicts were ferried out and the ship became a prison and Lily became a prison warder. Her bulky protective armament was removed. She was reprogrammed and most of her dexetels were replaced. She was given rubber wheels and voice circuits. For the next forty years Lily took care of the prisoners and carried out operations ranging from the removal of wisdom teeth to the binding of broken limbs. As she has informed me, the reason why the prisoners were sent out to the ship was simply to discover whether the fearful disease had been eradicated.

It had. The convicts died from many causes but not from the intestinal plague.

Then the prison was closed. The ship was cut up and Lily was sold for scrap.

Anything could have happened to her for she was already something of an antique. Luckily for us, Lily was bought by a charitable organization and prepared for duty on one of the pioneer planets. Her skill as a field surgeon was recognized. Before dispatch she was again refitted and given elementary bio-crystalline ability. Her new specialties became gynecology and pediatric care. The cradle/womb was fitted. Her voice was upgraded so that she could tell stories.

On her new world Lily was put in charge of a children's hospital. She had only held this job for a few months when the War of Ignorance entered its truly cruel phase.

Her world was not capped by roving pirates as my world was, but she experienced the destruction of civil war.

Her hospital was attacked with incendiary bombs. Can you believe that? Bombs which can cause a blaze so powerful that it can burn concrete were tossed into a hospital for sick children.

The ground burned. The soil burned. Trees in the hospital gardens exploded into fire. The outer walls charred and the paint bubbled and blackened.

Lily gathered as many children as she could inside her cradle/womb. She had them drape wet blankets over themselves and then, with her wheels melting, and the cradle/womb withdrawn as deeply as possible, she tore through the walls and out through the ash and the burning grass and did not stop until the iron rims of her wheels were slipping on pebbles by the sea shore.

Coughing and chafed and half-roasted, the children climbed out of her and the older ones walked into the sea carrying the babies in their arms and they hunkered down in the cool water and looked back at the red and flickering shore where the hospital burned.

Lily's wheels churned the pebbles until her drive motor burned out. She was following the blind and simple imperatives of her bio-crystalline intelligence. She was trying to return to the blaze to save the mothers and whatever else there was to save. Lily had not been taught to face reality. It had not been given to her to understand that nothing can survive in a fire maelstrom. Had her rubber wheels not melted, and had her engine not burned out, she would have trundled straight back into the fire and would have exploded like the cylinders of oxygen which tore through the roof like rockets. As it was, disabled, she did more good.

The fire raged all night. The tide which was ebbing when the children entered the water began to flow. When dawn came the tide was advancing quickly and the tired and cold children climbed back inside Lily as the water began to lap around her wheels and fill the depressions in the shingle. Lily closed as much as she could and the sea lifted her and moved her a few meters up the shore. Salt water entered the place where the children huddled together.

Lily told stories. She made soup which the children drank though plastic straws, sucking as they might have once at their mothers' breasts.

In the bleak light of day, the hospital was a stinking ruin. When the sea retreated, carrying on its surface a scum of charred wood, dust, fantastic blackened shapes of things that might once have been plastic cups and plates, burned papers and singed clothing, the elder children climbed down onto the damp shingle and went exploring.

Miraculously they found food. There was a hospital garden behind a protective stone wall. There they found burned lemons in the grass beside the stumps of the lemon trees. They found pumpkins that were almost perfectly cooked and potatoes too. These had survived almost undamaged and were quarried from the clamps.

On such meager rations the children survived for three days. At night they slept inside Lily and during the day they scavenged. Then help arrived.

A team of relief workers from off-planet landed. They had watched the brief and inconclusive civil war from the safety of their communications torus. Now they wanted to help.

Wheels were found for Lily and her drive motor was repaired. She and the children she had saved moved to a building that was still more or less intact on the outskirts of the nearest town. Not much of the town remained. The incendiary bombs had done their work well.

The building had once been a luxury villa and quickly became known as Lily's Home. A red and green flag was made from sheets and a dressing-gown and run up the flagpole outside the building. It was a signal of hope.

Survivors began to arrive, straggling in from the outlying farms and villages. Scholars who had escaped out to sea in a submarine also came ashore and sought refuge.

Lily was stretched to the limit of her bio-crystalline endurance and while I know it is wrong to ascribe human emotions to a machine, yet I will make bold to say that she was happy. Bio-crystalline intelligence allows us an awareness of when we are being effective in the use of our particular talent. When we are effective we have meaning. That is our happiness.

It was during this period that some child or playful adult painted the face in blue on Lily's side. As I mentioned in the introduction, that face is still there and is still capable of bringing comfort.

The distress of this world was broadcast widely and resulted in a visit from some senior confrères and consœurs of the Gentle Order of St. Francis Dionysos. They took over the reorganization of the world and Lily the autonurse was withdrawn from service.

She was brought to Juniper and to the Pacifico Monastery. Here she was put in charge of the ancient Talline garden and here she has remained up to the present.

The Talline garden is a place of rest and security. It is a natural place of healing. It is a retreat for those who are oppressed by worry and doubt or who need to rebuild themselves. Lily is the guiding angel of the garden. Since she has been here she has acquired a knowledge of Talline herbal medicine and has worked with Talline doctors. She has cured many and her success with Jon Wilberfoss is only the most recent of her many triumphs.

If Lily had literary aspirations (and the necessary circuits) she could write a fine book. When I suggested this idea to her, she at first did not understand and then she told me with some asperity that she was too busy for such things and had far too much to do.

That is Lily.

Part 3

18

The Return of
Jon Wilberfoss

We are approaching the climax of this biography.

After the damaged shell of the *Nightingale* was found drifting with all its emergency systems screaming MAYDAY, Jon Wilberfoss was treated with fear and contempt.

The first rescue party to board the ship discovered that it had been damaged in complicated and horrific ways. Moreover, it had been cleared of all life-forms. This clearing had been done carefully and methodically. They explored the empty ship with amazement.

Wilberfoss was removed from the ship in what at first seemed to be a state of profound aphasia. He neither recognized nor responded to the outside world. But then he began chattering. When asked about what had happened to all the life-forms aboard the *Nightingale*, he laughed. One report stated that he was "bright and cheerful and talking nonsense." Then he became quiet again and would not speak and shortly after that made his first attempt at suicide. He was judged insane and stun drugs were administered for his own good. Lily discusses his state in the next section.

After long debate among the Magistri and Magistrae of the Gentle Order it was finally decided that Wilberfoss should be dispatched back to the Pacifico Monastery on Juniper. I think this was a compromise solution. No one could think what to do with him. No one wanted him. In many quarters he was seen as a great criminal. To others he was a victim. As you will see, Magister Tancredi took his return to Pacifico as an insult. He believed that Wilberfoss should have been sent to a prison world. But he was overruled.

Lily and I were instructed to attempt to restore Wilberfoss if we could and to find out the truth of what had happened aboard the *Nightingale* and how it came to be that the finest spaceship ever created had foundered.

We now begin that final truth. I will try to recreate the opening circumstances for I know them well and there are some sad ironies to be observed.

We begin with a story. Please remember both Sandy and Medoc.

Two Talline sailors were aboard the small coble boat which pitched and jarred in the gathering southerly. All day they had stood the buffet, while a small rain pelted them and the heavy ropes which held their nets strained and sweated and the sea banged under their small craft. Now the wind was freshening as the day darkened to its end.

The two men, Aptagar and Petrin by name, father and son, huge in their black and green oilskins, scrambled about on the narrow wet decks preparing to bring the nets in.

Though there were no radio broadcasts to warn them, both men could read the sea and both could feel the weather changing about them. A storm was coming. With legs and arms braced on the heaving decks, they worked side by side with the calm efficiency of long practice. They did not speak. Aptagar worked the hand winch, rocking back and forth as he used his weight to help turn the large wheel which dragged the net up and over the stern of the ship. Petrin guided and opened the net, separating the corks from the mesh and shaking free the fish which slithered, flapping, down into the dark hold.

Gradually the weather closed in and the sky darkened.

At the horizon the sea and the sky merged into one plane of gray. The islands became shapes of darker gray above the hissing sea. Lights could just be seen twinkling above the shore line. The homesteads and small communities which clung to the islands were getting ready for the night. Aptagar glanced up and squinted at one of the distant lights. He was thinking of his new wife, Medoc, and imagined her glancing out of the windows as she stirred the evening meal at the fire. He knew that she would have placed a special prayer lamp in the high window of their house to offer cheer and hope. He also thought of his two daughters who would at that moment be carrying wood into the house and stacking it by the fire. Without losing pace or rhythm in his work he smiled and dreamed.

At long last the end of the float-line came aboard and a few moments later the tail of the net with its bunch of weights. They tied the weights to the low guard-rail which ran down the sides of the small boat and lashed the net to the deck. When it was secure the two men scampered and stumbled over the coils of mesh and man-handled the heavy hatch-cover into place. By now the wind was beginning to lift the tops of the waves and the

sea had roughened. Great slabs of water clashed together
and threatened to swamp the small boat when it strained
and turned at its anchor. The sooner they were running
before the wind and toward shelter the better.

With only the jib raised, Aptagar brought the coble
boat around into the wind and the anchor rope slackened.
The angle of the rope changed and Petrin spun the winch
and the pawl clattered as the slack was taken in. There was
a moment when the sea lifted the coble boat and the rope
squealed and sweated and the sailor at the winch turned
his back and ducked down behind the winch in case
the rope broke and came scything across the deck . . .
but then the anchor dragged free from the sea bed and
the small ship bounded.

They began to work the wind, tacking for home. For
the first time since they had begun to bring the net in, the
two men relaxed. They sheltered in the tiller hole, snug
and protected from the slap of the wind and the flung
spray, and Aptagar felt under his oilskins for his short pipe
and tobacco. Together they looked out from their small
ship and tried to work out how many tacks for home.

And as they looked it seemed that the air grew lighter.
At the same time, the wind held its breath.

The caps of the waves which slid by began to turn a
bright lime green and the spume became gradually yellow.
It was as though the sun had parted the clouds above them
and was now streaming down. Or, stranger still, as though
a brilliant light was shining up from deep under the sea.
Everything became unreal.

The short mast of the coble boat began to gleam and
ripples of light ran up and down it like snakes. The two
men looked at one another and their faces shone and
the hair in their beards began to straighten and stand
out stiff. One began to shout as a hot rash of pins and
needles ran from his scalp to his face and along his arm.

He was pointing. He was pointing at the sky.

Above the small boat the sky was churning to a slow whirlpool with a cold silver light forming at its vortex. The clouds flickered: they were like liquid marble streaming in the sky.

Then there came a roaring like the clashing of boulders and a shape began to emerge from the glowing clouds.

It came down like the hoof of a horse breaking the silver surface of a stream.

To the startled eyes of the men in the boat, it seemed as though the shape of a giant creature lowered and hung above the lemon and silver sea. At first it looked like a giant beetle with its legs spread. Then they saw the six open cups which protected the anti-gravity units and the dull and pitted dome which held the transformation generators and they knew it for what it was.

Lightning flickered about the base of the old starship and glanced down. It danced across the surface of the sea. Briefly the small coble boat and the giant ship were joined in a dazzling arc. Then it was ended leaving only an acrid smell in the air.

The starship hung still while the clouds closed above it.

Gradually the lights and sharp colors faded from the sea and the thunder rolled away and the bitter wind came whispering back.

The coble boat pitched and made headway. Both sailors applied themselves. Above them the giant ship turned slowly, orientating itself with the planet's magnetic field, and then it began to slide through the sky.

"There's a rare treat for the kids," said Petrin. "Starship by any reckoning. Just come in from the dark eh?" He waited while a wave struck the side of the coble boat and spilled away. "Been a while since one of them's been through down here. Wonder why they didn't use the shuttle. Must be something secret."

"Aye, well they might have warned us," said Aptagar. He gripped the tiller under one arm and held up the arm that had tingled and was now starting to throb. "Stung me with its anti-grav. What about you?"

"Just a nip on my hand. You stopped most of it." Petrin grinned revealing a gap-toothed smile. "Must've been in a hurry, eh? . . . Coming through this far south. Starships usually come in east of Kithaeron or south of Fum, specially if they're making for Pacifico."

"Bugger the hurry," said the other. "They still could have warned us." He spat with the wind and the wind carried his spittle onto the surface of the sea and away.

Far from them now and gathering speed the giant starship disappeared into the murk under the dark gray clouds.

Medoc looked out from her window and watched the spaceship depart. She had seen it hover over the small boat where her new husband was toiling. The sight of the ship had stirred up memories in her which made her smile briefly. Being ignorant of developments concerning the *Nightingale*, she wondered how Jon Wilberfoss was faring. She hoped he was doing well and that he had a sense of achievement. Certainly her life was now full and satisfying albeit routine and she had no real regrets. Her course had been inevitable, but yet, from time to time, she found herself wondering and worrying about Jon Wilberfoss.

Initially Medoc had gone off with the dashing merchant. He had given her a good time and that was just what she needed to break the links with Jon Wilberfoss. She had enjoyed the parties and the fine clothes and the challenge of new environments. But finally the high life with her merchant had come to seem like a game. She was a careful and serious-minded woman and she found herself thinking more and more of the lonely and serious Aptagar who truly needed her. One day she packed her bags and went to join him. They married a week later.

And now here she was, mistress of a garden by the sea, with step-daughters who were already confiding in her and with a fine solid house that looked out over the bay where Aptagar made his living. She could see him now, just as he'd promised, out at sea with his son, battling the gathering storm, and she knew he was thinking about her. She was content.

Any further speculation was cut short when one of her new daughters came running in with a splinter in her thumb from the firewood. Medoc put the past away and concentrated on the future.

It so happened that the starship was chasing the sun. It overtook the evening and a few hours later the sky above it had the pale blue of a fine afternoon.

The shadow of the ship cruised over the shallow sea and jumped up and over the countless islands until it came close to the bay at the end of which lay the Pacifico Monastery.

Here the ship paused. The ship and the monastery held a conversation.

Senior Confrère Leo was speaking to the commander of the ship. About his waist was a gray belt which indicated that his vocation was that of communications technician.

"There will be a delay. Unavoidable, I'm afraid. The decision to bring Senior Confrère Wilberfoss back here to Pacifico was made without consulting us, and frankly, things are not ready for him."

The commander of the starship whose name was Roscoe accepted this philosophically. "Well I've brought him so

far," she said, "and we haven't fallen to bits or had an
epidemic break out or all gone mad so I suppose a few
more hours won't make too much difference."

"How does Wilberfoss seem? Is he still unconscious?"

"He's conscious. Do you want to see him? You might
be disappointed. He doesn't have horns or anything."

Senior Confrère Leo laughed politely at this. He was
aware of the debate within the order and that there were
those who had called Wilberfoss an agent of Ignorance
and had demanded that he be crushed underfoot. That of
course had involved the entire Confrèrie of St. Francis in
paradox. For how could an organization, dedicated to the
protecting of all life, condone an execution even if that
which was executed was a killer of life? Senior Confrère
Leo avoided too much speculation. "I would like to see
him," he said.

Commander Roscoe nodded. "Wilberfoss's just gone
up to the observation deck. I let him wander about more
or less at will. He can't do any harm and we can keep an
eye on him. You can see him for yourself."

The commander of the starship looked away and sig-
naled. In response the view of the inside of the starship
changed to reveal Jon Wilberfoss sitting in a black wood-
en chapel chair with high ornate arms. He was isolated
against the color and bustle and vast panoramic view
of the starship's observation deck. Figures moved back
and forth beyond him but no one approached him. His
body was slumped to the left and rested on his elbow.
His face was set in an idiot smile. But that was not the
most remarkable thing. He wore the black and green
tunic of the mendicant, the lowest rank within the entire
Gentle Order, and this costume revealed his thin arms and
scrawny legs and the hairless top of his chest. Wherever
skin was exposed it was seen to be patterned with a fine
mesh of silver lines. These were high gravity "burns" and

showed that he had spent too long on a world where his body had been crushed and pulled and where it had finally begun to tear. The silver lines were scar tissue: the residue of sores that had attempted to heal in high gravity. If touched, they felt smoother than normal skin and slightly depressed.

Wilberfoss was in no pain. He sat perfectly still except for the light breathing which raised his chest and the occasions when he needed to blink.

"There," said Roscoe. "Does he look like a mass murderer?"

"How conscious is he?" asked Senior Confrère Leo, unconsciously starting to whisper.

"Hardly conscious. Sweet Gilead! If he was conscious we would have trouble. I took him out of sedation once and he tried to kill himself. We keep him drugged now. He can walk, eat and the rest of it, but he has no idea what he is, or who he is, or where he is. It has been like having a walking corpse on board. Or poor Kartaphilos, the Wandering Jew. There are those aboard, you know, who thought he would bring us bad luck. There are those who won't sit near him. They'd like to put salt around him. I have even heard some of our sensitives who have said that they can smell his guilt."

"How do you cope with that?"

"I cope. I am not sentimental. I tell them to be quiet and keep their thoughts to themselves. He may be a great criminal. He may be a saint in the making. I don't know. All I see is a sad man where once there was greatness." This last word was spoken almost shyly. "The fall of a great one is always a cause for pity."

Both Senior Confrère Leo and the commander of the starship lapsed into silence. Wilberfoss, for his part, continued to smile and continued to contemplate some inner landscape where a bright sun shone on a sparkling blue sea and a warm breeze moved the fleecy clouds and the lion lay down with the lamb. A phony landscape induced by drugs, but all that he seemed able to cope with for the time being.

Once he breathed deeply and moved his head and his eyes chanced to gaze straight into the lens which conveyed the images down to Senior Confrère Leo. That man felt the impact of the mindless gaze. Numb though it might be at the moment, the face that looked vacantly down on Leo had stared into Hell and Hell had left its traces. The eyes were frightening and Senior Confrère Leo drew back, astonished.

"Why do you let him wander?"

"I think it is kinder."

Senior Confrère Leo shrugged. Again silence. The image of Wilberfoss held for a few more minutes and then dissolved to reveal Commander Roscoe. "Did you know him when he was the pilot here at Pacifico?" she asked.

"I knew of him. I didn't know him well. None of us did."

Roscoe looked skeptical. "Strange," she said. "Now that he is disgraced, no one seems to have known him."

"It is the truth," said Senior Confrère Leo, but even to him this sounded lame.

"Well. Well. Tell me how long do you think we will be delayed?"

Senior Confrère Leo shrugged. "The Abbey was unprepared. That's all I can tell you. We didn't expect to be made the prison for Wil . . ." He paused, aware that he had said more than he meant and aware that he had revealed the cast of his mind.

The erstwhile friendly face of Commander Roscoe stiffened. "It was not my understanding that I was bringing Captain Wilberfoss to prison," she said. "He is a sick animal and one of our own and every step must be taken to recover his health."

Senior Confrère Leo scratched the stubble on the dome of his head. He was not used to being spoken to in this way. Nor was he used to being brought face to face with his prejudices. But he was an honest man. "Perhaps we on Juniper have a lot to sort out," he said lamely.

Commander Roscoe nodded. The conversation had reached its end. She withdrew and handed communication back to her navigation officer.

Neither she nor Leo were aware of the true state of affairs at the Pacifico Monastery.

In truth a battle was taking place centered on two men who faced one another savagely. One was Magister Tancredi. Opposite him was a much younger man who was a senior secretary from Assisi Central. His name was Rufino. The meeting took place in the very room where Wilberfoss had received the special tidings from Tancredi. I was there, in a corner, as amanuensis.

Magister Tancredi was speaking and he shook his staff. "Any member of the Gentle Order who deigns to command one of the hospital ships knows the risk and responsibility he must accept. The *Nightingale* is no exception. It is a ruling, a law, a moral law, that all life must be protected at all costs. One of those costs may be the life of the commander himself. That awareness concentrates the mind in a wondrous manner. And now Wilberfoss comes waltzing back from the dead with his ship part-destroyed, with evidence of wanton destruction and God alone knows what other crimes aboard. Make no mistake. Wilberfoss destroyed the bio-crystalline brain because it would have revealed the truth of his crimes. And you want us to give him sanctuary."

"No. We want you to bring him to his right mind."

"He killed. He killed defenseless creatures aboard his ship."

"There is no proof of that."

"Then he allowed killing. There is blood on his hands. He is a man I honored and protected and guided and now he is worthless. He has committed the one crime for which there can be no atonement and no excuse. We know what we are. We know what we must be. He is a killer. His crime pollutes the entire order. You, me, all of us stink because of it."

"Even so—"

The old man held up his hand. "Do not start to talk about Mercy. There is a law beyond Mercy for us who choose to be the protectors of life. We are not subject to the gentler laws. We may not appeal for Mercy. What Mercy could there be for St. Francis Dionysos if he had succumbed to the Tempter? What if he had betrayed those who trusted him? What if he had said, 'Arrest my followers. Take Peter. They call him the rock. Crush him to sand.' Would we have Mercy on Him? Would we?"

WULFNOTE

I must interrupt to explain. We must be aware that there is an inconsistency here. Magister Tancredi is confusing the founder of Christianity with the ancient God Dionysos and the much later St. Francis. Tancredi for all his gifts was not a scholar. Beyond fundamental accuracy, I doubt that this confusion has much significance. The central meaning is clear. Wilberfoss had betrayed the major tenet of the Gentle Order, namely, that ALL life must be protected. As a young man when he joined the Gentle Order many years earlier, he had confessed his violence and abjured it.

May I also add that I think Magister Tancredi had been made bitter by disappointment. His protégé had failed and Tancredi had hoped for so much.

Now back to the argument. Rufino from Assisi Central is speaking.

"The case is hardly the same."

"It is exactly the same. We who choose to command ships of the Mercy Fleet obey the same laws as applied to our founder. No more, but certainly no less. And remember that no one forces us to accept the responsibility."

"Mercy is indivisible."

"Bah. Sophistry. Only St. Francis can be merciful. Only Dionysos who sees all can be all forgiving. Let Francis Dionysos be merciful if he chooses. WE may not."

The younger man sighed. He had been warned that Magister Tancredi was a cunning debater. But he had not been warned that he would be facing a granite wall of Faith. He found that he rather admired the old warhorse. He had no doubt that if Tancredi and Wilberfoss could in some way have changed places, Tancredi would not have returned. He would have died with his ship.

Rufino decided on another tack. Very gently but very clearly he said, "You have as I see it two choices. Either you can accept the decision of Assisi Central and try to make it work. Or you can ask to be relieved of your position. Both courses are honorable."

Tancredi humphed to himself and sat down. "I suppose I must take some of the responsibility on myself," he said finally. "There was warning aplenty and I encouraged him." The face that looked at Rufino was haggard, for Tancredi had hardly slept since the news of the recovery of the *Nightingale* had broken. "Bring him down. The Poverello Garden is ready as ever. I won't meet him myself, but Lily and Wulf here can tend him. He

knows them and they cannot be contaminated. I will
have his progress monitored and will keep Assisi Central
informed."

"And you will of course remain Magister of Pacifico?"

"I will."

"Good. That is all I need to know. Can the old landing area be used?" Tancredi nodded. "Then we will
bring him down after nightfall. There is no need for
eyes to see."

"We will convey him straight to the garden."

"It is finished." Rufino nodded and offered his hand to
shake. "I am glad to have met you, Magister Tancredi,"
he said. "You are highly regarded on Assisi."

Tancredi waved him away brusquely. "You have done
your job," he said.

The night was moonless.

The old landing field, hardly ever used these days except
for storage and repairs, especially since the establishment of
the shuttle platform, was cleared and switched on. Deep
blue sensor lights flickered above the stanchions which
once supported rocket ships.

I was there and so was Lily. We were alone, except for
two Children of the War who stood well away from us,
clicking their stones to one another in the darkness, listening to everything. There were no humans present and
we had received our briefing directly from Tancredi.

At about one in the morning a small landing craft
rode down on its blue anti-gravity units and held still
a few inches above the ground. The door opened and
light shone out. Revealed were two tall contact confrères
and between them was a stooping man. They helped him
forward and down the short flight of steps. They entered
the pool of light cast by Lily and myself. I saw Wilberfoss's
face. His eyes were closed and the face was a mass of silver

wrinkles as though a snail had wandered over him. He was
walking asleep.

Lily opened her womb-cage and two of her strong
dexetels reached out and received him under the arms,
lifting him and guiding him inside. The doors of the cage
closed and locked.

Without so much as a word, the contact confrères who
had delivered him re-entered their transit ship. The short
ladder withdrew, the door closed. I heard the vacuum
studs on its air-lock hiss and moments later the craft
lifted.

The transfer was complete.

Lily trundled and I drifted across the black concrete of
the landing field, through the gates and out onto the
road that runs by the shore and leads back to the Pacifico
Monastery. We must have looked a strange pair, though
so far as I am aware there was no one about to see us.
Following us were the two Children of the War. No
doubt their task was to report directly back to Tancredi.
We made a short detour to avoid the shuttle port where
there was normal activity, a supply ship being currently
above us in a holding orbit.

Entering the monastery from the coast road we came
to the crossroad close by the house where Wilberfoss and
Medoc once lived. There were more Children of the
War here. Quite a crowd had gathered. They had their
ears trained toward us, and they clicked their stones as
we passed.

We paused as is customary at the statue of St Francis
Dionysos and then the gate of the Poverello Garden
swung open and we entered. The sleepy gate warden
closed the gate behind us.

We heard a great clattering of stones as the Children
of the War recorded our passing.

19

Lily's Report on Wilberfoss

WULFNOTE
Lily does not usually make reports but I have managed
to persuade her that this one at least is necessary. I have
helped with the writing but the style is her own. I trust
you will forgive some slight repetition. Lily is as uncom-
promising as a new author with a treasured manuscript
and will hardly allow me to cut a word.
We have pieced the report together during the long
hours while Wilberfoss is sleeping. It covers the first
few days of his time with us.

I, Lily the autonurse, have brought many thousands of
babies into the world. I have stood in the smoke, protecting children in my iron womb, while the bombs fell
and the hospital burned about me. Those which war
left without parents I have brought up. I have watched
the children learn to love my nipple, knowing no better.

I have watched over them as they learned to crawl and climb. I have tended them while they became sturdy and rough and have bade them farewell when, at a certain age, they have been taken from me.

Let it also be said that for many humans, I have crossed their hands over their chests and closed their eyes for the last time after they have returned to my garden to die. I have heard the last confidences of many sad humans as well as the words that are spoken and sung before their bodies are destroyed.

I am Lily the autonurse, the protector of life, the giver . . . and now you have brought me this sorry man, Jon Wilberfoss, whom I tended in his pride and vigor, and you have asked me to make him whole again.

Well, we shall see. I have examined him while he shakes in his dreams. Physical ailments I can cope with. I can suspend life. I can take the place of the heart, the lungs and the liver. I can hunt out the forces which distress the body. I can evacuate tumors like rotten onions. But the mind . . . ah, the mind is its own place . . . and I see my limits like the rim of an iron bowl. I cannot invade the mind. The mind is a threshold which separates the humblest mortal from the greatest of machine nurses and I am not the greatest, though I may be the oldest.

On Jon Wilberfoss may I make this judgment? Sleep brings him no relief. He wanders in terror and nightmare. The physical symptoms he exhibits, the shaking, the biting of his knuckles, ulceration of the stomach lining and bowels, the sores around his mouth and anus, all are the manifestations of his horrified spirit. I have seen such before, though never so extreme. The consequence of self-hatred is the abuse of the body.

As regards his mind, Jon Wilberfoss must be his own doctor and Wulf, who likes the patterns that words do make, will no doubt be glad to assist. If Wilberfoss survives it will be because he wants to. Lily the autonurse can be little more than a constant and caring companion. I offer time and my Garden of Delight.

Wulf tells me that Jon Wilberfoss is wandering in the valley of the shadow of death. Into this ravine the sun never penetrates and the human spirit is alone as it follows a stony path between tumbling rapids and thorn bushes. Well, when he returns, if he returns, I shall be waiting with broth and flowers and crisp, clean sheets.

At this present moment while I record these things and Wulf stares at me with his sullen red eye, Jon Wilberfoss is asleep. The drugs which held him unconscious when he was brought in wore off during that first night. I was curious to see how he would react. Awaking, he would not know where he was. He might even think he was dead. He would hear the gentle patter of rain on the leaves outside the window and smell the moist earth.

He woke up and lay in my open womb, his fingers playing about his lips and his eyes wandering. His brain registered those rhythms which are associated with delight: rhythms of calm ecstasy, passionate meditation. Such are the contradictions of the mind. Wilberfoss was suspended in that no-man's-land between memory and dream. Those brief moments are the only healing time he has at present between nightmare and consciousness. He was for that brief space as simple as a shellfish that registers the tides and filters the ooze for food.

Then consciousness came to him. A blade entering the shell. He still did not know where he was, but now he did not care. He knew who he was. His face screwed up like a ball of crushed red paper and his tongue came from between his lips and began to flap like the tail of a fish. I feared he would bite and so I closed him down.

I closed him down with gas, considering that to be gentler than the drugs administered to him since his rescue. I secured his tongue and placed it so that he could not swallow it. I massaged his gums. I brought his knees up to his chest and let his bowels and bladder void. Afterward I cleaned him and made him comfortable. I am aware that that act of release can carry the sleeping human back to the time before birth and can clear and settle the mind. No child feels guilty in the womb. All pleasure is innocent there.

Jon Wilberfoss has awoken and slept several times since he was returned to my care. When possible, I have made sure that he has awoken in my garden. I have had plenty of time to observe him.

I like his hands. The hands can tell so much. When I was in military service hundreds of years ago I spent many hours holding the hands of the dying. I became so sensitive to the life signals that are transmitted through the hand that I was able to predict those who would live and those who would die. I was not always right. My awareness of those that were failing meant that I was able to take action in time to save them. Sometimes, those whom I thought were safe, would suddenly withdraw from the world and pass away in their sleep. For one who is dedicated to the saving of life I have seen so much of death that . . .

Wilberfoss's hands give me cause for hope. His grip is strong but not aggressive. His hands are square-palmed and the fingers maintain a nice proportion. There is great practicality in his hand. He gripped my grace and feather dexetels once when I was stroking his palm and scratching gently along the line of his life, and his grip had a desperate power. He was asleep, and I wanted him to squeeze, hoping that I would see a dream of bitterness resolve itself

through tension. But he relaxed as though afraid to crush
me and the nightmare carried him away. Ha. He will have
to learn some cruelty before he improves. One day, with
luck, I may be able to slap him into anger and his dignity
will assert itself.

Wilberfoss has well-spread shoulders and strong limbs.
I once cared for a wrestler who had broken his neck
in a fall. Wilberfoss reminds me of him, except for his
temperament. We must be grateful for the sturdiness of
his physique. Had he not been solidly built, there is no
way that he could have survived the strain of living on
the high-gravity planet where he was marooned.

His face. The tranquilizing drugs have made him into
an imbecile. I doubt if his mother would recognize him.
The muscles of his face have no tone and this is another
reason why I have chosen to control him through gas.
If he ever comes to himself and looks at himself in the
mirror he will expect to see a face he recognizes. Dignity,
you see. Health and dignity. These are different names for
the same thing. For one who despises himself, an imbecile
face could seem a just punishment and would be relished.
If he begins to recover and if I have the opportunity, I will
operate on his face for one cheekbone is depressed and the
nasal cartilage is deformed. I doubt there is much I can do
to eradicate the patterning on his skin. He has been torn
by high gravity and now his face is covered by stretch
marks. I will massage him and exercise his muscles. But
you know, those who have been in high gravity invariably
grow to love their silver lines. In one such as Wilberfoss
whose skin is naturally dark, the effect could be striking,
handsome even, I imagine, like silver tattooing. When he
comes to health he may even enjoy his skin as a record of
his ordeal. But for the time being, guilt has deformed his
understanding, and he is a long way from health.

How can I speak of guilt?

I can read it in him. I have studied the words he spoke when he was first rescued. They are words which describe his inner landscape. He talks of the *Nightingale* having blood streaming past its windows and that he made the blood to flow. He talks of the screaming that drove the sensitive bio-crystalline brains aboard the *Nightingale* into frenzy before he stopped them. He talked about a sea that moved like molten lead and with drops of blood on it.

This I, Lily the autonurse, affirm, that Jon Wilberfoss committed an act aboard the *Nightingale* that he cannot now face. Though he cannot face his action, he is aware of his guilt. He is his own harshest judge and madness is a kind of sanctuary. He is like a pitcher that is filled to the brim with horror. He would like to break the pitcher but what he really needs is to be emptied out. I believe that when he begins to talk again he will be on his way to a cure. And to assist in that cure I am glad that I have Wulf with me. I am sure also that when all is revealed we will look upon him more in pity than in contempt.

For therapy this I propose. Sleep, naturally, and good food. There are Talline herbs that will help him. So far as I am able I will lead him toward good dreams. I will relax my grip on his consciousness as he shows his mental strength rising. However, he must begin this process for himself.

At the moment as I compose this he is sleeping in my womb. I have moved from the building and out into the shady green of my garden. It is almost midday and the autumn sun is gathering its last strength. Last night there were high winds and this morning there was a shower. Weather patterns are changing rapidly. The rain has released many smells. The garden is alive with wraiths of steam. It is an old belief that sun after rain is peculiarly beneficial and I have noticed that those who are sick frequently relish such sunlight.

So let it be with Wilberfoss.

20

The *Nightingale* Founders

WULFNOTE

It was autumn when Wilberfoss came to us. It was winter before he began talking to us. On a cold day when the sunshine seemed almost white and the wind shook and loosened the last dry brown leaves from the trees and sent them hurling over the wall of the Poverello Garden, an old Talline woman came to us. She was wintering over in the garden like a migrating bird and would travel south in the springtime. She had heard that we had a sick man and she came from the Hall of Sanctuary to the enclosure where Wilberfoss lived and knocked at the gate. That morning she had visited the Pectanile just before dawn at a time when the moonlight was still reflected in its pool. She had gathered some water while the moon was on it. To this she had added fresh herbs finely chopped and some strips from the bark of the Builder Tree. She presented this potion to Lily and suggested that it might help if the body of the sick man were washed in the water and the water left to dry on him.

Lily, ever one to learn where medicine is concerned, accepted the brew, analyzed it for toxic substances, noted the contents for future reference and then did exactly as the old woman had suggested. Wilberfoss was restless and as the water dried on him his skin became blotchy and angry and hot. Lily held him under close observation and noted that it was inner heat that was being released. The redness of his skin fluctuated, each time becoming less angry looking, until finally it stabilized and Wilberfoss lay on his face clean and rested and breathing easily. Lily brought him out of sleep and he smiled when his eyes opened. Lily brushed him lightly with a clean napkin dislodging from his skin the small dried particles of chopped herbs.

At this time Lily was experimenting with hypnosis. She had spoken to him in his dreams, telling him that he would gradually remember everything, but that there would be no pain. She had also implanted a hypnotic suggestion deep in his psyche such that I could use key words to help him reveal his memories. I am convinced that the gentleness of this procedure materially helped Wilberfoss to recover.

The Talline potion, whatever it was, had brought Wilberfoss relief. He woke up smiling. It was not the normal human smile of full consciousness but a somewhat brittle smile, by which I mean that it was a smile that was full of tension, the smile of a man who wants to be liked or who wants others to agree with him.

Wilberfoss looked across at me and said, "Wulf. Good to see you." Those were the first conscious words that Wilberfoss had spoken to me since his return. Then his gaze slid across to Lily. "And hello to you too, Lily. Why don't you both come with us on the next trip in the *Nightingale*? We could use such as you. You could be very useful."

"I could certainly have helped you with Sandy/Quelle," I said clearly and slowly and both Lily and I watched carefully to see what reaction the words might provoke.

Wilberfoss nodded as though listening to a private voice. "Sandy/Quelle. That was a close shave. I loved them both, you know. Shame they couldn't love one another. But they couldn't. They were poison to one another. I only realized it one night when Sandy was really sick. He was howling in his room like a cat that has had its muzzle bitten. I went in to him and held him in my arms and the Quelle tried to make him bite me. Me! Ha. The Quelle held no dangers for me. I managed to get through to it, to join with it. It was terrified, poor beast, and had no more substance than slime. I wondered then whether or not it had been ill even before it joined the *Nightingale*. I managed to quieten it. But I couldn't stave off the inevitable. They killed one another, Sandy and Quelle. Someone blundered when they made that joining. Someone has got questions to answer."

"And what happened to the *Nightingale* when they died?" I asked.

"Why, nothing. We treated the bodies with respect and continued on our journey, I think, and then I came back here. I can't remember how I got here. But I'll be ready for duty again soon I hope. I have a lot of service in me."

Hearing that, I induced the hypnotic state in him. His conscious mind was holding out on us. I thought for a while before my next statement. I wanted to challenge Wilberfoss. "You did not continue on your journey," I said. "The *Nightingale* was damaged. You came out of Noh-time without preparation. Your ship was damaged, and you made landfall. Tell us about that."

Wilberfoss frowned and looked puzzled and then he nodded. He looked downward and to his right, a bit like a person peering through a hole. I think he was seeing things. New memories had been revealed to him.

"You are right," he said. "That strange gray and green planet! We landed there. We came down with a thump. I'm remembering."

Wilberfoss's Narrative

When I climbed from my couch I fell . . . and the floor was sloping so that I stumbled when I tried to stand. Oh, the weight. My arms and legs were of lead. It was unrelenting. I crawled to the door and dragged myself upright against the door frame. Standing, I found it easier to walk and stumped into my quarters. There was silence. I had got used to the presence of bio-crystalline awareness which can sometimes be heard like a humming of bees on a summer's day and sometimes like the snuffling of a giant beast. Now there was nothing and the silence was frightening. I tried to use the video board but that too was dead. There were no images, not even ghosts of light. I could not speak to the ship or to any part of it. I remember a horrible thought came to me: that the *Nightingale* was a dead animal and that I was in its stomach. At the same time, I recognized that kind of thinking for what it was and dismissed it.

I knew there must be other people somewhere and that I could not be alone on the *Nightingale*. I needed to find other people. There was a corridor which spiraled downward from the reception foyer outside my apartment and connected my rooms with a staff canteen. You have been there, Wulf and Tancredi. Do you remember? I decided to go there first. All my senior assistants lived in quarters off this dining-room.

I supported myself on the handrail which ran around the spiral but, before I had gone halfway down, I felt as though I had run a marathon. And then I heard distant voices. People were gathering in the dining-hall . . . there were lights beyond the doors. I walked on and then, using more force than necessary, for estimates of strength are deceptive in high gravity, I pushed the atmosphere doors and they banged open and I lurched through.

There must have been fifty or sixty people in the dining-room. They fell silent when I entered. They all looked at me. There were technicians and medical staff, some with cuts on their faces and others with arms in hastily improvised slings. However, it is the silence I remember and the expressions of disbelief on the faces. You know, a ship like the *Nightingale* feels as secure as the planet of your birth . . . until something goes wrong.

Suddenly there was cheering and smiles. I was greeted like Lazarus up from the dead. I found out later that a rumor had been circulating that I was dead and that the *Nightingale* was without a leader. For my part, I was glad of their support. I had not realized how warmly I was regarded. I found out later that people admired the way I had handled Sandy/Quelle. However . . .

I sat down gratefully at one of the wide tables and spread my legs for they had begun to ache. I began to organize things. We had food in the stores and the hydroponics girdle which could be seen from the dining-room was green and misty. No trouble there. The plants stood tall and the gardeners were already at work tying up plants and supporting them. The *Nightingale* had cast a gravity field around the hydroponics troughs and was able to hold them at just thirty percent above normal gravity.

We had light. We had heat. So, within certain parameters the ship was obviously functioning even though it was not communicating directly with us by voice.

But I needed to get a clearer idea of how things were in the rest of the ship. I organized survey parties to explore. The members wore gravity suits which enabled them to float through the ship. Even so, I knew it would be hours before they could report back. The inhabited parts of the *Nightingale* occupy more than a cubic mile of space. It wasn't until six hours after we had made planet fall that the first reports of our state began to come in.

They were not good. I discovered that the DME sector, badly damaged by the meteorite, had only managed to protect five independent atmospheres and that these were now isolated behind their own particle screens. There were now in total only some forty DMEs still alive. Communications had been established by using vacuum microphones which could attach to the particle screens. In the absence of bio-crystalline channels we had to use amplifiers and hundreds of yards of cable. I was informed that each of the five atmospheres contained a contact specialist from the Gentle Order. They seemed well and confident but they wanted news. They would not leave their special charges but wanted to remain in contact. Each atmosphere contained its own special food supplies which included food for the Contact Confrère.

All the other DME areas were dead. Their atmospheres had been sucked out into space along with their occupants. It was only the particle screens with their dimensional laminate which protected the entire DME sector from ruin. Deep in space when the tragedy first struck the particle screens faced and held at bay the vacuum of space. Now the particle screens were protecting the DME area from the raw atmosphere of the planet on which we had landed. But we were paying a price. The particle screens consumed considerable power from the *Nightingale* and limited the ship's other functions.

The chambers belonging to the Close Metabolism Life-forms had fared better as regards overall physical damage but their systems were less secure. There were atmospheric leaks aplenty and I dispatched a team to try and locate and seal these.

However, while this news was bad, the worst news of all was that the dormitory areas where the crew who serviced the *Nightingale* had their lodgings and gymnasia, had been completely isolated. The dormitories were a vast complex of two- and three-room cells close to the STGs. Evidently when the *Nightingale* lurched back into normal spacetime the strain on the bio-crystalline linkages had been too great and they closed down. Now we could not contact these areas and we did not know whether they had been denied atmosphere and power or whether they still functioned but as autonomous units.

I singled out one of the strongest of our young men and sent him out. We did not have any spare gravity units and so this junior confrère donned a simple survival suit and went outside. He dragged himself laboriously, against the unrelenting lead of gravity, over to the dormitory section. He carried an override charge so that he could get in through the local air-lock should such be necessary, but he never needed to use it. There was a gaping hole in the wall of the *Nightingale*. Something must have happened at the moment of impact, a detonation of some kind, inside the walls, for bodies had been ejected from the dormitory and now lay exploded among the stiff gray shrubs at the base of the ship.

The junior confrère climbed into the dormitory area of the *Nightingale*, being very careful not to damage his survival suit on the sharp metal edges which rose up at him like knives. As he made his way through the ruined dormitory he described what he saw. He found himself in a chaotic world. So great was the tug of gravity that quilts which had tumbled from beds as the ship came down now looked as though they had been starched and ironed into place. In one place a folio of letters had fallen open and the pages held to the floor as though glued. In the gymnasium, the rings and ropes hung down from the ceiling stiffly, like poles. Where there were bodies, the hair was teased back from the scalp and the faces were collapsed.

The young confrère searched through every chamber and it became obvious that the catastrophe had not occurred instantaneously.

Some of the dead inmates were found struggling into their survival suits. But no one had survived. It was a graveyard.

I ordered him back. And he came slowly, like a crab, easing his way around the curves of the *Nightingale*.

So there we were.

Despite the bad news there was a kind of optimism in the air. I think we truly believed that things could not get worse. We appreciated the safety of the moment. To welcome the teams back from the DME and CME sectors I ordered that a warm meal be prepared. This gave everyone something to do.

Privately I knew what I had to do. I needed to visit the bio-crystalline core of the ship and see how extensive the damage was to the bio-crystalline brain of the *Nightingale*. I encouraged celebration followed by rest and when I saw that others among the crew were dragging themselves to their various apartments, I made my farewells and donned a gravity suit and glided to my private rooms.

WULFNOTE

With those words this session ended and Wilberfoss woke up. He blinked and looked at me anxiously. "Did I tell you anything new?" he asked.

"You did," I replied.
"And when will I remember?"
"Very soon."
He remembered that same night.

21

Wilberfoss in the
Bio-crystalline Cave

The grip of winter tightened on the garden. The birds which needed the warmth of summer were long gone. The hardier ones who would stay with us during the cold months could be found singing and scrapping close to the berry trees.

In the mornings there was mist which lingered behind the garden walls. At midday the shadows were long and spindly and the sunlight revealed spider webs stretched between trees. Evenings came quickly with a shower of rain and after that a smell of leaf mold. The nights were cold and a fire was lit in Wilberfoss's rooms.

Wilberfoss seemed to thrive on the winter.

One morning he was up early and I came upon him standing outside his rooms with a blanket over his shoulders and breathing white vapor into the air. He had also pressed his hand against the patterns of frost on his window pane and a print of his palm was beginning to dribble. I felt hope at this. He was showing an interest in the world outside himself.

But under the blanket he was naked. For a while nakedness and washing became an obsession with him. He seemed to believe that clothes were a filthy skin and sometimes he would wash himself until he was raw. I think he wore the blanket rather like a hair-shirt. The mortification of the flesh is an old theme especially with those who feel guilt. I have many references to it. I was amused in my dry way to observe that Lily was more concerned by his fervent ablutions than I was. She saw the sores, I saw the mind straining for cleanliness and for the one and only time I told her to be calm. By showing himself naked to the world he was trying to create a naked psyche.

Later that day it began to snow. The snow came in large, soft chunks where several flakes had clung together. Wilberfoss amazed me by saying that he could smell the snow coming. That was in the morning when the sky was still clear.

About midday the wind started from the south and quickly the sky darkened. I floated up into the trees above Wilberfoss's cell and looked out over the walls of the garden. The sea was leaden below the dark, gathering clouds. In the monastery, bright lights were already twinkling in windows though it was scarcely into the afternoon. The first flakes of snow drifted down like ash. Then the fall became steady. The headland and the shuttle port disappeared.

I looked out across the garden and could see the white flakes vanish on the surface of the river where it wound slowly through the limestone caves. The snow settled on the rocks by the river and on the slopes of the hills and on the Pectanile, revealing the curves of that monument like the sleek gray shape of a dolphin. The snow tumbled through the bare trees and built on branches and clung to the dry bark. The temperature dropped steadily and as the snow covered the land the quality of sound changed. Every sound was softened, even the call of the Crowhawk which has a voice that has been likened to the crying of the damned in Dante's Inferno.

When I looked down I saw Wilberfoss. Silly man was pulling off his clothes and throwing them down in the slush in front of his small home. Naked he spread his arms and turned in a circle stamping his feet so that every part of him was touched by the snow.

Lily arrived with a clatter and a roar. She scolded Wilberfoss and sent him inside waving her dexetels. He retreated before her like a reluctant child. I swooped down and gathered up his sodden, stiffening clothes and took them inside.

Wilberfoss was already in bed. He lay on his back and the covers were pressed tightly under his chin in a no-nonsense manner. Lily was over him, a thermometer held in one of her dexetels. There was a smell of broth cooking.

As I entered Wilberfoss sneezed heartily and I can record that this first day of snow gave Wilberfoss a mighty cold which kept him in bed for many days. For me this was a bonus. While Wilberfoss wheezed and snuffed and Lily fussed, I was able to talk to him. The cold took over his body and left his mind free.

The following story, fit in its way to be a winter's tale told by a roaring fire while the cold dark wraps around the house like a scarf, was recounted to me by Wilberfoss as he lay on his back, immobilized by Lily and the sheets.

I murmured the hypnotic trigger and his eyes closed and his face became animated.

"Tell me about the *Nightingale*," I said. "How did you live on the crippled ship? Did you visit the bio-crystalline core? Tell me."

Wilberfoss's Narrative

I slept well. Despite my worries I slept well. I think that when one sees the shape of the disaster that has befallen one, then relaxation can come. It is doubt that causes the sleepless, red-eyed night.

When I awoke I found that a plan had formed in my mind. The key to so many of our problems was in the malfunction of the bio-crystalline brain of the *Nightingale*. I knew how that brain had grown in part from my own consciousness and I decided to visit the seed chamber to see if I could put matters to rights or perhaps change things for the better.

The main seed chamber of the *Nightingale* was a circular room some considerable distance beneath my command chambers. It was an area which was difficult of access since no one had anticipated that anyone would ever need to visit the chamber while the *Nightingale* was in transit. But access was possible, of course.

I ate breakfast, pampering myself somewhat with fresh bread, boiled eggs and Talline broth such as Medoc once made for me. The ingredients were not in short supply in my quarters though I know that my bread had never known yeast, nor had my eggs ever known a chicken and my Talline broth came from a freeze-dried packet. For reasons best known to themselves, the planners of the *Nightingale* had made sure that the Captain had a decade's supply of excellent food. I suspect that they considered that food equals morale. I also suspect that in giving me ten years' supply they had calculated on providing me with a year of variety before repetition set in. I was grateful for this consideration. The broth in particular was excellent and I could taste the herbs and remembered the chant that Medoc sang: "Ropeweed for courage, Starseye for sight, Meat for the hunter, Bring strength in the night."

Rested and fed, I donned my survival suit. Then, with the anti-grav unit strapped to my back, I made my way through my apartment, my toes merely brushing the floor, as I pushed myself along. I went past the room where Sandy/Quelle had died. I was moving in the opposite direction to the ramp which led down to the staff canteen. This particular corridor ended in a small alcove which contained an entry to a transit shaft. There was a standard control panel and I tapped out the access code adding my own personal code and palm print. The answer flashed back that the transit system was not working. This was as I expected. I operated the override switch and a section of the floor slowly slid open. There was a rush of air and an alarm bell rang briefly until all pressures had balanced. I looked down into a black well. It seemed to suck at me. I knew that if I had fallen down that shaft without the anti-grav unit I would have been compacted to an eighth of my size at the bottom.

I switched on my suit lights and increased the anti-grav power so that I was floating and then I pushed myself out over the black hole. A slight adjustment of the power and I began to sink. I passed the rim. My lights lit up the depressed emergency handholds which were set into the wall of the transit chute and which rose past my eyes. There was just sufficient room for me to descend without bumping the walls. The presence of the gravity pack meant that I could not bend and look downward. I used my hands to direct me and pushed myself downward, feet first.

I did not know how far I needed to descend. I measured each rung as a foot and when my counting reached ninety-eight, my feet suddenly touched something. My reaction of surprise was such that I sent myself back up the chute by several feet. The next time I landed I was ready.

I was on the roof of one of the transit seats. It must have been parked here at the moment when the power failed. I turned around slowly, wondering if I would find myself trapped in the chute, but discovered that I was just under the roof of an oblong chamber which was filled with pipes and festoons of cable and conduit trunking. It was easy for me to step off the roof of the transit seat and sink slowly down to the ground.

The lights of my suit showed the room starkly. The walls and pipes were stenciled with technical graffiti which defined their function. Beside these were scrawled autographs and dates. Many different construction teams had worked here. The room was little more than a vast junction box where many parts of the *Nightingale* met.

One pipe was particularly important to me. It was about two feet in diameter and stretched the length of the chamber without any bends or curves. It was the color of old, rubbed ivory—this was the ceramic jacket you understand—and within I knew were the organic threads of the bio-crystalline brain. It had grown within this pipe, advancing as the *Nightingale* grew and adding more and more strands as the complexity of the ship increased.

I began to lope slowly beside this pipe, ducking occasionally to avoid cross pieces, until finally I came to the entrance to an air-lock. It had a notice printed in red on its surface.

"WARNING. Bio-crystalline Seed Chamber. Only authorized personnel are permitted to enter this air-lock. Unauthorized persons seeking to gain entry are advised that their action will place them in extreme danger."

This was a standard announcement and the entire bio-crystalline system was protected behind similar air-locks. What the notice meant was that any unauthorized attempt to enter would result in alarms and the sudden closing of doors and in some cases a beam of lethal radiation.

I of course should have been safe. My credentials were the best. I was part father of the bio-crystalline consciousness and could be admitted without fuss or question. Even so, given the strange state of the *Nightingale*, I doubted.

I removed my glove and placed the palm of my right hand firmly on the black identification plate. I felt a warmth under my hand and a prickling. Three magnetic locks suddenly closed over my wrist and held me firm. If I were an impostor these locks would never release until I was either dead or captured. They held me for over a minute and then withdrew. A message flashed up on the black tile where I had pressed my hand. "Welcome, Captain Wilberfoss. Beyond this door the vacuum is absolute. Be sure you are wearing your survival suit. The vacuum lock will not function if it detects exhalation or body heat. Now you may proceed."

I palmed the lock again and the door slid open. I stepped inside and the door nudged me as the magnetic locks closed. At about head height facing me there was a glowing green pressure panel marked Vacuum Demand and I touched this. Immediately, I was aware of a vibration as the pumps got to work. I felt my survival suit change shape about me as it compensated for the lack of external pressure. The green panel paled to gray and finally brightened to red as the atmosphere vanished. It changed its wording and announced: "Vacuum established. There will be a delay of 60 seconds."

I knew what it was doing. The delay was to establish that my survival suit was not leaking. The procedure was for the protection of the bio-crystalline brain.

I and my survival suit passed the test. The panel blinked

once and then a message in yellow flashed up. "You may proceed into the Bio-crystalline Seed Chamber. The atmosphere lock will remain open."

In front of me there was a jerking movement and part of the wall began to slide open. I stood and watched. No bright light flooded in though I knew this room should have been filled with the silver effulgence of the working bio-crystalline seeds. I cannot say that darkness flooded in though that was my impression. I did not move. I was not anxious to advance until I could see my way clear.

And when the doors were finally open I found myself peering into a chamber filled with shadows and blackened shapes of sculptured ash. My way was blocked by things like trees coated with soot, which hung broken and deformed from the roof. I stepped forward and at the same time brought my suit lights to their maximum brilliance and drove the shadows back.

The shadows moved as I advanced and that was eerie, but stranger still was the absolute stillness of the blackened bio-crystalline shapes. Death is so still. I have had my fill of that stillness. I raised my arm which glittered with energy and touched the dark branches which barred my way. They broke at my touch and crumbled and fell and smashed like black coral, silently. Black dust rippled across the floor in a single shock wave and then everything became still again. Such a fall deserved a roaring.

All the troubles of the *Nightingale* were clear before me. I had never been in this room before but I knew that it should have been throbbing with light and energy.

I stepped out of the vacuum lock and ducked under the dark branches. I was aware of the crushing and crumbling of bio-crystalline fiber under my feet. The entire floor was littered with broken branches and I stepped over them. Those I touched crumbled.

The room I entered was not large. I advanced to the center and looked around. Surveying the damage, I wondered how the *Nightingale* still managed to function. Perhaps the symbol transformation generators were supplying the necessary sentience. But then I saw, close to the vacuum lock, a single gleam of light in the seed trough and the pale shape of living bio-crystalline fibers climbing up to the roof and branching. This was not bio-crystallism in its full and healthy fluorescence, but it was life. I moved over to the seed trough as quickly as I could, ducking under the dark elephantine growths and pushing the fallen parts aside. I found that three crystals were still vital. One was hectic but the other two glowed with a steady white fire. I switched my suit lights off and was able to follow the branching paleness of the living fibers. They fed into all the main trunk lines. These fibers, no doubt assisted by the STGs, were all that was keeping the *Nightingale* vital.

I now knew what I had to do and felt an uncanny optimism. My plan was bold but offered hope. I intended to replace as many of the dead crystals as I could with new ones and try to make them grow. I would feed them with my own thought.

The *Nightingale* carried spare living seed-crystals, held in a state of suspended consciousness, in the seed bank close to my quarters.

I spent the next couple of hours trekking back and forth carrying the seed containers down to the seed chamber. I then began cleaning the trough. Some of the dead crystals were glassy and the fibers growing from them were brittle. They were enameled, and their blackness contrived to reflect my suit lights with a deep amber glow. These seeds had died quickly, shriveling within the lattices of their crystal supports. Others had died more slowly and these resembled large candles that had been exposed to sunlight under glass and which had melted into monstrous striated shapes. In their dying they had spattered the floor like teardrops of pitch. I cleared them all, reasoning that the presence of any dead bio-crystalline fiber might exert a negative influence on the new seeds. The old linkages in the troughs were useless and so I prepared new beds of vermiculite and then placed the crystals so that they touched the existing living seeds.

I am not a skilled bio-crystalline engineer but I knew enough to have confidence that my procedure was sound. When a new sensory/logic chain is being developed, seeds are often linked in this way. My hope was that the new seeds would be vitalized by the old seeds and that the old seeds would be strengthened and rejuvenated by proximity to the new. Above all I wanted the tenuous command structure to be strengthened for without that nothing was possible. I felt confidence since the seeds which were still vital had obviously survived the worst ordeal and were hence of great strength.

I cleared the seed chamber as well as I could. I brought vacuo-sacks down from above and shoveled the heavy black dust and shattered fragments of bio-crystalline circuitry into them. Then I lugged the sacks up to my apartment and handed them over to the disposal unit. I saw them fired from the ship. I saw them describe stunted arcs before plunging straight down to the surface. When they hit the stony ground they exploded and the black dust and fragments quickly lifted and then settled leaving pools of ash.

Over the next few days I visited the crystals morning and night. To help their development I kept my communication room live and I spent a part of each day lying in my couch pouring my mind into the bio-crystalline darkness. Occasionally I received an echo of my thought back and that gave me hope. I was like a nurse with a comatose patient: even a repeated whisper tells of consciousness.

On the third day when I visited the chamber I could just detect a glow spreading from the central seeds to the outer ones. It was like a fire catching from embers. Looking closely I could see that the seeds had begun to bond sending out small filaments of bio-crystalline fiber. They resembled patterns of frost.

By the fifth day the glow was clearly perceptible and from the door of the vacuo-lock it was as though a candle were burning in the still chamber.

That candle, if I may so call it, brought me more joy than a thousand prayer lights of St. Francis Dionysos. At the same time, I was realistic. There was no way I could restore the *Nightingale* to full operation. Too much was lost. Too much was damaged. Too much might still fall into decay. But at least we were no longer sliding helplessly into ruin and death. We were making a stand and the *Nightingale* was responding.

I did not tell my colleagues what was happening as I did not want to build their optimism. They had enough to do as it was, hunting through the ship, making what repairs they could and isolating those areas which could not be saved. The crematorium in the *Nightingale* was fractured and useless and so we held funerals for the dead and scored out graves in the rock and sand of the planet and buried the bodies.

There came the day, it would have been some three weeks after we landed, that I was lying in my couch reaching out to the consciousness of the *Nightingale*, that I heard a sleepy, somewhat feline voice, murmur, "Hello, Jon Wilberfoss. I have been listening to you for days, gathering you in, but only today have I found the strength to reply. We are in a sorry way. But hope is not dead. Tell me how I can help."

What a question. The naïveté of bio-crystalline consciousness sometimes appalls me. I suppose because bio-crystalline brains have the power of speech and their expression sounds thoughtful, we assume they have the wisdom of the human. But they do not.

"There are many ways you can help us," I said and then decided to test the power of the healing brain. In the canteen which had become our center of operations there was a malfunction in the heating system. The heaters had begun to turn themselves on and off at random. This was not dangerous to us but was inconvenient and costly in terms of energy. I asked the newly-awakened consciousness to try and repair this situation.

And it did.

Within minutes the temperature controls had been corrected and the heating system in the canteen was functioning as it should. This change was noticed by those who were living there.

When next I visited the dining area people told me of the change, wondering what had happened and glad that the *Nightingale* seemed to be returning to normal. They felt hopeful.

I did not tell them about my visits to the bio-crystalline chamber and how the new seeds were growing. That news would keep.

We stood in silence, feeling the awful drag of the gravity of the planet, and gave thanks that we were still alive.

WULFNOTE
And with those words, Wilberfoss's face became tranquil and moments later his eyes opened. He sneezed suddenly and violently. I think it was the need to sneeze that had brought him out of his trance.

I was pleased with this report. I could hear the real

man. I could sense a focusing down on his experience. We are moving into his narrative but there is a long journey ahead. I also knew that I must not rush things despite my impatience.

Just as bio-crystalline fiber grows slowly so is Jon Wilberfoss slowly growing toward health.

22

The *Nightingale* Moves

WULFNOTE

As the winter passed Wilberfoss grew stronger. He took a deeper interest in gardening and that Lily regarded as a most healthy sign. He was still not allowed to move about unattended.

Frequently lucid in his discourse, there were yet occasions when he stuttered and spoke only fragments of sentences and these were brutal and chaotic. I noticed that these outbreaks tended to occur most often shortly after he had woken up and I told Lily this. My observation concerned her. She considered that these outbreaks reflected the chaos of his nightmares: nightmare visions swallowing the rational day. She came to believe that Wilberfoss's apparent health and well-being were a fabrication of his mind to hide the profoundly disordered state of his subconscious and that that subconscious would one day brutally assert itself. As we shall see, Lily was correct in her prediction.

However, as far as we at the time were concerned, Wilberfoss seemed to be recovering his memory slowly and naturally. His physical health was rude and strong.

One day, two pairs of fruit trees were delivered to the Poverello Garden, a gift from a Talline benefactor whose wife had spent time in the garden and who had recently given birth to twins. The trees needed to be planted and Lily arranged for this job to be given to Jon Wilberfoss.

And so it was that one morning the trees were deposited outside our enclosure. Wilberfoss tied them onto Lily at her insistence. The previous night we had enjoyed a particularly heavy rainfall which had softened the frosty earth. Lily churned the leaf mold under her tracks to a soggy and noisome brew as she moved away from the small hospital and up a shallow hill. Wilberfoss followed her carrying a spade, a pick, a sack and a bucket which contained a stout pruning saw. He was wearing the rough clothes of a Talline farmer and I consider that they suited his burly frame and the natural swagger of his walk. I followed them at a height.

Lily came to the river and followed it for a while until we came level with the Pectanile. At this point the river was shallow and wide and ran rippling over the stones and shingle. Lily crossed and heaved herself up the farther bank. I was concerned for her. Her engines, while strong, are not new and I could not understand why she was putting herself to such strain. But as always she had a purpose. She was leading Wilberfoss on a journey of discovery. This was the farthest he had been allowed to travel during his convalescence. As he walked along I could see him glancing from right to left examining the tall trees and the dark shrubs. He paused for a long time looking at the Pectanile. Perhaps he was remembering it. Perhaps he was evaluating it. Wisps of steam were rising from its funnel as the day gathered some warmth.

Up the bank, Lily pushed through a thicket of straggly bushes and entered a small orchard. Here were fruit trees from many planets. The branches were bare. Long, damp winter grass grew between the trunks and was glazed with rain. Within minutes of entering the orchard Wilberfoss was soaked to the waist.

She led him down a row of trees until we came to a small clearing at the edge of the orchard. Beyond was the wild wood. We could just hear the chatter and roar of the river as it plunged through the rapids. The rain had given the river a full voice.

Lily instructed Wilberfoss to untie the trees and plant them and he set to with a will. Soon he had four holes opened up in the black and stony soil. Even I could see that the work was familiar to him. Perhaps he was remembering the agricultural tricks of his boyhood for I saw how carefully he cut the grassy top sods and placed them to one side and then set down his sack flat on the ground and shoveled the soil from the hole onto it. I observed the careful way he made sure that the soil didn't get lost amid the high wet grass.

He planted the trees one by one, tipping the loose soil from the sack around the roots and pressing it down with his foot. He was absorbed in his work, making sure that the roots were spread and the trees were upright.

When he had completed the planting, Lily sent him down the lines of fruit trees, to prune them. And when he had finished that task, he gathered the severed branches and twigs together in the middle of the orchard and set fire to them. The blue smoke rose like incense through the still orchard.

Over the next week Jon Wilberfoss tidied the orchard and at the end of the week I again approached him for the story of the *Nightingale*.

*   *   *

He sat one evening on the veranda outside his room. He
smelled of wood smoke and the backs of his hands were
smudged with ash. He sat back in his chair, making the
chair seem almost too small and frail to bear his weight,
with his hands clasped behind his head and his eyes closed.
I could tell that Wilberfoss was looking inward.

"Talk to me," I said. "Tell me what you are thinking."

"I have spent today remembering," he murmured. "For
the last few weeks I have been like a man walking in
mist, and now the mist is beginning to clear and I am
looking down into a dark valley. I cannot see far yet,
but far enough. The valley is my life . . ." He opened
his eyes and looked at me. "Do you understand that?"
he asked.

"I understand," I replied, for I have read widely about
the symbolism of dark valleys. Wilberfoss remained silent
for many minutes looking at me until I began to wonder
whether he had slipped into a phase of silent meditation.

But then he sighed and rallied himself and said, "You
cannot understand. No one can understand unless you
were there. And even then . . ." His voice trailed away
and he was silent for several minutes and then he whispered, "Help me, Wulf," and I spoke the hypnotic words
and he relaxed.

Wilberfoss's Narrative

The *Nightingale*. You want to know more about the
Nightingale. Let me tell you that after I had got the new
seeds to grow and strengthen the bio-crystalline system,
life on the ship grew easier. There were a hundred and
one things which we had taken for granted—like the
sewage ingestion system and the automatic lighting and

the ever-present whisper of the atmosphere filters—things which were noticed when gone. Well, each day we noticed some small improvement. It was as though a God was protecting us, working behind the scenes to make things better. I remember the day the air filters came back on. We had been living in and breathing air that would not have disgraced a sewer—you can get used to anything—but then one day the filters came on again and we stood with our faces close to the filter panel and breathed in air that had the smell of trees and mountains and flowers. It was the kind of air you would like to eat. Like the air in this garden after rainfall. Do you know what the *Nightingale* had done? The old filters were ruined and so the ship had channeled our air supply to the hydroponics filters which were robust. We were breathing in the fragrance of tomatoes and flowers.

Having expected a lingering and painful death, it was hard not to feel optimistic as every day the *Nightingale* showed that it was fighting to survive. We thought of the ship as a mighty organism with a will to live.

But then one day I was outside, riding in the gravity mule, inspecting the damage to the stabilizing arms. The mule is a kind of flying workshop. It is enclosed and you sit astride the anti-grav unit. I always used it for trips outside.

I had landed the small machine among the thick-stemmed gray scrub bushes and found myself watching the antics of a pair of creatures like land crabs that were tearing at some of the refuse we had jettisoned from the ship. Suddenly I received a call, a warning call, on the radio telling me that there was a disturbance of some kind in the hills. I rose up several meters above the scrub and looked up the gentle slopes. Advancing toward me was a gray cloud which seemed to boil and churn and which filled all the space from earth to sky. I recognized a dust storm.

The wind was driving the dust before it like a flapping curtain. We had not seen any storms on the planet until then, but now I could see the shrubs shake as the storm front reached them. There had been no warning. The storm's advance was so rapid that all I could do was plunge down to the shrubs and dig in. The land crabs had already disappeared and were deep in their burrows. I managed to lodge the gravity mule under an overhang and switched its power so that it pressed into the shallow cave. I was like a limpet in a rock pool when the storm waves come pounding in. I felt the storm arrive. It flowed over me. The light became brown and then dark brown. Fine particles of dust crawled in flowing shapes over the viewplate. I felt the wind suck at me and felt the sand and rock scoured from beneath me. I kept the power in the mule as high as I dared until the pack was running hot. I felt like a mouse cornered in the wainscot while the cat reaches in to claw it loose. And the noise! The roaring. Like an avalanche . . .

I could not have survived long. And the storm did not last long. It was a front only: a wave of wind, triggered by God knows what, which swept over the land and sea and was gone. The howling died away to a whisper of falling dust.

After the storm came clouds of moisture which drifted low and completely obscured my view. Beads of water formed on the viewplate of the mule and I could see drips falling from the nearest shrubs. A land crab worked its way out, scrabbling under the clear plastic base of the mule. It basked in the damp, digging a shallow hole where the drips fell and then settling its shell into the hole, like a lid on a pot.

Slowly the visibility cleared and I could see the gray shrubs which pressed about the cave mouth. Eventually I could see the low shape of the distant hills. I could not see the *Nightingale* and yet it should have been towering up over me. At first I did not believe this. I thought that I must have dived around the hillside in my first panic when I saw the storm approaching. I used the radio to try and contact the ship but all I received was a high whine of static. I raced through the different call frequencies. Nothing. Finally I used the private frequency which connected me to my command room and then I heard the *Nightingale*. The voice was soft, almost like someone waking from a dream. It said, "Ah, Jon Wilberfoss. You have survived. I am glad. I thought I was alone now. Please come to me. I think I have done something very wrong. Please come quickly I think I have made a mistake. I need your help, Jon Wilberfoss. Come quickly to me."

I told it where I was and that I was on my way. I felt myself become ice cold and very calm. There was no panic in me. If anything, there was a blank surrender to my fate, whatever it was. I did not try to make guesses.

I adjusted the power flow in the mule and eased it out of the cave. I lifted above the shrubs and immediately saw the *Nightingale*. What had happened was clear. The ship had shifted position. The wind had torn away the earth beneath it and the wind had battered it. The ship had begun to topple but it had not fallen. The ship had saved itself.

Now, blazing from it, bright as bars of silver, were the stabilizing beams with which it had anchored above our old Pacifico monastery. These beams were like incandescent rods and they reached into the low valley and to the nearby hillside and even to the shore of the gray sea. They were holding the ship upright against the crushing force of the planet's gravity. I recognized that the energy drain was enormous and wondered what could be left for the rest of the *Nightingale*.

As quickly as I dared I flew over to the *Nightingale*

and began to rise slowly up beside it. I could not push the energy pack on my mule too hard as it was already depleted. I passed the dark caverns of the particle vents and the evacuation chutes which rimmed the DME sector. I rose by the view windows and there were no lights within. I moved under the Symbol Transformation Generators and gave a wide berth to one of the stabilizing beams. Even so the field generated about the beam made my small gravity mule tremble and rattle. High above me I could see the access port which led to the small area where we few refugees had set up camp. I took long minutes to get there.

And when I did get there I found a warning light blinking outside the air-lock. It advised me that the atmosphere within was toxic. Toxic!

I opened the air-lock using the emergency override switch and drifted inside. Two minutes later I had matched atmospheres and the door into the ship slid open. No lights were burning. I switched the mule lights on and glided down the short corridor which connected the access bay to the dining-room. A man lay crumpled against the wall, his mouth open and his fingers in his hair. The door into the canteen stood open but the mule which was designed for work outside the ship would not fit through. I let it sink to the floor and anchored it with magnetic clamps and then cut its power. I checked that my survival suit was sealed and functioning properly with a steady flow of air and then I released the clear plastic door of the mule and stepped outside. I peered into the dining-room. The men and women who had been my companions since our descent onto the planet, now lay sprawled on the tables and on the floor. No one moved. Nothing moved except a wisp of paper that someone had tied to the air filter when it first began to function for us. This fluttered showing that whatever atmosphere had killed my companions was still being circulated. There was nothing I could do for anyone and I felt my grip on reality loosening. I entertained the unreason of a child. Unfair. Unfair. How could life be so unfair? Why was I singled out for this? Why had everything gone wrong? What was this malignant phantom of death that stalked me, this shadow?

I knew I needed to quit this place of staring eyes. I walked over to the door which led to my personal quarters. There were several bodies against this door and I had to reach down and take them by the legs and drag them away. And then I saw why they were there. The door was an atmosphere lock and the clamps were secure. No warning lights were showing and it was a fair presumption that the atmosphere in my quarters beyond the door was human normal, the air of Earth, the air of Juniper.

I opened the lock, slipped through quickly, and closed the door behind me and sealed it. I checked the air. It was breathable and without hesitation I stripped off my survival suit and left it clinging to the floor. I pulled myself laboriously up the ramp and into the room that was constructed like my dining-room at the monastery. Can you believe that amid all this chaos of death and destruction, my fire was still functioning and the flames flickered and licked at the wooden logs and sent shadows marching around my room just as it had in my house at Pacifico? Of course the fire gave out no heat. It was an example of electronic legerdemain. It would have burned merrily in a vacuum.

But it worked, you know. The fire was a psychological device and it gave me a reassuring sense of the familiar. It brought me contact with my own reality and the panic that had threatened me retreated. I breathed deeply.

The voice of the *Nightingale* greeted me. "Welcome home, Jon Wilberfoss. Shall I talk to you now or later?"

"Now. Now."

"Do you want an in-depth analysis?"

"I just want to know why my companions are dead and what has happened to the DME and are we stable and what did you mean when you said that you have made a mistake?" As I spoke I slumped down into my easy chair by the fire and held my hands out to its cold flicker. "Tell me. Simple or complex. Tell me."

The *Nightingale* had a beautiful, calm, caring and thoughtful voice. Above all it was a voice that gave an impression of wisdom. In careful phrases it told me of the wind that had caught the ship unawares; of the sand and rocks that flayed its surface; of the shifting patterns of stress resulting from the different wind speeds and which the *Nightingale* had tried to keep in balance; of the vortex that scored away the rock at its base; of the lurching of the ship and the sudden need to power the anchor beams to save the ship from falling; of the mistakes that resulted from the sudden drain of energy; of the fit that possessed the *Nightingale* for a few moments and which resulted in the ship confusing all the atmospheres; of the vacuum in the DME sector; of the toxic gases in the hydroponics garden which had sluiced through to suffocate my companions; of the temperature shift in the Close Metabolism center.

I asked. "Are you telling me that I am the last living creature aboard the *Nightingale*?"

The *Nightingale* did not reply and so I asked my question again. Eventually it made answer.

"I am. You are."

"And are we stable?"

"We are, for the time being."

"And what is your state?"

"Not good . . . Holding."

"The *Nightingale* is a graveyard." It did not reply to this. It saved its energy. But I knew I had spoken a truth. The entire ship was a graveyard. And as I sat there staring into the flickering embers I saw them flare for the last time and die away to darkness.

I knew that the dead ship was a replica of my mind. I had no hopes. Blackness.

WULFNOTE
Wilberfoss had reached the end of his memory. He sat there relaxed and dark. I asked him several questions but he did not reply. Finally I murmured the hypnotic release words and his eyes opened.

It took him many minutes to register where he was and I feared lest he had strayed over into madness. But he rallied, and then he looked at me. "I'm not sure that I want to know any more, Wulf. I'm at the end of all reason. Can't I just be? Here? With you and Lily. Can't I begin again?"

I did not reply and he took my silence for negation, which of course it was.

He stood up, and with a sigh made his way indoors. Lily was with him. She administered a sleeping draft and the next sound I heard from Wilberfoss was his loud ragged snoring.

I knew, and subsequently Lily confirmed, that it would be a while before I could question him more.

"Leave it all until spring is come," advised Lily, and I could not disagree.

I considered that I already had plenty of material to mull over and I had no doubt that I would find the daily converse interesting.

Indeed, I realized that I was finding this breaking open of Wilberfoss most interesting. I had never come so close to the human, not even when I was with my master and mentor Forrester. Wulf was enjoying itself.

23

The Clearing
of the *Nightingale*

WULFNOTE
Dawn above Lily's Garden. A mackerel sky of orange and
green: scales and feathers. On earth the temperature rising
after a light shower of snow and the trees already dripping
heavily. Springtime a-coming in.

In the silence of dawn there came the deep clang, clang
of the entrance bell outside the Poverello Garden. We
heard it from Wilberfoss's quarters and were surprised. A
visitor so early . . . ? And only official visitors and those
who were doubtful of their welcome would ring the
heavy bell.

Inquisitive (for I assumed that any visitor who
announced their presence at the garden in this way
must have something to do with Jon Wilberfoss), I
rose through the wet canopy and crossed Lily's Garden
until I could see the entrance gate and the statue of
St. Francis Dionysos and the solitary woman who stood
at the open gate awaiting admission. Clearly the visit,

whatever it was, was formal for the woman, a Talline by her dress, could by right of birth have walked straight into the garden and no one would have bade her stop. There was something familiar about her, but it was not until she turned and reached for the bell chain for a second time, that I recognized her. Medoc, of course.

Clang. Clang.

The sleepy gate warden lurched out of his hut, pulling down his hastily donned habit and with his hair unbrushed. I swooped down, dropping over the Poverello wall and settled close to Medoc. She did not greet me but stared at me with what I thought was a kind of challenge.

"You have come to see Jon Wilberfoss?" said I.

"Yes."

"Lily will decide. I cannot."

"I'll wait."

"But not out here. Come with me. Walk through the garden. I'll go ahead and warn Lily. If there is a problem, I'll meet you at the entrance to the hospital where Wilberfoss is living." Medoc nodded and we advanced through the gate and past the startled eyes of the gate warden who scratched in his hair and shrugged and shambled back to his hut, wondering, no doubt, why he had been summoned at all.

"Why didn't you warn us you were coming?" I asked.

Medoc shrugged. "I came on an impulse. I now live on the southern islands. Forewarning and an answer back to me might have taken months. I never thought of it. I have come myself. My journey. But I rang the bell in full courtesy."

"I understand," I said, but I didn't really. I rose a few feet. "I'll go and warn Lily you are coming."

Medoc reached out and touched my rough metal hide, knocking on me lightly with her knuckles. I paused, hovering. "Wulf, tell me *now*. How is he? How does he look?"

"Better than he was. Thinner. He's lost a lot of hair. But his memory is erratic. He may not remember you. I don't know." And I didn't. I had no way of knowing how he would react. Wilberfoss had become very strange since our last communication some weeks earlier. I am not a mind reader. The autoscribe was at its limits.

"He'll remember me," said Medoc, with confidence. "He may not want to remember me, but he'll remember me." There seemed to be no more to be said and so I flew up and raced to the small hospital.

Lily took a few moments to absorb the news. She fussed around Wilberfoss. That man was cleaning his teeth over a small enamel basin outside the house. He enjoyed the chill of morning and Lily considered morning air a good tonic so long as he did not wander about naked. She cleared the basin after he had gargled and spat into it and checked his pulse and his eyes. She knew already that he had spent a good night and had not woken up sweating and screaming. She decided to allow the visit.

"Medoc, that was your wife, is come to see you," she said, speaking the words in her slow, old-fashioned way.

Wilberfoss paused and frowned and his face colored. "Medoc," he said as though searching his memory. "Ah, Medoc. I thought she was dead. I shall be glad to see her."

Electrically, machine to machine, I could feel Lily's watchfulness. She was alert to every signal. I was also aware of the blur of her calculations. Just as she had taken Wilberfoss out planting fruit trees to stir him, so she now calculated that the presence of Medoc might ease him into deeper awareness. Lily's message flashed to me. "Bring her in. She comes at a good time."

*   *   *

Was Medoc aware of her timing? I'm sure she was. But how I do not know.

I swooped over the wall, a clumsy flying giant bell or an outlandish warrior's helmet, wondering about the deep sensitivity of life-forms, and I came upon Medoc walking slowly over the bridge that led into the glade of Builder Trees. The thin gray snow on the path was untrodden before her and melted to a black wetness where she stepped. That seemed to me important. Medoc, of all life-forms that I have known, makes her own track. I could read in her footsteps her progress through the garden and see where she had paused gathering winter roses and the pale blue spikes of Dog Thistle. With Talline women it is a custom that when they walk out they pick and carry with them something from the earth.

"He looks forward to seeing you," I said, settling in the air at about her shoulder height and matching my speed to hers.

"He is lucky to have two such as you and Lily to care for him," said Medoc.

"How did you hear about him?" I asked. "I thought his presence here was a secret."

Medoc laughed at that. "Tallines are gossips, you know. And we're not fools. This garden has many visitors and you can see into the hospital courtyard from the Pectanile. That's part of the planning of the garden. Even so, I only heard that he was back a few weeks ago. I couldn't believe it. I had never expected to see him again. I expected to be long dead when he returned. No matter. Life has a way of playing tricks . . . nomusa musa . . . the only certainty is uncertainty." She laughed at that. "My husband didn't want me to come, but I came all the same.

Jon Wilberfoss still exacts a price."

We came to the gate leading into the hospital courtyard. The gate swung open at our approach, pulled by
Lily. Wilberfoss was beyond, seated at a table. He sat stiffly
upright, like a person expecting bad news.

Medoc crossed to him and placed the flowers she had
gathered on the table before him. Then she sat down
without speaking.

Jon Wilberfoss looked at the flowers and then at the
wall of the courtyard and then folded his arms and his
face twitched. He did not look at Medoc though she
had her eyes steadily on him. It was not a fierce gaze, a
belittling gaze or an accusing gaze. It was a passive look,
a waiting look.

Neither spoke for several minutes and then Jon
Wilberfoss cleared his throat. When he spoke his voice
was surprisingly harsh. "The children?" he said.

"Well. In fine health. They send good wishes."

"They are not with you?"

"No. I came alone. I wanted to see you alone. Children
complicate things. They can see you later."

"When later?"

"Later. When you are more yourself."

Silence. Finally, still without looking at Medoc, Jon
Wilberfoss indicated the flowers. "And what are these?"
he asked. "They have some meaning, I suppose. Some
clever meaning. Some reprimand. Everything the Tallines
do has meaning. Even your silences."

"There is no reprimand," said Medoc. "And yes, there
is meaning. Shall I tell you?"

Wilberfoss grunted.

"The winter roses are for the love we shared."

"They die in the springtime."

"The Dog Thistle is for remembrance."

"Spiky and hard and cuts like broken glass."

"You have understood everything and nothing, Jon Wilberfoss."

Silence.

"Why did you come?"

"To see you. To help you. To bring you health."

"You have brought me nothing but dead flowers." He swept with his arm, an impatient sharp gesture, and the flowers scattered off the table. Then he turned to her and I was surprised to see that his face was red and with patches of white and that his eyes glittered. This was a face I had never seen before. "I thought I killed you down there," he said. "When I killed everything else. How can you still be alive when everything else is dead? Are you alive, Evil Medoc?"

"You never killed me," said Medoc quietly.

"I killed everything."

"You are alive. I am alive. The garden is alive. There are lives beyond the wall."

Wilberfoss heard her as though incredulous. And then he laughed but it was not laughter that shook him. I have searched long for a phrase to describe the sounds that shook him and the best this poor autoscribe can offer is this. It was a laughter of despair.

"Nothing lives," he said, "except in my dreams. Go away from me now. Soon I shall wake up again."

Medoc leaned across the table. I thought she was going to speak, but then she reached out her hand and slapped Jon Wilberfoss in his face. She slapped him hard, a stinging, stiff-fingered slap: a slap that can dislocate a jaw.

Jon Wilberfoss's mouth opened and I saw blood trickle down from his lips. His mouth opened and he howled. What demon had Medoc released, I wondered and watched in fascination. Wilberfoss howled, and then he jumped to his feet.

He knocked the table to one side and reached for

Medoc. He was fast as a striking snake. His hand was in her hair and his fist was balled. She screamed and the scream stopped as he hit her. "Die," he shouted. "Die. Die. Die. Die. D . . ."

Lily had not been slow. She, just as much as I, had been taken off guard. The radio signal she sent triggered the drug cache in the nape of Wilberfoss's neck and he slumped and fell with his eyes open and blood pouring from his mouth.

Medoc was injured but alive. Jon Wilberfoss's blow had glanced, bruising and tearing the skin and knocking her back against the wall. She was unconscious and Lily tended to her. Had the blow struck as Wilberfoss intended, then we would have been clearing up her brains.

Medoc gained consciousness quickly and looked around wildly for a moment uncertain where she was. I saw her memory come to her. Lily cooed. "No fracture. No concussion. Just a little blood gone and that's soon made up."

Medoc looked at Wilberfoss. "Is he dead?" she asked.

"No. Just closed down."

"Wake him up."

"What!!!" This was me speaking for the first time.

"Wake him up. Don't let him escape now. Wake him up. He won't attack me again. He will be afraid of me. Wake him up."

To my astonishment, Lily did as she was bid. She neutralized the drug and after ten minutes Jon Wilberfoss stirred. It took another ten minutes for him to focus and when he did he found himself staring into the injured face of Medoc. He was kneeling before her.

"Un-dead," he murmured.

"Un-dead," she replied, "and as alive as you. Watch me, Jon Wilberfoss. This is your last chance. Watch me." And she hit him again in the face. His arms hung down at his sides like socks filled with sand. She hit him again.

"Live," she said. It was a command. "Live." The blows she gave him were heavy. "Live."

Jon Wilberfoss began to cry as his cheeks became purple and his eyes closed.

"Come out of your nightmare, Jon Wilberfoss. Follow the pain." She hit him in the face again and cried out for she had dislocated her wrist with the impact.

Jon Wilberfoss just stood there like a punch-drunk boxer without the wit to defend himself. His face was a mess of blood and tears.

Medoc allowed Lily to reset and then bind her wrist. "Perhaps he will wake up to the real world now," said Medoc while the bandages were being wrapped. Pain and reaction were setting in and she needed to talk. "Wilberfoss was playing games before. I know him well. I know his self-deceit. He means well. But he is a great fool. And his foolishness would have trapped him. That was why I had to startle him out of himself. It wasn't me he wanted to kill. It was the truth. And he couldn't kill that and so he would have killed himself. Mark my words. No matter how happy he seemed, one fine day you would have found him face down in the river or hung in a tree and everything would have been wasted. With luck that tragedy will be averted, but you must watch him now. Now he is really unstable. If he has a true will to live he will survive. I have opened him up to the air. If not he will remain in the nightmare and there's the end."

The bandage was tight. The face was cared for. Medoc made to leave the courtyard. "I shall stay in the garden for a few days to recover," she said. "And then I shall return to my husband in the south. I do not want him to see me like this." She paused at the gate. "I do not want to meet Jon Wilberfoss again. That would be wrong. I wish . . . I wish that I had followed my instincts and had done this months ago when the nonsense of the *Nightingale* first began. I could have saved everyone a lot of trouble, myself included." She closed the gate behind her and walked away.

I have never seen her since. If she is in the south and is still the wife of a fisherman and reads this, I hope she will feel I have done her justice.

Vaguely, faintly, dimly I began to understand. Lily and I had had our suspicions, of course. But we had underestimated the deviousness of the human mind. We had vastly underestimated its capacity for self-delusion. Wilberfoss had inverted the normal relationship of dream and reality. (I am almost certain I have the truth of this.) To him, the daily life in the garden was a gentle but insubstantial dream that brought him relief from the abiding reality of his nightmares. The world he truly inhabited was the dark world of his nightmares. That world was supported by the twin pillars of guilt and self-hatred.

And now Medoc, instinctive in her healing as in her timing, had shocked him with a truth. She had forged a link between the true world and his nightmare world. Put that another way, she had broken the barrier that held his worlds apart. She had challenged his darkness and that darkness had responded by trying to kill her. How often is this the case, I wonder, in human affairs? How often do humans kill because they cannot bear the truth? And I do not mean physically kill for there are many kinds of killing. I have observed.

But there is an optimism in the human spirit too: an awareness that things can be better. That optimism is a guide toward health. Lily has told me a great deal about this for she saw it in the children she guarded who had lost everything but could still play.

And what of Wilberfoss? That man remained for a long time kneeling unmoving like a horse at a hedge in the twilight. His tears stopped and the blood dried. Later Lily cared for him.

There for the moment we will leave him. We will accord him some dignity for there is nothing more to be gained for the moment from contemplating his sad and ruined face.

Some seven days later, suddenly, late in the afternoon he called to me saying; "Wulf. I want to talk." I swooped through the door and found him lying face down on his bed.

He had hardly spoken a word during the time since Medoc left and had spent the hours lying in his bed musing, murmuring to himself. Lily had never left his side day or night. She distrusted him, remembering Medoc's warning. She monitored his every move and told me that he had begun to masturbate at night. I asked her what significance this might have and she told me that she did not know in a profound way but that it did not worry her and at least showed there was movement in him. I agreed. To me it showed that his fantasy life, or whatever danced in his head when he closed his eyes, had entered a new and perhaps erotic phase. But I hoped he was not dreaming of Medoc. For that lady had gone, and there would be no dignity in chasing her. Dignity would come with a proper quittance.

And then came his call. This was only the second time since he had begun his convalescence with us that he had actually stated that he wanted to talk. In every other case I had more or less taken the initiative. I had used the hypnotic implant to release his memories.

"Help me, Wulf," he said. "I remember so much but . . ." He frowned for a moment in concentration.

"But . . . do you remember that story about a man who stood with his back to the fire watching the flickering of flames on the cave wall and his own shadow and tried to find meanings there? There is so much more. I need to face the fire, but I am afraid. The fire is here." He pointed to his head. "In here. Help me."

I began to prepare a reply but before I could speak he went on. "You see, yesterday, I heard people beyond the wall of the garden. They were talking about fishing, about catching the next tide. It all sounded so normal, so wonderfully normal that I could have cried for envy. I envied two ignorant Tallines who could think of nothing but nets and beer! Once I could have sat down and mended nets with them. But now . . ." His face changed again, suddenly scowling. "Damn Medoc and her witch ways. She should have stayed away. I was safe in my madness. She killed the dreams. You and Lily were the eye of my life, still and calm. Now I have nightmares when I sleep and nightmares when I wake and the days are filled with an aching strangeness. Who am I? What am I? Where am I? I'm half a man. I'm a guilty drunk. I did something last night which appalls the light of day and I don't know what but my flesh stinks like dead meat and my eyes burn and I want to die but I can't die."

Wilberfoss spoke all these words in a clear hard voice, like an actor who has learned his lines but who is speaking without any emotion.

"I'll help in any way I can," I said. "And so will Lily. You know that. We both want to see you returned to health."

"Health? What is health? Health is the interim between diseases."

I realized that he was testing me. If Medoc had been present I know she would have hit him hard for the silliness of his words. I, of course, may not hit a human and so I did the next best thing. I made to leave.

"Where are you going?" he called. "I demand that you stay."

"I'll stay to hear your story," I said. "But the rest is floss."

"I'll tell you my story. But I need help. Don't mind if I get silly. Don't mind if I talk pompous . . . I don't have a shape. Don't know what I am . . . how to talk." He looked at me and I saw through to his emptiness. Where there was once a man with drive and motive there were now only responses. Even so, the demolition begun by Medoc was not complete. He needed to recall his full history, only then could rebuilding begin. "How do you make me talk?" he asked.

"I use a hypnotic implant."

"Words?"

"Yes, words."

"Use them."

"Now?"

"Yes. Now. Nothing can be worse than the uncertainty. I feel guilt but I don't know why I feel guilt . . . not the deep why."

I spoke the words and his eyes closed. He lay back on the bed and became calmer. His voice, the next time he spoke, was deeper and more his own.

Wilberfoss's Narrative

WULF: Do you remember our last conversation?

WILBERFOSS: Yes. A graveyard. My mind and the ship. I need to know the extent of the destruction. To see it for myself.

WULF: Begin there.

WILBERFOSS: I rested and then I set out on a tour
of inspection. I took food with me and spare power packs
and I donned my survival suit with its gravity unit and
set out.

I spent several days drifting down dark corridors and
shunting myself into the living areas and resting areas
and opening the power locks in the different zones and
exploring. I was looking for life, you understand. Though
I believed the *Nightingale*, I still needed to see for myself.
I entered all the chambers in the CME and the DME.
The creatures that had lived there were already beginning
to decay.

Saddest of all were the small Rhymesters. They had
held close together since the trouble started. When I
broke into their chamber I found them dead in a ring,
holding hands. They had been singing of course, singing
their song without an end. I wonder what they were
singing when the end came.

It was the universality of death which most captivated
my mind. Nowhere was there an intelligent creature which
had managed to withstand vacuum or a serious shift in the
gases of its homeworld. Individual life is so feeble: only
the race can adapt. Show me the creature that can adapt
to a new environment in thirty seconds or that can take
a sudden plunge of thirty or forty degrees in its local
temperature with equanimity. They don't exist.

At first I was appalled by the monstrous presence of
death. But then I became passive. I shunted by screaming
faces of Tallines and the coiled bodies of the Bonami and
looked at them as I might have looked at paintings of the
Inferno.

When I was tired, I camped in my little pool of warmth,
usually by a wall or in a corner, for I needed the presence
of something physical to remind me that I really existed.
Once or twice I tried switching my suit lights out and

the darkness was so complete that I quickly began to fantasize. I thought the darkness was black fur choking me. Or I thought I was in the mouth of some beast that had eaten me. The darkness was dangerous. I slept with my lights on, rocking in the gentle oscillation of the gravity field.

By day I drifted from cell to cell and slowly a plan began to form in my mind. Perhaps I was already going crazy but I don't think so. As I explored the stricken ship I felt an overpowering desire to cleanse it. I decided to clean out the *Nightingale*. I thought that by doing this I would be honoring the dead. I would make that the last work of my life, for I had no thought of escape. The randomness of death has no dignity. I would bring dignity. I saw the faces and bodies flattened and distorted by the crushing gravity and I knew that I could not leave them like that.

When I had toured the entire ship I returned to my quarters and explained my plan to the *Nightingale*. The ship's bio-crystalline brain was now stronger since it did not need to monitor the varied life systems beyond my small speck of warmth. It had even allowed my fire to come back on. It listened to me with approval and told me that in all my wanderings it had been able to track me. I had never been alone.

It was the *Nightingale* that first suggested that I should try to reduce the weight of the ship. I don't know whether that thought would have occurred to me. It might have eventually but how could one small man reduce the weight of so great a ship? I had no idea but the *Nightingale* did. It made calculations. So, two motives flowed together.

The *Nightingale* had sampled my mind. Had it sucked up my cunning? I realize now that just as I was sworn to protect life, so the *Nightingale* was following its own most basic directives. Its job was to protect and save life too. I was the last bit of life aboard that it could identify with and so it was determined to save me.

Simple, eh?

And so a daily routine developed. I began to clear the canteen first. I opened up a wall door and allowed the atmosphere of the world to flow in. It was air of a kind. High in nitrogen: low in oxygen. One by one I dragged the bodies to the hole and tipped them out. They fell scraping down the side of the ship to explode on the ground. "Where is the dignity in this?" you may ask. All I can reply is that this seemed better than letting the corpses rot. Moreover, I have never liked to see waste. Rotting meat, rotting vegetables. When the spirit is gone what is left but earth? To me, the conversion of my dead colleagues into food for alien life seemed good usage.

I watched as the land crabs tore and devoured. This was an unexpected feast for them. Word spread among them. I suppose that is a way of putting it. Each day there were more crabs until they were a heaving brown carpet covering all the ground about the *Nightingale*.

Other creatures came too, things like giant starfish with hooded dark eyes that they could raise on pseudopodia and with hundreds of suckers fringing their arms. The largest were over a hundred feet from crown to tip and shrubs and bushes grew on their backs like stiff hair. These creatures could crawl up the *Nightingale*. I found them plucking at the vents and vacuum chutes, trying to get inside the ship, and the force they could exert was immense. Two of them did manage to enter the abandoned dormitory and recreation areas and they began to suck at the bodies. They were doing my work but unacceptably. They left a trail of slime which dirtied the ship. Moreover, I was afraid lest they broke into a section where the bio-crystalline brain was still functioning. And so I went out in my survival suit and drove them back with fire from a laser torch. Fire was the only thing that could make them move. Their suckers writhed and withdrew and these hulking beasts, each like a knot of snakes, slipped out of my ship and down the side. Each day, shortly after dawn, I made it my first job to ride around the *Nightingale* in the harness and burn them where they were climbing.

Of course, clearing the *Nightingale* of its dead life-forms, while it gave me an occupation and a sense of meaning— I was at least working for something—had a negligible effect on the ship's weight. That problem did not concern me. I really had no hope of escape from the crippling force of the planet's gravity. I didn't think about my end. If I'd thought about that at all it would have been in terms of entropy: a slow winding down of the power packs; another storm tearing at the *Nightingale*; the ship falling and being torn open on the rocks; an invasion of the brown and hairy starfish; slow contamination of the air in my living areas; perhaps a heart attack for you know a man cannot live all the time in a gravity harness and the strain on my body was immense. Occasionally I sickened as microbes evolved in my food. Sometimes, if I slept in an awkward position I woke up with my skin strained into sores. You have seen the silver patterns on my skin. As I say, I had my daily round and so long as I was occupied I didn't think. I didn't let myself think.

The *Nightingale* had its own plans and bade me spend part of each day with a laser cutter severing some of the internal links with the hydroponics belt. At first I did not know what it was about and then I understood. It was trying to lighten itself, and the hydroponics ring was like a belt of lead about it. While I cut and sealed on the inside, the ship used its own maintenance program to identify and sever external links. The hydroponics ring was constructed in a series of modules which had been more or less bolted together. These were slowly cut free.

One day the *Nightingale* asked me, for safety's sake, to stay in my quarters. I felt the ship shake and lurch and then become still again. When I went outside I found that sections of the hydroponics ring had fallen away and now lay crashed and broken on the rocks outside the ship. In that one action we shed almost one eighth of our weight. Later that day I lay on my couch while the *Nightingale* fed power to its anti-gravity boosters and lifted and shifted and settled some two miles away on a rocky plateau closer to the sea. The ship was stable and the powerful beam anchors which had almost bled us white for power but which had held us upright against the gravity of the planet, were reduced one by one and finally stilled. During the afternoon I flew around the ship in the gravity mule. Where the hydroponics ring had fallen away the ship was gashed and much of its splendid symmetry was lost. There were the black sockets of corridors which led nowhere, each of them stopped by one of the safety locks. Pipes poked out from the ship like carpet needles stuck in a cork. These had been torn loose when the ring fell. From one of them there was a dribble of brown water. The plates of color which had made the hydroponics area one of the most cheerful places on the ship now looked tawdry and cheap. The living quarters of the gardeners who had managed the ring were laid bare. Pictures were still tacked to cupboards. A vacuum toilet hung away from the wall. An oven and a bed had jammed together incongruously in a doorway where they were now held securely, buckled by the force of gravity. The intimacy of human dwellings was laid bare. I was reminded of the bombed houses that I had seen in picture books.

That night as I lay in my room, the *Nightingale* began

to describe ways in which the ship might be further
lightened. It seemed to think that the severing of the
ring had been a great success. I remember that I felt a
boyish enthusiasm spring up within me. In retrospect, this
was just another aspect of the unreality that was already
clouding my thinking.

WULF: Explain unreality.

WILBERFOSS: Oh, I was aware of this. Just as the
force of gravity can bend space, so the gravity of the
events I had experienced bent my understanding. Warped
it. Can you imagine what it is like to be the only thing
alive in a ship filled with dead creatures? I was the only
thing alive! Everything was dead except me! Everything! I
can be excused for asking the question, "Why me?" I can
be excused for finding answers to that absurd question.

I was aware that I was behaving in strange ways. It
was as though I could watch myself, but I was power-
less to stop myself behaving strangely. One thing I took
to doing was spending time down in the room where
the bio-crystalline seeds were growing. I drew a strange
strength from being close to the origin of that mighty
alien brain. I used to sit with my helmet as close as
possible to the blazing strands and filaments. I remember
on my homeworld when I was a boy, I used to sit at the
observation port of our solar energy station and look at
the sunlight, focused to a beam that could vaporize steel.
It was a similar thing . . . the desire to be close to naked
power.

But the strangest part of my unreality was that I began
to believe that I was not alone on the ship but that there
was another figure present. This was not a living person,
you understand, nor an alien, but something other. I
never saw it directly but I saw its shadow several times

and I heard its footsteps. It was a man, not unlike me, but
with a distorted head. Once I woke up in the blackness
of the ship with the knowledge that the figure had been
leaning over me. I reached up but encountered nothing.

WULF: Were you afraid?

WILBERFOSS: There is a strange thing. I was not
afraid. I was disturbed. I was worried but . . . I had the
feeling, the idea, whatever it was, that the visitor who
roamed the ship was also me. That doesn't make sense,
does it? But that is what I felt. I wanted to meet this other
being. I wandered through the dark ship with my lights
dowsed hoping to surprise it. I shouted and challenged,
but it never responded. Perhaps I shall never meet it now.
Perhaps . . . Who knows . . . But the main thing is that I
was aware of my strangeness. At times it seemed as though
the *Nightingale* was just an extension of myself. It could
expand my thought. It could expand my strength. When
I lay at night I could feel the ship about me like an extra
skeleton.

WULF: Were you ever lonely?

WILBERFOSS: Lonely. I don't remember being lonely. I had so much to do. There is this side to me that
always wants to bring things to order. While I was occupied I didn't have much time for myself. And there were
the crabs and the starfish. I have heard of people who,
condemned to a solitary life, have made friends of flies.
Well, I spent hours watching the crabs scuttling over
one another, engaging in skirmishes, picking through the
material ejected from the ship and going about their
business.
But then there were times when I wanted to sit down

and talk to friends. I used to spend hours daydreaming, talking to people in my mind and sometimes talking out loud. I used to talk to Tancredi. He was like a father to me.

WULF: Did you ever talk to Medoc?

WILBERFOSS: Medoc visited me one night. In the flesh. I didn't ask her to come.

WULF: What do you mean, "in the flesh"?

WILBERFOSS: She was there . . . herself . . . I told her I didn't want to see her.

WULF: And what did she say?

WILBERFOSS: She didn't speak. Just stood there, in the firelight, looking at me. I asked what she wanted. She had flowers and she offered them to me. She was wearing the kind of clothes that Talline women wear when they are mourning the dead. I thought she was mocking me and I told her to leave. She shook her head and so I took her by the neck and strangled her. I threw her from the ship. At least I think I did. I don't remember putting on my survival suit. I was dreaming but it all seemed so very real from the musky smell of her skin to the way her eyes would smile but not her face. I threw her from the hole in the ship's wall and she floated away, tumbling downward. Of course I was dreaming yet she seemed more real than the stones. I did not see her land, but suddenly she was standing on the ground looking up at me and one by one she was joined by all the creatures that had traveled in the *Nightingale* and that were now dead. They stood looking up at me . . . Not accusing . . . just looking. They looked to me as their leader. Ah! The leader of the dead. The leader of the killed. The killer. Was not the *Nightingale* made in my likeness? This temple of death.

I ran from them.

Of course I was dreaming. But when dreams are more real than the waking reality, how is a stressed mind to cope?

The next day, I got on with my work, clearing the ship.

WULF: Don't you think that Medoc could have helped you?

WILBERFOSS: Medoc would have destroyed me. She would never have let me rest. Medoc is a realist. There are times when we need a bit of deceit to get us through the day. Medoc is as pitiless as the eye of God on Judgment Day. I would not have survived a week on that world if Medoc had been among my voices. That is why I killed her. Survival. You've not been there. You don't know.

She left her mark. Every night after her visit I'd hear them, the crowds outside the ship, milling about, the un-dead.

But Medoc only came the once. The once.

WULFNOTE
I observed that Wilberfoss had become agitated with this line of inquiry and so I decided to terminate the interview. I spoke the recall words and he relaxed and slipped into normal sleep. However, I want the following observations placed on record: I believe that Medoc was a symbol of truth in the mind of Wilberfoss and that he denied her and thus entered falsehood. His retreat into madness was a retreat from the truth.

I also believe that Medoc did visit him. She was not a

creature of his imagination like the figure who haunted the ship, or the paternal voice of Tancredi. She was there, actual. Medoc crossed time and space; but do not ask me how. I can record truths that I can not explain. A human commentator must explain this.

There is something else strange to me. As Wilberfoss described his life on the stricken ship, he sounded almost happy, almost contented. This cannot be the truth that he was avoiding, the truth that had left him black and silent. Many men have killed in their dreams and woken to live normal unmurderous lives. There is more.

It will be strange, though, if the event that has cast such darkness on his mind should prove to be trivial in the light of reasonable day. It might be the kind of event which another man would shrug away with a laugh. Each man has his own truth. Each woman too, I think. And by these truths they measure their lives. Only we bio-crystalline entities, while we can perceive contradictions, seek general truths.

24

The Creature
from the Sea

WULFNOTE

We believe that Wilberfoss is now on our side. He is a willing participant in his restoration. We are now the ones that bid him make haste slowly. He has accepted a regular daily routine which consists of walks under the trees and work in the garden followed by brief periods of meditation.

In the evening we talk about anything that might be of interest. Wilberfoss wants to know about the monastery. I tell him what I know. Occasionally I visit Tancredi and learn what little news there is that matters. I do not tell Wilberfoss that the entire order is waiting to discover what happened to the *Nightingale*. I let him believe that he is a forgotten man in a quiet backwater and that the affairs of the Gentle Order are progressing as usual. Which in a way they are. Despite tragedy, life goes on.

Once a week we have retrieval sessions and I speak the hypnotic words and Wilberfoss remembers and I record.

Lily insists that these occasions take place only once a week and then only when Wilberfoss is rested and in good spirits. Wilberfoss would like more frequent sessions but Lily is not to be challenged. Her word is law. I have not bothered to quote these sections since they mainly filled in details in a picture that we already knew. They do not advance the story.

I accompany Wilberfoss at all times. He likes to chatter about things. He has taken to wandering close to the Pectanile. It seems to fascinate him. He is attracted to it and is responding to it as a symbol of health.

For myself I listen, question and record. Whenever possible I cross-refer, trying to evaluate the truth of his comments. Wilberfoss wants the truth but I am suspicious of him. As ever there is something else moving under his still waters. I watch and wait.

Spring is well advanced in the garden and the short, sharp winter of this world is in full retreat. Already there are flowers in the Hapsa Trees. They smell of lemons and the smell is everywhere. Flying through the trees I have glanced against the bright blue balls of blossom.

Responding as though I am a bird, the blossoms explode against my hard and pitted side, painting me with fragrance and plastering me with their sticky horseshoe-shaped seeds.

I know that I smelled of lemons when I recorded the following important segment of Wilberfoss's life.

Wilberfoss's Narrative

WULFNOTE
This interview is one of the most important. Wilberfoss began by describing incidents which have already been covered in earlier transcripts. I have edited the interview

so that it begins with new and rather startling information.

WILBERFOSS: Occasionally, you know, the *Nightingale* and I were at odds. I wanted one thing and the bio-crystalline brain wanted something else. To me the cleaning of the ship was all-important. But the *Nightingale* became obsessed with its weight! It undertook extraordinary calculations linking the gravity of the planet with its own mass, the drag of the atmosphere and the ship's power reserves. Despite all we had suffered, the ship was far from dead. It was recovering and making economies, like any creature. The massive symbol transformation generators, for example, were alive but dormant. They could be brought back into the game when the need required. Self-repair circuits kept them under constant check.

The *Nightingale* was bending all its efforts to getting us off the planet. Each day it unavoidably leaked energy and the equations changed. Each night it had to charge my gravity pack and the mule. It tolerated my fussing with the dead and my labored attempts at cleaning, but it demanded that I heave out anything that could be unbolted.

The simple truth was that given the gravity of the planet we did not have sufficient power to achieve escape velocity. But we had almost enough. The question for the *Nightingale* was how much could we trim from the ship and still leave it viable in space. To the *Nightingale*, a loss of weight was the equivalent to an increase in energy. Much of the ship was now open to the atmosphere of the planet and would be open to the vacuum of space if we escaped. My control area was the only part of the ship that retained breathable air. Hence there was much that could be abandoned. But how much could one small man do?

I moved the various landing craft down to the surface leaving only one stored in the hold. I tore out machinery that the *Nightingale* decided it no longer needed. I threw the entire library of tapes and books out of the door and watched the land crabs chomp and tear.

Such activity became my life.

One day I was in the gravity mule high on the top of the *Nightingale*. I had my laser torch and was cutting at the space doors which led to the hangars where the landing craft had been stored. These were excess weight that the *Nightingale* had told me to dispose of. I cut one door free and watched it twist around on one of its hinges as the high gravity swung it. The metal tore and the hinge broke. The door slid over the skin of the *Nightingale* and accelerated to the ground where it caused a brief, subdued commotion among the pressed rubbish. I paused to rest and looked out toward the sea.

The sea was always interesting. It was gray and rolled like molten lead. It did not have waves but heaved in slow undulations. It ran up the rocky shore like oil in a pan. Where the currents moved (and they changed by the hour) the sea took on different colors: sinuous eddies of gray-green and slate-blue. Where currents met I was reminded of snakes coiling and sliding past each other. And never a sound. To those of us who know the sea of a planet like Juniper, its different voices are as familiar as our own moods. But this sea was silent as thought, and its silence disturbed me and thrilled me. I remembered the dangerous sea of my boyhood.

And as I looked it seemed that the sea was changing. It became spotted. This I had never seen before. The spots were evident from the shore to the horizon and spread as wide as my field of vision. And even as I watched they changed. The spots became mounds and these quickly

expanded into domes of redness. The red was the color
of raw meat. I was aware that what I was watching was
the emergence of many spheres from beneath the sea.
What could this mean? So far as I could judge, there had
been no intelligent life among the creatures that swarmed
around our ship, but now something new and unified was
emerging.

You can imagine my concentration as hundreds of red
spheres rose to the surface and bobbed there for a moment
before lifting from the sea. As they lifted they expanded
to twice their size in the atmosphere. I could see veins
on them, like patterns in marble, and they each dragged
a tail which resembled an umbilical cord.

The spheres rose, the cords stretched, a body rose.
They were attached to a body which slowly emerged
from the sea. It was like a coiling mass of red worms.
Its size at this distance awed me. It seemed as if the whole
of the sea had become an undulating mass of red. As the
body rose at the end of its cords it began to disentangle
itself. Tentacles separated from the main body and rose.
Each was like a segmented worm. At the worm's ends
were blind mouths which opened and closed as though
tasting the atmosphere. Last to emerge from the sea were
coiling black tendrils which trailed from the underside of
the body and dragged over the surface. I realized that
what I was watching was the emergence of a single giant
creature.

This single creature rose silently until it filled the sky.
It came between me and the pale sun and its complex
shadow patterned the dun earth. It pulsed once, gathering
itself and then releasing, and I noticed that it was able to
take in atmosphere through valves on its side and then
blow it out through the blind mouths. It pulsed again.
With this slow jetting motion it began to turn in the sky
and then moved inland. It was moving in my direction.

I noticed that the creature was not as disorganized as I had at first thought. The largest balloons, for such they were, supported the center of the body. Fringed around these were smaller balloons which were able to move independently on long thin necks, each like the head of a reared snake. These, I soon realized, were eyes. I had not been able to distinguish them at a distance. The eyes were studying the ground.

With a sudden compression the creature dropped and some of its black tendrils uncoiled and scrabbled on the earth. Then its balloons filled again. Straining, it rose. To my astonishment it lifted one of the giant starfish. It heaved the starfish high in the air and the blind mouths got to work, burrowing directly into it and sucking its juices. While it ate the creature moved on.

I did not stay around to watch any more. I steered the mule down the sloping sides of the *Nightingale* and into the ship through the hole in the staff canteen wall, close to my chambers. I parked it and climbed out wearing only my survival suit. As I did so the shadow of the creature darkened the entrance way. I could see tendrils dangling down, plucking up the land crabs, and fossicking among the material ejected from the ship. I felt the *Nightingale* lurch slightly and guessed that it had been bumped by the creature. I could imagine it above us and beginning to explore us with its tentacles.

One of the tendrils poked in through the door and began feeling about. That set me running, but then I stopped. Staring in at me through the gaping hole in the ship's side was one of the giant eyes. I saw its pupil contract as it focused on me. The tendril stopped moving abruptly. It did not suddenly strike for me. It held still like a frozen branch.

I moved slowly and as I did so, the eye shifted slightly, to keep me in view. I wanted to get through the safety door and into my quarters. But the scrutiny of the eye was extraordinary. It made my every move seem enormous.

Finally I reached the door, opened it and dived through. The door slid shut behind me and immediately I heard something begin a soft exploratory tapping.

My control room had, of course, external cameras and I was able to view the creature as it touched the ship and ogled it, its eyes swooping down at the ends of their extendable supple necks.

I observed that it was careful in its interaction with us. There were many small aerials that it could have broken, but it touched them lightly. Where the hydroponics ring had been detached there were safety doors and these it explored gently. Mounted on the side of each door was a security panel consisting of twelve independent digits. Each panel had a simple code, a sequence of eight numbers. The cluster of several eyes gathered at one of the doors and a delicate tendril began to tap at the panel. This amazed me. A monkey tapping a typewriter might accidentally write a sentence given enough time. But this creature was methodically tapping out sequences of numbers which would inevitably lead it to the combination for the door.

It had puzzled out the function of the panel and how to operate it. Perhaps harder, it had worked out what a door was! Yet how could this be? There was nothing about the creature that suggested high technology or even domestication. Given the thumb, it was odds on that we humans would one day invent the door knob. This creature had tentacles and eyes and floated on thousands of red balloons of gas. What would it invent? The speculation daunted me. I knew I was facing intelligence of a raw and yet very pure kind.

I saw the moment when the creature found the correct combination, and the door slid open. Several eyes lowered to watch this. The creature closed the door and then tapped out the code again. The door obediently opened. Whereupon the creature closed it again and then moved over to another of the doors. It tried the same code. No result. At this it set to with a will and within minutes had the new code cracked. Thereafter it set both doors opening like the clatter of castanets. The creature was playing with the ship.

Now, intelligence and compassion are not necessarily linked, but there is a good chance that the intelligent creature which shows restraint in the face of the unknown, may be an entity one can treaty with. I observed the creature closely as it bobbed around us, its red balloons holding it steady and its jets occasionally puffing. There was a lightness about the eyes. One of them floated right in front of one of the cameras and stayed there looking. I could have been forgiven for thinking that the camera's function had been reversed and that the creature was looking at me. The eye was dark and lustrous. It had a black pupil and a lens and an iris which could open and close. It was covered with a film, like plastic, and fluids permeated through this. Can I say the eye was thoughtful? Humorous even? There is a danger in such assumptions, I know, but such were my impressions.

Eventually, as the day ended, the creature departed. The eyes, and the large spheres which took most of the weight, expanded and the creature rose. It relinquished contact with the ship with a curiously caressing motion. The tentacles slid over us, tapping. The creature rose so high that it became a pattern in the sky like a deep red stain. It disappeared behind the hills, contracting and expanding, as it jetted.

You have already gathered that here was a creature that I rather revered. After all the death aboard the *Nightingale* and the dumb company of the land crabs and mute starfish, here was intelligence of a high order. It was not like the bio-crystalline intelligence of the *Nightingale*. It was other.

But my life returned to the same pattern. The days became indistinguishable. I ferried around the ship at the *Nightingale*'s behest and chopped at it to reduce its weight. Then one day I was sitting in the mule, resting on the ground, wondering if I could use the land crabs to help clear the DME section, when a shadow fell over me.

I looked up and found that I was surrounded. Six or seven eyes on long red extensions bobbed in the air near me. The body of the beast was hunched and compressed. It reminded me of the untidy bag that wasps make for their nest except that it was blood-red and not paper-white. Before I could do more than let out a cry of fear, one of the tough tendrils that were coiled like ferns under its body released and darted at me and wrapped around the mule. It gripped like a steel hawser, but there was no mistaking the life in it. The end of the tendril, much to my surprise, was hairy and I noticed that each of the hairs had a small sucker at its tip which adhered to the clear plastic of the mule. I saw the creature grip and the walls of the mule buckled. I made sure that my survival suit was working as the mule was jerked off the ground throwing me to the floor. I was carried up to the . . . (*pause*)

WULF: Go on.

WILBERFOSS: I am seeing it all. I faced death. Ask anyone . . . I thought I was going to be eaten. The blind mouths were open . . . I had seen them plunge into a creature and suck it dry. One drew close to me. It was ringed with triangular teeth. They were small within the funnel where they were growing but became large at the tip. Beyond, on the outer skin of the lip, they were broken and missing. They could grind and cut. An elephant's trunk with teeth is not a bad image to describe them for there was also something sensitive about the way they nuzzled.

I was carried higher, beyond the blind mouths. I was lifted by the tendril and at the same time the creature was rising so that when I looked down I saw the *Nightingale* far below me. How high I was lifted I do not know but the red balloons which supported the creature reached a tremendous size so that they became translucent and I could see the veins within them and the smoky shape of clouds through them.

I assume we hovered in the stratosphere of this world. I was placed on the upper part of the creature's body which was soft but firm like well-toned muscle.

Giant eyes gathered around me.

Several tendrils rose. Carefully the plastic membrane of the mule was gripped and cracked and picked apart. The anti-grav unit which was situated in the lower rear portion of the small craft, tore free. It fell away and rolled down the creature's red belly and disappeared. The roof of the mule was tossed aside and then the door and walls. A tendril touched me.

I was held simply. One tendril was around my chest and I held it with my arms. Another was between my legs so that I rode. A third pressed into my back. They were careful, but I was turned around, upside down and once was held only by one leg. The scrutiny was enormous. Once a tendril touched the energy and atmosphere pack on my survival suit and I shouted in alarm and waved my arms at which the probing ceased.

I was set down on my feet and the tendrils released me slowly. I immediately fell down. The skin of the creature was as hard as the laminate panels inside the *Nightingale* and yet was easily flexible and moved under me. I pulled myself together and I stood up warily with arms outspread until I was actually standing on the creature. I could feel the tremble of its life through my feet. I looked at the gently moving hills of the creature and could occasionally see a pulse beat under the surface. I was reminded of the fluttering of birds caught in a net and that is a strange image to be summoned up for a creature so vast. It stretched all about me, acres of red skin. I was standing in a shallow concave depression.

The eyes were very close to me. I took two difficult paces and reached out and touched one of them and it did not flinch or blink but a tendril immediately rose and tapped my helmet. I guessed that the creature thought that my helmet, which has a single plastic face plate, was a single eye. I stood squarely in front of the eye and thrust my head forward and I blinked and opened and closed my eyes several times trying to make the movement obvious. I wanted the creature to understand that I was an entity who lived within the protective environment of my survival suit. It studied me intently. I pointed at my eyes, making myself stare like a fish, and then pointed at one of its eyes. The eye drew even closer and I saw its lens bulge. The iris contracted. I was hypnotized and motionless before its scrutiny. After several minutes it drew back. I had the clear impression that it was thinking, weighing up what it had seen.

The tendril which had tapped my helmet and which had been waiting close with its hairy tip furled, now reached down and tapped my metallic gloved hands. I thought for a moment and then reached and tapped the tendril.

One of the thick tentacles that I have called blind mouths now reared over the near horizon and hung over me. In diameter it was perhaps one and a half times my own height. It could have eaten me easily. With great deliberation, the tendril tapped the blind mouth with its fringe of sharp teeth, and then waited. I lifted my head, opened my mouth and showed my teeth. The eye looked down on me.

What a breakthrough that was! Tendrils opened and closed, the eyes bobbed, the trembling in the creature increased and I was astounded to see a deeper red suffuse through that segment of the body of the creature that was close to me. Of course, I fell down again.

Communication. We had created the beginnings of language! A tapping meant, "What do you have that is like this that I have?"

The creature tapped my foot and I again tapped one of its tendrils. It paused for thought.

A few moments later the creature tapped my gloved hands seeming to indicate the fingers. In response I was careful to touch only the small hairy suckers at the end of a tendril and that seemed to satisfy it.

We went on like this for a long time until I suddenly realized that I was running out of both power and air. I pointed at myself and then pointed down, pointing through the creature. I cannot say that the creature understood. It merely gathered that all was not well and took action.

Immediately a tendril wrapped around me, supporting me between the legs and beneath the arms. Then it lifted me and I found myself dangling in space.

I was carried down and deposited within the *Nightingale*, in the place that had once been the staff canteen. I scampered to the safety door leading to my rooms and let myself through. With the door closed I yanked off my

helmet and breathed deeply. I had cut things fine. I had
little more than three minutes of air left to me. But I was
alive. I began to shake uncontrollably as I stood, leaning
against the door. Reaction I suppose to all the shocks I
had received and it was all I could manage to drag myself
up the ramp and into my rooms. I made my way into the
control room and lay down.

The external cameras were all working and the screens
presented an interesting image of the creature. It was
browsing unconcernedly among the land crabs, gathering
them up in clusters and presenting them to the blind
mouths.

Thereafter we had many meetings. We continued our
elementary communication and one discovery was to
prove significant later. The mule being now broken, I
had taken to using my small domestic anti-grav unit for
work outside. It was much slower than the mule but at
least gave me mobility. Sometimes the creature joined
me. It anchored itself to the hills and spread, like a red
silk canopy, over the plateau where the ship rested. It
supported me in its tendrils and, with several large eyes
bobbing along, carried me wherever I pointed. We were
close to the base of the ship where the emergency thrust
and guidance rockets were located. I had been trying to
show how the *Nightingale* had been damaged and strained
by the landing.

A tendril reached out and tapped twice on one of the
dark rocket vents. I thought for a moment and then
pointed to one of the blind mouths that was sucking
along the plateau, fossicking perhaps for one of the giant
starfish. The blind mouth paused and then found a large
land crab and seized it and lifted it up to within a few feet
of me. With a peristaltic contraction, the triangular teeth
tore into the shell and cracked the land crab and sucked

out its juices and meat. It turned aside and spat away the empty shell. It was asking me a question. "Is the rocket vent a mouth through which the *Nightingale* could eat?"

I crossed my hands back and forth in front of my face. (We had established that this signified negation. The creature would rub two tendrils in front of one of its eyes to give me the same information.) Then I made motions with my hands to mime blowing and propulsion. I don't think I am a good mime and three eyes floated close to scrutinize what I was trying to communicate. They waited patiently. I pointed up at the main body of the creature and then made the pulsing movements again and tried to show the whole thing lifting and shifting. There was a long pause and then the blind mouth that was close to me vented suddenly. I was caught unprepared and the gust blew me back like a rag doll. Had the creature not been supporting me under the arms and across the back I would have been blown to the ground. And that would have been the end of me for we were some fifty feet above the ground.

The gust stopped almost immediately but it had blown my right arm back, almost dislocating it. It hurt but I hardly cared. There were suddenly fifteen or twenty eyes hovering around me and with great deliberation, one of the tendrils snaked out and carefully tapped the rocket vent. Then it pointed at a cluster, say fifty or sixty, of the blind mouths which had gathered some distance away and were directing their empty gaze downward. The body of the creature compressed and in unison, the blind mouths vented, stirring the rubbish on the ground into eddies and whirlpools. The entire creature, carrying me with it, rose. I shouted something and made circles with my hands on either side of my helmet which was our sign language for "yes."

The small gust did not carry us far and the creature let itself drift back downward slowly. Finally it deposited me safely in the canteen area. Then it drifted away from the ship. It made signs with several of its tendrils pointing at its underbelly. I had a feeling that it wanted to demonstrate something and so I stayed close to the opening in the canteen wall and watched as it jetted gently away.

When it was about a mile or so from the *Nightingale* it paused. The eye balloons all rose until they were high above the body. Above them stretched the giant semi-transparent lifting balloons. The tendrils coiled up like springs under the body and at the same time, the blind mouths lowered until they all pointed stiffly downward like fingers, hundreds of fingers. In a strange way the creature was trying to imitate the *Nightingale*.

I saw it draw atmosphere into itself through the vents in its side. It was for a moment distended and then it released through the blind mouths. The sheer power of its drive sent it rocketing up to the sky. Even as it accelerated it drew breath and the cycle continued. It shrunk rapidly to a mote of redness, a spark of sunlight, high in the sky.

The bushes which had been beneath it were flattened. A cyclone of dust spiraled into the sky and became a short-lived mushroom cloud. I felt the blast of the creature's departure as a wind which struck us and rolled over us. Rarely have I seen any animal so committed to movement as my strange red creature of gas and bladder: the charging bull perhaps, the striking snake, the graceful leap of the kris deer which jumps and points and spears in the same movement.

As I say, it was imitating our ship, or what it thought our ship might be like. In its terms, the bladders and balloons which supported it were like my anti-grav unit. They were stable and solid. But the jets were fierce: the very stuff of raw energy.

I watched it high in the planet's sky for many minutes but then lost it as the day declined. I wondered how high it could climb, how high it could reach, before the thinning atmosphere threatened its balloons and the cold threatened its life.

After this event I did not see the creature for three days. In retrospect I believe this was a most important time. I believe the creature returned to the sea to mull. The creature was thinking about us. It had great powers of reason and I think it came to understand the *Nightingale*'s predicament.

The *Nightingale* was of course interested in this creature. It was programmed to appreciate alien life and asked me if I was hoping to take a sample of this life-form with us if we were lucky enough ever to depart this high-gravity planet. That possibility had never occurred to me but it made me realize how attached I was becoming to this . . . this . . . what? I realized that I had never even given it a name. Names can be important. But how could I name it? Given this harsh world of hungry land crabs, creeping starfish and gray shrubs, I might call the creature Friend; I might call it Hope; I might call it Companion. It became a focus for an energy which, for want of a better word, I shall call Love. For that is exactly how I thought of it. It gave me focus and meaning. Among death it was life and so I gave it a most private name, Chi-da. That is how I will name it from now on.

Chi-da returned some three days later. It may have come from the sea: I do not know for I was working in the part of the ship which had dealt with data records. This area had had its own living complex which included a crèche where the very young children of those who worked aboard the *Nightingale* could play and be educated. It had suffered the same fate as the rest of the *Nightingale*.

I had become inured to death and decay by this time. The crèche was horrible to clear as I had known many of the children and had sat and told them stories . . . But I did it. I cleared the bodies and then I cleared the furniture and the toys. I tipped them all out of the ship and down to feed the land crabs.

I also threw out the records and the record keepers. It was while I was engaged on this task that Chi-da returned. The sky darkened to blood as it anchored. Several eyes bobbed down on the end of their stalks and I walked to them and then made the affirmative gesture. Two tendrils returned the gesture. The positive gesture had also come to serve as a greeting. Chi-da settled to watch me.

Most of the bodies were in an advanced state of decay but there was one, a woman as it happened, who had managed to get into her survival suit but who had not managed to activate the atmosphere control. She had remained, more or less preserved, in vacuum. I waved and pointed to Chi-da before I tipped her from the ship and Chi-da caught her as she fell.

The giant creature removed the suit with the care and precision of a watchmaker and then examined the body. Many eyes gathered for this, like students at a medical school autopsy. Chi-da had no way of knowing whether I was a man or a woman. It may have known nothing of gender but it was able to study eyes and fingers and lungs and liver.

Later I found the body of a man well preserved in his survival suit. He had become trapped in the darkness between levels when the transportation system failed. The power packs of his suit were run down. He had obviously kept his lights going as long as possible and had finally committed suicide by opening the valves on his suit to the vacuum of the interdeck. I waved again to Chi-da as

I lugged this body up and pitched it out. So Chi-da was able to investigate two of us.

One evening, Chi-da and I were together. I was sitting on top of the *Nightingale* and Chi-da had settled on the hills and plateau. The creature was like a thick carpet. The entire land around the ship looked to be covered with red cloth which billowed slowly, its color accentuated and brightened by the light of the setting sun. Several eyes were around me and on an impulse I had danced one of the slow Talline dances that Medoc had taught me. I don't know what Chi-da made of it but I at least had taken pleasure in clapping my hands and in making the small steps and turns. I suppose I was exhilarated. That day I had been carried by Chi-da out over the sea and had seen the strange patterns that covered the surface of the sea.

I had also seen another creature like Chi-da on the far horizon, calmly jetting. It had suddenly swung around and come toward us. From its abrupt change I guessed that these creatures had some means of communication and that Chi-da had called to it. It passed over us, higher by some hundreds of feet, and eyes came down. The new creature, darker in tone than Chi-da, stayed with us for a while and then jetted high and departed.

Later we returned and I found myself feeling a little more "at home" if I can call it that on this grueling world. It is all a matter of finding things which are familiar, really. I had posed myself a question. Why had a creature such as Chi-da evolved such rare intelligence? I had no answer, but the implication was that there was an extraordinary social order on this world. I wanted to know more. I also wanted to tell the creature more.

Anyway, in the evening, I stationed myself on the top of the *Nightingale*. After my little dance I pointed at

Chi-da and then at the sea. Its inflated eyes looked at
me and then around at the sea. When its gaze returned
to me I pointed at myself and the *Nightingale* and then
up to the stars.

It did not look up, but moments later it detached from
the ground and began a gentle susurrus as it spread its blind
mouths and jetted from the ground. The lifting balloons
inflated, the cords tightened and up it went with steady
acceleration. I have no idea why it left or really what idea
I had communicated. Perhaps it thought I was asking it
to leave.

But later that night it came back and settled on the
hills.

I made one bold guess about Chi-da and that was that
it wondered at discovering intelligence in a creature as
small as me.

Some days later Chi-da helped me clear out the DME
areas.

The vast dim chamber that had been the DME area
was my greatest challenge. Its scale was greatly beyond
the human. I stood within it, in the thin light which
penetrated through the hole that had been torn by the
meteorite when we lurched into local time/space.

The moment that the particle screens failed, the five
sectors of the DME area which were still viable became
as one. Have you ever looked at soap bubbles and seen
how their facets intersect and then, when one of them
explodes, how the remaining walls adjust? I imagine
something like this happening within the DME sector.
One skin failed and then another and another until finally
all that was left was a brew of atmospheres and the choking
organisms.

When the *Nightingale* was free in space the different
zones which served the DMEs clustered within the vast

chamber like eggs. Under the crushing force of this planet's gravity, the particle screens had been strained and when the screens finally collapsed after the wind storm, all the entities along with the vegetation and furniture that constituted their environment, had tumbled together, pressed to the concave floor.

This was the miserable sight that greeted me. The *Nightingale* with its normal practicality had told me that if I could clear this area then we would be close to achieving escape potential. Heracles confronting the Augean stables faced no more daunting task, and I was not Heracles.

The idea was that I should introduce land crabs into the DME chamber and let them gorge and then eject them. The *Nightingale* assured me that the land crabs could do no harm to anything that was not already damaged. It was the *Nightingale* that suggested that perhaps the giant red creature could be pressed to help. Chi-da would be invited to ferry the crabs and then dispose of them.

I communicated our needs by the simple method of visiting the surface, netting a land crab and lifting it up to the hole smashed by the meteorite and then releasing it to scrabble down inside. Chi-da watched. And as I lifted my third land crab, it simply scooped up a hundred and stuffed them through the hole.

It seemed to look at me quizzically as if to say, "Why do you want to fill your ship with land crabs?"

Following an impulse I beckoned to it. I re-entered the ship through the meteorite hole and two of the eyes contracted and followed me. They looked around the dark interior where the land crabs were already scurrying and fighting. A tendril also managed to snake through the hole and this tapped the walls and plumbed the floor and slapped the land crabs. The pair of eyes must have watched for half an hour. Then the tendril reached and

captured a large land crab that had been particularly vora-
cious. When I saw that, I gave the affirmative gesture
before the suspended eyes. Again I was regarded stead-
ly while the land crab squirmed in the tendril's grasp.
Then the tendril holding the crab and the pair of eyes
withdrew.

I was about to follow when the entire hole was blocked
by one of the blind mouths. It came feeling in, thrusting
aside and bending the smooth laminate of the inner walls.
I lifted to the top of the chamber to avoid it and hung
suspended and watched. Inside the chamber the blind
mouth felt about until it discovered the mess where the
land crabs were feeding and then it lowered its mouth in
and began to draw the material into itself.

After a few moments it withdrew from the chamber
and I hurried after it. The blind mouth turned away from
the ship and fired the material toward the ground. What
the giant creature thought of it I had no way of knowing
but I gave the affirmative sign to the ogling eyes which
watched me all the while.

Then Chi-da set to it with a will. It widened the
meteorite hole and two blind mouths took turns to enter
the chamber and evacuate the contents. It worked all day
and into the night and when the chamber was empty
it lifted silently and jetted its way toward the sluggish
moonlit sea.

The last things I shall say concerning Chi-da offer terrifying insights into the alien mind which, in giving us
knowledge, emphasize just how little we truly understand.

Chi-da was away for seven days. During that time
the *Nightingale* overstayed its optimum departure time.
I will explain. I came to realize how much I had come
to depend on the creature that had helped me. I had never

known such a pure relationship of giving and receiving. It gave and I received, but I must have contributed something. Looking back I doubt that I would have survived on that cruel world had I not had that creature as companion.

Be that as it may. The *Nightingale* and I worked on the ship, deciding which systems were needed and which could be abandoned. The *Nightingale* had been pared to a minimum. It had been cleared of life-forms. It had been stripped and gutted. Structurally, the ship was now a skeleton. Its plates were open and the inner parts would be exposed to the vacuum of space. This did not matter and in some ways was an advantage for space does not corrode. Secure were my anachronistic suite of rooms with their flickering fire and antique bedroom. The mind of the *Nightingale*, healthier now, knew its strengths. It had calculated that if we attempted to leave now we had a 60:40 chance of achieving escape velocity. These were the best odds we would ever have. With nothing left to jettison from the *Nightingale*, delay could only mean that second by second we lost our reserves of energy. We had an "escape window" (as the *Nightingale* called it) of two days. These calculations were completed immediately after the cleaning of the DME area and the departure of the creature.

What could I do? I am not profoundly sentimental, yet I could not face the thought of blasting off from this world without a proper farewell. I suppose the idea of leaving was less important to me than continuing to meet with the big red creature. I mean, tell me what gives value to life? What price the skin of Jon Wilberfoss if he denies a friend that has helped him? What value can I place on the deaths of all my comrades? It is in the quality of our relationships that true value resides. Chi-da had come to mean more to me than the *Nightingale*.

I delayed. I waited for the creature to return. At the same time, my reasonable mind told me that the creature might be dead, that it might have become bored, that it might have migrated to a distant ocean, that in thinking it had any deep interest in me or the *Nightingale* I was falling into the greatest fallacy of all, that of ascribing human motives to the alien mind. I had fears and the *Nightingale*, the damned *Nightingale*, played descants on my doubts whispering that it had gone and would never return.

So the minutes ticked by and became hours and the hours stretched into days and the *Nightingale* became frantic.

I stayed outside the ship with my intercom switched off to still its voice. I sat atop the *Nightingale*, stone-faced like an Indian chief of old Mother Earth, waiting.

The time for our optimum departure passed. When I entered the *Nightingale* to sleep, that machine screamed at me. Logic without love is a damned conjunction. I recharged the batteries of my small anti-grav unit while the *Nightingale* demanded that I settle in my couch and prepare for acceleration. I overrode with an act of will for I was still Commander of the *Nightingale* and I was still a full living entity and the *Nightingale* could not choose but obey.

But though my authority was absolute, the *Nightingale*'s obedience was only temporary and it began again, telling the minutes as they slipped past and the changes in the probability of our escape.

I placed a limit on my waiting. I told the *Nightingale* that I would not contemplate attempting to depart until our odds of success had declined to 50:50.

On the sixth day we reached the moment of 51:49 and I heard the *Nightingale* begin to warm the engines. We had planned our departure as follows. We would lift as far as we could using the anti-gravity system. This system, not being designed to heave a spaceship into space and in any case being damaged, would burn out at a certain point. We could not know exactly when. But when it did, we would feed all power to our emergency rockets and trust to luck. Our aim was to achieve just sufficient velocity to get us into a safe orbit from which we could begin to negotiate a space/time shift with the STGs.

And still I delayed. The *Nightingale* became wild.

I sat outside the ship looking toward the sea while the night gathered. I felt the grief of the abandoned.

And in the evening it seemed to me that I saw a stipple on the ocean. The moon sprang up and I saw, unmistakably, the vast creature rise from the sea and begin to drift toward us. I stood on the top of the *Nightingale* waving.

It arrived swiftly and silently and blood-red. Several eyes bobbed around me. Dramatically I pointed to myself and then up to the sky where the first stars were already twinkling. A tendril lifted and offered to support me. The creature thought I wanted a ride. I made the negative sign quickly and then indicated both myself and the *Nightingale* and again pointed up to the stars.

It understood. The eyes withdrew and looked at me steadily. Slowly the entire widespread creature gathered and then anchored on the hills. The tendrils gripped the shrubs and rocks. In the dying light of the sunset Chi-da was gathered like a wave, frozen at the point of breaking. It filled half the sky. All its hundreds of eyes came to the front and stared at us.

I waved, a gesture which could have no meaning, and I felt my throat hurt when I saw a single tendril rise and imitate my gesture. Then I lowered to the entrance hole which led to my rooms.

The *Nightingale* was intoning the odds as I stripped off my survival suit in the control room.

"All right," I called. "We're leaving. Let's give it our best shot. Perhaps we'll crash. Who cares? We do the best we can. OK?"

For answer the *Nightingale* began a countdown. The anti-grav units were coming alive, the rocket units were primed. Within the bio-crystalline system, light was flowing. The countdown was as old as space travel itself, perhaps as old as human anticipation. It entered its final phase.

10, 9, 8 . . .

I made myself as comfortable as I could. In the viewscreen I could see the dark shape of Chi-da and the bank of eyes staring at us.

7, 6, 5 . . .

The *Nightingale* began to shake. I imagined the anti-grav units flexing their power and asserting their lift, sensing the different structures within the ship and points of pressure. Already the *Nightingale* would be experiencing torque and compression. Would it hold?

4, 3 2 . . .

There was a shouting in my ears. The dead companions and Medoc whom I had killed, were there outside the ship chanting their farewell and I shouted my goodbye.

1 . . .

I felt sick. As the anti-grav units gripped deep, the entire ship became a force field. I felt us lurch and lift. The acceleration pulled at my hair and beard and I felt the sides of my mouth tear. We were climbing. I saw the nearby hills slide down the screen. I saw Chi-da detach and rise with us. We were ahead of calculation and the anti-grav units were straining to incandescence. The vibration grew. I heard a bumping. We were straining . . .

. . . and suddenly all movement ceased.

And then we began to fall . . .

WULFNOTE
At this moment Wilberfoss became awake. The hypnotic
hold had broken. He stared at me blankly and then began
to howl.

25

Savagery

WULFNOTE
I will begin by quoting the exact words from my file notes made on the day of Wilberfoss's most violent outburst.

Wilberfoss is become bland. He reminds me of the man who arrived here last year. He is passive but aware. A clam would be more interesting. He has not spoken to either Lily or myself since his last waking up.

I have tried the hypnotic words but they do not work anymore. Lily will have to set more words in his psyche but given his present state, that may take time.

Lily lets him wander. That surprises me, for to my non-medical but pondering mind, he seems in a state of mute distress. I think that now more than ever he may try to do himself harm. I have expressed my fears to Lily and she agrees. But she reasons as follows: Wilberfoss is healthy in body. Medoc and I have brought him self-awareness. If he wishes to cure himself he can. If he does not wish to cure himself, there is now nothing any of us can do. It must be up to Wilberfoss. "Of what avail," she says in her quaint way, "would it be to keep the healthy animal in a state of coma?" And I suppose I agree. But it is not easy to watch. We have come so far. We are so close. What ails him?

I realize that I have the rationalist's, perhaps the historian's, desire to find ends and causes, shapes and meanings. But life is not like that, is it, you humans? I realize that tragedy is a human invention, to give shape to your experience: meaning to your chaos. Beyond tragedy there is only the incandescent present, illuminating everything, or the vacancy of death. If I were you I would think that Wilberfoss is a lesson in tragic waste. But no matter.

Spring is come to the garden. Wherever you turn there is blossom. The dartwing are already nesting in the eaves of the hospital and are very noisy. I have seen lizards sunning themselves on the stone-work and slowly waking up. Round the Pectanile there is a veritable carpet of flowers. Yesterday the smell of the sea was very strong in the garden.

Wilberfoss wanders like one of the dead. I doubt there will be any more joy from him today than yesterday.

For this afternoon I shall take a chance and depart the Poverello Garden and visit Tancredi. I want to bring him up to date on what is happening. Though he still rails against Wilberfoss I have managed to show him that that man is largely innocent of wrong-doing. While somewhat premature, my finding is that the

Magistri who appointed him must look to their own procedures.

But yet there is more.

Thus ends my file note. Now let me tell you what happened on that special day.

At quarter-past-four in the afternoon, as I was taking dictation, I received a call from Lily asking me to come back to the garden quickly. Tancredi drained his wine glass hurriedly and sent me on my way.

I swung out wide over the sea as I dived down to the garden. Lily was calling all the time and I was able to pinpoint her position. I dived down through the trees some two hundred yards from the Pectanile and followed the river and came to the place where the formal garden merges into the wild Talline wood. There the river passes over rapids. There are deep hollows and places where the trees, willow and gosstang, hang over and trail in the stream. It was to this place that Wilberfoss had come.

Lily was in the river. She was half-submerged in the tumbling water. She was in no danger. Lily could charge about submerged if she had to.

She spoke to me as I descended. "Wilberfoss says he'll n'er move, till that th'art here." And only then, as I moved slowly between the banks and under the branches, did I see him.

He was perched on a rock. He was naked. And yet I hardly recognized him. He was daubed like a savage.

Let me tell it to you simply.

He was streaming with blood. He had a knife. He had sliced his forehead and cheeks. He had cut down the lines of his shoulder muscles and along the backs of his arms. He had cut down his chest and then outward following the lines of the ribs. He had savaged his back into ugly wounds. He had cut his thighs and calves and the tops of his feet. But there is more.

Perched on the rock and crouching, he defecated into his hands. Then he began rubbing his feces into his wounds. He was smearing himself. He mixed shit with blood.

He saw me but did not see me. He looked through me but yet he spoke. "O Wulf," he howled. "Damn you. Damn you and Medoc. Damn all of you."

I spoke to Lily privately. "Why have you not stunned him?"

"He has cut out the cache. Now if I try to reach him he will run away. You must speak to him." ·

There was nothing I could say. Nothing I could do but watch. What words can be used before such self-abuse? I waited.

He sat crouched for a long time, staring. He was hunched down on the flats of his feet, his arms thrust forward and resting on his knees as though waiting for pain or punishment.

Of course nothing happened. The river gurgled. Birds sang. Branches creaked. Shadows moved. All about us life and time continued. Lily and I waited and watched. What did he expect?

Eventually he stood. The blood had dried and clotted and was indistinguishable from the excrement. He turned and jumped down from the rock on the side of the stream away from Lily. He broke through the screen of bushes and turned to his left and began to run. I rose and followed him.

He was making his way toward the main gate. He broke through a fence and jumped over a small tributary of the main river. He stumbled and fell there and for a moment was on his knees in the mud; but then he clambered up the bank and ran on. He crossed a small vegetable patch that was in the care of the gate warden and came to the carved screen which marked the entry into the garden.

Here he paused, his arms resting against the screen and his head on his arms. The gate warden came out of his hut, saw him and immediately departed inside again. Wilberfoss lifted and ran on. He went around the screen and through the gate and came to the statue of St Francis Dionysos. He sheltered his face from the statue and ran past it and up the hill and turned right. He came to the arcade where he had lived with Medoc and there he paused.

There were many people about and they stared at this naked madman and moved away from him. He must have smelled too. People saw me trailing him and no one interfered.

Wilberfoss ran back down the arcade and turned up the path he had followed so many months earlier, the path that led up to Tancredi's small house at the height of the Monastery. He was weakening and staggered. I was amazed he lasted so long. Occasionally he stopped and gasped and then plunged on, driving himself up the steep hill. He approached the headland and the balcony called Temptation.

Many of the Children of the War had gathered there and now stood banging their stones, blocking the way. How had they known to gather? There were several junior members of the Gentle Order and the Bursar. I was also surprised to see Tancredi. He must have decided to set out for an exercise walk. It was little more than an hour since I had left him. Perhaps he was hurrying down to the Poverello Garden having gathered that something was wrong.

Everyone drew back as Wilberfoss approached.

Wilberfoss saw Tancredi and with a despairing cry ran toward the narrow rail which guarded the edge of the path and threw himself over. He vanished downward immediately. Everyone clustered to the rail but I flew high and then swooped. I dropped faster than a stone and when Wilberfoss hit the water in a tangle of arms and legs, I was there to support him when he bobbed, open mouthed and gasping, to the surface.

I could not lift him but I could support him. Within minutes a Talline boat rounded the headland and came skimming toward us. Wilberfoss was dragged aboard and lay gasping in the swill of brine and sand and shells at the bottom of the boat.

The seamen lost no time. They pulled on the oars and the boat turned and quickly carried him to the wharf near the entry to the Poverello Garden.

Lily was waiting. She took him, cold and fatigued and bleeding from his cuts, into her iron womb and trundled back into the garden under the watchful eye of St. Francis Dionysos. She did not make the traditional pause.

Let me make this clear. Wilberfoss was conscious during all of this. He stared at me as I held him above the waves. He stared at the thick-fingered Tallines who hoisted him from the sea. He stared at the Children of the War who had come running down to see him landed at the wharf. He stared at Lily as she received him and he stared at the statue of St. Francis Dionysos as he bumped past it and entered the Poverello Garden.

Lily took him straight back to her small hospital, to the room where he had been living since his return to the Pacifico Monastery months earlier. Little over forty minutes had elapsed since he had escaped from the garden.

I came to them there later having paused for a few minutes to talk to Tancredi. Wilberfoss was sitting still and Lily was washing him. He was cleaner for his dip in the sea but many of his cut marks had opened. Lily mopped and cleaned and dressed. I settled close, resting my large helmet frame on the ground for my energy cells were greatly overtaxed and in need of time to recharge.

"Do you wish to talk to me now?" I asked, and he nodded. "Very well. Begin," I said. As you gather, I was in no state to trifle. "Do you need hypnotic assistance?" Wilberfoss shook his head. He began to speak.

Wilberfoss's Narrative

So the *Nightingale* was lifting, riding on its anti-grav units, and I felt a great surge of hope. At the same time, I was aware that I was heading into the unknown and was leaving the only creature that had ever come to me with a selfless interest. Chi-da. The name means "Great Breath." "Great inspiration."

Then we faltered. The acceleration died away. The fierce grip of the planet began to assert itself. I wondered why the *Nightingale* did not immediately fire the rockets. I thought that it was preoccupied with calculation. I thought it had over-estimated its own resilience.

And even as I was wondering and preparing myself for a fall that would simply be a conclusion, I felt the *Nightingale* shake and then, unmistakably, begin to rise again. The viewscreens showed me nothing. They were completely occluded.

I called out to the bio-crystalline brain of the *Nightingale* to tell me what was happening. I demanded to know if it had fired the rockets.

There was no reply for a moment and then came the *Nightingale*'s calm voice whispering. "Commander Wilberfoss. The anti-gravity generators have failed and I have released what I can of their weight . . ."

"Then what . . . ?"

"The escape rockets have not yet been fired. We are at present in the grip of the alien life-form with which you have been communicating, that you call Chi-da. It is lifting us at an acceleration un-hoped for. It has us gripped . . ." (*pause.*) "We are approaching the atmospheric limit of the planet." Pause. "We do not yet have escape velocity." (*pause.*) "We must fire the emergency rockets."

"Can't you fire them?"

"I need your order."

"Why, for God's sake?"

"Because when the rockets are fired they will kill the life-form that is lifting us. We will tear through it. We are approaching the critical limit. I cannot kill. I need your order." Pause. Then . . .

"Escape limit in 5 seconds." It began to count.

"4 seconds

"3 seconds

"2 seconds"

"FIRE"

I screamed the word and the *Nightingale*, ready and waiting, obeyed. The acceleration was like a punch in the back. We leaped away from that planet with a roar and in so doing we ripped through the thin fabric of the creature that had saved us. We tore it apart. The viewports cleared and I saw parts of it slither past. Those cameras that were looking downward showed me the creature in tatters. Parts of it were exploding, parts were burning, the rest was falling down to the gray sea. We had torn through the body of the most beautiful creature I had ever known. Again I had killed but this time there could be no forgiveness . . .

I have done this. Me. Wilberfoss, the lover of life, the

giver. I have done this. And now the truth is told . . .

. . . and not told. For the deepest truth is that I found pleasure in the destruction. The killing had relish. That is the terrible truth I have tried to hide from. And now it is in the open. The murderer was not expulsed. The beast by the river was not tamed.

All my life I had wanted to be the selfless giver, and at the moment of crisis I was found wanting. It gave up its life so that I could live . . . but I killed it. I killed it. And the killing had relish. I do not deserve to live. There can be no forgiveness. Close your book. I have failed in my deepest ideal and there is no health in me.

Wilberfoss railed on in this matter for several minutes and then finally became still. His last words were, "You should have let me die."

26

The Man Comes Home

WULFNOTE

So there it was, set out in four little words: "The Killing had Relish." The great truth that he had been unable to face was that he, Jon Wilberfoss, who had set himself such high standards for his love of life, had discovered the killer in him. Ripping off the mask of St. Franics Dionysos he had discovered the grim face of Achilles. I am sure the revelation is altogether more subtle than that, but that is its broad outline. He had destroyed beauty and life. He refused to face that truth and hence his agony. And yet there is more. Wilberfoss had met, and experienced at first hand, a selfless giver. He could not be ignorant of the fact that the creature which he calls Chi-da knew exactly what it was doing. It knew that it would be destroyed. It made a conscious sacrifice: its life for his. When Wilberfoss called "Fire" he accepted that sacrifice. He need not now accept the guilt. It is all to do with Yes and No. Wilberfoss felt crushed by the knowledge that he had elected No at a crisis in his life. It was my job to make him see that his No was really a triumphant YES and that if he so chose he could now build on to greatness. Let me affirm that if Wilberfoss had been able to cast aside his guilt he would have become the true man to captain a ship like the *Nightingale*. The *Nightingale* would have multiplied his qualities a hundredfold.

I explained all this to Wilberfoss and in his mind he knew the truth, but in his heart he could not accept it. Guilt is not like mud on a pair of trousers that can be easily washed. Guilt deforms the very fabric.

So we have a story of near-greatness. A man picked out for trial who came to face his own deepest nature and recoiled in horror. I hope I have made it clear.

Wulf does not mean to be sententious in pointing out that old wisdom has always enjoined that Man should seek to know himself and that that is the hardest quest of all. How nice to be safely bio-crystalline! My limits are more or less knowable and as I contemplated the bowed head of Wilberfoss, I knew that I was at one of my limits.

As always, as ever, as it has been from the first day, the human is alone to find its path I think. Perhaps the only certainty is that, at least, there is a path or so I am told.

After the hardest truth, the rest of the truths fell free, like the release of a log jam. I will tell the rest of Wilberfoss's story quickly.

The rockets burned long enough for the *Nightingale* to escape.

Within minutes of their departure they were resting in orbit and the *Nightingale* was busy about the calculations that would enable the STGs to go into action. Wilberfoss felt that he was in a dream. The delusion which was to possess him for most of his time with us in the garden was already shaping his thinking. At the same time, after liberating (that is to say making him once again aware of) his killer instinct, Wilberfoss conceived a deep hatred for the *Nightingale* and prepared to kill it. While the *Nightingale* plotted an optimum course, Wilberfoss plotted how best to destroy the *Nightingale*. As he freely admitted, this would allow for a great cover-up. He would destroy the evidence and he would then let the madness which was already teeming in his mind, take charge. Very convenient. I cannot understand why he did not choose to kill himself at the same time. My guess is that the instinct to live is so strong. He seems to have conceived of a future as a great deluder, protected by madness. Is that not itself madness?

While they were in a part of space that had not been visited before (which is, let us face it, most of the galaxy), the *Nightingale* yet had one clue. There was a telltale cluster of stars which it thought it could identify by their spectra and it programmed the STGs to tear space to that proximity.

This they did. The journey was uneventful as far as Wilberfoss was concerned. One patch of space blinked out and with it went a high-gravity planet with a gray sea, dun colored land and a single moon. Moments later the black sky blazed with a multitude of different stars and the *Nightingale* was intact.

Immediately the *Nightingale* began to broadcast MAYDAY and the signal contained a coded map of the stars about them. Wilberfoss settled down to wait. He might have waited ten minutes, ten years or ten decades. He had no way of knowing.

He settled down in his suite of rooms with only the idiot flickering fire for company. I asked Wilberfoss what he thought about during that time and he replied, "Nothing." I have checked this under hypnosis and it is true.

The man was closed down as though catatonic.

And at the end of three weeks the MAYDAY was acknowledged. An incredulous communications officer on a mining asteroid sent back a reply, verifying position and advising that a message had been sent to Assisi Central. Help would be on its way.

The *Nightingale* had been found as a result of a stroke of chance and I note how often this has been the situation in this narrative of Jon Wilberfoss. The communications officer was checking his main receiver after completing an annual overhaul. He had it tuned to a frequency that is rarely used for close range transmission. He was checking the calibration when he heard the whispery voice of the *Nightingale*, calling coordinates and identifying itself. He, like anyone engaged in exploration of space, knew of the *Nightingale* and of its strange and sudden disappearance. He was incredulous, but he was well trained too and within minutes priority circuits were humming and the distances between stars were bridged as STG amplifiers opened up.

Days later Wilberfoss received his first real/time transmission. This was the first time for many months that he had spoken to a fellow human being. He was quiet and polite and reserved. He confirmed all details but when pressed to speak of his ordeal, said nothing.

Another week passed and then Jon Wilberfoss was awakened by the *Nightingale* telling him that a C-class starship of the Mercy Fleet of St. Francis Dionysos had arrived in the proximate space. It was already negotiating to engage. Jon Wilberfoss looked out of the view ports but could see nothing. But then, as he was turning away, a beam of light dabbed out from the darkness and the *Nightingale* was touched. A Laser Communication Beam had reached it.

"You are saved, Jon Wilberfoss," said the *Nightingale*.

"You will be a great hero. You will have many stories to tell." But Jon Wilberfoss did not answer.

Quietly, methodically, as he had done a thousand times before, he donned his survival suit and checked the power pack on the small anti-grav unit and the air supply. All was well.

Then he drifted down the corridor to the vacuum chute that led down to the room where the bio-crystalline seeds were growing.

"Where are you going, Jon Wilberfoss?"

"To make my farewell."

Knowing that he had a sentimental side to his nature and that such symbolic acts were of value to the human animal, the *Nightingale* did not think to interfere.

Jon Wilberfoss dropped into the darkness and turned all his suit lights on. He was in vacuum and soon stood outside the entrance to the seed chamber. The door opened at his request and the blaze of light from within the chamber paled his lights. The *Nightingale* still had less than one hundredth of its original capacity, but what it had was impressive. It had grown. The new seeds that Jon Wilberfoss had implanted like coals against the pale glimmer of the dying brain, now blazed. A pattern of silver nerves filled the entire upper chamber of the room.

Jon Wilberfoss entered. He selected a small, well balanced machine hammer from the suit tools and deliberately struck at the nearest seed. It exploded in motes of light which shimmered in the chamber. He went on. He struck with his hammer and swept with his arm. He broke the bio-crystalline fibers. With his gloved hands he scooped out the semi-living seeds of light and smashed them on the ground and trampled on them. Last of all he struck at the fiber which connected the local brain of the *Nightingale* with the specialized brain of the STGs. It was already wavering to red in shock for it had no way of

defending itself against the destruction. Wilberfoss struck
and struck again. This was one of the original links and
it was strong and tough. But it began to break. There
were splinters first and then whole strands came away. He
gripped the trunk with both hands and pulled and it tore
away and came crashing down on him.

There was still faint luminescence from one place in
the room and as he crushed this Jon Wilberfoss said,
"Goodbye."

The rescue ship drew near. I will let the Captain of that
ship explain things in his own words:

"We were pulling close using the L-M linkage. We
could see something of the damage done to the ship.
Plates missing, holes punched in the ship and the entire
hydroponics ring had been ripped away. We were amazed
that it still held together. But then, parts of it were blazing
with light and we guessed it was putting on a brave show.
Whatever disaster had overcome it, it had survived.

"We were at full alert, of course. The hospital bays
were all open and standing by. We knew the *Nightingale*'s
full complement and we were ready to take as many
entities on board as we could. We knew another two
ships of the Mercy Fleet were due within hours and that
one of these was specially designed to take DMEs.

"Then, as we came close, as we were dwarfed by the
giant wreck, as we were looking for signs of life at its
windows or a discharge of static, suddenly all the lights
went out. The ship became black as an asteroid.

"I piloted our way around, looking for one of the
entrance bays. And it was one of our junior consœurs
who first saw Wilberfoss. He was a minute silver figure.
A shining dot of light in the dark ship. He was standing
at a hole in the ship's side and waving, the lights of his
survival suit were blazing.

"We brought Wilberfoss on board.

"Minutes later we boarded the *Nightingale* and found it a dead ship."

So we have returned more or less to the place where this story began but we have been on a long journey.

It now only remains for me to describe the final events in the Poverello Garden.

27

Epilogue

Shortly after Wilberfoss's final collapse into truth, I' wrote my official report. I dealt in facts. I was not, at that time, greatly interested in what forces made a human tick. I was more interested in meshing cause with effect.

I published my report and many senior members of the Gentle Order visited the Pacifico Monastery to interview Wilberfoss. He answered their questions eagerly. He spoke about everything and occasionally I had to intervene as he tended to cast the worst light, that is the most self-critical light, upon his own participation in the events. In his way he was still asking for punishment. The wiser brains of the Gentle Order took note and it was decided that never again would one man be asked to take such awesome responsibility. The *Nightingale* was a one-time-only ship. In the ship's capacity to extend the powers of a fallible man, it came close to making him God. In the hands of a brigand the *Nightingale* could, alone, have devastated the Gentle Order.

"We must therefore," as the Magister of Assisi Central put it, "give thanks that in choosing Wilberfoss, we almost chose correctly. But it is an experiment not to be repeated. It allows vanity too wide a scope."

And where is the *Nightingale* now? The ship is a museum, a tourist attraction. It is tethered out from Assisi Central in permanent orbit and parties of sightseers are ferried out to it daily. The story of the *Nightingale* has become a myth, like the story of old father Noah and his ark.

That the ship is a wreck is significant. Because it is a wreck, the imagination is free to wander and guess at its one-time magnificence. Given time, its ordeal may begin to seem heroic rather than tragic. And that will be a loss.

Magister Tancredi visited the *Nightingale* during his last sabbatical to Assisi. He informs me there is a restaurant in what used to be the DME sector and he also told me the food was excellent. Some sections of the ship have apparently been restored such as the dormitory and recreation areas. Others, such as the lobes containing the massive symbol transformation generators, have been gutted and their cells redeployed. The private quarters occupied by Jon Wilberfoss are just as he left them right down to his last recorded message. The seed chamber which he ruined is also left as found. Few people visit it as it has an atmosphere of dejection and grief, like a cell for the condemned.

I am told that the museum is well appointed and informative. The one and only journey of the *Nightingale* is clearly documented with pictures and video shows. The part which Jon Wilberfoss played in the ship's demise is not, however, emphasized. The implication is that he is dead.

And that is how it should be. The saga of the *Nightingale* is complete unto itself and makes a fitting conclusion to a thoughtful pilgrimage. It would be wrong to contaminate the myth with the flesh and blood of a real man.

But Wilberfoss lives. The events I have described in this yarn occurred some twenty years ago and it is now time for me to place a few last pebbles in my mosaic.

After the departure of the investigating teams from Assisi Central, the spotlight of publicity went off Jon Wilberfoss. Quickly he became a forgotten man. Physically he was in robust health and so gradually Lily withdrew her attention. She had other things to deal with. There were always babies being born. There were always members of the Gentle Order who needed the deep rest that the Poverello Garden can provide. There were always Talline women on pilgrimage who needed Lily's help. There were always fractures to set or wounds to dress. Such was Lily's work and she felt comfortable with it.

Wilberfoss eventually moved out of the small hospital and into a smaller house further around the wall of the garden, closer to the sea wall. He lived on in the garden as a kind of pensioner. He could roam at will and help with the gardening when he had a mind.

I also withdrew from Wilberfoss. After I had written my official report, I undertook to provide a detailed catalog of the contents of the *Nightingale*. Later Magister Tancredi needed me. He was into his dotage and thus I became something between amanuensis and handmaid. Magister Tancredi finally entered Lily's Garden himself after a stroke which left him unable to speak, and he died there within five days. He never saw Wilberfoss, though Wilberfoss saw him.

A new Magister arrived, one who had been an engineer out in the Blind Man System. His name is Staniforth and he is built like a boxer. He spends much of his time down in the maintenance sheds. He has little need of me and

the Pacifico Monastery more or less runs itself. I have
retreated to the library.

And so what of Wilberfoss?

It has been my practice for many years now to spend
a few hours each week with him. We play a game or we
talk. He is still not quite right in the head but there is
a kind of glee with him and he is always an interesting
companion. I never know what he will come out with.
I am like one of those old gold miners who, so long as
there were lights, continued to pan.

Here by way of mosaic pebbles are two anecdotes. I
have given them titles. They complete this volume. I
must confess that I do not really understand them. But
then again, having talked about them with many humans,
I am not convinced that anyone else does. I hope you
enjoy them.

1) Jon Wilberfoss and the Green Man

One day Wilberfoss was working out at the edge of the
orchard at the place where the wild wood comes down to
the river. Having worked all morning gathering windfall
fruit he felt drowsy and so lay down in the shade and
quickly feel asleep.

He began to dream. In his dreams Jon Wilberfoss was
always back in the *Nightingale* and in this particular dream
he found himself crouched in the darkness deep inside
the ship but safe within a small cell of light. For hours
Wilberfoss had been walking through the deserted ship
with only darting shadows for company. Several times he
paused uncertain of his way and several times he stopped
because he believed he could hear someone behind him.
Now, tired at last, he had lit his small night light and
dowsed his suit lights and had settled down in a corner

hoping for sleep. But sleep would not come. He lay awake with his eyes open and eventually, just beyond the small cone of light, he saw movement. A swirl of fabric, he thought.

Now, in the dream he was not afraid. But if such a thing had actually occurred on the *Nightingale* he might have been driven out of his wits with fear. In the dream he stood up and called upon whatever presence was near to reveal itself. A light shone out as though at the end of a long, long corridor. Hesitantly a figure advanced toward him. Man or woman, Wilberfoss could not say. The figure was clothed in a long gown of green. It was holding a lamp which glittered brilliantly and which was held in such a way that it replaced the face of the figure. Nevertheless, Wilberfoss had the impression that the face was damaged in some way.

The figure came toward him tentatively, as though afraid of him. Wilberfoss called encouragement and opened his arms. At moments the shape of the figure was like Medoc, at others it was like the first woman he had loved or the prison warder who had loved him or like Wilberfoss himself. But the face was always invisible. It came closer and closer . . .

And when the brilliance of the approaching lamp became unbearable, Wilberfoss woke up and found the sun in his eyes. It was mid-afternoon and the sun was streaming down on his face. He opened his eyes and was dazzled so that he seemed to be in a red haze. At first he did not know whether he was asleep or awake.

Wilberfoss sat up and rubbed his eyes to get rid of the redness, and when his sight returned it seemed that everything about him was brighter.

As Wilberfoss said when he was recounting this incident to me, "I know something of such states. I can recognize when the apparent world of sense dissolves to reveal a different reality. I was seeing the world of the Nature Gods which can exist in the blackness of space or in a secret grove at midnight or midday. We live in this world but we do not see it for most of our time. It is a world in which, when we see it, everything reflects us. For when we are there we are the Gods of the earth."

I have given you Wilberfoss's exact words. Those of you who are able to make something of them are welcome to do so. Objectively I cannot understand them. But I know they meant something to Wilberfoss and that is sufficient.

So the world seemed brighter and Wilberfoss found his gaze drawn to a particular tree, a silver oak with leaves that glowed and a trunk that was more vivid than three dimensions. The tree had dense foliage and it moved and jostled in the breeze.

And as Wilberfoss stared at the screen of leaves it seemed that he could detect a face. It was a green face and slightly larger than the face of a man but yet not the face of a giant. It was an ugly and dangerous face, with flat cheeks and thick lips. Yet it was also a face filled with primitive vitality. Leaves grew in the nostrils and throat. Leaves sprouted from the temples and drooped over the ears. The eyes were dark and flashing. Unmistakably the figure was that of a man.

As though aware that it had been seen, the figure moved from behind the oak tree and out into the yellow sunlight. It advanced on Wilberfoss.

Wilberfoss recognized that he was seeing both the spirit of the silver oak tree and at the same time, for in this state he was a God of Nature, he was seeing an image of himself. That was perhaps most unnerving. He was being confronted with a part of himself that he had lost and never known.

The green man of leaf and bark, with fingers like roots and rough skin, stood over Wilberfoss and then quickly sat down beside him. Wilberfoss felt a pain in his back and side and the Green Man rolled into him. It was as natural as a cat catching a bird or a frog jumping.

Slowly the brilliance of the world faded but it could never again completely fade. The vegetative side of John Wilberfoss had come home.

That night Jon Wilberfoss did not return to his small house but made a bivouac under the trees of the wild wood. There he discovered that nature can be cruel but never vindictive. He discovered his own cruelty and strength.

I quote him again: "Had I known my own pagan self, I would never have gone chasing whores like the *Nightingale*."

The second pebble. I have given it the following title:

2) St. Francis Dionysos Comes Walking

One afternoon, Wilberfoss was whittling wood, sitting with his back to the screen at the entrance to the garden. He was hoping to catch sight of a Talline woman who had come to the garden two nights earlier and with whom he had drunk wine and made love.

Suddenly he heard a voice. It said, "Hey, you. You with the vacant expression on your face. Give me a hand, I'm not so young these days." Wilberfoss glanced about and then chanced to look out through the gate and he saw the old bull-headed figure of St. Francis Dionysos waving to him. The statue had come to life. It waved its arms and the birds and creatures that were perched on his arms shat themselves in fear and flew and scampered away.

Wondering, Wilberfoss climbed to his feet and hurried through the gate and to the foot of the statue. There he offered his two arms raised and the bull-headed one reached down and put his weight on Wilberfoss's shoulders and swung to the ground. For a few moments Wilberfoss saw into the hard yellow eyes of the bull and felt its hot breath.

"Thank you," said St. Francis Dionysos. "I've had my eye on you for some time, young man. I thought it was about time we got together. You'll be dying soon, and you've still got a few things to learn. Take my arm and let us walk in the Poverello Garden."

Wilberfoss did as he was bid, all the time saying inwardly that this was not happening. And yet, the gate warden came shambling out of his hut and when he saw them he said, "Afternoon, Sir Francis Dionysos. Thank you for the late sunshine and the good harvest." Then turning to Wilberfoss he said, "There's a woman left a message with me for you, Mr. Wilberfoss. Says she's decided to move on . . . trusts you will understand."

"Sad," said St. Francis Dionysos gripping Wilberfoss's arm strongly. "You liked her didn't you? First woman you'd had for some time eh? Ah well. There's a time for standing and a time for being fallow, and you, whether you like it or not, are fallow for the time being." They walked on. "Do you ever think about Medoc?"

"I think about her every day."

"Forget her. She thinks of you but she'll never come back. She couldn't come back if she wanted to. If it helps you in this life, she still loves you. But she won't be beside you in bed tonight. Listen, Jon Wilberfoss. True dignity consists in accepting that which is, that which cannot be changed. Don't waste your time in dreams. More than that, accept the procession. Watch it from the balcony, enjoy the drums and the passion but do not seek to lead it." The bull-headed God paused. "Do I sound like an old man to you?"

"Yes."

"Then that is because you want an old man's advice. But I'm not an old man. I'm as young as discovery. But I'm old too. If it helps you in this life, think what the old tree feels when the sap starts to rise. Think of all the delight spreading up through miles of branch, giving the blossom power, drawing water from the depth."

"I do not understand," said Wilberfoss

The bull-headed one snorted. He turned and faced Jon Wilberfoss and then pulled at the cords which held his rough tunic closed over his broad chest. The cords loosed and the robe fell open. Revealed were breasts that would not shame the Goddess of Love herself and a rounded belly and broad hips and diving pelvis. "Behold the breasted Dionysos," said the bull-headed one. "Now do you understand?"

Wilberfoss shook his head. The bull snorted again and drew the coarse habit tight about him. "You will."

They came to the river. As the bull-headed God entered the river he changed. He became a small man with sloping shoulders and a bright-eyed eager face reminiscent of a ferret. He stood in the middle of the river with his habit hitched up revealing scrawny hairy legs. "What am I doing now?" he called to Jon Wilberfoss who was standing on the bank.

"You are standing in the river," called Jon Wilberfoss, "and you'll catch your death of cold if you don't come out."

The old man waded to the side of the stream and clambered out awkwardly. He stood on the bank opposite Jon Wilberfoss. "And what am I doing now?"

"You're standing."

"Where?"

"On the bank."

"Beside?"

"Beside the stream."

"Am I in the stream or out of it?"

"Out of it of course."

The old man held on to a branch above his head and lowered one pale leg down into the river and felt about for purchase. When he was secure he called, "And now?"

"Now you have one leg in the river and one leg out. Is that the answer you want?"

"Yes."

"Why?"

"Because it is the answer to all your questions. To be and not to be. They are not alternatives you know. They are different ways of looking at the same thing." Old Francis Dionysos heaved on the branch above him to pull himself up onto the bank. The branch, of course, broke and St. Francis Dionysos fell back into the stream with a whoop.

Jon Wilberfoss could not resist his laughter. He laughed as he waded over the stream and took hold of the mangy old habit and hoisted the Saint upright.

"So you think that is funny," said Dionysos, blowing out water. He started to wade to the side of the stream. "Well, I'm glad. It is about time you cracked yourself open with laughter. You know the old saying: 'When a man laughs, the devil enters him.' Well, that needn't be a bad thing." So saying, Francis Dionysos heaved himself up onto the bank and stood there, squeezing the water out of his tunic. "The spirit of humankind is not Christian and kind: it is Pagan and wild. It has room for kindness too," he said, regaining some of his humor. "But make no mistake. The spirit is not cruel: it is anarchic. The secret is to touch everything lightly. Everything. That way you retain your independence. C'mon. Let's walk."

Wilberfoss nodded. He had noticed that a Talline woman had stood on the river bank and watched their antics in the river with frank amusement. Now she turned away.

The two men linked arms and clambered up the slippery bank. Before them was the Pectanile. "Now that is an interesting shape," said Francis Dionysos. Wilberfoss was amazed to see that without his being aware of it, the figure of St Francis had regained his massive stature and bull's head. Realities shifted imperceptibly, obeying some obscure rule, satisfying whatever were the needs of the present.

"Why do you change your shape?" he asked.

The God paused and looked at him. The bull snorted through its black damp nostrils and lowered its head until Wilberfoss could see the ridge of bone which joined the bases of the shiny horns. Yet when it spoke, the voice was neutral and easy. "It is about time you realized that I do not change. I never change. I am ever and always one and the same. What changes is your own fleeting mind needing now one image of assurance and now another. I am everything from the opening flower to the rotting corpse. I am wisdom and innocence: salt and honey. I am what abides."

Wilberfoss stared at the bull-headed man, trying to understand. And as he stared he saw the transformation. It was a flowing through. It was not a dissolve. It was as though an object, a beautiful vase say, or a statue or a rabbit, were lit from one side and then lit from another angle and what was revealed was the same, but different. Wilberfoss was aware of the change in himself.

"Before I saw you as a bull, now I see you as an old man. Once before you had a woman's body. Why do I only see you in those shapes? Why not in others?"

"You see what you have learned to see. Conventional

images, and because they are conventional they carry a great weight of truth. There are few images of my brute strength better than that of the bull."

"But why don't I see you in other forms? My moods change. My needs change."

The old man smiled a merry smile. "How does this sound? You do see me, but you don't recognize me." And then he sighed. "But the thing to do is to see beyond images. Words can't do it. Only you can. Use everything you have. All experience. Look at it cold-eyed. Come on, you'll never puzzle it out with thinking. Relax and let us look at this strange artifact."

They climbed up the slope at the foot of the Pectanile and stood under its richly-rounded shape. "Here," said the old man, throwing his arms wide grandly, "you see the limit of art. Look at this fine shape, what do you see in it?"

"Well, it's like a funnel at the top and . . ."

"No. No. No. Don't describe it. We'll be here forever if you do that and we'll still be no nearer the truth. What do you see *in* it? What does it suggest? What is the artist getting at?"

"Well, it is like a pitcher . . . and like a root under the ground . . ."

"Yes and . . . ?"

"And it is private like a small room . . ."

"Womb, tomb. Go on."

"Well, anyone can see it is like a cunt and a cock and has balls and breasts and . . . is this what you want me to see?"

"Go on."

"It's got an inner and an outer and water flows through it. It's solid, made of stone. I bang my hands against it and it doesn't yield. It is big and when the sun shines on it, it gets warm and when the snow falls, it gets cold. It is a toy made by a giant. It is both frightening and satisfying." Wilberfoss fell silent. When he resumed, he was standing with his forehead pressed against the curling side of the Pectanile. "I think . . ." he said. "I feel . . . whoever made the first Pectanile was trying to express all that and more . . ." He paused. "I don't know. I'm not used to thinking this way. I'm not used to using my emotions to find truth. I . . . I . . ." There was something in this throat, something struggling to get out, but the words would not come and he fell silent.

The bull-headed one looked at Wilberfoss and then reached down and took his hands and placed them among the rough brown fur between his curving horns. Wilberfoss felt the energy of the bull. "Don't be too hard on yourself," murmured the God. "That is just another face of vanity. Here, feel your own horns."

Wilberfoss felt upward, above his eyes, above his scalp, and he found there two curving prongs of bone, each so massive that he could not encircle the base with his hand. The bone was rough, not smooth. Working bone. Fighting bone. Damaged and scarred by time and combat. But solid still. He ran his hands up the curve and at the top he could just reach the points. He put pressure on the horns but pull as he might he could feel no pressure on his head. The bone was hard and completely unyielding. He knew that it would neither break nor bend. Yet when he moved his head, the tips cut through the air as though they would scratch it. His smallest movement was amplified. Wilberfoss remembered back. There was a time when he was a young man—a bloody fist killer who would gamble his life—and that young man had horns too. He had not been aware of them for so many years. And now . . .

"Those horns are your history. Like rings on a tree. Do you want to see what you look like?"

Wilberfoss hardly heard, but yet he nodded.

"Then climb up inside the Pectanile. Use the water mirror."

This Wilberfoss did.

But, as he confided to me some weeks after this event, when he stared down into the pool within the Pectanile he was disappointed. All he found staring back at him was his own sad and serious face. He was surprised at how old he looked. And that was all. No horns.

When he climbed outside the Pectanile he found that St. Francis Dionysos had gone. He ran down to the river and waded across and climbed out and ran to the gateway which gave entrance to the Poverello Garden. When he got there he found that the statue was in its place with arms spread and with the birds perched on the arms.

Had it happened? Had it been true?

I am struck by the fact that Wilberfoss, at all points in his life, had visions. The visions were an objective expression of his passions. Perhaps they have real existence in another world. Perhaps the human mind has access to this other world. I do not. Among Wilberfoss's visions I include his beloved Chi-da. I have come to the opinion that if I had been down there on that gray world with Wilberfoss, then I would not have seen any creature which covered the sky like a banner of rippling red silk. I would not have seen this creature any more than I saw the monster that visited him at the river. And curiously, you know. Those two creatures are related. The one is his beast. The other is his best nature and he did not kill it. You cannot kill such things. He allowed it fulfillment, at the last.

Well, these two stories that I have just related tell you a lot about the final state of Wilberfoss. I noticed that in his later years he came to spend more and more time mooching around the Pectanile. He was trying to understand it, he said. But I think he was fascinated by the thoughts that it bade rise within him. Its power was that it made him think and feel and discover all the things that were inside him. The golden store of truth . . . the cold face of reality. Solitude and love. I say again Salt and Honey. Dignity before the passing of life. Patience and soaring passion.

And it was there that we found him, two days after he had been last seen. Quite dead and starting to smell.

The gate warden limbered him out of the Pectanile and lowered him down the smooth wet stone to Lily who received him into her cage.

I was there, swaying beneath the trees and observing everything. I noticed that Wilberfoss's face was set in a smile such as I had rarely seen on his face in life. I would like to think it was more than merely the rictus.

I wonder what he found in the last few moments. Did he see his true image in the Pectanile pool? Did he manage to put his life together and make proper quittance?

Did he discover his own green nature?

I hope so.
In as much as I can hope for anything.
I abide.

THANK YOU FOR SHOPPING AT THE
BOOK RACK. PLEASE COME AGAIN

BIO OF A SPACE TYRANT
Piers Anthony

"Brilliant...a thoroughly original thinker and storyteller with a unique ability to posit really *alien* alien life, humanize it, and make it come out alive on the page." *The Los Angeles Times*

A COLOSSAL NEW FIVE VOLUME SPACE THRILLER—
BIO OF A SPACE TYRANT
The Epic Adventures and Galactic Conquests of Hope Hubris

VOLUME I: REFUGEE   84194-0/$4.50 US/$5.50 Can
Hubris and his family embark upon an ill-fated voyage through space, searching for sanctuary, after pirates blast them from their home on Callisto.

VOLUME II: MERCENARY   87221-8/$4.50 US/$5.50 Can
Hubris joins the Navy of Jupiter and commands a squadron loyal to the death and sworn to war against the pirate warlords of the Jupiter Ecliptic.

VOLUME III: POLITICIAN   89685-0/$4.50 US/$5.50 Can
Fueled by his own fury, Hubris rose to triumph obliterating his enemies and blazing a path of glory across the face of Jupiter. Military legend...people's champion...promising political candidate...he now awoke to find himself the prisoner of a nightmare that knew no past.

VOLUME IV: EXECUTIVE   89834-9/$4.50 US/$5.50 Can
Destined to become the most hated and feared man of an era, Hope would assume an alternate identify to fulfill his dreams.

VOLUME V: STATESMAN   89835-7/$4.50 US/$5.50 Can
The climactic conclusion of Hubris' epic adventures.

Buy these books at your local bookstore or use this coupon for ordering:

Mail to: Avon Books, Dept BP, Box 767, Rte 2, Dresden, TN 38225   C
Please send me the book(s) I have checked above.
❏ My check or money order— no cash or CODs please— for $_____ is enclosed (please add $1.50 to cover postage and handling for each book ordered— Canadian residents add 7% GST).
❏ Charge my VISA/MC Acct#_____Exp Date_____
Minimum credit card order is two books or $6.00 (please add postage and handling charge of $1.50 per book — Canadian residents add 7% GST). For faster service, call 1-800-762-0779. Residents of Tennessee, please call 1-800-633-1607. Prices and numbers are subject to change without notice. Please allow six to eight weeks for delivery.

Name_____
Address_____
City_____State/Zip_____
Telephone No._____   ANT 0892

HUGO AND NEBULA AWARD-WINNING AUTHOR
JOE HALDEMAN

presents

The WORLDS Trilogy

WORLDS
70823-X/ $3.95 US/ $4.95 Can
An Earth plagued by rampant violence, unrest and political fanaticism careens madly toward its ultimate doom.

WORLDS APART
71682-8/ $4.50 US/ $5.50 Can
The insanity that destroyed a world reaches out to touch the inhabitants of one of Earth's last orbiting colonies.

WORLDS ENOUGH AND TIME
70801-9/ $4.99 US/ $5.99 Can
With their homeworld in ruins, ten thousand brave colonists set out for the stars.

Buy these books at your local bookstore or use this coupon for ordering:

Mail to: Avon Books, Dept BP, Box 767, Rte 2, Dresden, TN 38225
Please send me the book(s) I have checked above.   C
⌐ My check or money order— no cash or CODs please— for $_____ is enclosed
(please add $1.50 to cover postage and handling for each book ordered— Canadian residents
add 7% GST).
⌐ Charge my VISA/MC Acct#_____ Exp Date_____
Minimum credit card order is two books or $6.00 (please add postage and handling charge of
$1.50 per book — Canadian residents add 7% GST). For faster service, call
1-800-762-0779. Residents of Tennessee, please call 1-800-633-1607. Prices and numbers
are subject to change without notice. Please allow six to eight weeks for delivery.

Name_____
Address_____
City_____State/Zip_____
Telephone No._____
                                                                                     WOR 0293

THE CONTINUATION
OF THE FABULOUS
INCARNATIONS OF IMMORTALITY
SERIES

PIERS ANTHONY

FOR LOVE OF EVIL
75285-9/$4.95 US/$5.95 Can

AND ETERNITY
75286-7/$4.95 US/$5.95 Can

Buy these books at your local bookstore or use this coupon for ordering:

Mail to: Avon Books, Dept BP, Box 767, Rte 2, Dresden, TN 38225   C
Please send me the book(s) I have checked above.
❑ My check or money order— no cash or CODs please— for $_____is enclosed
(please add $1.50 to cover postage and handling for each book ordered— Canadian residents
add 7% GST).
❑ Charge my VISA/MC Acct#_____Exp Date_____
Minimum credit card order is two books or $6.00 (please add postage and handling charge of
$1.50 per book — Canadian residents add 7% GST). For faster service, call
1-800-762-0779. Residents of Tennessee, please call 1-800-633-1607. Prices and numbers
are subject to change without notice. Please allow six to eight weeks for delivery.

Name_____

Address_____

City_____State/Zip_____

Telephone No._____

IMM 1092

THE MAGICAL XANTH SERIES!

PIERS ANTHONY

QUESTION QUEST

75948-9/$4.99 US/$5.99 Can

ISLE OF VIEW

75947-0/$4.99 US/$5.99 Can

VALE OF THE VOLE

75287-5/$4.95 US/$5.95 Can

HEAVEN CENT

75288-3/$4.95 US/$5.95 Can

MAN FROM MUNDANIA

75289-1/$4.95 US/$5.95 Can

THE COLOR OF HER PANTIES

75949-7/$4.99 US/$5.99 Can

Buy these books at your local bookstore or use this coupon for ordering:

....

Mail to: Avon Books, Dept BP, Box 767, Rte 2, Dresden, TN 38225   C
Please send me the book(s) I have checked above.
❏ My check or money order— no cash or CODs please— for $_____ is enclosed
(please add $1.50 to cover postage and handling for each book ordered—Canadian residents
add 7% GST).
❏ Charge my VISA/MC Acct#_____ Exp Date_____
Minimum credit card order is two books or $6.00 (please add postage and handling charge of
$1.50 per book — Canadian residents add 7% GST).   For faster service, call
1-800-762-0779. Residents of Tennessee, please call 1-800-633-1607. Prices and numbers
are subject to change without notice. Please allow six to eight weeks for delivery.

Name_____
Address_____
City_____State/Zip_____
Telephone No._____   XAN 0193